YOUNG JUNIUS

YOUNG JUNIUS

SETH HARWOOD

TYRUS
BOOKS

Published by
TYRUS BOOKS
1213 N. Sherman Ave. #306
Madison, WI 53704
www.tyrusbooks.com

This is a work of fiction.
Any similarities to people or places,
living or dead, is purely coincidental.

Library of Congress Cataloging-In-Publication Data has been applied for.

12   11   10   1   2   3   4   5   6   7   8   9   10

978-1-935562-28-3 (hardcover)
978-1-935562-27-6 (paperback)

For my families —

Harwood and *Palms*

ACKNOWLEDGEMENTS

Thanks to Mrs. Varella, Mrs. Haynes, Mr. Hutch, and that whole thuggish bunch at the Longfellow School way back when. Mrs. Varella actually made me believe I could be a good English student, and Mrs. Haynes tirelessly read us *The Good Earth* and *A Tale of Two Cities* out loud every day in a class called—what else?—Reading.

Thanks to Scott Sigler for paving the way and showing me how to win an audience, then turn the publishing world on its head. Big ups to J.C. Hutchins, Evo Terra and all the other podcast novelists taking the world by storm.

Thanks to everybody at the Writers' Workshop, especially Marilynne and Jim.

Eric Campbell believed in this project early on. From him to Ben, Alison, and Ashley, the team at Tyrus has been nothing short of awesome. Thanks for letting me take it out of the box!

Shah Anderson, Tresca Behling, Drew Valderrama, Phil Riberra and a great many online fans provided me with superb information on subjects too strange and varied to include here. Needless to say, all of these improved this book by leaps and bounds.

Margot Welch, Mark Coggins, Jerry Scullion, Shaukat Ghaswala and Bob Ostrom provided artwork and photos for which I'm grateful.

Shirley Bruce was first on PayPal the day the Special Edition went live. The Palms Family listened to me read this book as I wrote it, Digital Dickens style, as well as spurred me on in their desire for more about Junius Ponds.

Steven J. McDermott originally requested a short story for *Storyglossia's* crime edition, which later became chapter one of the novel. Thanks to him, and to Anthony Neil Smith for early encouragement and not messing with the piece.

Thanks to Stacia Decker for being the best agent I can imagine—for blasting through an early read of this novel and helping me edit it down, then supporting me through each and all of my changes and market moves. She's a fast reader and one of the best editors I've seen in action.

Thanks to my Dad for so, so much. Especially for getting me away to Tanzania when the time was right. To Jess for coming along and supporting me all the way. Thanks to my Mom for always being there.

And finally, thanks to Cambridge, the city, where I was lucky to spend a part of my youth.

1

"You have to figure it out, is what it comes down to."

Junius fingered one of the long tassels of the curtain ties. In one of the funeral parlor's front rooms, his older brother lay in a coffin, not yet twenty and done with all the living he'd ever do.

Here in a side room, it was just him, Willie Stash, and a small, ugly nine.

"I try this, you put me on?"

"Shit," Willie smiled his signature smile, the one that showed the big gaps in his top *and* bottom rows of teeth. "You do this one, I put you in charge of Teale Square. How that sound?"

Junius smiled. He had no crew, just the cheap nine on the table—if he took it—and his boy Little Elf. But the gun gave him so much more than he'd had yesterday, even *with* a living brother.

He picked it up. *Beretta*, it read along the side.

"All right."

Outside, Elf came up to Junius before he made the corner. He'd been waiting on the steps of the funeral parlor for Junius to finish with Willie. They walked a block before either of them spoke.

Then Junius stopped, turned toward his man. "This," he said, pulling up his shirt to show the Beretta tucked into the front of his jeans.

Elf nodded. "Then we find who killed Temp?"

Junius looked up the block. At the corner, two of Willie's boys stood talking to one another, trying to look as though they owned the real estate they stood on. For all purposes, they did.

A BMW stopped in front of them, and a white face stuck out the window—a college kid looking to score. Willie's boy shook his head and sent him around the corner. In the liquor store lot next to Food Master, someone else would hand him a bag and take his money.

Junius shook his head. He turned away and started walking, the hard metal pressing into his abdomen, cold against his skin. He knew the safety was on, but still it felt strange. "He wants us to make it right."

Elf looked away, toward the projects on the other side of the street. In the middle of a courtyard, five boys played twenty-one on a netless hoop with a soccer ball.

"Fuck it then. Where we start?"

"The towers."

Along Alewife Brook, they made their way toward the T station, walking opposite the big cemetery for the first few blocks, until the sidewalk ended and they had to cross four lanes to avoid the mud. Elf had on his new Forums, so he was real particular.

Junius looked below the sidewalk into the dirty brook that separated the street from the cemetery. It didn't so much flow as creep, an old bicycle and a rusted shopping cart sticking up out of the muck.

The headstones along the grass were old but in good condition. No room inside for Temple, only long-dead white people. Temple would get cremated, and then Junius didn't know what. But it was better they had the body; his mom didn't have to suffer more uncertainty or a missing persons investigation that would yield nothing after months.

The walk to the towers took them into Arlington, just a block into the dry, white Switzerland of the surrounding neighborhoods.

They went up Mass Ave. and down a back street that let out on a path behind the T. In the mornings and afternoons, commuters lined this route, but in the mid-afternoon of a Sunday, the two had it all to themselves. They passed through marshland, with twin banks of reeds by their sides.

"Yo," Elf said. "Show me the gat."

Junius stopped. He was eager to look himself, to get a feel for the grip and the touch of the steel. Temple had always kept him away from guns, made him swear off their violence. Now, he pulled it out from his belt and showed Elf, holding the barrel parallel to the ground, aimed back toward where they'd come.

"Damn, yo. Let me hold it."

"No." The handle felt small in his grip, as if it were made for a boy's hand. Even at fourteen, Junius stood six foot three, the equal of many grown men he saw, and not skinny like the rest of the kids he'd come up with. His bones held man muscles; whether he'd earned them or not, he had the gait of one who had. His legs bowed and his arms rarely fell straight.

When he looked around them through the reeds, his head dipped below his shoulders and his back hunched. He was like a spring— ready to pop.

Elf backed away a step as Junius pulled the slide and chambered a round. Willie had shown him the safety, and now Junius clicked it off. He touched the trigger, testing its shape not its tension, and turned the gun over. He held it sideways, like on TV.

"Yeah."

Then in one motion, he swung the gun over his head like the arm of a clock going from nine to land at three. He straightened his elbow, aiming toward the station. As he did, he squared his shoulders. With his arm level and the gun straight, it felt real; he held it up and down, ready.

"That's how you do," Elf said. "Now let me hear you clap."

Up ahead, Junius saw nothing but reeds. He squinted, aimed, and pulled back the trigger until he felt it tense, took it just to the point where he thought it might fire. He had never shot a gun.

His breath hung in front of him in the dry, cold air.

He didn't know how it would kick, only that it did. It would be *loud.* He tensed his face—partly from fear and partly to aim. Then he lowered the weapon.

"Shit," he said. "We kill some commuter, we be fucked."

He took his finger off the trigger and slipped the safety on. He wanted to eject the live round but didn't know how, only that the safety was supposed to keep it from shooting.

He slipped the gun back into his pants and walked up the path. Behind him, Elf sucked his teeth in disappointment.

As they came to the big, gray parking structure of the station, Elf pointed out two of Rock's boys hanging where the commuters came out to get their rides or catch a bus. Rock did steady money from the business set like this. So if Marlene controlled two of the three towers, Rock still did well running the station and 412.

Willie ran pieces of Somerville, not much compared to the towers, but enough. If Junius found out who did Temple and took that man down, he'd have Teale Square, some of the best territory in his hood. At fourteen, that was more than even Temple had amounted to.

The two crossed toward the station and headed for Rock's boys.

Junius recognized Derek and Ness as they got closer. Ness used to be Eliot when he was young, but then when he started to roll, people called him Ness because of his long neck.

Elf called out, giving them the nod.

Derek shook his head. "Fuck you niggahs want?"

"We looking to find Rock. Want to see what's been going down."

"Down?" Derek stepped back and looked at the ground. He checked Ness and then stared at the others. "I don't see nothing here but rent, motherfucker. Rolling product. You want to try and take this?"

Junius stayed quiet. He watched Derek talk his shit, point his finger at Elf and tell them they should go back to their side of the border.

"We just want talk," Junius said finally. "It's about my brother."

Then Derek stopped. He wiped his mouth and shut it all down.

"Yeah," Junius said. "That's what we here on. That's why we going through to the towers."

Derek looked around. Junius could see a white guy in a suit waiting to talk to Ness, looking to buy, but Derek waved him off. "Come back later."

"Who I talk to?" Junius said it slow, definite. The voice was one he didn't recognize, one he didn't hear as his own.

Derek said, "You go to the top, son. Tower two. Take your ass up in there and all the way up. You ask the Oracle."

"Marlene?"

"Shit. Oracle to you, motherfucker. Whatever she say be your fate."

Elf took two steps back. Neither of them had thought of going all the way to the top.

Junius nodded slowly at Derek and Ness. They'd been fair: no threats, no need to show the gun. "That all?" he asked.

"Ha?" Derek's mouth almost popped with the sound. "Is that all?" He shook his head and started laughing, turned to Ness and pointed at Junius. "This motherfucker," he said.

Ness laughed and they slapped palms.

"Yeah, niggah," Derek said when they finally calmed down. "That all. Just take your ass to the Oracle."

Junius turned to the towers, his hand at his belt, and listened for any fast movements behind him as he started up the sidewalk. About four steps later, Elf called peace to the others and started to follow.

The Rindge Towers stood three tall buildings, each one a city: twenty-two stories of apartments, hoods, crews and trouble; a corner on every staircase. Whoever pushed and ran these controlled much more than Teale Square, more even than the bulk of the Davis-Teale-Tufts triangle that Willie called his land. Much more than weed to the white boys and whatever they needed for parties on the weekends.

Whoever held the Rindge Towers supplied to the serious Cambridge junkies and suburban drive-thru addicts—the ones who snorted, smoked and shot up, who would bring you every dollar they *could*.

"Shit," Elf said when he caught up. "The top? Fuck you think be up there?"

Junius heard Ness call to the suit. He took a quick look back and, though Ness slapped a dime into Mr. Suit Man's hand, Derek still watched them. He gave Junius the nod, pointing his chin toward the towers.

"Top," Junius said, "means we go all the way."

They crossed in front of the Polynesian tiki bar and approached the highway.

"You ever been up there?"

"I been inside a couple times," Elf said. He showed the palms of his hands. "But not like this."

Across the street, the three brick towers stood tall, each one covered with hundreds of windows on a side: windows that betrayed nothing, just endless rows of lives and capped-over air-conditioners that didn't work.

The light changed and traffic stopped. Junius began to cross. Elf hesitated, then hurried to catch up. On the other side, he stopped.

"Yo, J," he said.

Junius turned.

"Yeah?"

"I think I'm a head back."

Elf was sixteen, two years older than Junius, but they'd been together almost all their lives, like brothers, even with Temple around. Junius nodded. "I hear you."

He walked ahead on his own.

Junius saw Lamar in front of 412. Lamar who lied about his age to play in the Rindge Ave. league games. Where Junius was the man-child lying to say he was old enough to play, Lamar was the eighteen-year-old who cheated not to leave. Junius was good enough that everyone looked the other way. With Lamar, they left it alone because he carried a Glock.

As soon as he saw Junius, Lamar headed toward him across the parking lot. He called his name out, asked what Junius was doing on the wrong side of the world.

"What you want?" Lamar asked, when they were face to face.

"I'm looking for Marlene. Come to find who shot Temp."

"Yeah?" Lamar laughed. "You going to see the Oracle?"

Junius started to pass, but the bigger man cut him off with a forearm to the chest. He pulled up Junius's shirt and looked at the nine.

"That for real? You crazy?" He pushed Junius back, and then Lamar had his hand on the gun's grip, but Junius caught his wrists and kept Lamar's fingers away from the trigger guard. Lamar pulled on the gun and pushed Junius. They both stepped closer to the highway. Junius did not let go.

"Now, motherfucker. You let this shit go, and you walk. You leave, I take your gun and *don't* cap your ass. You fight, I drop you like the bullshit you is."

Cars whizzed by. Junius pulled on the gun, but it didn't move. Lamar was strong. He tried to twist it. Same result.

"Go home."

"What up, niggah?" Elf stood next to Junius, shoulder to shoulder with him in front of Lamar. "My man and I going in today."

Lamar let go of the gun and stepped to Elf. He laughed. "Fucking munchkin-land. Ain't I showed you not to come up here before?"

He threw a fast elbow at Elf's head and Elf flinched back, but Junius didn't hesitate: as soon as Lamar's hands were off the gun, he pushed him back toward the towers. He'd been boxing for two years and knew the right moves, but none of them came; he reverted straight back into the streetfighter he'd always been.

Lamar stepped back shaking his head. That was when Elf caught him under his chin with an uppercut and then followed with a quick left hook to the body that came in as soon as Lamar's hands went up.

The hook was enough to double Lamar over.

Elf stood before him, his fists ready and one foot forward. "Go on," he said to Junius. "I got this."

"No you ain't." Lamar touched his chin and spit on the ground. He stretched his neck and stepped to Elf.

Junius looked at the two of them. Lamar had two years on Elf and at least fifteen pounds.

"Go!" Elf waved off Junius. "This me, niggah. That—" he angled his chin at the towers, "is you."

Junius stepped into the drive, still watching as Lamar stood tall over Elf and threw his first punch. Elf caught it on his arm and didn't hesitate; he came with a left jab to Lamar's chin that rocked his head back and then stung his cheek with a fast right. Lamar stumbled.

Elf ran at Lamar and crossed him with a left hook to the head. Lamar folded and spit blood.

It was then, while Lamar was bent, that he drew his gun.

"No—" Junius called, but it was too late.

Elf froze at the sight of the weapon, and Lamar stepped forward. He whipped Elf across the head with the barrel, then slashed the gun's butt up into Elf's mouth.

Junius saw blood.

Lamar doubled Elf with a hard left to the stomach and tried to knee him in the face.

As Elf struggled to catch his breath, Lamar raised the Glock. They were far enough from anything that wasn't towers for him to drop a body and not fear.

Junius stepped toward Lamar and drew his nine.

"Stop," he called. "Hold up!" He tried to sound hard.

Lamar howled and backed off, shaking his head. "Now you fucked up *two times*."

As Junius stepped to the walk, he had the nine leveled at Lamar's chest.

"You pull a gun on me? Oh, now fucked yourself, young one." Lamar's lips curled into a snarl. He spit. "Think you really use that?"

"Step off."

"Yo, fuck you!" Lamar started to turn his gun on Junius. "Shoot me now, or I carve you up like my boy did your brother."

"What?"

"Think you have any choice about this now?"

"Who? Who killed Temp?" Junius jumped forward.

Lamar saying "his boy" could mean anyone in Rock's crew: Black Jesus, Roughneck, Milk, Hammer, anybody. Junius waved the gun. "Who?"

Elf fell from a bent-over position onto his ass. He spit a stream of blood onto the ground. A thin trail hung from his chin. His eyes blank, he said, "No, J."

"Listen to your man. He speaking truth. Like this you walk out."
Lamar smiled. "Maybe. This shit go further, they gone carry you out
on a board."

Junius traced the arc of the cold trigger with his thumb. He
flicked off the safety.

"*Or*, maybe I be fucking with you. What you think?"

"This for real," Junius said, trying to sound steady. He knew what
he had to do. Behind him, someone in the towers would have Lamar's
back, and someone that person's back after that. But right now just the
three of them made this scene. The February cold offered that small
piece of justice.

"Yeah, niggah," Lamar said. "Shit be real now." Junius could see
the black O of the Glock's barrel as Lamar raised it up. He knew
Lamar's next move.

Junius fired.

The crack of the report cut the day, and Junius jumped from the
sound. Lamar spun fast, his right hand shooting up to his left shoulder.

Elf's eyes went all disbelief and fear. He knew how much that
shot had just changed.

"Yeah," Lamar said. He started to turn back around with his
Glock when Junius fired again: three fast shots. Now that it had
started, there was only one way for it to end.

Only one shot hit. Junius knew he'd fired wild, but let off two
more shots as he saw Lamar's chest. The second hit him hard, knocking him back off his feet.

Derek and Ness would be coming fast now, and others too.

"Get up," Junius yelled at Elf.

He walked up on Lamar, kicked the Glock out of his hand. With
labor, Lamar wheezed and spit blood on his lips. "You dumb, dead
niggah."

"Who killed Temple?" Junius asked, holding the gun in Lamar's face. His voice sounded distant, not his own.

"Fuck you." Lamar reached for his gun.

Junius kicked him in the side. He pressed the gun to Lamar's cheek and asked again, "Who killed Temple?"

"Fuck him *and* fuck you."

Junius knew the next shot would kick. There was going to be blood—enough of it to bring a war.

"Get ready to run."

Elf scrambled to his feet. "Don't—"

Without looking down, Junius pulled the trigger one last time. The sound was louder, and something wet hit his neck.

Junius saw it all in Elf's eyes: more than he needed. Whether he didn't look down that last time because he didn't want to—because seeing death on his brother's face was enough for one day—or because he couldn't, Junius didn't know.

And it didn't matter now.

They ran. Without knowing if anyone was behind them or not, they ran. Give Elf the credit: short or not, the boy could go. They took off in the direction of North Cambridge, up Rindge Ave., away from Alewife, Derek and Ness, away from the towers. They passed the cheap supermarket with drunk homeless out front, wasted in the middle of the day off cough syrup, and crossed Rindge Ave. through traffic while cars honked, Junius tucking the nine into the back of his jeans. From the front of the towers they could hear shouts and people yelling.

Into the gravel parking lot of the park, they rushed past the baseball diamond, through the outfield, and jumped the fence to the M.D.C. pool where mothers from the towers brought their kids to pee in the summer. It was closed now, black covers over the empty holes in the ground. They ran across the concrete to the fence on the other side and jumped it to the grass.

Junius looked back fast when he landed and saw no one coming—no chase, nothing to fear—but ran on. He turned in the direction of the neighborhoods and pushed Elf forward.

"Come on." They ran across the high school football field of frozen mud, out of the park and to the quiet neighborhood streets on the other side from the T. Junius knew these back streets from spending time with a girl he'd started to mess with, Adrianna, who lived a few blocks up. These were three-story, two-family houses where white people lived.

They stopped running a few blocks in, and Elf put his hands on his knees to catch his breath. He spit blood on the ground. "Damn," he said. "This what it comes down to?"

Junius pulled Elf's shoulder. "Come on. We got to tell Willie."

"Fuck you, niggah." Elf shook him off. He ran a hand across his broken lips and showed Junius the blood. "See this, yo? This *my* blood. We can handle that. But now? Now Lamar dead? Fuck. Look at you."

Junius looked down and saw Lamar's blood on his coat.

"What I'm a do? Niggah wanted to shoot us both. Now we got to tell Willie so he can be ready to deal."

"No." Elf shook his head. "You got to run and keep on."

"What?"

"Serious. Get ghost. Break out and don't never come back. Rock's boys know you around, they gone make serious shit for us *and* for Willie. They won't stop at nothing until they done."

"Done?"

"Yeah. Until shit be even."

Junius's lungs burned. He looked at the rows of quiet houses.

The idea of running to New York City came, but even that was a world so much bigger than Boston, a place he feared dealing with by himself.

"I got to talk to Willie. Shit, he gave me the gat. What he think happen?"

Elf spit again and nodded. "Niggah got a gat, he gone clap."

He straightened up and they started to move again, not running, but faster than a walk. What was the point in running? If someone wanted them gone, they'd just drive to Willie and tell the man. That was what Junius didn't like: Derek and Ness would say who killed Lamar and then—it didn't matter who—someone from Rock's crew would come asking, asking with guns.

They went up to Mass Ave. and crossed into Somerville. Junius felt safer here, but still like someone could come up behind them and start shooting.

"Hold up." Elf wiped blood off his face with his T-shirt. "Yo, do I look fucked up?"

Lamar had cut a good gash into Elf's chin with the butt of his Glock, split both lips open. The lips were puffed out and bloody, but the gash on Elf's chin looked worse.

"You look good," Junius said. "This give you some character."

"That means I look fucked up." Elf spit on the ground again, this more phlegm than blood. Junius told him to press the sleeve of his sweatshirt against his chin to stop the bleeding.

"Willie ain't gone like this. He ask us why the fuck you did it. Why you thought you had to."

"And what I'm a say?"

"Shit. Say you too young and dumb to know better. It's a truth."

Junius shrugged, rested his hands on his knees. "What if it ain't? Say I *meant* to kill him? That one of us had to get fucked, I decided it was him. Plus—"

Elf waited, his breath puffing out of him in short clouds.

"Plus he was fucking with me about T. Don't fuck with me about Temple. That shit ain't right."

Elf nodded and gave Junius a pound. "You right. But Willie might not like it. You know how hard Rock gone come back."

They both knew the answer involved every bit of a war that Willie could handle.

At Willie's office in the back of Armando's Pizza, Junius let Elf tell the story.

The nine sat unloaded on Willie's desk, clip by its side. Willie picked it up and smelled the barrel as soon as Elf started to talk.

"This best be good," he said.

Elf took his time filling things in, explaining about Derek and Ness more than he had to and describing in great detail how Lamar changed the situation by pulling his gun. The whole time, Willie stared at Junius, daring him to speak.

"I busted shots," Junius said, as Elf told Willie that he squared up with Lamar. The cuts on his face told that story—more than enough said.

Willie grimaced. On either side of the desk, Omar and Jackson stood tall.

"I pulled the gat and Lamar called me out. He had the Glock so I had to dead it, right? First to deal, first to do?"

"First to die." Willie shook his head. He shook a Kool from his pack, tapped it against the desk twice and then raised it to his lips. Jackson leaned down with the lighter. As Willie exhaled, he sat back in his chair. "What you learn?"

"He knew who killed Temp. Said one of his boys."

Willie nodded and took a long drag that showed his teeth. "Then it's not all a loss."

"But we need to go up in the towers and ask Marlene now. Right?"

"Huh uh." Willie shook his head. He asked Omar and Jackson, "You want to visit Oracle?"

They both shook their heads like they'd rather go clean an apartment.

"Exactly," Willie said, tilting all the way back and running his fingers up the cigarette. When he got to the top, he started to play with the lit cherry, touching and shaping it with the tips of his fingers. "You play with fire ..."

Junius waited.

Jackson crossed his arms and stared at where Junius sat. It felt like Jackson looked right through him, as if all he could see was the chair. "You do this for Temp?" Jackson asked. "Cause that shit can't be stopped now."

"We end it when we know who did this," Junius said.

Willie sucked his teeth. "Easy, young gun. Two things we not gone do now is get up to Marlene or dead up this Temple shit. They took one of ours, now we took one of theirs. You did good." He nodded. "Now it's done."

Elf looked at Junius out of the side of his eyes. "But they gone come back now."

Willie rocked in his chair as he considered his cigarette. Then he angled his head to one side. "They might. And who you think they want?"

Elf's shoulders slumped.

Junius sat up straighter. "That's why we go to Marlene. We ask her to Oracle this shit up and speak on Temple. She tell us what needs doing and then Rock fall into line. He can't fight her judgment."

Elf looked at Junius again but stayed quiet. Willie didn't move for what seemed a long time. When he did, he looked at his boys first and then at Junius. He raised his eyebrows.

"Two things. One is how this look about Lamar. Rock's boys come to me in peace, asking about one of they own, I got to speak on it.

"Other is if you doing this still for Teale Square, I give it to you. But this get much bigger and none of us sell shit. This ain't about money then, if it is now."

Junius knew the next question as sure as he knew Lamar was dead. "What you tell Rock's crew then? When they come ask?"

If they wanted him, Teale Square or nothing it wouldn't matter. Junius wouldn't have the weight to fight back, and Willie knew it.

Willie stretched all the way forward across the desk, took a last hard drag from the cigarette and ground it out in a glass ashtray. He let the smoke out through his nose, like an angry bull, and stared Junius down.

"Only one thing I can say then. Got to say you went solo, lost it when you heard about your brother. That's the only way I can play the hand."

Junius could feel Omar and Jackson getting closer, looming above him. He wanted to look at Elf, but knew he couldn't break Willie's stare. If Willie was serious, this was his verdict; it was final. If he was kidding, waiting to see how Junius would react, to know what he'd do, he had to sit tight, hold it down while he waited for the joke to break.

It didn't.

Willie stood up. "That's it." He clapped his hands off and wiped his palms on the back of his jeans.

Junius knew he still couldn't speak, couldn't ask Willie for a second chance or protection. This was it. He either had to stand and protect himself from Rock with his own strength, go into hiding, or leave town.

Three choices and none of them good.

He picked up the nine that Willie had left on the desk and put the clip back in. "Guess I be needing this."

Outside, Elf wouldn't say anything until they were back at his house, up on the pitched roof above his and his brother's bedroom. His younger brother was playing Nintendo, getting way too far into Mike Tyson's Punch Out. Like they always did when they wanted to smoke a j or get away from people, Elf and Junius climbed out the window and up the fire escape to the roof. Up here they could see over the parkway and into Arlington, to the green hills in the distance. That was if they looked north. If they looked west, they could see the projects behind the Food Master, a run-down retirement residence, and, far off, the three high-rises of the Rindge Towers.

Elf sat down heavily on the shingles and touched his chin with his wrist. Junius was surprised to see his hand come away dry; somewhere in all this, his chin had stopped bleeding.

"We should get that fixed up," Junius said. He stayed standing, his feet on uneven parts of the roof, resting an elbow on his knee.

"I be all right."

"That shit will scar if you don't get stitches."

Elf looked up with thin red eyes. It surprised Junius to think Elf might have been crying. "Shit, you think I care about my chin now?

Big Willie just put us out on our own against Rock. We either stand up or get shot down."

"I can't—"

"How we won't get shot down? How we don't die in this?"

Elf spit toward the edge of the roof but didn't make the gutter. He shook his head.

Junius crouched next to his friend, both feet on the same section of roof, his hands on his knees.

"You know I want to ask Marlene. Go up in there."

"And you think it can happen? Think it just end there?"

"I don't know. But there's only one way to find out."

"Yeah, that's right." Elf stood up and spit a big gob off the side of the roof. "Fuck's a matter with us. We just go up in there blazing with that nine, the one—how many bullets you got left in it? Five? Go past Rock's boys and Marlene just up and lets us in, gives us a free pass to get out, tells us who killed your brother, and we go kill his ass too. Then it be all square. That how you see it?"

Junius stood again. He held his hands high over his head and let the cold February wind blow through his arms. He turned toward the projects and the towers and took a deep breath.

Even without stretching, he was taller than Elf. He had the strength to hold his own against anyone in his grade, all but a few of the eleventh-graders. He liked school, too. Liked the idea of playing football next year if he could keep his grades up and didn't miss class; he had even made some Bs to keep his mom happy.

His mom, the woman he hadn't seen since his brother's funeral that morning, the woman who wailed and sobbed the whole way through the ceremony.

No way he'd give his mother another body to mourn.

"Fuck," he said. "I don't see it any other way. I'm not crazy and I don't want die, I'm just saying all this other shit has to go. It's what I have to do. You right: we stop now and Rock get to us. We keep going, maybe we get left alone."

"Or Willie let us back in out of respect."

"True."

Elf pulled a j out of his coat. "How we go up is how we come down. You can't go into the towers and make all that. How that happen?"

He put the whole j in his mouth like he wanted to hide it there, then brought it out slow between pursed lips, making sure it wasn't too dry.

He cupped one hand around it and flicked the lighter a few times. He got the flame to last only as far as the joint, if that far, and then turned to Junius. "Give a hand?"

Junius cupped both hands around the j. This time Elf brought the flame to its tip and inhaled, took a few quick puffs.

"Thanks."

He nodded with his mouth full, his cheeks puffed out, and held the j into the wind, let the breeze carry off a stray ash. When he exhaled again, he took a deeper toke and a longer inhale, pushed the smoke down into his lungs.

He held it out to Junius, and Junius shook his head. "I'm cool."

Elf's eyes narrowed. He let out the smoke. "Niggah, you not gone hit this?"

"I got to stay clear in my head now. This big."

"Just chill. Sit back and lounge. Nothing going anywhere while we up here."

Facing out over the rooftops, Junius knew it wouldn't last, that he was going to have to act.

"Let me ask you," Elf said. "What made you come back? Why you didn't just get up in them towers when we was there? Why you fuck with Lamar again?"

Junius closed his eyes, pictured the scene with Lamar standing over Elf, going for his Glock.

"Had to," he said.

Elf took another hit, swallowed as much as he could, and sat back to hold it in his lungs. He shook his head as he held it, Junius waiting.

"Nah," he finally let out the smoke in a gasp. "I can't let you do this on your own. Hit this j and then we figure out where we sleep tonight."

"Bullshit." Terrence was on the phone when Junius and Elf came in off the roof. "Nah, niggah. You can't be serious. I'm looking at him right now."

"Bitch," Elf said. "Hang up that phone." His brother looked at him with slow eyes like he was watching TV. "Now!" Elf leapt across the room and hung up the phone by hitting the cradle. "Fuck you talking about, niggah?"

Junius took a step back toward the window. The fact that even high Elf could move like that, snap on his brother so fast, stunned him.

"I—"

"Who you talking to?" Elf grabbed his younger brother by the face, squeezing his cheeks together. His brother beat at his arm with the phone handset, but Elf didn't stop. "What you talking to them about?"

Terrence tried to talk, but his words came out smush-face. Elf let him go. "Speak!"

"I was talking to Ramon. He say your boy shot Lamar." Terrence looked at Junius with an expression somewhere between fear and awe. "You did that?" he asked.

"Fuck," Elf said. "Course he didn't kill nobody. You crazy?" He smacked his brother across the temple for good measure. "How you tell people that shit?"

Junius didn't know what to say. Suddenly he felt like he was the one who'd gotten stoned on the roof.

Elf looked over at Junius. "Don't matter what you didn't do, now. This fuck told somebody your ass up in here, then this be where we can't stay."

"What? I—" Elf's brother stammered.

"Who Ramon know?" Elf asked him. "Who told his ass that Junius did something? Huh?"

Terrence shook his head.

"Exactly. Right now he telling someone else that J here, and *some-body* getting ready to come find us."

"Shit," Junius said. He didn't want to go back out into the cold and find another place to hide for the night, but if Elf was right, then that's what they'd have to do.

"I—" Terrence tried again.

"You stupid." Elf clapped his brother on the side of the head, almost knocking him out of his chair. "Come on, J. We out." He tilted his neck at Junius and headed for the stairs.

8

Marlene looked out at the roofs of the other two towers: the additional one she held and the one Rock's boys controlled. In both she could see flames burning in the windows, the occasional lighter brought up to a pipe filled with what they'd started calling crack.

Crack: solid cocaine rolled into a ball and mixed with shit, cutter, ammonia. Smoked. The fastest high, the worst down, the most people fucked up she'd ever seen this fast. Marlene wasn't selling rocks to people in her towers, not supplying her own with the white death that went for less than weed, fucked you up ten times worse, and left you begging for another blast.

No, she wouldn't work that way; she wouldn't take her own people to that place and make them beg. But Rock would, and now she needed to clear him out. Her people were already walking over to 412 and buying from his crew.

She ran a fingertip across her upper lip. In her hand, she clutched the remote for the lighting and shades. She'd made her penthouse by breaking out a wall and joining two of the public housing units together, and she could call it that all she wanted, but looking out the windows into North Cambridge, into a town of two-family separated houses, she knew there was more than what she had here.

She slid the blinds closed with a button. With another button, she brought the lights up, just enough to add visibility to the ambience she'd set up with her row of candles on the mantle and the two on stanchions above either end of the couch. Laid out across the tan suede, Anthony snored lightly, the candlelight shimmering in the sweat across his chest.

He looked good and she knew it, the way his chest thinned to two narrow hips and fine legs. She'd be able to get him up again, awake and aroused, and that would distract her from Rock for another half hour, maybe more, but it wouldn't solve anything. Seeing those pipes blazing in *her* windows, knowing that poison instead of basic, simple weed was going into the lungs of *her* people sent a shiver through her. All out of simple greed.

"Fuck," she said. "This can't stand."

They called her Oracle because things she said came true. These days, in most cases they did because she made them, controlled the manpower and violence to get her wishes accomplished, her plans realized. But even before all this, she had something people believed in.

Once, as a girl, she won an AM radio at a street fair by picking the right paper bag off a table filled with a hundred. People asked her for the rest of the day to do their picking. Each time she did they wound up with something they wanted—not the rubber bounce balls, or the other cheap toys from the supermarket machines, but fancy brushes and nice mirrors, little remote control cars on wires. The good stuff.

After that, at age eight, she started having dreams. When she dreamt that her uncle, her mother's brother, would be killed, she did not say a thing. Then, a week later, he was taken by a truck while driving home.

Drunk driver, the police said, but the white man behind the wheel never went to jail. Nothing happened to him.

Her mother cried for weeks.

For close to a month, she would not leave the apartment; she'd stay in her room, come out and drink coffee, an occasional beer. When she ate, it was cereal. She sent Marlene's older brother to the store for groceries and he'd come back with real food: eggs, cheese, macaroni, even hamburgers, but her mother wouldn't eat. These things sat in the refrigerator getting old until Marlene took pans out from under the counters, put things into them, and did her best to follow the instructions on the boxes, to make do when they called for ingredients she didn't have (two sticks of butter?), or guess at how to cook things like hamburgers that came without instructions at all.

Her brother laughed at the table, quietly so their mother wouldn't hear, and told Marlene they were the worst meals he had ever eaten, even as he wolfed down whatever she put out. He'd be careful at first, slow to fork into the crisp pieces of meat she scraped onto his plate, but still he ate them, every one.

For the whole time her mother cried, Marlene blamed herself for not telling her family about the dream.

Then a year later, the dreams came back. This time they featured her brother.

Malik had always been a basketball player, one of the best in the towers. He regularly stayed out late holding court up at Corcoran Park.

In her dream he played basketball for a school with uniforms and a crowd. His team was losing. They were only down a few points and Malik had done something good, something she didn't see because the crowd stood above her, cheering. And then they groaned loudly as a group, and a woman screamed. She heard someone shout Malik's name.

That was how the dream ended. She had it twice on successive nights and this was enough to make her frightened. Even with the dream of her uncle, she hadn't seen anything twice.

She told her brother, begged him not to play for the school team that year, but he'd committed himself to trying out for varsity at Cambridge Rindge and Latin, the school where Patrick Ewing had played and Rumeal Robinson was a star. So what if Malik was an inconsistent student his first two years; he'd decided to try out and had been going to class. His mind couldn't be changed.

Then the tragedy began.

Malik made the team and played more and more as the season progressed. By his senior year he was averaging fifteen points a game. He was asked to play for UMass Boston. The problems started when he left Cambridge, moved out to play for Salem State.

At home was where things changed. With Malik gone, nothing remained behind but the resentment. No one liked somebody from the towers to make it, even if Malik's success was anything but guaranteed. Just that he had an option was enough for people he'd come up with—the other players and runners and even those who dropped out of school before Malik went back to class—to turn on him.

So when he did finally get hurt—in a game for Salem State when he went up for a dunk over a crowd and severed his ACL on the landing, basically fell from the rim to the floor in a terrible position and destroyed his knee—he returned to find the towers gone sour around him. People were secretly happy at his failure. Over time, when he didn't play basketball again, he grew welcomed. They accepted him as one of their own, a loser to the world but a life-long member of the Rindge Towers; as long as he had not actually made it free, the fact that he came close was a cause for respect.

This was his tragedy, as well as his greatest success.

From his return, he started taking over the drug game in his own tower, 410, and when he achieved that, he took over 411, installed Marlene and their mother in the double-unit at the top to rule its game. To their mother, this was the second tragedy of her life, the one that pushed her into the misery from which she never returned.

Seeing her son turn back to the towers and become a part of the game was more than she could handle. She retreated again to her room, crying, refusing to eat but once a day. She started to wither into a frail old woman. Her social security checks piled up on the kitchen table—she wouldn't use them and neither Malik nor Marlene needed or wanted the money.

That was when Marlene had another dream. In this one she pictured her mother in a field, the sun on her face and flowers in her hair, the wind blowing around her. She was smiling. Marlene heard a voice in the background, a woman calling to her mother from a house.

The second time she had the dream, she knew the voice was her aunt—her father's younger sister, still living in Mississippi—though they hadn't spoken to or heard from her in nearly twenty years.

When she woke up, she knew what they had to do. Her mother needed to go south, back to the state where she grew up, where she'd lived before her ambitious husband moved them north to try his luck in Boston, where he wound up driving a bus for the MBTA.

When the cheerful postcards started arriving from Mississippi and they knew their mother was happy, Marlene became even more important. Malik recognized her as special, possessing more knowledge than she could be explained to possess.

He had started them calling her the Oracle, and she became a big part of his new hold on the game.

Without their mother to worry, Malik grew ruthless, his hold on the towers increasing until the last two with power were Rock and himself.

Rock had 412, and Malik controlled 410 and 411 with the power of Marlene's visions and his iron fist.

9

Elf led Junius up his block into Somerville, further from the projects, toward the neighborhoods that were nothing but houses where white people lived. They passed the big hall for Jehovah's Witnesses, and Junius heard music inside and thought he saw people dancing.

Elf pulled him on.

"Fuck. What happen when Rock's crew or someone from Willie show up at my house? They gone fuck with Terrence. And if my mom answers—" Elf didn't finish the thought. Instead, he just said, "Fuck," which covered it.

Junius snapped out of whatever haze he'd entered. If Elf's mom had to deal with boys from Willie or Rock's crew, then things were bad for Elf as far as going home again. His mom had already put him on a probation.

"Where we going?"

"Shit if I know." Elf cut onto a side street and stopped by a brick wall. "I was thinking we could break into a house. Find one where no one's home and break in through the basement."

"Yeah? Or maybe we go to my mom's."

"You don't think they be waiting? Watching your moms to see everything she does?"

Junius felt the cold whip through his jeans and wrap around his legs. He knew it was too cold for them to stay out much longer. "How about we break in though *my* basement? Go around through the back way?"

"What if Rock's boys waiting up in there for us?"

Junius shook his head, trying to force the thought out of his mind. "Then that's where we going. I don't want my moms bothered by no fools." He got up and started for his house: up the cross street it wasn't more than a handful of blocks over and a few streets up.

"Come on," he said.

They crossed the bottom of Junius's block as quiet as they could. He pulled his hood up and walked quickly, looking for people in parked cars—a lit cigarette, a head, any sign of someone—but didn't see anything. He agreed with Elf that they worked better individually, so he crossed the street again and headed up Thompkins—one block over and in the direction of his house.

As a kid, he'd jumped yards too many times to remember, trying to outrun another crew, lose someone he'd robbed or even get away from the police. Hopping the fence at the back of his mother's small yard was an old trick. The only wrinkle this time was he'd have to break in through the back door instead of going around to the front and using his key.

He scanned the cars on Thompkins. Nothing. At the right house, number 334, he waited beside a parked Cadillac.

In five minutes, longer than the amount of time they'd agreed on, he saw Elf coming up the block.

Junius's legs were cold enough now to be itchy. Even inside the pockets of his thick jacket, his hands felt like blocks. He could see his breath cloud in front of him, like steam from a pipe.

Then Elf was beside him. "That the house, right?" Elf pointed his chin at 334.

"Yeah. You see anything by my mom's?"

"Nobody. But that don't mean they not there."

"Yeah."

Junius wanted to appear calm and in control. It was, after all, his idea to come here. If something was wrong inside, if some of Rock's boys were waiting, he owed it to his mother to fix that, to keep her safe.

He hunched over as he walked. Beyond the garbage cans, to the side of 334, was an unlocked gate. Like the rest of the neighborhood, the people who lived here knew a locked gate wouldn't stop anyone. Junius opened it and passed inside.

Walking along the side of the house was technically the point where he started trespassing, but Junius didn't care. Elf came right behind. Light shining through the windows settled on the side of 332, less than five feet from where Junius slid along the base of 334 toward its yard.

There, he took one look around, knowing where he'd see the light on the back of the house with its automatic sensor. He knew it would come on as soon as he crossed the yard, but hoped no one was watching. If they noticed the light, maybe they would think it was a raccoon or somebody's dog.

Junius tried to stay away from the house as he crossed the backyard, but when the light came on, he broke into a run across the grass. He vaulted over the fence to the frozen space behind his mother's.

1 0

Gail Ponds-Posey sat on the couch in the dark when the knocking started. It seemed strange to her that someone would knock, but with this old house the bell couldn't always be trusted.

She sighed.

Less than twenty minutes ago, the last of her mourners had left. These were the other women from the neighborhood who cared enough and knew how she felt. It seemed there were too many of them—women like her, in their forties, already dealing with too much loss. She knew those her age who were grandmothers raising grand-kids in place of sons or daughters who'd gone off, not ready for the responsibility, or come up dead.

Now she'd lost one of her own boys in addition to her husband, a man not so unlike these kids today. He'd never been ready to raise a child, let alone *two* boys. Aldo had steadily drunk himself further and further into a stupor, lost too many jobs to keep track of. Finally she asked him to leave. Two boys was enough of a burden; a third, grown and old enough to know better, just couldn't be abided.

And so she did what she had to: joined the other women in being alone in this world with her children. Whether the fathers had gone to jail, run off, or gotten themselves killed, the result was the same for the women: the job of raising the children became theirs alone. They helped one another as much as they could, pitched in with small favors, remembering to call each other before making a trip to the supermarket, but they all were tired. Too tired. The nights and days of working, the lines and endless fights for state support wore them down all the same. Too many of the boys' needs either happened too fast to ask for help with or just caught her blindsided when she got off a shift and came home to a mess.

The knocks came again, louder this time. She wondered if they would decide she wasn't home, if the lights being off would help them realize she'd gone to sleep, didn't want any, or just needed to mourn on her own. She decided to wait for that realization to come to whomever it was outside, but the knocks continued.

That she did the best she could was no consolation. Seeing Temple laid out in a coffin, her first-born son in his only suit—still too short at the sleeves and tight around his chest—and her husband showing up halfway through the wake, drunk, hardly able to stand, taking a swing at another man before being forcibly removed, all of it amounted to the worst day of her life, the lowest she'd felt in as long as she could remember.

She knew God worked in mysterious ways, that anything he gave her was more a challenge and a path to her fate than anything she caused, but still she couldn't help feeling the fault was hers, as if she could have done something better along the way.

She should have left the neighborhood, taken the boys to New York to make a go with her sister. But she knew better. With her one son left, the one who was a man too soon, she wouldn't do different.

Taking Junius to New York City now would help her lose him; he would leave her to come back to these streets—the only world he knew.

The knock came again and she heard her name called by a voice she couldn't recognize. A voice that said he knew she was inside. It was a man's voice, sure enough. Someone, she could tell already, who meant no good.

She rose off the couch and heard her knees creak. "Please," she said under her breath, "let this man leave me alone."

She crossed the small living room into the short hall, turned, and saw the silhouette of two heads through the window of her front door.

"You inside there? Gail, these men know you at home." She closed her eyes, cursed at the sound of her ex-husband's voice. He almost sounded sober, a detail she knew couldn't mean anything good.

Junius stood at the back door with Elf right behind him. He tried the knob, knowing it would be locked.

This would be the hard part: breaking in without waking his mother or being heard by anyone else. If the key to the back door was the same as the front, things would be too easy. Of course it had to be hard. Cold as it was, things would continue to be hard.

No one had a key to the back door. As far as Junius knew, one had never existed.

On the other side of the thin wooden door was his mother's back staircase that led down to her basement and its warmth.

"Let me try."

Junius stood out of the way for Elf. He shook the door, tried to turn the knob, and then took a card out of his pocket and jammed it into the crack between the door and the frame.

"Nah," Junius said. "Shit opens the other way. You can't do it like that."

He looked up at the fire escape to the upper floors. Going in through a window, then coming down the back stairs to the basement meant going in through someone else's rooms, running into a neighbor in the middle of the night or waking someone up. That route would definitely not work.

"Fuck this," Junius said.

He pushed Elf out of the way and threw his shoulder into the door. The sound wasn't as loud as he thought; it worked like he'd hoped. On his second try, he heard a small cracking in the frame, and with his fourth try, holding the knob in his hand and thrusting his whole side into the door, he broke the lock through the frame and the door came open. Four tries, four sounds he hoped would be muffled enough by the house, the hall, his jacket, and the noise of his neighborhood at night.

He stuck his head inside and listened. Warm air came out around his face and something inside smelled familiar: his mother's smell, maybe the scent of the products she used to clean. He held his breath, trying to taste this smell as he listened for whatever sounds would come.

Eventually he let his air out.

"Let's go." Elf had already said it once, but Junius made him wait. Now he opened the door and entered the house. Immediately on his left was the door to the basement that no one ever locked. He sent Elf down the shaky wooden steps.

He came to know these steps well last summer when he brought Dawn over to his house to fuck in the basement. Temple had explained to him how it worked: the times he knew his mother would be home, he went down and unlocked the back door ahead of time, then took Dawn around back later and into the basement to do it on the old rugs. When they fucked like that he had to make sure she stayed quiet. They could hear his mother walking around just above them, the floorboards creaking over their heads.

Once he forgot to check whether his mother would be doing laundry. On that occasion, hearing her open the kitchen door, he'd known immediately, pulled out, and hustled Dawn up onto her feet, so that when his mother creaked down the basement stairs they were both behind the big gas furnace, holding their breaths. Dawn was naked from the waist down, crouched beside the furnace, and Junius had just enough time to pull up his shorts.

Dawn wanted to laugh, and Junius knew if he looked at her he'd lose it, so he kept his eyes trained on the heater and the small flame that burned inside it. He listened to his mother load the washer, then add detergent and, finally, start it up. He breathed when he heard this sound, then more freely when his mother went back up the steps.

By the time the back door off the kitchen had closed, Dawn burst into giggles with her hands over her mouth and her eyes watering. Junius looked at her—her curly brown hair and long eyelashes, and below her yellow tank top her pale white legs—and he knew she was worth it. He took his shorts off again and led her back down onto the rugs.

Now he did his best to close the broken back door, found the brick they used to prop it open in the summer and used it to prop the door shut.

As he started down the stairs, waiting a few breaths for his eyes to adjust to the dark, he thought he could hear voices from the front of his mother's apartment. From the direction of the living room and above them, he thought he could hear the sound of a man's voice.

A dim light showed through the small window on the side of the house, whatever moon- and street-light made it through the narrow gap between his mother's house and next door. Junius led Elf past the furnace, toward the washing machines.

Above them, he could hear someone pacing—heavy footsteps creaking the wood. Some *man* was walking in his mother's living room, talking to her. He heard another voice from the direction of where the couch would be. The second voice was a man's as well, just a little bit familiar, but not one that Junius could place.

"What do we do?" Elf whispered.

Junius shook his head.

"You hear your moms?"

"No."

Then Junius heard a soft voice. It was his mother and she sounded like she might be crying. Junius felt his blood pressure jump a notch. Someone was up there and they were making his mother cry.

"Let's go," he said to Elf, heading back toward the stairs so he could get to her apartment.

Elf stopped him with a hand on his chest. "What we do? Think it's Rock up there he be happy to see us?"

"I don't care."

"You want your mother to see you shot? That fix things?"

Junius clenched his teeth. He had a habit of grinding his teeth in his sleep; his mother used to stand by his bed at night, listening to the sounds and fearing what he would do to his mouth. Now, he clenched them and ground his bottom molars against the tops. He'd noticed that he did this when he was stressed.

"Fuck. If they up there with her—"

"Chill, man. We wait them out, hang here for a while. Maybe by morning they gone."

"Morning? Yo, fuck *that.*"

Elf started for the rugs, maybe thinking about lying down, and Junius thought of Dawn.

He checked his watch and saw it wasn't even midnight. Still, it was time for his mother to be in bed. He took the gun out of his waistband and felt for the button to release its clip. He wasn't sure how many bullets he had left, but he popped the clip out and felt the round hood of the first bullet, its soft, smooth tip.

He didn't know how many men were up there or how many bullets it would take. They'd be armed and there were at least two of them. He knew that much.

1 2

Junius asked himself what Temple would do.

His brother taught him to care for and look after their mother. She'd been through enough today with the funeral, Temple gone and now someone she didn't know keeping her up at night, making her cry. Even if Elf was right that waiting was the best move, it wasn't a choice Junius could make. He wouldn't sleep, rest, or sit down with his mother upstairs in pain.

He hoped they wouldn't do anything physical to her.

In the quiet, he tried harder to hear what was being said. I Ie heard mumbles and then his mother said something clear: his father's name.

Junius swore. He took a step toward Elf, who was lying on the crusty carpet that Junius wanted to tell him would be stained with so much jizz, but didn't. Instead he kicked him.

"Get up," he said. "That's my moms."

Then Elf was up. They both listened as someone above them raised his voice and yelled, "I know you going to tell me where he be!"

"Derek?" Elf asked.

Junius recognized the voice too. "That niggah."

Then he heard another voice, a man who wasn't his father, Derek or Derek's boy. It was someone older, maybe even older than Lamar, definitely a full soldier in Rock's crew.

Junius swore again.

"Three of them?"

Junius nodded.

"What we do?"

"We get up there." Junius started toward the back stairs, slow at first, and then faster at the back of the house. Elf moved slowly in the dark.

At the top of the stairs, Junius turned and climbed the two steps to the door that led to his mother's kitchen. Two thoughts crossed his mind: that someone might be waiting for him on the other side, and that he'd be safer going around to the front and trying to case out what was happening through the windows.

He put his ear to the door and listened for someone in the room. Derek probably didn't even know about the back door. And walking around to the front of the house meant he might be seen by someone watching the street. If Derek was upstairs, Ness had to be close.

Junius tried the knob. It was unlocked.

He opened the door a crack, waiting for something to happen. When nothing did, he peeked inside—just his head and the gun— and saw only the dark kitchen, a light across the floor of his mother's small dining room. His mother always kept the apartment clean, took pride in the fact that she had the extra room and a nice table to set for when they had company.

This was her home, and Junius wouldn't abide someone coming in and holding her hostage. If they wanted to find him, they were about to.

Junius showed Elf the gun, and Elf held up a small planting shovel he'd picked up in the basement. Junius shrugged.

He pushed the kitchen door open and pointed to a spot where they'd be able to see the living room. Junius moved to the spot, kneeled, and Elf came behind him, both of them low beside the table. Looking beneath it, Junius saw the backs of Derek's legs in baggy black jeans.

In the dining room, the mourners' food was still laid out: casseroles, store-bought trays of cold cuts with clear plastic tops, fried chicken. Junius realized he hadn't eaten since that afternoon. His stomach grumbled.

He pointed to the set of legs and to a spot in the hall next to the living room's other entrance. His mouth close to Elf's ear, he whispered, "I go that way. When I move in, you go through the dining room and hit Dee from behind."

Elf nodded.

Junius moved low and quiet, on the balls of his feet, his fingertips just brushing the floor. In the hall, he hugged the wall of the living room, then stopped and leaned against it when he reached the doorframe. On the love seat, his mother cried softly, repeating that she didn't know where he was. He heard his father ask her to help him, and then a choking sound. The unmistakable click of a gun cocking. His mother *hated* guns.

The only word that flashed through Junius's mind had four letters and his mother didn't like.

He knew acting with a plan was always better, knew from the kung fu movies he watched every Saturday that the fighters who rushed in were the ones who didn't last. But some of the heroes did rush in, took care of everything before they had time to consider a strategy. Some of the best just fought everyone they came across, took on everything in the world. Junius liked them.

The best part about these fighters was their rules, a code they had, which Junius also liked. He knew if there was anything like a set of rules for his game, it included people not fucking with somebody's mother, especially not an older woman in a grieving state.

He shook his head as he raised the gun, leaned back into his haunches and straightened his knees.

Then, when he heard Derek say, "Tell us old woman, or this old man gets dead," he bolted up and around the corner into the living room.

To his left, the first thing he saw was a man who wasn't Ness choking his father and, in the middle of the room, Derek with a .45 raised and pointed at his father's head. From behind him, his mother cried out.

Junius aimed at Derek, but he didn't have time to shoot before Elf came in low from behind and tackled Derek to the floor. His mother screamed for them to stop.

Derek and Elf battled on the rug for control of the .45 with Derek waving it wildly around the room until Junius stepped up and kicked it out of his hand. His mother wouldn't want *any* shooting going on in her house. But then the man holding his father stood and pushed Junius over the coffee table and onto the empty couch. He was off balance after the kick, and that was part of why he went down, but also the guy who shoved him was *strong*. The man held his father up in front of him in a headlock and put his other hand behind the old man's head. Aldo's eyes went wide.

"You want me to kill this old fool? Because I pop his head off right now." The man started to squeeze. "How about that?"

"Clarence, stop this!" his mother screamed.

Junius raised his gun to point at the man called Clarence. His father was partly in the way, but from so close it was an easy shot.

"No!" his mother cried again. She closed her eyes and crossed herself.

Clarence laughed. "Yeah," he said. "Don't shoot me in front of your mother, young buck."

That was when all hell broke loose on the floor: without his gun, Derek started to fight wild against Elf. The two of them knocked over the coffee table.

Elf was on top for a moment, and then it was Derek with the upper hand. He had Elf beneath him, choking, then pounded his face into the rug. He only did it once, but that was enough to reopen Elf's split lips.

When Junius saw that, he was the one to call out. If they got blood on his mother's rug, that'd be as bad as killing someone. He kicked the coffee table back over and it hit Derek, giving Elf enough time to scramble away and get his hand over his mouth.

Junius sat up. He aimed the gun at Clarence.

"You don't want that, J. Tell your son, Aldo."

"Just do what the man says, boy. Listen to them now."

Gail Ponds-Posey opened her eyes and hit Elf hard across the back of his head. "Boy, you get your ass off my rug if you be bleeding!" She followed the slap with a box of tissues thrown at Elf's face. He just managed to knock it out of the air before it hit him.

Clarence laughed, still holding Junius's father.

"Who *are* you?"

"I be the devil, son. The first and the last. *I will fuck you up.*"

"Clarence! Don't you talk that way to my boy." Gail Ponds-Posey stood up fast, maybe too fast, because the man she'd called Clarence shifted Aldo's head into his other arm and shoved her back down onto her love seat. She landed with a loud huff, and Junius jumped onto his feet, crossed the room with one step, and shoved the man back into the wall, pushing the loaded gun into his face. The frame of a hanging art print broke and fell off the wall, its glass shattering onto the floor.

"No!"

Junius didn't look at his mother this time. He met Clarence's bloodshot, yellowed eyes. Again he found himself in a situation where the gun had put him somewhere he didn't want to be, somewhere his choices were actions he didn't want to take.

Clarence pushed his father down onto the rug. To Junius's right, Derek looked like he might make a move, so Junius cocked the hammer of the nine. "Don't push up, Dee. You just sit."

He pushed the gun against Clarence's temple. "You the first and the last?"

Elf went under the man's chair and got Derek's gun. He stood with it in one hand, a fistful of tissues held over his mouth in the other.

Junius pushed Clarence harder against the wall, lowering the gun barrel down his face to push at his lips. "Momma, I swear I don't want this," he said. "And I didn't want to shoot Lamar, but he strapped and I'm strapped and—"

"Where you get a gun at?"

Junius shook his head. "The point be that now I have it things changed. Truth is, I just want sit down, eat something, go up to bed. But now we got these fools in our house, probably more outside." He pushed Clarence down into a chair.

"You shouldn't've did this," Clarence said.

"Sure." Junius stepped back. "I shouldn't have did lots of shit. But I did. So now what I'm going to do?"

"You can fight like you was a man, boy."

As soon as Clarence said it, Gail Ponds-Posey was up off the love seat fast, across the short distance to his chair, and slapped him hard across the face. "You come in *my house?*" she asked. "To tell *my son* how he should act as a man? I done lost one boy this week and I am *not* about to lose two." She stood over him, pushed Junius behind her. "*Now get up off my chair and get the fuck out my house!*"

Clarence started up slowly. Elf still held Derek's gun on him. "Put that gun down!" Gail Ponds-Posey yelled. "You take out those bullets and give this boy back what belongs to him."

Elf looked over at Junius, and he shrugged, so Elf slid the clip out of the .45 and ejected the round from the chamber. He turned the gun around and set it before him on the floor.

"Come on, Dee," Clarence said, rising. Beside him, Aldo was still getting up off the floor. "You better do what she says, now. Clear who got the pants up in this house."

"I—" Aldo started to respond, but his wife cut him off with one wave of her hand.

"Don't you dare think about responding to him." She turned back to Clarence. "Don't think I wouldn't tell your mother all about this if she were still alive today, Clarence Williams. She be turning over in her *grave* at this behavior. Unbelievable."

Clarence stood tall, his head almost a foot above Gail Ponds-Posey's, but he kept his eyes down. "These ain't your streets, ma'am. Things changed now."

"That may be so, young man. But this is still my house. Do you hear me? You do *not* come in here and make this your street corner. Understand?"

Clarence nodded. He waited for Derek to stop and pick up his gun, then they walked toward the front door. There he turned back to the living room one last time. "We be waiting for you, junior. We there whenever you want to come outside."

Gail Ponds-Posey pushed Clarence toward the stairs.

"Get out of my house," she said. "And leave a grieving family to grieve!"

1 3

Malik had been doing fine in the towers until the unthinkable happened: the police arrested him without warning. No dreams, no insight that it was coming, Marlene just as stunned as her brother. That the case against him for conspiracy and drug trafficking dropped him in Billerica for a seven-year stretch came as even more of a surprise.

And suddenly Malik was gone. Marlene could visit him, a simple forty-minute drive out Route 2 was all it took to get to the prison, the glass between them as thin as the width of her finger when they faced each other, phones to their ears.

He was calm there. The respect he owned in the towers translated to his life inside. Enough of his people had already been arrested in a steady stream of men disappearing over the years, that they populated a crew in the prison, enough of a force to see Malik got what he needed and didn't get hurt.

So the inside wasn't bad. When he eventually got a phone, Marlene's visits to Billerica slowed. He controlled the towers *through* her, their plans concocted daily by phone.

They held 410 and 411, though Rock came at them once, twice. Malik's men trusted Marlene, especially Seven Heaven, his second in command, his enforcer, his gun.

And for the past three years, that was how things stood: Malik, Marlene, and Seven Heaven at the top of their world, not aspiring to destroy Rock but holding on to what they had. Malik felt keeping Rock in the picture helped them, gave the appearance of competition, the sense that they didn't control enough of the towers to invite any outside attention from gangs in Boston or the 808 crew, a group that controlled the biggest set of projects in Cambridge, the huge six-building complex along the Charles River on Memorial Drive.

But that changed when Rock brought his namesake into the game. When every fiend in the towers found he could get twenty times the blast from cocaine at a lower price, he went right for that Ready Rock, the candy that came in little vials.

She saw her customers stray to Rock and go immediately downhill: they forgot their lives, their jobs—if they had them—and turned to stealing and other crimes to satisfy the never-ending itch.

It got bad fast, and Marlene wondered why she was the only one who saw the trend when she looked out through her windows. Sure, some of the older residents, the grandmothers and grandfathers saw it, called the police when they were assaulted in front of their buildings for whatever cash they held, mostly the gains of social security checks, but Marlene knew—just like everyone else—that these complaints would do nothing, that she might be the only one with the power to make any change.

"You ok?" She felt Anthony's hand brush her shoulder, smooth her hair back out of her face. "Why you look so worried, beautiful?"

She looked down at his chest, avoiding his eyes, and noticed that between his legs he was stiffening already, again. She moved forward to kiss him, brushed his lips and ran her hand across his back. She kissed his pecs and his nipples, started to head downward when he put his hands on her shoulders and held her where she was.

"Marlene. You can tell me. I know you don't think I can help here, but maybe I can."

He smiled. Sure, Anthony would think he'd have answers to the problems in her towers. As one of the few black members of his class at Harvard Law, he thought he had answers for everything, that the books he studied had real power over places like this, forgotten civic ideas like the Rindge Towers.

He thought the DA's office could help, that a few good arrests would lead to small solutions that would build and build until—guess what?—all of her problems and the problems of the towers' residents would be solved.

Marlene didn't know what she found most troubling: his idealism about her world and how naive he seemed, or the chance that his view of the problems included her.

He winked and she knew Anthony really thought he could help, thought he knew what she had going on. He didn't even know how she made her money or came to afford what he liked to call "her penthouse in the skies of ghetto heaven."

He knew Malik was her brother and why he'd been sent to Billerica. Sometimes she even entertained the idea that he might be trying to use her, that he secretly hoped to get inside her world and draw enough evidence to break his big, career-making case for whatever law firm or prosecutor's office he wanted to join once he got his JD.

But if he was using her, she supposed they were even.

When they met in Harvard Square the night Marlene snuck out on her own, against the advice of Seven Heaven, the one thing she saw in Anthony, other than a beautiful face and perfect body, was the fact he was someone else, *someone from outside*.

So she used him to explore another world, to see how life looked through a different set of eyes—and, sure, the sex was good enough to keep him around just for its sake alone, just as long as he didn't try to bring a case against her.

"I'm fine." She ran her fingers through the short hairs on his chest, a ploy she knew he had a hard time resisting, and stretched up to kiss him again.

He let her kiss him twice before he cupped her face in his hands. "I know you have a problem, lovely. I just want you to understand that I might be able to help you out of it."

"I know." She nodded her way out of his hands. If there was one condition that their relationship had to exist on, she knew, it was that she never let him inside what was real.

14

"Now what the fuck you got yourself into?" Junius's mother had just shut the door on their company and now she turned to her son, demanding an answer.

"I—" Junius said.

She slapped him across the face.

Elf shied away into a corner of the room. Aldo Posey stood with his head down. He looked like he was trying to fall asleep on his feet.

"Please tell me you did not just bring those fools into my house," she said, looking at her husband. "*Aldo!*"

He jumped to attention. "I— They— they found me at the bar."

"*Sorry!*" Gail said. "You are *sorry!* Now tell this boy to go get himself killed the same week we just lost Temple."

"I—" Aldo Posey didn't say anything else.

"That's right," she said. She told Junius to stand up, even before he'd finished sitting down. "Don't make me tell you again. You hungry?" she asked. "Make yourself a plate and then come back to tell me what all this show is about."

"Yes, ma'am."

Junius crossed into the dining room and to the table of food that his mother's friends had left after the funeral reception: enough food for a week, food for at least four people. Junius took a fried chicken breast and a drumstick, some cold cuts, potato salad, and a biscuit. Elf followed.

In the living room, his mother had righted the coffee table and was fixing her magazine stacks. "Sit," she commanded. Junius and Elf sat side by side on the couch. She asked them what they wanted to drink and then went and brought them Cokes from the kitchen. "Now tell me what all this is about."

Junius explained he and Lamar had been in a fight that Rock didn't like, and that that was where Derek and Clarence had come from. He didn't say anything about Marlene or anyone getting shot or the other towers. When he finished, he just looked at her.

"I don't *want* to know who killed your brother," she said. "You know who it was? It was *this*. All this around you, what you bringing into this house, what you see on the streets is what took your brother from us." She waved her arm to include both ends of the block, whatever else might be outside. "That took him and now it taking you!"

Junius chewed. He knew better than to answer his mother when she was explaining her views on the world. She'd be talking about church next and how it all went wrong when he'd stopped coming to Sunday mass. He watched his father start to nod off behind her. Back in a chair, he was actually starting to fall asleep.

When his mother saw where he was looking, she turned in time to see Aldo's chin hit his chest. "My Lord!" she said. "God knows he been no good to you. Didn't set something right. But didn't I show you not to get involved in this mess?"

Again she waved to the street outside, their world, all the bad things.

"Yes, ma'am." Junius nodded.

His mother walked to the windows and looked outside. If he had to guess, he thought Rock's boys would have left, gone home for the night, or gone back to tell Rock that Gail Ponds-Posey, a grieving mother, was now part of their problem. Not that Rock would care. He'd know Junius would have to come out at some point, and when he did, the mother rule wouldn't apply.

She drew the blinds shut and sat down heavily on her love seat. "My Lord."

The truth was she was tired. She'd seen Temple taken from her this week and now these men, these pieces of trash, had come into her living room and threatened her, her son, and his friend.

Her husband? He was one of them, a piece of trash like the others, blowing into her house with the wind. A good broom or a wave of her hand was all it took to sweep them back out. But behind her, on the other side of her windows, were the streets, *their* world: the places she couldn't clean, protect her son in, or change.

"My my my," she said. "Aldo." He was asleep in his chair. Even with the lights on around him, that man could fall asleep in the middle of a train station. She shook her head. Maybe she hadn't done enough to set him straight. Maybe that's what had set her sons in the wrong direction. She didn't know. Some of it had to be him, his responsibility.

Her son chewed, drank his soda. He looked like a boy still, just a child, but he'd held a gun at those men. She shut her eyes tight, trying to push away the image of him holding the gun on Clarence. Clarence Williams: a boy she'd seen come up on the streets just like the others, his mother a good woman until the day she was shot dead on the street, killed for being on the wrong block at the wrong time.

Clarence. Sure, they could have done more for the boy, someone could have brought him home and given him a bed. *Someone* had to have an empty bed in their home. But no one had.

It all made her want to weep. She shook her head, looking at her son's friend, the one they called Elf. She knew his mother. Barely older than Junius, he'd held a gun too.

The worst of it, she knew, was still to come.

She stood up and told her son to go up to his room when he finished eating. He and his friend should both sleep upstairs. She would see him in the morning and they would straighten this out then.

She left her husband sleeping on the chair and went to start putting the food away in the kitchen.

Junius woke when his mother opened the curtains beside his bed. Sunlight shone onto his face, and he knew he was done sleeping. He looked at the clock: not yet seven.

"It's early," he said. Then he saw his mother's eyes: cold, decided.

"Get dressed and come downstairs."

He left Elf asleep on the floor and went downstairs in a pair of shorts and an old T-shirt from the baseball league. He stopped in the bathroom to piss. When he got out, he could see on her face he'd made a mistake.

"I got twenty minutes to tell you this, so you listen up."

He sat down across from her, rubbed the sleep out of his eyes. "Yes, ma'am."

She tapped the coffee table. "This here is fifty dollars." Two twenties and a ten lay atop of an issue of *Ebony*. "This enough to get you to your aunt's house in Brooklyn. When you leave here this morning, and I mean in the next hour, before any of these jackasses out there get up," she waved to the street, "you go straight to South Station and get on a Greyhound to New York City. You hear me?"

Junius nodded.

"You walk straight to the subway, do not stop, you buy a ticket and leave as soon as you get downtown. I may not be perfect and the Lord knows you sure done wrong yesterday, but this be the only way. You have to leave here now."

His father grunted in his sleep, and Junius noticed him in the bedroom at the back of the house, sleeping in his mother's bed.

"You don't wake him now neither. Leave him be. He got problems enough on his own."

Junius looked down at his hands—strong hands that should be able to fix this, to keep more trouble from coming. "What about you?"

His mother wiped her cheek. If there was a tear there, he hadn't seen it. "We be ok here. This my home."

"When can I come back?"

She shook her head. "It's not safe for you here no more, and I rather see you at your aunt's when I come visit than see you laid out like Temple. Can't have both my boys like that." She took a deep breath and her shoulders sagged; for a moment, she looked small. She rubbed the bridge of her nose and this time Junius thought he saw the shine of a tear.

Then she sat up straight and exhaled. "No more," she said, restored to herself again. "Time for you to leave."

She checked her watch and stood up, dressed for work already, even after the funeral yesterday and last night's action. There were bills to be paid.

With Teale Square no longer a possibility and Willie Stash not getting behind him, Junius knew this old woman in her flower-print dress might be his only support. This woman he might never see again.

Her and maybe Elf.

Junius held his mother, brought her as close as he could and felt her small body in his strong arms. He couldn't remember exactly when he'd gotten to be so much bigger than she: wide enough that her shoulders didn't cover the space of his chest, tall enough that his chin was higher than the top of her head.

She stood back and pulled away from him, checked her watch again. "This the only way," she said. "Now go."

"I got to get dressed."

She frowned. "Then do it. But don't procrastinate. Get yourself to the station in the next hour. Move before anyone else is awake."

Upstairs, Junius dressed quickly. He took a fast shower, pocketed his mother's fifty dollars, pulled on yesterday's jeans again—they were his favorite—and a clean sweatshirt over his favorite Celtics T.

He looked at the nine on the dresser, removed the clip and counted five bullets left—he'd fired seven times. He considered the gun, knowing he'd had enough shots to destroy his mother's living room last night, to fill it with bodies.

Junius shook his head. The gun just caused trouble.

"Yo." Elf sat up, rubbed his face. "What's up?"

"Time to go," Junius said. "I got to catch a bus."

"Shit. Where you going?"

Junius told him about his aunt, his mother's speech, and the fifty dollars. Elf nodded the whole time.

"I'm a come," he said when Junius had finished. Just like that.

"Then get dressed. We gots to go."

When Elf was pulling his clothes on, Junius hid the nine in a dresser drawer under his T-shirts.

His father was asleep, snoring, when they came downstairs, and Junius didn't wake him.

It was light outside and had been for a few hours. But it was cold. The wind whipped down the street and through his jacket as soon as Junius stepped outside. He locked the door and pushed his key back in through the mail slot. He wouldn't need it again.

Junius zipped his jacket all the way up and pulled on his black knit cap. Elf did the same, his hat a brown Boston College skull cap that he wore with the BC logo on the side of his head.

Neither of them had gloves, so they walked with their hands in their pockets, headed up the street in the direction of Porter Square and its new T station with the big, red sculpture spinning outside. The T would take him to South Station, where he was supposed to catch his bus.

In a Ford at the other end of the block, Derek dozed, his eyes barely open. Ness was fully asleep in the passenger seat, taking his turn while Derek watched. Clarence had said to turn the car off every twenty minutes, so they weren't spouting exhaust and drawing attention to where they were, but come three o'clock in the morning and cold as shit outside, Derek made the executive decision that not freezing their asses off was more important.

They kept the car idling five hours, the heat on, and now the gas gauge dipped down close to empty, but Derek didn't care. He was warm, and if he was a little sleepy, that was how he was *supposed to* feel at this hour in the morning.

His eyelids slowly fell, then he forced them open again, and then they fell. In another half hour, it'd be Ness's turn and he could sleep. For now, he pushed himself.

As soon as he looked again, he saw Junius and his little butt buddy locking the front door, pulling their hats on and walking up the block.

"Shit," Derek said. He punched Ness in the leg. "Wake up, niggah."

Ness started. He sat up, shaking his head, asking, "What, what?"

"Look who just came outside," Derek said. Less than an hour ago, he'd seen Mrs. Ponds-Posey step out onto her porch and lock the door behind her, then head up the block to go to work. He'd thought about going in after them, breaking into the house and shooting those bitches, but feeling comfortable in the heat and not wanting to move for a while had won that war. Now, seeing the two of them, it was most definitely time to make a move.

"Get ready."

He turned the key to start the car, not remembering it was already started, and the ignition made a loud, grinding complaint. Fortunately, Junius and Elf were too far away to hear.

"Yeah." Derek nodded, backed the car up enough to pull out of their space, and drove slowly into the street. "Here we come, motherfuckers."

He idled now, keeping some distance as they walked. They would make a right at the end of the block to head for the T, and when they did, he would move.

"You awake?" Derek asked.

Ness grunted.

"Go find a pay phone." He handed Ness the card with Clarence's home number on it. "Call Clarence. Let him know what we found."

"You serious? You want me to call that mothefucker right now?" He shook his head. "Just drive on past those niggahs and I put two caps in them simple."

"Nah. I said call our man." Derek waited for Ness to finish getting his gloves on before he moved the car again. Even then, he just drove forward a half-dozen feet. "Get out," he commanded.

When Ness finally got out, he turned back. "Where I meet you?" he asked, holding the door open, letting the frigid air blow into the car.

"I be up the block, follow these bitches to Porter Square. Tell Clarence we meet him in the T." Derek nudged the car forward just enough to rip the door from Ness's hand and slam it closed. As he pulled off, he saw Ness hold up both middle fingers and then grab his nuts in the rear-view.

17

Early mornings were her favorite time of day, the only time she'd come down by herself and walk among the people outside. Marlene loved being close to those who really knew the towers, the ones who *belonged* here: the retirees, who always woke early; the workers, out of their apartments before eight AM to get to their shit jobs at fast food chains, Jiffy Lubes, downtown garages, gas stations; even the people coming home from nightshift work, these were the people she respected.

She held her fur around herself, pulled it tight to her neck and faced into the wind, looking out at the parking lot. Some of the retirees pushed rolling carts toward the bridge that crossed the train tracks to Fresh Pond Mall and Star Market, where they'd buy their food for the week with food stamps, welfare checks. The social security helped too, but it was the combination that enabled them to get by, and sometimes that wasn't enough. In her pocket she had an envelope of crisp twenties, ready to give cash to any who asked, whoever had a need. In the early mornings, she'd be sure to give money only to those truly in need.

She watched a rusty Toyota pull in from the street and find a parking place. Its driver got out slowly, a tall man dressed in thick Carhartt layers, coveralls and a jacket over that. He worked at Logan. They'd spoken once. Everyone knew who she was, she expected, but some of them were polite enough to pretend they didn't. Even with the fur.

He worked loading and unloading planes for UPS, packing boxes to ship through the night. The last time she'd seen him he walked fast, comfortable; now he limped, moved slowly toward her building. He lived with his wife, a cleaning woman who worked days and second shift. They saw each other only on the weekends.

As he came up now, his hat low over his face, he barely met Marlene's eyes, just offered a short nod.

"Your walk," she said. "What happened?" Her hand instinctively went to the envelope in her pocket, even seeing on this man's face that he'd be too proud.

"Fell," he said. "Few weeks back." He stopped in front of her. Tall and wide. She guessed he'd weigh two-fifty, maybe more. He played basketball somewhere, at some point. She'd seen him with her brother at the courts.

"You played with Malik, right?"

He nodded. "Timothy." He pulled off a glove and offered her his hand. His cold, hard skin scratched her palm as she shook it, but she looked him in the eyes. "Morning. Nice to see you." He took his hand back and pushed it into a pocket, then turned to resume toward the building.

He didn't get ten feet before a boy, a kid who couldn't be more than twelve, thirteen, turned out from behind one of the pillars. How long had he been there? Without saying a word, the boy held up a baggie and took a bill from the man's hand. Timothy didn't even stop his forward progress, just accepted the exchange like a worker would accept a free paper at the T.

"Alright," the boy said. "Have a good one." Then he saw Marlene and his smile disappeared. He ducked behind the pillar.

"Stop," she said. "Come here."

He did as he was told, looking up with a blank face. "Yes, Miss Marlene," he said.

"Who are you?"

"Jeremy. I'm Jesse's boy."

Jesse: one of her runners, a guy barely Malik's age who'd been a few years ahead of her in school.

"How old?"

"Thirteen."

"You go to school?"

He shrugged. "Most days. This week school vacation." From the smoothness of the exchange with Timothy, she knew his attendance record wouldn't improve when vacation was over. He saw what she knew. "I go or I don't go," he said. "Them teachers don't care. They think I stupid."

"How's your math?"

"Good enough," he said, holding out a roll of cash.

"You know him?" She nodded at where Timothy had been, and the boy told her he sold to the man every day.

"Since the pain," he said. "This what he need to get by." He patted his other front pocket.

"What you carry?"

The boy held out in his hand: dime bags, twenties, nickels, a few baggies with red and yellow pills that she took.

"What are these?"

"You know. Ups, downs. They the regular, like Dunkin' Donuts."

Marlene wanted to say no, to take the pills away from the boy, from the people in her building. But she knew if she did they'd get them from someone else. She'd talk to Malik about it.

"You holding rock?" she asked. This was what she really wanted to know.

"No, ma'am." He shook his head, looked down. "If they want that, I say go get it from him." He pointed at the far tower, the 412.

"They do it?"

He nodded.

"They come back after?"

He shook his head. "No. Huh uh. They get that shit, they don't come back. That's why you should hook *me* up with it. Help sales like Christmas."

She gave him back the pills. "Go home," she said. "Tell your father I said you're not working today, and that next week you go back to school."

The boy looked like she just took his best friend. "I hate school!"

"You need it," she said, gripping the top of his head and turning him back toward the building. "Now go inside and get warm. Get some sleep. Play a game or something."

She watched him go slowly, stubborn, looking back over his shoulder a few times to see if she was still there. With any luck she wouldn't see him out here again. He'd be back, she knew, but if she didn't see him then it wasn't a direct challenge to her authority. If she did see him, then Jesse would have to sit down for a listen.

She turned back to the parking lot. Nearing eight o'clock, the traffic was slow. Those who started work at eight were long gone, those who started later would be coming soon, heading for the trains and buses. But for now there was a lull. She watched her world. To the right, at 410, she saw quiet action: an old man pushing a cart and a boy around eighteen leaning up against a car, waiting to sell.

To her left, she could see 412, Rock's house, and a man running out of the building pulling on an old, tan jacket. He had a beard and a short afro, his body stocky but strong. It was Clarence—one of

Rock's closest boys. Malik had told her to watch him, said he wouldn't be afraid.

In his hurry, Clarence didn't see her. Just ran for his car, a gold Olds 98, that he started hard, backed out hard, and then tore out of the lot in, taking a right on Rindge and heading toward Mass Ave., away from Route 2.

1 8

Clarence rolled the 98 up Rindge Ave., too much in a hurry, too early in the morning to let this shit slide for anybody. So what if that old woman had known his mom, even been good to him when he was coming up.

He hadn't pointed the gun at her; it was Dee, even if he gave the order. He punched the pine trees hanging from his mirror when he hit traffic on Rindge, knocked the plastic baggie off his newest.

He counted eight trees waiting for the bitch school crossing guard to get the little assholes across the street and into school. When the traffic finally did start again, he smelled his fingers: they felt oily at the tips where he'd touched the trees and, sure enough, smelled like too much "Pine-Fresh" scent. He wiped them on his seat, hoping it would be good for the leather. What he wanted was a hit from his stash back up in the apartment, even just a cigarette. *That's* what his fingertips should smell like.

He knew he'd catch another light up at Mass Ave., but still thought he'd get to Porter before the kids, if Ness was right about where they were headed. Then he'd have a smoke—shit, a whole pack of smokes.

The light at the top of Rindge was next: sometimes you made it, sometimes you got fucked; today, Clarence made it. He made the right without even coming to a full stop, caught the red just before the Mass Ave. morning traffic came at him. Maybe this day would work out alright.

Two blocks up, he was in the left lane, slowing for the light, when he saw them—Junius and little Elf—coming up Mass Ave. He slapped the wheel into a hard left, cutting across the two oncoming lanes—another lucky gap—and just missed them. He swore, knowing he'd have run them down if he was three seconds faster through the turn. He hit the wheel and the horn. They both looked back, and he gave them a hard eye-fucking, thought for a second about just stopping the car and getting out to run grab them up. But there was another car behind him trying to make the turn, caught in the middle of Mass Ave. and honking its horn.

"Fuck!" he said again.

They cut across Mass Ave., and he saw them run down a side street as he started up Russell, driving the only direction he could, parked cars along both sides of the street and not enough room to pull over.

The car behind him lay on the horn the whole way, and Clarence had to white-knuckle the steering wheel to keep from getting out and slapping the shit out of somebody.

"That was Clarence," Elf said as they hit the curb on the other side of Mass Ave. and kept going.

Junius didn't slow. He cut down the other half of Russell at a trot, not looking back. Only a week ago, Temple had told him the old train tracks were getting hooked into Porter Square station for the commuter rail. He hoped it meant they could get into the station a back way.

He'd gotten to know Russell Street last summer, when he started messing around with Dawn. Her mom had an apartment in a house on the last part of the block, and they sometimes went there when she was at work. Now Junius didn't stop to look at the house, wonder if Dawn was home, or try to guess who she was fucking. She'd become a ho and nothing more. If he was a part of her transition wasn't his concern.

They hit the short fence that dead-ended the street, and Junius went high, his legs at one side, while Elf just hit it dead-on at his waist. When he was over the top, Junius saw the ten-foot drop to the gravel along the tracks. But with his feet already in the air and his hands letting go of the fence, there was nothing he could do. He floated for a split second at the top of his vault—that instant before he started down, he just flat out hung above the cold earth.

Then he fell. His Nikes hit gravel and he rolled to his side, wound up on his ass, looking back up at the fence in time to see Elf do his flip. He caught his upper body on the tracks-side of the fence—through the ivy—and then swung his legs around so they were beneath him. He paused for a second like that, perfectly in control. Then he let go and landed softly on the gravel. He turned to Junius. "Need some help?"

Junius just shook his head. "You work on that?"

Elf laughed. "Every day, my man. Every fucking day."

They walked the tracks along the gravel, puffing and winded, their breath billowing out of them into the cold.

At the station, they had to pull themselves up onto the platform. It wasn't even in use yet but would soon be a real stop along the commuter rail line. Opaque plastic tarps hung over the benches and covered the spots where signs would be installed. The entranceway to the rest of the station was roped off—red plastic tape stretched across it—but they went through anyway, up a dark set of stairs that didn't smell like piss yet, and to another plastic sheet. Behind it, Junius could make out the rest of the station: the high expanse of the main entrance and the token booth.

He used Elf's house key to cut along the bottom, about three feet from the ground on down. Then they crawled into the Porter Square stop on the Red Line, two outbound stops from Alewife and less than a half-hour ride from South Station.

19

Inside, the station was busy with commuters, briefcases, students. It didn't make sense for them to hop the turnstiles and draw attention, so Junius went to the booth and bought two student-rate tokens with a dollar, never showing his student card because no one ever bothered to ask.

He passed a token to Elf, checking the escalators up to the street for Derek or Clarence pushing through the crowd. Once past the turnstiles, they took the long escalators down to the subway. People said it was the deepest station in Boston: seven stories into the ground. It was the longest set of escalators Junius knew, and when he first rode them he'd been impressed. Now he just wanted to get down as fast as he could. They walked on the left with the commuters, Junius watching all around.

At the bottom, getting off past all the brass gloves and mittens, he saw Derek waiting in the crowd.

Derek and, on a second look, Ness with him, both scanning the inbound platform. Junius pulled Elf against the wall.

"What?"

"They here. Dee and Ness. I just seen them."

Elf closed his eyes and shook his head. Whenever he stopped to think, it worried Junius. For him, it all just seemed something he had to do.

"What we do now?"

Junius moved to the row of newspaper machines and squatted behind them. He could see Dee and Ness going up and down the platform through the crowd.

The sound of a train coming started with a low, far-off rumble and built steadily. Junius couldn't tell what direction it was headed or what end of the tunnels it came from. He waited.

When it came, the train was inbound as Junius had hoped. People around Dee and Ness started moving, hustling to get on. Junius pulled Elf behind him, and they made their move: around the newspaper machines and toward the platforms, then quickly down the escalators to the outbound level. They ducked as they rode, watching above for any faces peering down.

On the lower platform, they sprinted along the wall opposite the tracks and hid behind the handicapped elevator shaft.

"Now what?" Elf asked.

"Got two choices: either wait for the next inbound, try to time it right and ride the elevator up, hoping they don't see us—"

"You think Clarence be up there?" Elf scratched at the scab on his lower lip.

Junius shook his head. "Or we wait them out down here, hope they get bored or tired and think we tried something else."

"How we know they left?"

"We just wait."

Now it was Elf's turn to shake his head. "Or we get the next outbound and switch trains out at Alewife or Davis."

"That three choices."

"Which you like?"

"I'm thinking."

"Man." Elf brought his hands up to the sides of his head and pushed his hat down toward his eyebrows. "Shit. What you thinking? New York?"

"Brooklyn," Junius said. "That or we go and see Marlene, find out about Temp."

"You crazy?"

But Junius could see a gleam in Elf's eyes when he said it. There was something about this he liked.

"We just saw Clarence ain't at the towers. Dee and Ness right up there."

"You think Rock ain't got other boys?"

Junius nodded. "No. No, he do. He do. I'm just saying—" He shrugged.

The sound of another train coming began somewhere down the tunnels. Junius thought he could tell it was an outbound. The sound rose, its vibrations increasing.

"What you think?" Elf asked.

"About our choices?"

"Yeah. All four."

"I say this train come headed outbound, we get on."

"And then we switch, or we head to Marlene?"

Junius felt himself smile, already deciding where to head. "What you think? You want be sitting on the T when Clarence come?"

"No."

"I'm saying." Junius could see the lights of the train heading toward them on the outbound track, and he made ready to move.

20

The train stopped, the car in front of them nearly empty, and they got on. Junius watched the platform through the glass as the other passengers got on and off the train. When the car finally chimed and the doors closed, he sighed in relief. For a second he considered yelling up to Dee and Ness, just to pop shit, but then the doors were closed, and he sat down across from Elf.

"Yeah, niggah," he said. "We go backdoor *and* do the shit we originally intended."

"Marlene? You really bent on that shit?" He pulled up the hood on his jacket, then just nodded his head between his shoulders. He slumped forward to rest his elbows on his knees as the train sped up. By the time the view was just black tunnel walls, Elf was shaking his head, but Junius didn't want to start fixing any problems that weren't broken.

As the train pulled into Davis, Junius jumped over to Elf's side so both of their backs faced the platform. If any of Rock's crew waited, he didn't want to risk meeting their eyes. Elf pulled his hood up around his head again and Junius did the same, slumped back against the glass so it'd look like he was just trying to catch a little sleep.

When the car chimed and the doors were about to close, Junius looked up. There were only a few other people in the car: a tired-looking nightshift worker and a mother with her baby sleeping on her lap.

Then Junius chanced a look at the platform and he met Pooh's eyes—Pooh standing on the platform watching, looking at the train. As soon as he saw Junius, Pooh jumped forward and stuck his arm through the closing doors. Junius could see his hand inside and the red lights over the doors blinking. He knew the doors would open again in a moment and let Pooh inside. But on the platform, Junius didn't see anyone else, no one to get Pooh's back. He started down the car.

By the time the doors opened again and Pooh stepped in, Junius was already halfway down the aisle. The mother with her baby saw what was going to happen before anyone else and shielded her child with both arms. "Oh my God," she cried.

Junius didn't stop. He flat out ran the last part of the car and jumped Pooh with his whole body, laid him out over the divider between the seats and the door.

Pooh landed underneath Junius with his legs up over his head and his torso on the seats. Junius was caught on the divider, but had enough touch with the ground to pull himself back. The nightshift guy shook his head, swore, and then looked purposefully away as Junius came around the partition to start punching. Pooh flailed his arms, trying to block.

Junius connected twice before Pooh scrambled into a better position and started kicking at Junius from his back.

Junius stepped away, and Pooh slid off the seats and got to his feet. Then he backed into Elf. The train rocked and started moving, and Junius lost his footing for a second with the jolt. Pooh turned on Elf, who pushed him, and then Junius threw Pooh back down onto the seats and hit him hard on the mouth.

The mother with her baby started to scream now, past "Oh my God" to terror at what she might be witnessing.

Junius saw his friend's waist next to his head. "Yo, help me hold him down."

"Fuck! What we gone do with him?"

"That's what I don't know." Junius shoved Pooh's face into the seat, then pulled his head back and slammed it down as hard as he could.

"Let him loose," the night man said. "What you boys trying to do?" He had on dirty, blue coveralls and stood tall above them, taller than Junius even. His hands curled into big fists.

"Just ease back," Elf said.

"Who you telling?"

Junius took a moment to look at the guy, to really see him, and what he saw wasn't good: a big dude, not as old as he'd first thought, maybe someone who knew Rock.

"That Pooh?" he asked.

Now Junius flat-out stared. He let up on Pooh enough that he could turn to see the night man too. For a second, Junius started to wish he still had the gun. But he *didn't* have the gun, just had two hands full of Pooh's jacket.

"Fuck. That is Pooh."

"Stay back," Elf said, though the man was almost twice his size. He kept coming like he hadn't even heard Elf. He pulled Pooh up out of Junius's hands.

"The fuck going on here? Who you?" The night man looked from Junius to Elf and back. Pooh started to stand, but the man pushed him back down into his seat. "You wait."

Junius said, "Temple Posey my brother."

"Who he to you?" Indicating Pooh.

"Rock's crew."

"Rock?"

Pooh nodded. "This motherfucker bucked Lamar."

The night man did a double-take, looked at Pooh then back at Junius, hard. Out the windows, Junius could still see the black tunnel walls speeding by; soon they'd arrive at Alewife.

"Lamar?"

"Big L rest in peace," Pooh said.

Now the night man nodded. "That young gun, huh?" He looked Junius up and down. "And you even younger than he be!" He reached for Junius's face, but Junius flinched away. "Yeah," the man said. "Why you ain't in school?"

"Vacation week," Elf told him.

The night man didn't take his eyes off Junius. "That bullshit?"

Junius shook his head. "No." Then he added, "Sir."

"Where Temple at?"

"He dead."

"Shit." The night man seemed to shrink about the shoulders. "Lamar have something to do with that?"

"*Next stop, Alewife station. Alewife. Last stop on this red line train. Alewife is next.*"

The train jumped, then started to slow.

"Did Lamar—"

Junius shrugged. "I don't know. Trying to find that out."

"Man, this niggah," Pooh started to scramble up, but the man held him in place. "This niggah want to come up and get *fixed*. We can handle him."

The night man bent closer to Pooh. "You will?"

"Shit," Pooh drawled like the word was about ten letters long, most of them i's. "With the quickness."

Junius saw Alewife's fluorescent lights and new white tiles appear outside the windows. He blinked at the brightness.

"We want talk to Marlene," he said, feeling the brakes engage and the car suddenly stop short, then lurch forward. A crowd waited to board: the late-morning workers bound for Harvard, Kendall, and downtown Boston. "Ask *her* what happened to Temp."

The night man curled his lips. "Marlene good people. I rolled with her brother Malik, way back." The train stopped. Pooh squirmed to stand, but the night man held on. "How about I keep your boy here, we ride back to Harvard. Have us a talk." He turned to Pooh. "How that sound?"

"What?"

"Yeah," Junius said. "That would help."

"I owe Marlene. Your brother too. Tell her E-Parish say, 'What up?'"

"My man." Junius reached out and they slid palms together, then clasped hands.

"Be careful. But if you have need up in 412, go up sixteen and ask for Miss Emma. She see you right."

The train stopped and the doors opened. The mother with the baby got off at the other end of the car without looking back. People from the platform started to file in.

"*Alewife station. This train will not be making any more outbound stops. Alewife station. Alewife.*"

"Let me up, niggah," Pooh said.

E-Parish pushed him back against the seat with a big hand. "Wait," he said. "You and I gone talk."

"About what, *bitch?*"

Junius started out of the car after Elf, looking back at the big man one last time. He heard him say something to Pooh about Rock, Rock and crack, he thought, and then he was in the thick of the crowd, pushing his way through the boarding passengers to the clear part of the platform, heading for the back exit toward the towers.

Clarence took his time riding down the escalator at Porter. He knew
Dee and Ness were watching the platform, and if they came up on
Junius and Elf, his boys would make them wait. They better.

He was pissed off enough already that he'd missed Junius as he
turned off Mass Ave. When he drove around the block and came
back, they were nowhere in sight.

Next was the bad taste he got when he parked and came inside
without having his cigarette. Just wasn't time.

He sniffed his fingers, again disappointed to get the tame smell
of the air fresheners. Why these fucks had to move at this hour in the
morning, he didn't know. He wanted to go upstairs and chill out,
stand and watch the commuters while he smoked a few Kools, even
roll one up to get his day-high going. But this shit—the one thing
Rock put him on top of all week—just wouldn't go straight. He wiped
the back of his hand across his nose.

Some fool had put metal gloves in the middle of the escalators,
probably to stop people from sliding down the ramps. He'd done it.
Why shouldn't kids do it now?

He looked back up the long escalator to the top. It was a long
way. When you looked up, the roof was designed to look like white

birds outlined on a light blue sky. Some stupid shit. But looking down toward the tunnel, the design was old trains on white. More dumb shit. Someone made these images on layers of triangles, the top part sticking to the roof and the sides hanging down, making an image when they all lined up—whether you were looking up or down.

Just some dumb shit.

It was all part of the way they were trying to make things nicer now, nicer than when he was coming up. They even put in a T station near the towers. Now kids wouldn't have to ride the Rindge Ave. bus all the time; they could just take the subway like kings of the city. Clarence saw someone had already written a name on the tiles next to the escalator. That made him feel good, even if it wasn't a name he knew.

He'd have his boys would put his name all over Alewife station. That would get things going.

A woman bumped his shoulder heading down the escalator, running actually, like she really wanted to get her day going that much faster. The train wasn't even coming—you could hear it if it was—so what was she running for? Nothing.

Clarence was more than halfway down to the platform now. Dee and Ness better have those kids.

At the bottom, he saw a handful of commuters waiting on the inbound level. One was the woman who'd bumped him. She was reading the *Globe* now, her big bag slung over her shoulder like when she bumped him. He sidled up to her like he was drunk, said in a low voice, "Hey, pretty lady, you want to buy some crack?"

Her eyes practically burst from her face. She saw him, but tried to act like she hadn't.

"Smoke that rock, lady. That's what I'm talking about."

She shuffled her newspaper and stepped away, but Clarence didn't stop. He took a cigarette out of his jacket and said, "We can smoke up right here. Help you get through the day, you know?"

Her face went white. She glanced around them and started walking, her newspaper tucked under an arm.

Clarence called after her, "I do not sell marijuana! You think just because I'm black I sell drugs? Is that what you're saying?"

She started walking faster and it made him smile when he saw a few people turn away disgusted.

Dee stood down the end of the platform that she was headed, but Clarence decided to give her a break. He turned around and saw Ness halfway down the tunnel, just as the sound of the train began in the distance.

Clarence headed toward Ness.

"You see me?" Clarence barked, about ten feet from him.

"Huh?" Ness's eyes looked heavy, as if he might be partway asleep even standing here.

"I said, you see me come down just now?"

Ness shook his head.

Clarence wanted to hit him, but as he closed the distance between them, he decided to let it slide. He'd waited in Dee's car all night, and now it was morning. They'd have smoked out—it was the same thing he'd have done. So it didn't surprise Clarence when Ness told him he hadn't seen Junius or Elf.

Still, on principal, he gave Ness one good slap across the side of his head and lunged at his gut with a left that he pulled back only at the last second. Ness flinched just the same—at least he was somewhat aware.

Behind them, the train pulled into the station bringing sound and wind as it flew down the track and started to slow somewhere near the middle of the platform. People turned from the noise and a few young suits even covered their ears. Clarence shook his head. He saw Dee finally walking down the platform toward them. About time.

Above the train, the tunnel was a series of white panels that gave you the feeling of being a rat underground somewhere, trying to get out of a tube. Clarence didn't want to be down here any longer than necessary.

He spit over the handrail that separated the inbound level from the open air above the outbound one.

"Shit," Clarence said. He stepped to the railing. The few outbound passengers waited around the escalators, and he knew as soon as he looked down that that was where Elf and Junius had gone.

Dee finally came up. "What up, C?"

Clarence waited for the train guy to say his piece about the doors closing and the station before he spoke. "You didn't see them, right?"

Dee shook his head.

"Either of you watch *that* train?" Clarence pointed down to the outbound side.

They both thought for a moment, then nodded. They were lying. Clarence wanted to hit both of them or at least Ness again, but he took a deep breath instead. Then he clapped Dee on the ear.

"Fuck is wrong with you? These niggahs come down here, you think they take a commuter rail?"

"Nah," Dee said. "We checked and it don't stop here."

"Right. So you see them hit the inbound?"

"No."

"So then where they go?"

Clarence knew they could have stayed above ground, kept running along the tracks in either direction, but that didn't make sense in this cold. No, they had to take a train.

He hated the fucking tunnels. When he got back to the car, he would smoke a joint, too, he decided. These fucking punks were causing him too much trouble.

Of course they took a train: the only one they could.

Clarence turned to head for the escalators, and the train cars started to pull past. For a second, he thought he recognized someone in the last car, another young buck like Dee and Ness, this one sitting on the train like a dumbass.

Clarence shook his head.

The youth today: wanting to be soldiers when they didn't know shit.

22

In the station, Junius pulled his hood down over his eyes and hunched forward. He leaned into the crowd, trying not to appear tall. Elf wouldn't have that problem, but Elf also wouldn't be able to look around and see if anyone from Rock's crew was waiting. Junius knew they'd have someone out by the main entrance, selling shit even this early in the morning, so he went left off the train, toward the back stairs. Alewife had two exits, each letting out onto a different side of Route 2.

He tried not to stick out, didn't speak and didn't run, just shuffled toward the stairs. Someone ahead of them looked familiar, Rob from his baseball team last summer—a white kid who went to the parochial school in North Cambridge. Rob nodded as they got closer.

"What up?" he asked.

Junius wanted to ask if he'd seen any of Rock's crew. Instead, he said, "Nothing. Life."

"What you doing?" Elf asked.

"Not much. Waiting for this girl I know from up my school." Rob winked and put his hand out for Junius to hit it, so Junius did. "I think she'll let me stick that."

"Oh, yeah?"

Elf laughed.

Rob was fifteen, already in his sophomore year. His hair was tight on the sides, spiked up top. He had two lines cut in above his ear. He wouldn't know Temple was dead or about Lamar either. To him, everything was the same as always.

"Get yours," Junius said.

Rob gave Elf some dap, smiling a big smile. "Yo, I catch you."

Junius went up the stairs with Elf just behind. Most people came through the garage in the morning and used the other entrance, so these stairs on the opposite side of Route 2 were empty.

They came outside at the end of the frozen football field and trekked back across the grassy mud in the opposite direction they'd run the day before, hopped the fences for the pool again, crossed the deck, and came out by the baseball diamond.

The same homeless were out front of the Food Master, begging for dimes. By the afternoon, they'd be paying someone fifty cents to buy a cough syrup, then they'd drink it and pass out. Junius had made that buy for them once or twice when he didn't know better. Somehow the store managers were smart enough to cut off the bums from buying Robitussin, but they'd sell it to a kid from the towers pairing it with a loaf of bread every time.

"Hold up," Elf said, catching Junius's shoulder. "Who that?" He pointed to a guy at the bus stop by the towers, probably about eighteen years old. Junius knew him, knew he wasn't in school anymore and had never played baseball. Sometimes he sold shit out behind the diamond or around back of the supermarket. That meant he was either a runner for Rock or part of Marlene's crew. And they couldn't leave it to chance.

Junius shook his head. "I don't know him." They ducked into the dugout and watched. They could see their breath puff out in front of them and it made the wait seem long. After a time, the bus came and carted the guy and a few others off toward Mass Ave., heading for Harvard Square.

"Let's go."

They got up and walked toward the towers, Junius keeping his hands by his sides. He went slow, trying to watch everything around him all at once. He'd read comic books about soldiers fighting in jungles and *G. I. Joe* ninjas stalking their prey. He'd imagined himself like them, moving slow and calm, his awareness raised to new levels.

A car sped toward them and drove through a puddle of wet sludge. Junius jumped back from the splash, and it just missed him. A homeless man in a yellow watch cap pointed at them and laughed a broken-mouth laugh.

Up the street, Junius didn't see anyone selling or waiting to buy. Maybe sales didn't start this early in the morning. Maybe it was the right kind of day to find Marlene.

"Where they be?" Junius asked.

Elf nodded toward the towers. "They here. Waiting. Half they customers from the towers anyway, so they just wait in the lobby. Stay warm."

Across the street, they passed the old Chinese restaurant. It hadn't opened for the day yet, but still smelled good. Junius's mother had taken him and Temple there once on a Sunday for the buffet. The place had some *damn* good food. Junius remembered more than ten feet of choices and eating himself silly, piling his plates high. He tried to eat more than Temple but couldn't. It was a good memory. The kind he wouldn't be making with Temple anymore.

Junius stopped short, turned to Elf. "What you doing here, man? I mean for real. Why you come for this?"

"What you trying to say?"

"I mean why don't you just take care yourself? Why you come on this trip?"

Elf looked lost, his eyes focused on something far away. Then he said, "Come here," and pulled Junius into the parking lot, around a corner and behind the high brown walls that surrounded the restaurant.

Removed from the street's view, he pushed Junius into the corner. "What you mean?"

"You keep going back on this, man. Saying you don't want to be along, but then you do anyway." Junius spread his hands in front of him. "I mean this some serious shit. You can leave."

Elf laughed. "You a stupid niggah, you know that?"

He pushed Junius's shoulder, backing him into the wall.

"You think I go back now? Think I can? Maybe before that shit with Lamar, I'd have left. Maybe if I left it be when we up on my roof, let my brother and Ramon tell Rock where you at." He shook his head. "But not now, motherfucker. Now we *both* in this."

Elf's hands turned to fists, and Junius remembered how he hit Lamar, the good punches. He saw the cut still swollen on Elf's lip. He got himself ready for Elf to push him, ready for Elf to swing. But he wouldn't fight his man.

Elf stood his ground.

"Shit, man." He touched his lip with his tongue. "Fuck wrong with you. You don't think you better off with your boy?"

Junius shook his head. He turned away, avoided meeting Elf's eyes. "It's not like that. I just give you a choice. You want to break, I understand."

"Nah. You don't think I want to see what up with Marlene? Follow this shit through?"

"I mean—"

"No." Elf put his hand on Junius's shoulder. "We don't do this. I got shit else."

They pushed out onto Rindge Ave. and headed straight up the block. Junius knew he had as much chance of seeing someone from Marlene's crew first as Rock's. Problem was, he didn't know what Marlene's crew would do if they saw him.

Rock's people? That he knew.

But Marlene's could do nothing, something good, or something very bad. He was hoping for nothing.

"The fuck you used to do up in these shits?" Junius asked Elf as they walked.

"Used to mess with this ho."

"That what Lamar was saying?"

Elf shrugged. He laughed and brushed the tip of his nose with his thumb. "Yeah, yeah. It was." There was a pause for a couple of steps before Elf said, "I fucked his sister."

"What?" Junius stopped short, his hands going up to his head. He remembered Lamar standing over Elf and how mad he looked, saying something about Elf knew not to come around.

"You did what?"

"You ain't know? This goes back a couple summers. Wanted to get my nut. You know."

"But Sharon?"

Elf nodded. He started to smile, then stopped himself.

"Fat Sharon?" Now Junius started to laugh, and Elf's smile broke through. In a moment they were both laughing. "Fuck. Damn, yo. How old was you?"

"Shit. We was like thirteen." Elf kept stepping, and Junius jumped to catch up.

"Yeah." Junius didn't know what Elf was up to that summer. He'd started playing on a traveling team for Junior League baseball and lost track. Plus, fucking Fat Sharon wasn't something you talked about after. Still, it surprised him. "You tell anyone?"

Elf laughed. "Would you?"

Junius spit onto the sidewalk. "So it was good?"

"I was fourteen. Fuck I know? Just bust my cherry. Shit good *enough*. Up until Lamar."

Junius could see the parking lot ahead, cars and the first of the towers: 410—one of Marlene's. They had to watch what they did and how they moved. Junius put his hand on Elf's shoulder.

They ducked behind the first row of cars in the lot to watch the front of 410.

Junius didn't remind Elf that he was only fourteen now, that even when he was *thirteen* he knew better than to fuck Fat Sharon. Shit; even at twelve.

He didn't say anything about it, or about Dawn or Adrianna, the girls he'd fucked, who were in a whole other league.

None of it mattered now.

But he had to ask. "How long until he knew?"

"Lamar?" Elf laughed, then said, "Shit, about two weeks."

They both broke up laughing again, and Junius sat in between two cars to get it out of himself before getting up to look around.

"So you fucked her like four, five times?"

"Shit," Elf said. "I'm hungry. You?"

Junius stood up. "Maybe Marlene have pancakes."

"Yeah, right."

When Junius looked across the cars at 410, he saw a black BMW roll into the lot, creep up to the front and stop. It had tinted side windows, but through the windshield he could see a white guy was driving.

The car idled for a minute, clouds puffing out of the muffler. Finally the lobby door to 410 opened and one of Marlene's soldiers walked out.

Junius knew the guy from around but wasn't sure of his name. He was older, someone Temple knew. He wore a thick tan parka with grey fur up around the edges of the hood. He walked behind the car and came up the driver's side.

When he did, the driver's window went down. Inside, a bald white dude with a scruffy beard barely held his head over the door. One of his eyebrows arced halfway up to the top of his forehead, and he looked wild in the eyes. His hair wasn't like most bald dudes, with some around the edges. This was more like he'd shaved it himself. Not slick like Kojak, more like it happened only now and then.

The guy talked loud enough that Junius could hear his voice— nasal and angry—but not what he said. Marlene's soldier looked away, spit onto the asphalt, and shook his head. Junius heard him say the word "police" when he turned back to the car, and the white guy started waving his hands. Now Junius could hear him louder.

"Makes you think I'm a cop?" he said.

Marlene's guy turned again, leaned up against the car's trunk and stared at his fingers. Another soldier came out of 410: Big Pickup. He got the name when he bought a used Ford a few summers back. He drove that shit around North Cambridge, the only brother any of them had ever seen in a pickup truck, so the name stuck to him stronger than herpes.

The big part couldn't be disputed; he looked at least 6'6" and 250. He wore a Triple Fat Goose jacket inside out, with the geese emblem patterned all over his upper body.

"Yo," Junius said. He could feel Elf next to him, watching the scene go down. "Who that motherfucker with Pickup?"

"Meldrak," Elf said. "Niggahs call him Drak. He ain't right. Him you do not fuck with."

"Not when Big P got his back."

Big Pickup reached the front of the BMW. He stood in front of the car and folded his arms across his chest. The only way the car could pull out now was in reverse.

The white guy said something else, and Drak shook his head. Then the guy opened his door, and even got out, holding his hands up around his shoulders.

Drak walked away from the car, looking to the street. Junius ducked.

"Shit, now the time to move. While they watching this."

Elf was right. "But I want to see."

Elf swore and told Junius to come on. As he stood up, the white guy walked to Drak. Pickup said something, his arms still crossed, and the white guy stopped.

Just the fact that he almost walked away from his car, a loaded BMW with the engine running, certified this motherfucker as one of the crazier white people Junius had ever seen. Elf crossed behind a car, heading parallel to the BMW and toward 411. Every step he took brought him closer to Rock's territory.

The white guy came back to the door of his BMW. Even as cold as it was, he untucked his shirt and held his jacket open. Inside he wore a T-shirt with some kind of crazy eyeball in a triangle on it. He pulled his shirt up past the nipples and showed Pickup his skinny chest. The guy was pink and barely taller than his car.

"Yo," Junius said. "He your white brother."

Elf didn't answer.

Pickup just stared at the man like he was crazy. That was when he started to go for his belt to drop his pants. Junius got a chill just watching, knowing how Big Pickup would respond. And just like that, Pickup drew, held out a little black gun that looked like a toy. It wasn't.

The white guy laughed and held up his hands. "It's cool, man. It's cool, yo." He'd already undone his belt buckle and his jeans though, and his pants started to sag. Then they fell around his ankles. Junius could see his red bikini underwear from twenty feet away.

"You seeing this?" he asked Elf. "Can't believe this shit!"

"Come on."

Junius hoped Elf was watching where they went, because he couldn't take his eyes away from what Drak would do next.

Pickup had already put his gun away and was turning around, heading away from the car. He shook his head, and from the way his shoulders moved, Junius could see he was laughing.

Drak hit the white guy on the arm, saying something Junius couldn't hear.

The guy bent over and pulled up his pants. "Twenty," he said in his angry voice.

Drak watched him tuck his shirt in and buckle his belt. Finally the guy pulled out his wallet.

But when Drak took a bill from the man, he just turned toward the building.

"What? How about the handoff? You know."

The guy started to raise his voice again, and Drak stepped back. He pointed inside to Big Pickup. "You want to see *him* again?"

"Yo, hold up," Elf said, stopping short. He got down fast behind a car, pulling Junius with him.

"Hey, man," the white guy said. "I just want my shit."

Junius could see the two of them and the BMW, but he couldn't see what Elf was watching.

"Twenty," Drak said, holding out his hand.

"Man, I—" The bald guy pointed at Drak's pocket, the first bill, and then gave up and reached back for another twenty. "Fuck it. Let me see the bag this time."

Drak scanned the area fast, though if anything was going to happen it'd have gone down long ago. He reached into the back of his pants for a bag.

"Check this out," Elf said.

Junius turned around and peered over the hood of the car. "What?"

"Check out 412," Elf said. "I think something getting ready to go down."

24

Across the front of 411 and beyond a few rows of cars, Junius could see the front of 412 as a long white Lincoln with tinted windows pulled in. A couple of Rock's boys, Roughneck and Black Jesus, came out of the building through the double front doors.

Roughneck was just rough, that was how he got his name.

Black Jesus?

Black Jesus had Jheri curl worse than A.C. Green—all the way down to his shoulders.

Neither Roughneck nor Black Jesus were out selling. They just stood by the doors of 412, watching everything go down, barely paying attention to the BMW.

"What is this?"

"Wait." As Elf said it, Roughneck stopped and held his right hand up—just a hand, the one closer to the doors. Everything seemed to stop. Black Jesus looked at Rough then turned to face the same way. They both watched the car Junius and Elf were behind.

"*Get down*," Elf whispered.

Junius dropped lower, below where he could see the front of 412. He turned, put his back against the car and leaned against it, keeping his head down.

The white guy in front of 410 said, "Now, that's just not right!"
But from his position, Junius couldn't see the BMW. He saw Big
Pickup outside again, in front of 410, and heard Drak say, "Then just
go fuck yo self."

"You—"

Junius winced at the possibility of what might come, of how
badly this guy would get fucked up if he actually said nigger, but then
he just said, "You my man, all right? We cool?"

Drak was already walking away from the BMW, toward the front
of 410. He waved his hand as if he were brushing crumbs off a table.
"Ok, buddy," he said with a flat accent. "Keep it moving."

Junius heard the door of the BMW slam and its engine rev.
Pickup stood with his arms crossed on his chest, facing 412. He
didn't notice Junius or Elf.

"What's going on?" Junius asked.

Elf had almost flattened himself against the ground to see under
the car. "They just waiting," he said.

"They see us?"

"Huh uh. They checking Drak and Big Pick."

Then Big Pickup nodded in the direction of 412. "Morning," he
told Rock's boys.

Junius didn't hear anything come from the others. "Yo, peep this,"
Elf said. Junius turned and crept to the front of the car.

Roughneck had started to wave with his right hand, but not at
Pickup, at the building. Then the doors of 412 opened and a black
Doberman walked out slowly, a big one. The dog wore a gray fur col-
lar, and as it came forward, Junius saw the leash trail behind it. Black
Jesus opened the back door of the Lincoln.

"That's Bonnie," said Elf.

"Bonnie?"

"The dog, niggah. Bonnie the Doberman."

That was when Rock came out of 412 holding the other end of the leash.

Junius had seen him maybe twice before, not much more than that. He came to the Cambridge City Championships a year or two back, when Temple's team played Lamar's. Junius remembered the way Rock sat in the middle of the stands with all his boys around him, keeping everyone else too far away to touch him.

He had a girl on his arm Junius couldn't get enough of. She was like a magnet to his eyes; every time he looked, it seemed like he could see more of her body. He kept glancing back, thinking he was definitely going to see her nipple if she moved the right way in her shirt. He knew he wasn't supposed to do it, that staring at Rock or his girl would get him fucked up. So he tried not to, but damn if he didn't think about her all through the game and dreamt about her that night.

Rock wore a gray fur coat that fell to his ankles. He wasn't as tall as Roughneck or Black Jesus, but his coat was long and it looked soft. He had dark black glasses and a high-top fade that slanted to the side in the way the people were calling a Gumby. His skin looked like he'd just come out of a warm bath, like he was cleaner than anyone Junius knew. His goatee was just like the kind Junius wanted but couldn't grow yet.

His strut and the way his jacket matched the dog's collar made 412 Rindge Avenue look like an apartment building on Commonwealth Ave. That, or like the one on TV where the Jeffersons lived. Like Roughneck was his personal doorman.

Black Jesus held the Lincoln's door open and the dog jumped right in. Then Rock followed, never touching the car, his whole exit as cool as the other side of the pillow.

Roughneck hadn't moved; he still eyed Big Pickup. "Morning," he said, finally.

Black Jesus closed the door of the Lincoln and got in the passenger's side in front. The big car hummed and started to roll through the parking lot, Roughneck never turning, not even watching it go. He finally nodded again toward Big Pickup and then went back into the building.

"Shit," Junius said.

"Yeah. Shit," Elf said. "*That* is the motherfucker wants you dead."

2 5

They stood up slowly and looked all around. Big Pickup watched them from the front of 410, but Drak was gone.

"What's up," Elf said when Big Pickup kept staring. Pickup waved for them to come closer, even stepped partway to them. Elf led and Junius followed. He had to look up at Pickup.

"You Temple's brother," Big Pickup said, not asking.

Junius nodded.

"Heard you had trouble."

Junius waited to find out if it was safe for them to stand out here, where Roughneck or someone else from Rock's tower might see them. Pickup had big cheeks and hadn't shaved in a while; stubble ran the length of his neck from one ear to the other.

When nothing happened after a few breaths, Junius went for broke. "I was hoping I could see Marlene."

Pickup nodded. "Yeah," he said. "I figure I knew that." He stood calm, still as a summer day, even with each breath visible in the cold. He studied them like he was reading a book, just scanning the pages without even moving his eyes, just absorbing it all in. When he turned to Elf, Junius felt like a weight had been taken off him.

"Either you holding?" Pickup asked.

Elf shook his head.

Junius said, "No."

"I search you and find a gun, I break your fucking hands."

Junius nodded.

"You understand me? That's where I start."

"I hear you."

Pickup turned to Elf.

"I understand," Elf said.

Big Pickup nodded.

"Come on."

In the lobby, Pickup raised his chin to a couple of his boys, more of Marlene's soldiers. Junius knew she had crew stationed here at all hours to watch who came in, that they also did some selling and told buyers where to head for their fix. He avoided their stares, and the way they looked at him as if he was a ghost walking.

"Five-oh here yesterday," Pickup said, after pressing the elevator button. He didn't look at Junius or Elf when he spoke, just faced the twin metal doors. "Shit come down someone get killed. Everyone on the force looking for who killed Lamar, taping off the body, all that shit."

"What people say?"

"Oh, you *best* bet someone popped the name Junius Posey. People talking about the brother of the boy killed up in Ball Square." Now Pickup finally turned toward Junius. "I was you, I be far as fuck from here."

"Didn't see no cops out there today."

Pickup snorted. "Still early. They be here after they donuts."

"Yeah, right," Junius said. "They come find me good as they found who dropped Temple."

The elevator chimed above their heads. Twenty-two floors and only one elevator in the whole building. Junius wondered why the police weren't investigating *that*.

Pickup shrugged. "I tell you clear as day, they be back. Best watch who knows you up in here."

When the doors opened, creaking and grinding against their frame, Pickup stepped in, then Junius and Elf followed. Everyone knew Marlene had a penthouse in 411, so Junius was expecting them to go all the way up. Instead Pickup pushed the button for sixteen. Junius was about to ask why, but Elf caught his eye. Elf had a blank face on that said *don't even think about asking questions.*

As they rode up, no one spoke. Big Pickup clearly wasn't much of a talker.

What surprised Junius was they had the elevator to themselves; it didn't make any stops between the lobby and sixteen, just climbed steadily, if a little slowly, up the floors. Above the doors there were no numbers that lit up. In fact, from the inside of the car there was no way to know what floor you were at or approaching. All you could do inside was wait. In the lobby, it'd been the same: no indicators to let you know when the doors would open.

On its own, the elevator was clean, its walls free of graffiti. Junius knew *he* wouldn't write anything on them if he knew Marlene could see it.

At sixteen, the doors opened and Pickup led them out. The hallway was dim, natural light only coming in through one small window at each end, the two separated by at least thirty-five feet of drab carpet. Along the length of the ceiling, fluorescent bulbs flickered on and off, humming. The carpet below Junius's feet was thin, worn, a dark shade that could have been brown or black—there was no way to tell in the light. Junius followed Pickup, and Elf walked behind.

Finally Junius asked, "I thought Marlene all the way up top. Penthouse in the sky."

Pickup glanced back over his shoulder at Junius and kept walking. Close to the end of the hall, he opened one of the apartments and stepped into an empty room with a tan carpet thicker than the one in the hall. Junius padded into the empty space. In the middle of the living room were three chairs: one that looked comfortable, like a nice chair you'd buy at a fancy store and two wooden chairs that could have come from anybody's kitchen table.

The kitchen looked small and clean, unused for cooking. The living room windows were blacked out with garbage bags taped in place. The room wasn't dark, though, because of its emptiness. Just the three chairs in the middle of the floor and nothing else, not even a TV. The three other doors off the room were closed.

"What up now?" Junius asked.

Pickup said, "Show me your clothes."

"What?" Elf looked like he didn't want to.

"I mean take your shit off, niggah. Strip down and show me each piece of your clothes when you take it off."

"Huh?"

But Junius could see they'd just gotten all the explanation there was. He started to unzip his jacket, already pulling off his hat with one hand. He showed Pickup his hat inside and out and handed over his winter jacket to have its pockets and lining checked. Pickup started squeezing his hands through the fabric and down the sleeves.

Junius undid his belt. If asked, he would strip naked and spread his butt cheeks to see the Oracle.

Marlene had finished showering and was sitting in her living room when the phone rang. She'd been planning her discussion with Malik for that afternoon, what she wanted to say about Rock and how best to approach the topic of the crack invasion that she saw around her. The question wasn't necessarily of taking over Rock's tower, but of whether crack could be stopped from spreading—if it was even possible.

From inside Billerica, Malik didn't know all she was facing in this new drug or what it did to their people. But sometimes he surprised her, and if there was one place a crack addict would wind up, Billerica was it. If he'd seen it with his own eyes, he'd know something needed to be done. If not, he'd know as soon as their sales numbers changed.

Seven Heaven came out of the office and stepped across the carpet.

"Pickup downstairs with the young buck who waxed Lamar," he said. "Boy name Junius. His brother Temple. They from Willie Stash crew."

She turned to face him, noticed that she'd been wringing her hands. "Temple that got killed?"

Seven Heaven nodded.

"This kid did Lamar?"

"Most definitely."

Marlene exhaled, then found herself nodding. "What he want from me?"

"Been asking to see you. Wants to see the Oracle."

She sighed. The older she got, the more tired the Oracle idea became. She hadn't had a dream about anything significant for years now: no visions, premonitions, or lucky picks at any street fairs. She was just a person, but people still wanted to come to her, expected her to be special.

Stupidly, they believed in her, and either because she didn't want to take any small hope away from them or didn't know how to stop it, she had yet to refuse an appearance.

Seven asked, "What you want me to say?"

Marlene was still nodding. There was no doubt in her mind what she had to do. "Tell them I'll be down."

She exhaled. Behind her, the door to the office closed after Seven Heaven.

She shook her head, leaned back into the soft couch. Rock was always ready to pop off, eager to start the kind of gun play and killing that could cripple business for weeks at a time. He truly did not care.

The police could come down, park in front of the buildings, shut down their space altogether, and Rock's anger would not fade. He was stubborn, she knew, and maybe from his point of view it made sense. Maybe from the place he saw things, with just one of the three towers, he had a lot less to lose. She shut her eyes. Trying to predict what would make sense to the man called Rock would get her nowhere.

But as sure as she knew anything, she knew that he would want revenge on Junius for killing Lamar. He'd already been to Willie Stash, she'd heard, and Willie did the diplomacy, left his young soldier out in the wind. And Rock left Willie alone. Why not? He avoided any small war Willie could bring *and* had Junius all to himself to put a target on. No worries, no danger of anyone coming back for revenge.

The boy was alone.

She thought hard about who he was, but couldn't come up with a face. It made perfect sense that he'd come to her now, seeking shelter and support against Rock, support that she couldn't give. Maybe he'd also want to know who killed Temple. If he was truly crazy, he'd still be filled with a desire for death and the stupidity to think she knew more than a person would.

If he was that far gone, she'd tell him who did his brother and then she'd sit back and see what he would do.

26

Stripped naked with his clothes in a pile before him, Junius watched Pickup squeeze through his jeans, wondering if the big man would actually check his drawers. Junius knew *he* wouldn't.

Pickup threw the jeans at Junius's chest. "Get dressed," he said, kicking his pile of clothes, not touching the blue and white boxers.

He started on Elf's jeans as Junius hurried his clothes back on and shoved his feet into his Nikes.

When Pickup finished Elf's jeans, he stared at the two of them.

"This what you wanted, young guns?" He shook his head, then turned and walked out of the apartment, back into the hall, and shut the door behind him. Junius heard it lock from the outside, saw there was only a keyhole on the inside of the lock.

He checked his pockets to make sure everything was still there: his pen, his little pipe, the money his mother had given him for the bus.

Elf dropped onto the floor to pull on his jeans, socks, and sneakers—he was already back into his drawers.

"The fuck is this place?" Junius asked.

"Antechamber, probably. Back in the old days they had special rooms like these to make the suckers wait before they got to meet the king or someone."

"Marlene?"

"Oh, fuck yes. In this case? She the queen."

Junius crossed the room to try one of the other doors. It was locked, but even without opening it he could smell a strong scent of weed. "Damn," he said. He took a deeper breath and smelled: some of the sweetest and strongest fresh herb he could get his nose around, the smell like the door was a baggie itself, the room just full.

"There so much weed behind this door," Junius said, "we could catch lift just standing here."

"Oh word?" Elf got up fast, checked the door while he was still pulling on his shirt. His eyes popped. He tried the handle again. Still locked. "That is some *good shit.*"

Elf crossed back to the middle of the room and put on his jacket and hat. Then he walked to the back wall to sit on the floor below the blacked-out windows. Junius crossed to the second door: it was locked and didn't smell of anything he could recognize.

"When she gone come?" he asked.

Elf just shook his head, his eyes already closed.

She walked into the apartment at the end of the hall, in past Seven Heaven after he unlocked the door and stood back out of the way. The small one they called Elf was sitting down. The other one, Temple's brother, stood in the center of the room. She had to look at him twice to convince herself he was only fourteen. Even then she remained uncertain.

He looked resigned, as if everything had been determined already; no room for going back or changing how he'd move forward. He stared right at her, unabashed.

"I'm Marlene," she said.

"Tell me who killed Temple."

"Ho!" Seven Heaven held up a hand. "That ain't how you speak now. You best show respect."

Junius glanced at Seven, then said his own name. He waited for her to speak. She turned to Elf, who promptly stood and nodded.

"You two came here to talk to me?"

"They say we go to the Oracle to find out who killed my brother."

Seven Heaven turned to her and raised an eyebrow. He was the only one who understood what Rock's Ready could do to their whole economy, that it could kill the goose that laid the golden eggs. These boys presented an opportunity to change that; they were practically standing before her asking for guns and a set of names to cross off her list.

It was almost too easy.

"Rock," she said.

The smaller one's face went wild. "*Rock?*"

She nodded. "He the one you want. You want to know who did Temple? That your answer."

"He pulled the trigger?" Junius asked.

Seven Heaven stifled a smile. This boy was smart. They both had to recognize that. They could either use it to their advantage or get caught behind it at some point down the line.

"You right," she said. "He wasn't the trigger. Didn't step behind the gun and do it his own self, but let our towers want his crack and he kill us all."

"What? Who shot him?"

The boy didn't blink, didn't ask about the crack, what Rock was doing, or who she was worried about. He asked who held the gun that killed his brother. It'd be easy to tell him Lamar, tell him he'd done that part of the job and send him straight on after Rock, but he might not believe that. Give him too much and he'd think things were too easy in this life, might even get soft. Looking at her now, he was anything but that. His eyes didn't waver or leave hers. He had no quit.

"Black Jesus," she said. "He the one shot Temp."

"Why?"

Now Seven Heaven didn't smile or even look her way; he just studied the boy, trying to figure how far he would go.

"You wanted who did this, I told you. He did it because Rock said to."

Now Junius looked at Seven. Seven nodded. "Rock fixing to take on more spots," Seven said. "He come at us, now he coming at Willie. Your brother just in his way."

"Nah," Junius said. Now for the first time since she came in the room, he looked down at the floor. There was some feeling in him, some bend. That could work to her advantage. To get anything done right in this world, you had to have a part of you that was human.

Seven said, "No rhyme or reason in this game, son. You should know."

"No rhyme or reason to you coming up on Lamar, was there? Now he got people who want to come back at you." She paused for a few breaths to let it all sink in. "That's the game, young gun. It's all a circle. The snake that eats its own tail. You want this, you have to see it for what it is. And you already in deep."

He pursed his lips and started nodding in small movements. "Temple didn't go for no reason. I'm a be sure I see that."

Marlene stepped back. The way Junius looked at her—like he was ready to go through her, through the door, and out into Rock's building to do whatever needed to be done—gave her pause. For a second she considered going back upstairs and finding out what *really* happened to Temple, the short answer that might give this kid peace and get him away from her troubles.

But that wouldn't do anything for the people in the towers—*her people*. They had to be able to live their lives. She had to fight the changes, the new poison and what it would leave behind.

That was what it came down to, what made her turn away and head for the door, leaving Junius with just a lie.

2 7

Outside, Clarence rolled into the towers' parking lot with Dee and Ness. He'd angrily sucked down a cigarette driving them over from Porter, watching Dee roll a blunt on the way. At least this boy was good for something.

When Clarence, Dee lit the blunt then passed it. Clarence took a big hit, swallowed, and pulled in another on top. He clenched his teeth and let some of the smoke seep up in front of his face.

"We gone fishbowl this motherfucker," Ness said from the back seat.

"Clambake," Dee said. "This Boston, bitch."

Inside the lobby of Rock's tower, Clarence could see Roughneck running the day trade, sending his boys out to cover the neighborhoods up to Davis and down to Porter. Pretty soon Dee and Ness should get back outside Alewife to make his money. If he came up short this week, Rock wouldn't just let it slide because he'd been chasing Junius.

"The fuck kind of name Junius?" Clarence asked. Smoke came out when he spoke and he considered whether asking was even worth that. His lungs were already starting to tire, but he would hold the hit longer.

Dee took hit and said around the blunt, "Fuck I know. Moms just got creative and shit. Trying to come up with something original."

"Junius Caesar!" Ness reached into the front seat for Dee's pass.

Clarence coughed. Something about Junius Caesar tickled him and he started to laugh, the smoke busting out of him in quick gusts. "Fucking hail Junius," he said, his voice high. "The niggah who would be king." He coughed and laughed.

Dee broke up laughing then too, spewing out his puff. "Some shit," he said, then handed the blunt to Ness, who sat back into the leather.

Clarence reached across Dee to the glove compartment and pulled out a baby vial of coke. Dee's eyes widened.

"None for you, son." Clarence unscrewed the cap and used the spoon attached to bring a scoop to his nose. *Bang. Zoom.* Now his morning was starting out right and becoming legitimate. He dipped the spoon back for another hit and did his other nostril. *Pop.*

He pushed in the car's lighter as he screwed the cap back on the vial.

Roughneck looked out through the front doors of 412 into the cold. A few minutes ago, Clarence had pulled up, and now the windows of his car were fogged. Fogged or smoked up: in the time he been able to see inside, Dee lit up a blunt. The dumb fucks.

Clarence broke the first rule: don't get high on your own supply. Probably never even watched *Scarface*, tried to know the rules or apply them to his life. Regardless of the rest of the movie, that one rule was worth everything, made all the difference between being a steady fuck-up like Clarence and an actual businessman like himself.

Already that morning he'd sent out six crews bound for various parts of Cambridge and Somerville, kids who would make good cash today with school out and everyone lounging at the crib, their moms and pops at work.

School vacation week was as much money as they could handle, and what was Clarence doing? Smoking his ass out in his ride.

Roughneck started to crack his knuckles—all the knuckles in his fingers—and do his stretches. He'd been taking classes at the Fred Villari in Union Square for four months now and was learning the forms, the katas. Fuck if old Fred wasn't a class A white Italian prick, but some of the teachers up there knew shit and could drop real knowledge about kicking ass.

Roughneck threw a punch combination that began one of his new forms and then pulled back. Doing the forms or acting like he was studying was definitely not cool here in the lobby. He liked to sneak up to the roof to practice. Even in the cold, he liked the open space and the feel that no one could see him.

From up there he could see the Fresh Pond Mall and the movie theatre he went to every Thursday night for the Hong Kong Cinema. He started going when they first showed *Scarface*, watched that shit every Thursday night for a month, and then when they switched to the Kung Fu, he always made the move to be there.

During the movie, people would start puffing, actually pull out their weed and puff right in the theatre. Rough wanted to say that he minded, tell them to stop, but he knew they were his own customers, from one connect or another, and how could *he* tell *them* not to smoke. So he learned to be cool with it. Even if he didn't smoke, he could still chill with his popcorn and the movies with their fake-ass sound effects and budget subtitles. It was fun.

He looked out at Clarence's car again, the Olds 98, and laughed. They were still inside smoking up the windows. He pushed the door open and headed out to see what the fuck.

"Yo, Rough!" his boy Milk said. "You want me to come?"

"No. You stay here."

Roughneck walked the twenty feet to the car in the cold. When he reached the 98, he rapped on Clarence's window. Inside, they were still puffing, Dee in the passenger's seat holding the roach of a blunt, Clarence laid back in his seat, smoking a Kool, and that fool Ness half-asleep in the back.

"Yo, C Dub," Rough said.

Clarence rolled his window down a few inches. He had the fancy new automatic windows in his Olds. Rough would be getting automatic windows in his car, once he had the funds for the black Pathfinder he was saving for. He had no real need for a car: he didn't go to school, bought his groceries at the store next to the towers, and could walk to the movies when he wanted to go. At nineteen, he had his whole world right here. But status was what any of this was about and since he first saw one, he knew the new Pathfinder was the car he had to have.

"The fuck you want?" Clarence said through the open window. Smoke puffed out of his mouth.

Roughneck shook his head. "Damn, Dub, is that any way to greet a brother?"

"You like a son, son. A stepchild to me."

Still shaking his head, Roughneck put his hands on the top of the window and pushed it down. Ever since he'd gotten the nod to be by Rock's side more than Clarence, it was nothing but bile from the older man. The window started to lower just a bit as Roughneck pushed on it.

"The fuck you doing? You trying to fuck with my ride?" Clarence's hand went for the window control, and Roughneck could feel its push. He held it where it was, a feat that was much easier than actually pushing it down. The door made a whirring noise, but the window didn't move.

"Ok," Clarence said, opening the window more. He brought his face closer to Rough and their eyes met. "Yeah, niggah," he said, and opened the door into Rough's thigh.

Rough stepped back, letting go of the window and bending over to absorb the blow. He smelled the weed smoke curling out around the edges of the door: a thick, strong smell.

"Not even noon yet," Rough said. "And you fucking rocked, old man. Smoking up all your profit."

"Yeah? Then maybe I should—" Clarence reached inside his jacket for what would most likely be a gun.

"Take mine?" Rough said, reaching into the car and catching Clarence's wrist. He held it inside the jacket, keeping the hand against Clarence's chest. "Take it, then." Rough bent down to put his face right in Clarence's. "Take it." He could smell more than just smoke on the old man, something deeper, more disturbing.

Clarence opened his hand and held up the other one. "Easy," he said. "I got nothing in here that'll to hurt you."

"What you got?"

"Matter of fact?" Clarence said. "Nothing. Ain't shit."

Roughneck eyed him carefully as he let go of the wrist. Clarence brought his hand out empty. "Hang on one sec," he said. "I'm a reach in here and get my blow, hit that, and then I'm a kick your ass."

Rough stepped back, crossed his arms, and watched what Clarence would do. He knew if there was a gun in the glove compartment and Clarence reached for it, he'd be able to start kicking the shit out of him before he could do anything.

In the back seat, Ness looked out at Roughneck expressionless, like this was all going down on TV.

Clarence opened the glove box and brought out a little black vial. He slipped off the top, tooted once into each nostril, then his eyes went wide and he shook his head once, quickly. "Yeah, blood!" he said. "You ever taste this shit?"

He shook the vial at Rough. When Rough didn't answer, he said, "Didn't think so," and got up out of the car. "I leave it in there, these monkeys get to it." He waved back at the other two. "Nah. Got to keep my shit right here." He patted his chest.

"You breaking rule one," Rough said.

"Fuck is that?"

Roughneck started to count off on his fingers, but Clarence came at him fast and kicked him in the shin.

"The fuck?" He looked down at his lower leg, and that was when Clarence stepped in fast and with a hard right hook that caught him in the ear. Roughneck blinked and shuffled to his side. The punch sounded like Clarence blew up a bomb in his ear.

Rough brought his hand up to his head, and that was when Clarence reached a left jab into his nose. Now Rough stumbled back, standing up straight. "The fuck?" He saw white in front of his face and tried to blink it away.

"Fuck with me?" Clarence said.

Rough tried one of the sweeping wrist-blocks he learned at Fred Villari, but it didn't connect.

"Look at me," he heard Clarence say.

He blinked a few times and could see Clarence standing in front of him, lighting another one of his Kools. "You don't fuck with a man's car. You hear?" Clarence had his left foot forward, like he was in a boxing stance. He shook the left foot and Rough watched it, then Clarence stepped forward and shot out another jab to Rough's nose. It staggered him, made things go white again.

"My 98 Olds-mo-bile! So!"

Rough heard Clarence's feet shuffle and then felt his chin blow up on the left side of his face. Another right.

"My 98 Olds-mo-bile is!"

"Yo, yo, hold up!" It was Milk's voice that Rough heard from just next to them. Rough blinked away the tingling in his nose and wiped his eyes. Clarence stood in front of him smoking, with Milk off to the side.

"That's all right," Clarence said, taking a hard drag of his Kool. "I was done with him anyway." He flicked the cigarette at Roughneck and it hit him square in the chest, then bounced off. Clarence turned and stepped back to his car, already shaking the black vial by his side.

"The fuck?" Milk said, reaching around to the back of his pants where he kept his gun. "I should?"

Rough felt like he was ready to pop, as if his skull might blow wide open with anger. He wanted to rip the car apart piece by piece, but he held it together. He put a hand on Milk's shoulder. "Unh huh."

If there was one rule that Rock's boys all knew, it was not to pull a gun on a soldier, not one of your own, no matter what. Keeping the cops away from the towers was one thing when you had to drop a body now and then, but if they actually started popping off at each other, they'd never get a free day. And since Clarence hadn't broken that rule, neither could Milk.

"Not today," Rough said. "Today we just walk away."

Milk's eyes widened like he couldn't believe what Rough was saying, and Rough couldn't believe it either. You didn't take a beating and back down or walk away. His mind raged with the things he *wanted* to do. But he had control.

Rough shook his head as he watched Clarence shut the door of his Olds, rev the engine, and peel out in reverse, leaving a trail of white smoke from its exhaust.

"We chill right now." Rough touched his ear where it still stung and brought his hand back to look at it: no blood.

He blinked and stared at the Olds as it pulled away from the tower and screeched out of the parking lot toward Route 2.

Junius looked down at the thick tan carpet in the empty apartment. Marlene stood in front of him and Seven to his right. Elf was next to him; he could see his boy's Adidas.

"I'm a make sure this shit didn't happen to Temple for nothing." He thought of his mother, her wish that he get out of the city, flee the scene for New York, and the way he'd have to walk with one eye on his back forever if he did, no matter where he ran. He shook his head. She couldn't lose another son to New York *or* a bullet. Now that he was here in the Towers and had come so far, his mind was made up: he would stay.

Marlene walked toward the door and Seven jumped to open it, then held it for her as she walked out. When she had gone, he let it shut. He turned back to them.

"This what you wanted, huh? This where you want to be?"

Seven had three lines cut into his eyebrow, to show how many people he had killed. Some crews cut it into their eyebrow, some gave each other tattoos. Big Willie's boys didn't do shit. They didn't want to wear any proof of what they'd done. But Junius believed. Looking at Seven, he knew the man had killed three, probably fools from Rock's crew.

"You got a snake biting your ass too?" Junius asked.

Seven laughed. He moved his chin like he was chewing. Maybe he meant it to be a nod.

"We all got snakes around here." Seven winked and then tilted his head toward the kitchen. He stepped around the divider onto the linoleum. When he clapped his hands onto the counter, Junius and Elf jumped. They walked to where most of the towers' residents would probably put a small table for eating and stood at the divide.

On the other side, Seven Heaven opened the freezer. Junius could see the refrigerator wasn't plugged in.

Instead the ice in the freezer was all black steel. Seven took out two guns—ones with long, extended clips in front of their handles. They looked like something Junius had seen in toy stores—like the water pistols he played with just last summer, running around up in Somerville trying to get ladies' shirts wet with fake pump-action uzis—only these were more real. The barrels were short, but Seven screwed a black extension onto the end of each—silencers. He took the clips out, cleared the chambers, and held the guns up in front of his chest to show they weren't loaded, and then he slid them onto the counter with the handles facing Junius and Elf.

Elf pulled his hands off the counter like he'd just touched a hot skillet.

Seven Heaven laughed. "Don't be shy, yo. You want to run in this world, you gone have to touch some steel."

Elf turned to Junius, bit his lip. "Yesterday we had a gat. Look where that got us."

"Got us alive today," Junius said, reaching for the gun closest to him. "We come fresh without and Lamar shoot us both."

You right about that. Shit." Seven reached behind him and slid open a drawer next to the stove. Inside was nothing but long black magazines. He laid three out in front of Junius. "These the loaded," he said. "Thirty-two in each, and you don't have to think about putting one in the chamber."

He picked up the gun in front of Elf. "Watch." With his right hand holding the gun, his finger off the trigger, Seven pulled back the bolt and jammed a clip into the bottom of the stock. The damn thing looked like it wanted you to hold it with two hands and fire from the waist.

When Seven had pushed the clip all the way up, he pulled the bolt out and it snapped forward.

"Round chambered now, son." He held up the gun and pointed it at the wall. "Bang."

Elf stepped back. He laughed.

"You keep grinning like a motherfucker, I'm a shoot you my damn self," Seven said.

Then Seven showed them the clip release near the trigger guard and pulled the clip out again. He slid the bolt back, releasing the bullet from the chamber, and lay the gun down on the counter unloaded.

Junius picked up the weapon closest to him. He took the clip and hefted its weight, trying to get the feel in his hands. The gun was already heavier than the nine Willie gave him—the piece he felt made him a man, took Lamar out, and started all this mess.

He pushed the clip into the well and let the bolt pop forward, testing the new weight. With the gun loaded, it felt more stable, balanced. He felt the urge to hold the magazine with his left hand. In two hands, the gun felt right, and like he expected someone would use it in a movie—shooting from the waist, mowing people down.

"Shit," he said. It couldn't be that easy.

Seven smiled. "This the Tec-9, motherfucker. Silencer equipped. You don't fuck with these. No one see you, hear you, know you around. You hop in and hop out like a cat." He shook his head. "Semi-auto, son. That means you just pull that trigger and pop off long as you need." He leveled a cold stare on the two of them, his hand still on the second gun. "Understand?"

The gun Junius held was all black, not cold and not warm, hard in his hands. Along the silencer, holes had been punched in the metal. Junius imagined shooting. "Fuck, yes," he said.

Seven spoke again, this time louder. "You *understand?*"

Junius looked all along the length of the gun, saw its brand name stenciled into its side. "Don't have to tell me twice."

"Good. Because I won't."

But when Junius looked up at Seven, he was staring at Elf.

Elf reached for the gun like it was some kind of drug that could get him addicted and spit him out somewhere in an empty sewer. He touched the handle with the tips of his fingers, brushing against the texture of the grip.

"Give me that!" Seven picked up the Tec by the barrel and grabbed Elf's wrist. He forced the gun into his palm and then curled Elf's finger around the trigger.

"You feel this?" he asked, shaking Elf's arm. "You hold this gat and feel it now, because this piece save your fucking life." He pointed the gun at his own chest, Elf still holding it. "Feel that?" He pushed Elf's finger back on the trigger and the hammer clicked on nothing.

"That's how it feel to pull a trigger on a man. Now you ever have to do it for real, you best not hesitate. You do?" Seven looked at the two of them. "One or both of you be dead."

Junius tried sliding the Tec down the back of his pants, but it felt big there, too heavy.

"Nah," Seven said. He grabbed the front of Junius's pants and pulled him closer to the counter, then reached behind him and took the gun. "This ain't no movie." He pushed the gun down the front of Junius's jeans, the grip sticking up above his waistline. "You have this right here, no fucking way you forget it."

Seven pushed Junius away. "That your power, son. You big now."

Junius nodded. He felt the gun press against his stomach, pulled out his shirt and covered it. "Yeah," he said. "I be set."

"Good. Now you best not point that shit anywhere near me." Elf held the other Tec-9 in his hand, still staring at it.

"Elf," Junius said. "What up, niggah?"

Elf nodded. Seven held out a clip, and Elf loaded it into the gun as Junius had, as Seven had shown them. "Ok," he said.

Elf held the gun at his shoulder height toward the weed room and aimed at the wall. "Ok," he said. "Ok."

Seven took Elf's hand and pulled the gun toward him. He pushed in the bolt and it clicked. "Safety," he said. "So you be safe." Then he pushed the weapon down the front of Elf's jeans.

Elf nodded, the silly grin finally off his face.

On the counter lay four more clips. Seven pushed them across to Junius and Elf, and they each took two and slipped them into their pockets. The clips were long and stuck out, but with their shirts un-tucked, they were hard to see.

Seven nodded. "You ready to do work?"

Elf looked at Junius, and Junius nodded. "Just tell us where we start."

Seven smiled. He said two words: "Black Jesus."

2 9

In the stairway of 411, Elf sat down on the landing between the eighth and ninth floors. "Hold up," he said, breathing hard. They'd only come down from sixteen, but Elf looked winded; he dropped his head between his knees. The Tec-9 stuck out in his shirt and Junius could see its barrel poking through his jeans.

Seven had taken the elevator up after he left them. Instead of waiting for it, they took the stairs. According to Seven, there were windows in the stairways below the sixth floor that they could watch 412 from, to see when Black Jesus made a move. That was Seven Heaven's big suggestion: sit in the stairs and watch 412 for Rock and Black Jesus.

Elf covered his eyes with one hand, then leaned back and pulled the Tec out of his pants. "See the size of this thing?" he asked, holding it in front of him, the barrel pointed at the ceiling.

Junius snorted. It was funny the way Elf held the gun, the look of surprise on his face.

"You don't want it?"

"Yo, fuck, man. You hear me?" Elf shook the gun. "They gave us machine guns! Look at this fucking thing."

"Shit. We start thinking, we go crazy. Can't think now. Just do."

Elf shook his head. "Shit. Then I gots to get *blunted.*"

Junius spit against the wall. "Downstairs," he said. "You can puff while we wait."

And so a half-hour later, they were sitting on the landing between two and three, watching 412 out the window for Black Jesus as Elf leaned back and tamped out his blunt against the railing. The stairwell had the weed funk now, and that helped fend off the smell of piss that had gotten worse the lower down they came. Junius hadn't hit the blunt, but just from the contact in the stairway, he felt a little eased out.

Since they started watching, a few people had gone in and out of 412, but not anyone worth recognizing—just a few folks Junius knew from around and people going off to work. Roughneck's boys were holding down the lobby, selling product. Milk did the work while Rough watched over.

Junius hadn't seen any sign of Rock or Black Jesus since they took off in the white Lincoln. They were still out somewhere, doing whatever Rock liked to do with his days.

Then Elf started to laugh. It wasn't his usual laugh or one that came from his chest, more like a giggle, like the nervous part of him that grinned at Seven and the guns.

When Junius looked, the stupid grin was back on Elf's face. He was caressing the handle of his Tec-9. He removed the clip and looked at the bullets. Then he unscrewed and re-screwed the silencer, then took it off and put it into his pants.

"Yo, tell me you ain't losing your shit."

"Nah." Elf shook his head. "Fact is, I'm starting to feel good about this. What we do? Shoot Jesus? Drop Rock? Put a few caps in his ass? Ain't nothing but a crazy day in the towers."

Elf bobbed his head a little trying to come up with words to match an imaginary beat. "Crazy ass day, niggah. Running games, holding Tec-9 in its holster. Body count. Shit popping up like a toaster." He smiled at himself, nodding.

Junius looked away. "You starting to worry me," he said. "Maybe we get you a different gun. Something smaller."

"Nah." Elf held the Tec in front of his chest with both hands. "Look at me, man. Look at this gat I be holding! Shit gone pop *off!* Loud. Fuck that silencer."

Below them the door off the lobby banged open and kids' voices echoed up the stairwell.

Junius pushed the gun down between Elf's legs. "Just be cool," he said. "Hide that shit."

Two boys started running up the stairs toward them, and Junius fell back against the wall, clearing a path between himself and Elf. Elf slid the Tec under his thigh, a move that wouldn't really hide it. There was nothing Junius could do.

"Yo, I heard Rock cap that niggah," one of them was saying. They ran up the stairs and then froze when they turned the corner and saw Junius with Elf. They couldn't be older than eleven. Junius had seen them before, but didn't know their names. The one who'd been talking still had his mouth open; his words hung in the air. Then his face changed. He looked like he was seeing a ghost.

"Yo," Elf said. "What up?"

"Ahhh—" the boys just stared at them. "We just chilling. You know?"

"I'm right here," Junius said. "You see me?" Junius held his hands out by his sides, his palms open. "You want to tell Rock to come get me? Here I am. Go ahead."

The boys' eyes widened. "Rock? I—" The taller one shook his head. "I didn't mean nothing about Rock and you, Junius. I mean, you my boy, right?" The boy started up toward him, his hand extended for a pound.

Junius gave it up, but then the kid tried to come in for a hug, and Junius held him off.

"That's cool." Junius didn't want to get too close, definitely didn't want anyone feeling the Tec in his pants. The boy would be upstairs making a phone call in a hurry, letting someone who knew someone know Junius was waiting in the stairwell, watching 412.

"You know me?"

The tall one tilted his head toward a shoulder, then nodded agreeably. "I know you from the diamond, seen you hit cleanup last summer for the Cubs. Games right across the way, you know? I watch them to see who hitting." He pointed behind him in the direction of the park. "You was."

Junius nodded. "Now you do shit for Rock? Living in Marlene's—"

"Nah, nah." The kid shook his head emphatically, his friend doing the same.

"It's not like that, yo."

"Nothing for Rock up in here," the other said. "We keeping shit tight for Marlene and Malik? No shit for Rock up in 411. We know that."

Junius looked at them hard and cold. "I be here now," he said. "But no one can know."

"No," the closer one said. "You my man. No one hear it from us."

Junius glanced at Elf and saw him staring at the others, caressing the Tec. Junius looked back out the window at the empty front driveway of 412.

"Seven and Marlene know you. We need to call them on this?"

"Nah. We won't fuck this up."

"It's cool."

They made to go up the stairs, watching Junius to see what he would do and stealing glances at Elf, who'd been quiet this whole time, just sitting and rubbing his gun.

"Go ahead," Junius said. He waved toward the empty stairs.

"Word," the taller one said. "Word. We check you." They took off up the stairs.

Junius waited to hear their steps fade before he said, "You trust those two?"

"Shit. I don't trust nobody." Elf brought the Tec out from under his leg, waved it between his knees like he was spraying shots all over the stairs—exactly where the two boys had stood.

"Fucking pigeons in here. Sitting pigeons watching this window." Junius looked outside again, saw no change in front of 412. "Yo, fuck this," he said.

"What you thinking?"

Junius angled his head up, toward the floors above them. "I'm thinking the roof."

"Roof?" Elf started to get up. "I like that idea." He pushed the Tec down the front of his jeans.

3 0

On his way up to the roof, Roughneck didn't talk to anybody. He left Milk watching the lobby, dispatched a few young ones to do the selling. After the bullshit with Clarence, he needed some time to himself, alone up top where he could work it out with a few forms.

He took the elevator up to the top and then the stairs to the roof. He threw punches at the air going up the steps, and then knocked the roof door open with his shoulder.

"Yo, fuck!" he yelled into the cold air.

Milk wouldn't treat him any differently after getting tagged up by Clarence, but he had his own conscience to live down. His blood burned at what had happened and that he didn't do anything about it. He couldn't, especially to an older soldier like Clarence. Rough knew a few of the punches had caught him because they were fast— they were good punches, no denying that—but what got him the most was what Rock might do if he actually came back hard on Clarence.

Fucker was just too close to Rock. Of course, that proximity rule extended to him too and Clarence should have considered that before throwing blows, but clearly Clarence didn't think.

He didn't consider his actions, just another reason why Clarence was an inferior soldier. But now he was an inferior soldier that had pounded on him in front of 412. Rough closed his eyes to keep from screaming. He picked up a pebble from the rooftop and threw it hard toward Route 2. He didn't even look over the edge to see where it went: if someone was real unlucky, it'd hit their fucking car, or worse.

He stepped to that side of the roof and launched into his first form, the punch combination that started off the Monkey Sequence. The Monkey was familiar to him but to get to the next level he had to learn the Tiger perfectly so he could test for his purple belt. Purple marked the turning point between know-nothing beginner and re-spectable mid-level student. He'd been going for close to three months now and was eager to make the jump.

Purple was a dark color, so different from yellow, white, or or-ange. Just the fact that you had a dark color around your midsection made you look like you were on your way. Dark belts were real.

The Monkey started with a series of punches and then slide-steps with blocks that led to kicks. As Rough started into these, he gradu-ally left his thoughts behind. As he went on, he started to punch harder, kick with more force. His body loosened up.

In ten minutes, he had his jacket off and was practicing the open-ing of Tiger. It felt good to sweat in the cold wind, to move faster than when he started, to go through the Monkey as fast as he could.

Now just the start of Tiger was his challenge: to go through it clean and as fast as he could. It was just seven punches, four blocks, and three kicks, with steps and changes of direction in between, but it made for enough of a challenge. He ran through the sequence in his head: punches, blocks, kicks.

Away toward the highway, he saw just blue sky, a fading pattern of clouds leading off toward the horizon. He turned and threw a kick in the direction of Boston, toward the Hancock tower and the downtown skyline. The roof's pebbles crunched under his feet. On one side of Boston, the Hancock and Prudential buildings marked the highest points, on the other, the Federal Reserve and the skyscrapers of the financial center marked the waterfront.

The steeple of Sanders Theatre at Harvard rose above the rest of what he could see of Cambridge. Fresh Pond reservoir stretched out to his right. He should jog around it, complete the two mile loop for endurance, but so far he had yet to do it.

He punched, threw his kick combinations, stepped and blocked until he heard a loud bang from the roof of 411 that jarred him out of his quiet world and back to the immediate world of the towers.

He dropped into a prone position, a push-up that felt like the right purple-belt thing to do, but he was all the way on the other side of the roof from 41. He couldn't see anyone, but he doubted if anyone from 411 would be able to see him.

3 1

Junius and Elf ran up the stairs until they got too tired, and then stole into the hallway on twelve to use the elevator. This hall was identical to all the others: empty, piss stains on the carpet, dim light coming in through the opaque windows at either end, fluorescent bulbs twittering on and off. As they waited for the elevator, Junius handled the grip of his Tec. He knew there wouldn't be anyone to fear in the car, but he did it anyway. Even if he was acting paranoid, he decided to go with it: better safe than dead was an easy way to look at it.

When the doors opened on an empty car, Junius relaxed a little. His nerves were up now and perhaps this was part of how things should be. He considered the fighters from kung-fu movies and how they walked on their toes, always holding their hands ready and looking around. It kept them alive, that was what mattered most. Junius bent his elbows and held his arms out from his chest. He positioned his hands in front of him, ready to move.

They rode the car all the way up to twenty-two and, just as the doors were opening, Junius remembered that this was Marlene's floor—where she lived. He ducked his head out and saw two soldiers standing with their arms crossed. One was Meldrak, the other Jason. They both tilted their heads, eyeing him like a cat stares down its prey.

"What you want?"

"We just—" Junius held out a hand to keep Elf in the car. He thought about going back down a few floors and picking up the stairs there, but it was too late. He stepped into the hall, holding his hands at his shoulders. Elf followed.

Junius nodded toward the stairs. "Marlene cool with us. Seven hook us up to watch Rock. Big Pickup too."

The guy closer to Junius pushed out his lips as he started to nod. Junius had seen him around: a Latino brother named Jason. He was Temple's age and they played baseball together one year. His skin was lighter than Junius's and his hair puffed out in wide curls.

"What up?" Junius said to him.

Jason smiled and the gesture broke the mask, almost like he just took it off. "They cool, Drak," he said. He put a hand on Drak's—a hand Junius saw didn't contain a gun. "This Junius. He Temple's younger brother."

Drak smiled too. Temple had warned Junius about him a long time ago, said he was just an angry motherfucker. Elf had said the same only a few hours ago.

"Temple's brother who kill Lamar?" Drak asked, his arms still crossed.

Junius didn't like the way Meldrak looked at him. "No, I—"

That was when Drak pulled his hands out from under his armpits to reveal twin guns. He pointed them at Junius and made a sound with his mouth like he was cocking the weapons. "Chhh-chhkkk."

"Motherfuck!" Junius ducked back against the side of the hallway, and Elf dove into the elevator.

"You shot my boy Lamar?"

"Yo, chill man!" Jason said. "Lounge!"

Meldrak shook his head, still holding the guns up. Junius saw twin muzzles, the black pupils, and he didn't like it. He wanted to reach for the Tec-9, but with his hands by his shoulders, he knew he didn't have time to make a move. He'd trusted Drak for being one of Marlene's soldiers, and now there was nothing he could do.

He thought about saying how Lamar tried to point a gun on him, and that's why he was dead, but bravado only came off in the movies. In this life he didn't want to piss off a man with two guns on him.

"Nah," Meldrak said, lowering his arms. "I'm just playing with you." He laughed. "Should've seen your face, though. You were thinking like a motherfucker."

Elf slowly came out of the elevator and tried to force a smile. "You a funny dude," he said. "Real funny. Yo, this is me laughing." His face was cold, no expression.

Jason hit his partner on the shoulder as he lowered the guns. "Yo, that shit is *fucked up!*"

"We're looking for the roof," Junius said.

"You come up in here, we got to fuck with you, right?" Meldrak looked around: at Jason and then back at Junius. He raised his shoulders like he was waiting for them to agree.

"You don't think it's funny, don't see the joke? Then *fuck you.*" He leaned toward Junius, said the last words with a light spray from his lips. Temple had said the only way to handle guys like this was to avoid them.

"Nah," Junius said. "You had us. No doubt." He nodded. "Want to check my pants? I think I got a little pebble in my drawers. I'm a thank you for that."

Meldrak smiled. "I can smell it, too." He winked, then moved back against the wall. "Stairs up there," he said, pointing down the hall with one of his guns. Jason turned away when Junius looked at him. He was shaking his head, probably more than sick of Meldrak's humor.

"Word. Thanks." Elf walked ahead of Junius, down the hall and away from Meldrak.

Junius heard Jason say he was sorry about what happened to Temple. He thought maybe Jason had been at the funeral, but couldn't remember. The whole day before was a blur.

3 2

At the top of the stairs, they did not have to break the lock on the door to get out to the roof. By the battered look of the door and the marks on the wall next to the lock, this happened a lot.

Outside, it was cold, but they were in the sun, and Junius took a deep breath when he saw the size of the world around him. In the blue sky, he saw thin white horizontal clouds receding toward the horizon like so many waves. He thought about the time his mother took him and Temple up to Salisbury Beach one summer and about playing video games on the boardwalk. They played in the water too, him and Temple, trying to throw sand in each others' eyes. His mother taught them to body surf on the small waves, and once he learned how to do it, Junius spent the rest of the day jumping onto the little rides. He remembered lying in his bed that night, Temple snoring on the other side of their room, and feeling the sensation of his body still floating in the water, getting carried up and down.

They were so much higher here than they got on the roof of Elf's house. Junius could see so much more.

"Damn, yo!" Elf said. "This like the time we went to John Hancock with school, all the way up that observation deck." He pointed toward

Boston, and Junius was surprised to see the whole skyline: the Hancock Tower, the Prudential, the other tall buildings he didn't know. You could see it all from up here—all of Boston. It didn't look far.

"That's Boston. Big as shit. What we doing over here?"

"Huh?" Elf laughed. "Because this be where we live, motherfucker, and we got problems enough here." He pointed his chin toward the edge of the roof. "You hear that?"

Junius listened and heard the music from below, Public Enemy, someone blasting the song about Chuck Dee's Uzi weighing a ton that everyone had been rocking since the summer. It sounded like someone was playing it from a car.

"Come on." Elf ran across the roof, the pale rocks crunching under his feet. It wasn't far to the edge. They sat down when they were close, arms resting on the short wall that ran around the perimeter.

Junius could see the white Lincoln far below, driving into the lot in front of 412, its windows down, the music pouring out. Elf pulled out his Tec and pointed it at the car. "You think?" he said, bringing his face down to the gun's site, holding the weapon with both hands.

"No," Junius said. "There's no way you make that shot. Not with that gun. You need a serious sniper rifle to make that shot." Junius put his hand on the gun to move it away from Elf's face. "Like this you just piss somebody off, let them know where we is."

Elf sucked his teeth in disappointment.

They watched the Lincoln pull up in front of 412, and Black Jesus got out. He went around to the back door and opened it.

"The fuck we supposed to do?" Elf asked.

Bonnie the Doberman came out of the car first, then Rock looked out after her. He checked around him in all directions before he came out of the car completely—all directions but straight up. Even if he had, he couldn't have seen Junius and Elf from this high above, their faces small against the edge of the building.

Bonnie pulled Rock out of the car, toward the tower, and Black Jesus held the door open for a woman who got out next. Even from this high up, Junius could tell she was a knockout: she wore a tight white ski jacket on her upper half, and was all dark cocoa legs down below it. She might have on a mini-dress, or something, or she could have on nothing at all. She had a little white hat pulled down over her straightened black hair.

"Damn," Elf said, as she followed Rock into the building. Black Jesus shut the door to the Lincoln and followed her in. Roughneck wasn't anywhere Junius could see.

With the door closed, the Lincoln drove back to the street side part of the lot and pulled into an empty space. Junius watched to see who got out, but the driver had a hat on, the kind of hat you'd see an actual chauffeur wearing on TV. No suit, just jeans and a goose down, and that fucked up hat.

It made Junius remember the first time he saw a limo on *Diff'rent Strokes* in the opening credits—that and the weird episode where they showed Mr. Drummond driving it himself. He never understood why you'd own a limo and drive it. Nobody would drive their own limo.

He pointed out the hat to Elf, who was already watching the driver, still holding his gun. "Yeah," Elf said. "That hat fucked up."

Rough got up but stayed low, moving slowly toward 411. As he got close to the edge, he noticed two kids on the other roof. They moved fast to the side closest to him and then ducked. One of them brought out a gun and pointed it toward the front of 412. The other one looked familiar, but it took Roughneck a second to realize that he was Junius, the one who shot Lamar.

Rock wanted him dead, had put Clarence on the job. That was

what Clarence was supposed to be doing today. Not sitting in his car smoking weed.

From the sound of things below, someone blasting Public Enemy loud enough to hear on the roof, Rough knew Rock was back from getting Berry, his new hot piece of ass from Boston.

Rough felt in his lower back for the small Beretta he kept there, and then remembered he'd taken it out, put it down with his jacket on the other side of the roof.

He swore under his breath, watched them put their gun away. It was a Tec-9 and there was no way they'd make a shot with it from the roof. Still, Rough felt a relief knowing they wouldn't try.

If these two were in Marlene's tower, then Clarence was going to have a hell of a time doing anything to them. Marlene's buildings were a definite no-fly zone. Rock sometimes pushed to test this, sold in her parking lots, even close to her lobbies, but going all the way to the roof was a stretch, a near-impossibility.

So Rough watched them watching the street. The sweat on his back cooled and cold air whipped along his skin. On the street below, Public Enemy got louder and then softer again as Mike Only drove to the other side of the lot.

Then their heads were gone.

Rough considered what might happen if Clarence caught these two, or if he brought them in to Rock himself. Maybe there was a way to help himself come out on top with these two.

Rough scratched his forehead, wiped sweat on his jeans. These kids didn't look like they needed to die. Maybe preserving their lives would be the best way for him to get back at Clarence.

He stood up.

"Yo!" he called over to the other roof.

They looked at him, their faces the only parts of their bodies above the wall. They were confused, their brows knitted above their eyes.

"Yo, what you doing here?"

Junius said something to Elf, then they both were quiet. They kept staring across the gap.

"Fuck you doing in the towers?"

Neither of them moved.

"You know these boys out to get you, right?"

They nodded.

"Listen up and I'm a tell you something."

Roughneck winked.

Junius wasn't sure he saw it right—they weren't that close—but if he didn't expect different, he'd be sure Roughneck had winked.

"I won't tell no one where you boys at. But you shouldn't be up here." He raised his hands. "Do what you feel, but you should get on out the towers."

Then Roughneck walked away from the edge, back toward the other side of his roof. He put his Triple Fat Goose on over his sweatshirt. For a moment, Junius saw a gun, and then it was gone.

Junius gripped his Tec. It was hot now and slippery from his sweat. He couldn't shoot Roughneck at this distance, and he hoped that meant Rough couldn't shoot him either.

Rough raised two fingers as if in salute and then went back to the rooftop stairs and was gone.

"The fuck you think of that shit?" Junius asked.

"I don't fucking know. Maybe that niggah crazier than you."

Junius laughed. "No niggah crazier than me."

Elf turned his back to 412 and sunk down against the pebbles, his back against the short wall.

"Ha!" he said. "Fuck!" He yelled the words like he wanted to test if anyone could hear him. He looked up at the sky and laughed. "Damn, man, you is a crazy niggah. It's true." He shook his head and kept laughing.

Junius sunk against the wall too. "Yeah," he said. "I'm crazy. This all is some crazy shit."

"Roughneck telling Rock where we at right now. His boys coming up in the elevators."

"Like we G.I. Joes or some shit. Snake Eyes right here!" Junius held up the gun. Laughing felt good against all the other seriousness, and he let himself go—threw his head back and barked at the blue sky. "Here I am," he yelled.

Elf scrambled up onto his feet. "Fuck! You just bark right now?"

Junius barked again, this time like a bigger, angrier dog. Elf stumbled. He held his hands up, still laughing, trying to get Junius to stop, and then he tripped and fell backward onto his ass on the roof.

His gun went off.

Elf rolled over and checked himself with his hands to see if he'd been hit. Junius heard a ringing in his ears. Elf's face had gone from laughing to ashen, and Junius dove forward, flattened himself against the hard pebbles. The shot would be heard down on the street; twenty-two stories below them and all the way down, Junius knew people would hear the shot.

Elf lay flat against the roof. "Shit."

"Told you not to take off that silencer."

"No, you did not. You did not ever fucking say that shit."

"Safety then, niggah," Junius said. He held his gun toward Elf to show him how the engaged safety looked.

"Shit, man. You think they—"

"Hell, yes, people heard that. All the way up and down, that shit be known."

"*Fuck.*"

"Yeah."

They lay there a while, listening to the sounds of the world around them. All was quiet, but Junius knew that didn't matter. Rock's boys could be rushing up the stairs or riding elevators to come after them.

"Nah. You did not say shit about no silencer."

"I—"

"No."

"Fuck. Come on," Junius said. He started crawling toward the door for the stairs back inside. When they were halfway to it, Drak popped out, holding his gun in front of his chest like a cop on TV.

"Yo!" Junius dropped the Tec and held his hands up, empty. "It's cool, man. Be cool."

"Someone up here buck shots?"

"Yeah," Elf said. "We saw that boy Roughneck up here trying to check out Marlene's tower so we had to let off at him."

Drak waved behind him for Jason to get low. In a moment they were both out on the roof, holding their guns.

"I don't see him," Drak said.

"Nah. He gone. Niggah scared."

Jason and Meldrak exchanged a look, then ran to the wall closest to 412. They got down and looked out over the edge.

Elf started to go with them, but Junius held his arm. "Stay here." He raised his chin at the other two. "Someone sees them, maybe they think they the ones let off."

Junius got up and brushed off the front of his jeans and his jacket. The pebbles of the roof had made welts into the sleeves of his coat.

Drak and Jason came back from the edge. "Nothing on Rock's side," Jason said. "Shit look quiet as kindergarten."

"Kindergarten ain't that quiet," Elf said.

"That's the point. You don't know what might come down."

At that moment, Junius saw movement on the opposite roof. Behind Jason and Drak, Hammer and two other soldiers came out the door with their guns up. It didn't take more than a second to see they had guns. They came out shooting; before he even got to the edge, Hammer leveled his gun and fired. Junius jumped at the ground as he saw blood spray across the pebbles in front of him.

The sound of Hammer's gun was different than Elf's had made, different than what Junius heard yesterday when he shot Lamar. Hammer was letting off multiple shots at one time. In front of Junius, Jason crumpled to his knees, a series of red spots already spreading across his sweatshirt.

"Shit, niggah!" Meldrak was down already by Jason, hitting him in the shoulder to wake him, but Junius could already see dead in his eyes. Then, before his body folded again, his head exploded out one side with a loud pop. Junius looked away, but it was too late: he could feel the wet and a small chunk of something hit the side of his face.

"Nasty," Elf said.

"Fucking Jason," Meldrak slurred.

The stream of shots from the other roof stopped.

"Motherfucker got that shit on full auto," Meldrak said. "Niggah got the modified."

"I got—" Elf held his Tec toward Meldrak, and Drak grabbed it right out of his hand.

"Let me see this shit." He put his own handgun, something smaller, in front of Elf. Junius saw the name "Beretta" stenciled across its side. Elf took it, and Junius wanted to smile.

He wiped his face with a sleeve and saw that it came away streaked with blood.

Meldrak kept low and moved carefully toward the edge of the roof. "Shit ain't full auto," he said, "but this clip *much* bigger than mine."

Before he got to the edge of the roof, Meldrak jumped up sideways, and popped off about five shots. They came slower than Hammer's, each one firing on its own, making a separate sound. Five individual bangs.

Someone swore on the opposite roof.

Elf looked to Junius, and Junius could tell he was pissed off about having a smaller gun.

"Fuck you niggahs doing," Drak called.

Junius swore. In front of him he could see the gun Jason still held in his dead hand. He took it and gave it to Elf. "Now you got two."

"Ok," Elf said. He looked at Junius, waiting to see what would come next, what Junius would do.

A series of shots echoes again from the other roof, more automatic fire. Elf was already starting a low scramble toward the edge.

"What the fuck," Junius said. "Buck shots."

Another volley of automatic fire tore through the air and took chunks out of the bricks of the stairway exit just behind Junius. Elf was crawling toward the wall, and Meldrak moved low along its edge. Junius wanted to get up and to see the other roof: who was there and who was shooting, but instead he scramble-crawled back toward the stairs and then around behind.

As he moved to its side, he heard a few more shots and more bricks breaking. With the doorway at his back, he stood against the bricks, facing away from the 412. On the roof of 410, he didn't see anything, but then he saw a sudden, small movement along the edge. He saw the glint that looked like glass in the sun, a lens maybe, or even—he was about to think—sight. And then he saw the muzzle flash of the rifle and heard the shot, not loud, more a hiss like the whisper from a silencer.

He cursed at the fact that Elf had started this with his mistake. Junius looked at his own gun's extended barrel, the silencer he hadn't taken off. The weapon was really long with the silencer sticking out, but he was glad to have it.

With both hands on the gun, one on the handle and one holding the clip, Junius ducked around and shot four times at the other roof, one trigger pull for each shot. The bullets screamed out through the silencer, making a high whine as they left the gun, something like a whistle. The kickback was so small Junius hardly felt it. Everything about shooting the Tec-9, was just too easy. Especially knowing he had twenty-eight more in the clip.

"Fuck." He slipped back behind the stairs again. He'd fired from the waist, barely aiming, but there was no one to hit. He didn't even see where the bullets went. But he'd fired. In the middle of all this crazy shit, he'd fired off four fucking shots at Rock's house.

Junius looked out again from behind the stairs: Elf and Meldrak were still lying low against the wall. Nothing moved on top of 412. Back on 410 he could see the glint of the lens, or sight, but nothing else.

Then something on 410 moved: a black thing like a dark coat rose just a little above the wall, moved to Junius's left, and was gone. It was watching sharks on TV.

Back toward 412, blood spurted out of what was left of Jason's head and pooled around his shoulders, a chunk of skull and hair missing. The rocks that had been white were now red all around him. Steam drifted up off the blood into the cold.

Elf shifted onto his knees tried to shoot double-fisted, both Berettas raised at 412, but Meldrak pulled him down onto the ground. Hammer rose up for a moment and shot across the ledge.

Junius wanted to fire, but by the time he had the thought, Hammer was gone.

Footfalls pounded the stairs in the building, and the door behind Junius slammed open. He heard pebbles crunching under feet and saw Seven Heaven and Big Pickup standing next to Jason's body, firing wild at the opposite roof with automatic Tec-9s. When their guns started clicking on empty, they ducked back into the stairway, and Junius could hear them cursing as they reloaded.

That was when Junius heard the sirens—a lot of them—coming from the street below.

"Fuck," Drak called out over it all.

Seven Heaven stuck his head out the door and yelled for them to get off the roof. Junius saw Hammer and a few of his boys running back into 412. He got ready to shoot, but then Elf and Drak were up and running across his line of fire. He lowered the gun and turned into the stairway, where he was pushed along past Seven and Pickup, down onto the landing of twenty-two.

"Shit motherfucker, shit," Pickup said. "Move!" He clapped Junius on the back.

"What about—" Junius asked.

"Let's go! Let's go!"

Elf and Drak came running down the stairs, and then Seven and Pickup started down.

"What about Jason?" Junius asked. "His body?"

"Shit," Pickup said. "Another niggah dead in the towers. That's what the police think. Won't do shit."

"Huh?" Even from inside, Junius could hear the wail from the cop cars twenty-two stories below. When they reached the hall, Seven and Meldrak broke off toward Marlene's.

Pickup led Junius and Elf down to twenty and to an apartment in the middle of the hall. He knocked on the door and a little boy opened it right away.

"What's up, my man?"

"Homeboy, your moms at home?" Pickup asked. The kid shook his head. "Hang out with these cool brothers then, alright?" They gave each other a pound, and Pickup pushed Junius and Elf inside.

Then he was gone.

The kid closed the door. Junius was in the middle of a living room that smelled like fried food and spices. On his right was a tan couch with yellow flowers on it and dirty covers on the arms. The couch faced a big TV set with a pair of pliers sticking out where the channel knob was supposed to be.

"Sit down, suckers."

The Price Is Right was on TV. "Bob mother-fucking Barker," Elf said, and he moved to the couch.

Marlene slid the drapes to the side so she could look down at the street below. Out on Rindge Ave. she saw three police cruisers lined up, ready for business. Seven opened the apartment door behind her.

"Time to go," he said.

She turned to see him taking her fur out of the closet. He held it up for her to slide into.

"This was *them*," she said, pointing in the direction of 412. "Rock's boys. Let Cambridge finest go up there."

"All three towers today," Seven said. "Our eyes on 410 dropped shots in this, too. With Drak and your people on our roof."

She squinted in her anger. "The kids? They went up on the roof? With guns?"

Seven tilted his head like did she really want to know the answer to that question. She didn't. Of course he gave them guns, but to kill Rock and Black Jesus, not to take shots at clouds.

"They started this?"

Seven held out his hands. "Too soon to know. Too late to stand here discussing."

"Ok." She finally came across the room to slip on her coat. "Where we going?"

"The usual," he said, and ushered her out the door.

Barker was setting up the second showcase showdown when the sirens finally stopped screaming from the street. Even on twenty, they were loud enough to hear over the TV, and the kid had to turn it up for him and Elf to hear the descriptions of the prizes.

Junius sat still with the gun in his hand, its silencer resting against his leg. Elf had tucked the twin Berretas into his jeans somewhere, but Junius wanted his gun in his hand.

He wasn't interested in the showcase showdown; instead he wanted to know what was happening outside, up on the roof, in the other buildings.

"When's it safe to leave?"

"When Big Pickup comes back for you, is my best guess. You'd think he'll be back soon."

Junius didn't say anything.

"After *Price* I like to watch *I Love Lucy*. You guys like Lucy?"

"She alright," Elf said. "I kind of do."

"Good. Not like she's sexy or nothing, but it's a laugh."

Junius turned to Elf. "The fuck you start up there?"

"Please," the kid said, not taking his eyes off the TV. He pointed to a crocheted sign above the television that read: *This is God's house. Please speak accordingly.* Junius waited for him to laugh.

"It means no swearing."

"Right." Junius tapped Elf on the shoulder, nodded toward the door and all that was beyond it. "What you *think* about that, man? This crazy, right?"

Elf turned his head all the way to one side and then back again, taking his chin to his shoulders. He touched the scab on his lip with a finger. "This what it be." He patted the front of his jeans, where Junius assumed he'd tucked the Berettas. "We past the point of no turning back. From here on out, we just got to act like we know."

"Show and prove." The kid nodded. "If you think you know what that means."

They took Marlene down the east stairs.

Big Pickup joined them on the way down, Drak and Seven going first, then followed by her and the big man. She wore heels and that was a mistake, of course, but the stairs were too dirty to go barefoot now, too much broken glass, and so she had to make do. Her calves were hurting by the time they reached ten and at five they were screaming for her to stop.

"Fuck me," Marlene said. "Why couldn't we just use the elevator?"

"Bullshit is that we didn't get you down in it first, when the firing first started," Pickup said from behind her. He lifted her in his arms, one forearm under her knees and the other along her back, and carried her down the stairs.

"Now this," she said, looking up into his face—not really such a bad face, actually—"is the way for a lady to travel."

She didn't miss noticing when Seven looked back at Pickup with contempt. "I didn't hear you say take Marlene out back when."

These guys were hardly breathing heavy, even after seventeen flights. *These* were the ones to keep around her. Somewhere along the way she had made a set of good choices with these three, Seven and Pickup especially, even if they didn't always get along.

"Plus," Seven continued, "Rock's boys find out we take her in the elevator first sight of a few shots, they gone be waiting one time and roll up."

"He right, too," Meldrak added.

"You got Raphael set up on the other side?" Seven asked.

Pickup grunted. "He be there."

At the basement, they took her past the boiler room and the janitor's closet to the maintenance tunnels underneath the towers.

There was no one at the door, and Seven opened it without using his key.

"Don't we usually—" she stated to ask.

"I'm on that," Seven said. "I'll find out who left his post."

On the other side of the door, Pickup set her down. He had to stoop in the low tunnel, the naked lightbulbs right alongside his head. The tunnel was maybe two hundred feet, and halfway through it they could already hear Raphael give them the all clear from the other side.

"Coming with Marlene," Seven answered. "You get the elevator?"

"Got it."

Marlene could see Raphael, one of her Latino boys, waiting at the end of the tunnel.

"Cops come at you yet?"

Raphael said they were sticking with 411 and 412 so far, and she liked the sound of that.

In the basement of 410, Raphael made a show of kissing the back of Marlene's hand. She wasn't sure why he did it, but he always did. Maybe it was his thing.

He led them to the elevator and they all squeezed in, Marlene at the back behind Seven and Pickup. She could barely see the doors around the two giants. She put a hand on each of them.

"You two both did a good job today," she said. "Be good to each other, alright? We're on the same side here."

They both shrugged awkwardly and nodded toward one another. She knew that was the best she would get. Pickup had high aspirations, and Seven got his spot by never being content himself. She'd have to find a way of appeasing the both of them. Making Pickup her head of security hadn't done it, especially since Seven kept putting his hand into that pot. She'd have to find something else.

Meldrak spoke, his voice scratchy like his mouth was too dry. "Jason dead," he said. "Big Hammer let off a full clip and tore his ass to pieces."

"Jason, my Jason?" she asked. "From twenty-two?"

"That's your boy," Seven said to Raphael—Jason was Puerto Rican too. "Round up the clan."

"Fuck you," Raphael said it like a matter of fact, like you would say "good morning" to a stranger, the antagonism between the black crews and the *boricuas* always there, even when they were working for the same set or living right alongside one another on the same floor.

The car stopped at the lobby, and Meldrak held his hand up at a few older women who wanted to get on. "Wait for the next," he said. Marlene wanted to stop him, to welcome the ladies into the car and see them safely to their homes, but the doors were already closing.

She'd glimpsed the bright of the sunlight in the lobby coming in through the glass, but hadn't seen any police or flashing lights. That much was good.

Maybe soon the ambulances would show up, but most likely that would still be a while, if they showed up at all. Not much an ambulance could do for a dead man, and all the more reason for the cops to just leave him be, up on the roof as a reminder for the rest. If they took Jason in, brought the body to the morgue, it just meant paper-work. She knew how things worked, even tried to explain them to her idealistic Anthony, though he'd never believe.

The doors opened onto the twentieth floor, Malik's floor: where he still had his apartment waiting for him to come home to.

Marlene followed Raphael and Seven out into the hallway. Meldrak and Pickup stayed behind in the elevator. They passed two more of her soldiers, Sean Dog and Corwin.

Sean Dog followed them into Malik's apartment, holding his rifle, the one with the big sight. He still thought he could hunt Rock's crew from the rooftops, insisted on carrying a big gun and trying to scope soldiers like a sniper. Marlene knew he'd never hit anything, no matter how long his scope. But it kept him happy, so she usually left it alone.

"I got one of them," Sean Dog said. "I think I clipped his shoulder. That boy bleeding bad."

"Uh-huh." Seven waved it off like a stupid idea.

Marlene sat at the small, four-chair table just outside her brother's kitchen.

"Yeah," she said, and sighed. "Tell me something else, though. Like what the fuck really happened up there."

Clarence sat in his 98 on the other side of Rindge Ave., watching the police cars all over the front of the towers. He'd driven up to Davis again after giving the fuck-off to Roughneck. Punkneck is what they *should* be calling him. He was about good for little else.

At Davis, he'd checked in at Mike's Diner and bought a fresh pack of Kools. Willie's boys were up there waiting, but said the two were still no show—the little fucks he was supposed to be finding.

He left Ness and Derek to hang and see if they showed. Truth was, he was probably better without those two if it came to getting anything done. Now that they were stoned out and slowed—damn if he was giving them a toot of his coke—he was better off alone. He sat in the heat of the Olds, listening to Marvin Gaye, watching the towers go up in flashes of red and blue lights.

"Motherfucker," he said in a slow drawl.

It was still possible that the boys had walked to Harvard or gone up the tracks walking, but Clarence didn't believe it, not enough to bet his day on it.

He *knew* they took that outbound train out of Porter. So where else could they have gone? Other than back to Marlene, there weren't many other possibilities.

He was thinking about giving up on the morning, just going up to his place to take a long shower and hit that Ready, or just hit that Ready and fuck off to the rest of the day, when he saw Pooh walking up Rindge on his own. He looked low, staring at his feet as he walked, his coat pulled up around his ears. Clarence honked the horn, and Pooh saw him across the street, then started toward the car. When he did, Clarence could see bruises on his face: around his temples and under one eye.

He thought about just rolling down the window and making Pooh wait outside, but he'd get colder that way and the kid looked like he could use a friend, so Clarence unlocked the doors using his automatic button.

He locked and unlocked them twice again before Pooh got to the car, each time enjoying the bump and click as the button activated. When Pooh opened the door, a cold wind blew in. Clarence told him to hurry up.

Pooh put on his safety belt when he was finally in the car.

Clarence turned down the music. "You not going anywhere. We right here, so tell me what you seen. Who came up on you?"

Pooh pursed his lips. "Came up on me?"

Clarence reached out, but then thought better of it. These kids nowadays didn't like to be touched; someone told them stories about fags and boys, so now they always got freaked out about shit. Now the thing that scared them most was someone thinking they were gay, or if they thought someone else was gay. Clarence snorted. It was a real concern for them. More evidence of how the world was fucked.

"Son, someone been busting up your face."

Pooh turned to his window. Anything to cover up weakness.

"Who you see today? They did this?"

"Yeah. I seen your boys."

Clarence got more interested. "My boys who killed Lamar? Young buck and his dwarf?"

Pooh nodded. "Junius." He wasn't more than sixteen himself, barely old enough to be trusted.

"You ride on that inbound train before? Thought I saw you." Clarence caught the shifter on the steering column, already dropping it into reverse to head toward Boston. "Where they at?"

"I seen them on the red line. They was coming out here. Probably up in the towers right now."

Clarence checked the kid's face for the hint of a smile or a sign he was joking, but it wasn't there. He had been through some shit. "I saw you go inbound. You see them up Boston?"

Pooh shook his head. "They was on the train out to here. I picked them up at Davis, but this big dude made me ride back to Boston with him, wouldn't let me get off."

"Big dude?"

"E-Parish, Marlene's boy or some shit."

"Yeah," Clarence said, nodding. "I know that niggah."

Clarence knew Eric Parish well: they'd come up together, separated by only two years, and Eric was always the straight one who worked at the supermarket in the summers, tried hard in school, got big lifting weights, played football—all that shit. But look where it got him: the motherfucker worked nights in a garage, still lived in the towers just like Clarence. Always had grease under his fingernails, hands that would never come clean.

That was what trying and hard work would get you.

Clarence stared at his own hand, his nails clean and manicured on the leather steering wheel of his new car.

"E-Parish do this to you?"

"Junius came up on me before I was ready. Caught me off guard."

"So what about E?"

"Made me get off at Park and wouldn't let me catch another outbound 'til he was gone. I been trying to get back up here like a hour!" Pooh shook his head.

Clarence smiled. He had to give it to old Eric. "He protecting them? Trying to shield those bitches?"

Pooh noticed the new pack of Kools on the dashboard, asked if he could have one. Clarence shook one out for each of them. They could use a smoke.

Across the street, the cops were already breaking up: six cars had responded to the call and now only four remained. An unmarked had shown up about ten minutes ago. That would be the detectives. They let a few of the patrolmen leave, then went in to keep working.

Outside the building, a tall black cop stood leaning against his patrol car in dress blues, his shaved head wrinkled like a raisin. Clarence could swear he was staring right across the street at them, directly into the 98.

The cigarette lighter on the dash popped out, and Clarence lit his smoke, then Pooh's.

"What's all this up here?" Pooh waved his cigarette at the towers, the police cars.

"Don't know. Just got here myself." Clarence lipped the cigarette to the side of his mouth and shifted the Olds into reverse. "Let's go see."

He backed out to make room and then drove out onto Rindge, waited for a break in the traffic and crept straight across into the lot for the towers. He drove slow, just rolling the car, enjoying the heat, turning Marvin Gaye back up a little to get more sound.

That bald cop stared them down the whole way, trying to eye-fuck Clarence into submission. Instead he drove right up and rolled down Pooh's window. The cop would like that, seeing the window go down automatically, knowing he couldn't afford it on his own car.

"What's up today, my black brother?" Clarence asked.

The cop stood still. Across the front seat, Clarence could see his chest, his arms still folded across it with his hat tucked under one of them, and below that his belt. His gun was right there next to Pooh's face.

"You eighteen, son?" the cop said to Pooh. "You know it's illegal to smoke tobacco if you're under eighteen?"

"Yeah," Pooh said. "I turned eighteen last month."

"Got any ID?"

"No, sir. Mr. Officer. I don't got no car, so I got no license." Pooh smiled a little at that one, and Clarence knew it was a mistake. The cop reached in through the car window and took Pooh's cigarette right out of his mouth. He dropped it to the ground.

"Now you need a license to smoke. So you better get one."

Clarence took a deep drag from his Kool and ashed it into the tray underneath the radio. He blew smoke in the direction of the officer. "Everything ok here this morning? As a concerned resident of these towers, I just want to make sure things is all right, you know what I mean?"

Clarence leaned over to the middle of the car and craned his neck to see the officer's face. The cop was still trying to eye-fuck him, his lips pursed like he wouldn't smile to taste pussy. He even had a short mustache shaved tight across his lip. This boy was all regulations. Clarence smiled, showing his gold front tooth.

"We got a call about a disturbance. You know anything about a disturbance here this afternoon?" The cop checked his watch.

Clarence stuck out his lower lip, shook his head just enough to convey the message. "No, sir. No, I don't. I'm just a concerned citizen trying to make sure everything is safe in my community."

"Johnson!" one of the other cops called from the building—a white cop, heavier and with his hair mussed, his uniform messier than the black cop's but with more bars on the shoulders. "Johnson, let's go!"

The black cop bent down now, leaned forward with his face at Clarence's level. He put his forearms on the car door at the window.

"It'd be a shame to have to pull you out of there," he said. "To have to search this car and see what we can find. Keep you standing out here in the cold." He wrinkled his nose like he was smelling the weed Clarence smoked with Derek and Ness. "Truth is, we got a call here today about a number of gun shots. You wouldn't happen to have a gun in there, would you?"

Clarence frowned. He took a last drag of his Kool and stubbed it out in the ashtray. "No gun today, sir." His .38 was under the seat, zipped into the cushion in a way he could get at it but that Clarence knew the cop would never find. "No, sir. No gun."

He hit the window button accidentally on purpose with his elbow, raised it just a bit into the cop's arms. The cop started, pulled his arms back fast.

"Gary!" the white cop called again.

The cop looked behind him to where the white cop was waving at him to come over—this white cop who would already be with the program and know what Rock was paying for.

"Be seeing you now, Officer." Clarence pulled forward. "Better go see what your boss wants."

The cop said something else, but Clarence was already rolling up the window, driving away from 411 to loop around back of 412.

He checked his rear-view and saw the black cop taking down his license plate, even as the fat white cop was already storming toward him, his face showing how pissed off he really was.

On the TV, Lucy and Ethel were stuffing their faces with chocolates. They were working in a factory on an assembly line and fucking up. Junius wasn't sure why, but for some reason they had to keep eating the chocolates to keep the line from going crazy. Instead they were going crazy on the chocolates. Elf and the kid were laughing their asses off, but Junius was somewhere else, thinking back to what happened on the roof: how they saw Roughneck and he told them to do their thing, even though he was supposed to be down with Rock and a friend to Lamar. How Elf let off with the Tec and what that had brought. He still saw what that did to Jason.

Compared to grown men like Seven Heaven and Big Pickup, Junius knew he wasn't shit. He knew too that Seven and Marlene had brought him in now; where Big Willie didn't have his back, they did.

Like it or not, he was indebted to them, and Marlene telling him about Rock and Black Jesus wasn't necessarily a favor as much as a command or her price for protection. He could do it though—make good on what she wanted—and if it wrapped things up about Temple, then that was ok too.

But he didn't know if he could do it with Elf along. They were best friends, but Elf looked at home on the couch watching daytime

TV, even with two guns in his pants. Seven gave them the Tecs with silencers for a reason, not just to make them hard to fit down their pants. But Elf didn't listen.

Elf noticed him looking over at the side of his face and turned toward Junius, winked like they were doing just fine.

But they weren't doing fine.

Junius had felt Temple's death that week, felt Lamar's, and now Jason's. He knew he'd be thinking about these, playing the shots back in his head.

Elf wasn't like that: he thought more about how the other pushers back in Teale Square and Davis would look at them. And that wasn't how your mind had to work if you were going to get through this—to survive.

Junius stood up. He rubbed out the wrinkles in the thighs of his jeans, saw scattered spots of blood on his right leg. That was what decided it.

"What up?" Elf asked.

"I'm going in the hall to see if I can find Seven. I want to ask him one question."

"What you want a ask him?"

The kid said, "Pretty much anything he can answer I can tell you as well."

"I just need to see what's going on." Junius waved at Elf to stay on the couch, but it wasn't necessary: Elf looked pretty much planted. "You hold up here, wait in case he comes back. Pickup too. If either of them roll up, just say I went to sixteen to look for them."

"You better not go up on twenty-two," the boy said.

"Yeah. I'll keep that in mind."

Elf turned back to the TV. "Ok. Check it out and come back before you do anything else, alright? Maybe we get some lunch soon. I'm hungry as shit."

"Sounds good. I'll come back and we eat."

"My mom left some chicken nuggets in the freezer that we can heat up. They just take twenty-five minutes."

"Word?" Elf held his palm out for some dap, smiling like it was the best thing he'd heard in a while.

Junius stepped toward the kitchen and the door. His own stomach had been churning since they started waiting on the roof, but he figured if he left it alone it would calm down after a little while, like usual. Breakfast was a meal he didn't bother with, and when the school lunch looked nasty, which was most of the time, he just waited to hit the pizza parlor across the street after school ended for the day.

He'd get a slice or two and an order of fries that he always ate right out of the white paper bag. He liked to tear off the top and then spill the fries out into the bottom, spray them down with ketchup, and eat it with a fork.

Yeah, he could get into eating, but the clock on the stove said it wasn't even one yet. His stomach would have to wait. Plus there was no pizza parlor near the towers. Whenever they played baseball, an ice cream truck sold slices; otherwise there was no place to get food in the Rindge Towers neighborhood at all.

Junius stopped with his hand on the knob. He took one look back at Elf sitting on the couch and opened the door. "I check you," he said.

Elf held up his hand, and then Junius was gone.

Rock sat at his glass table by the windows, drinking coffee and smoking a filtered Kool. He wore a gray robe over his boxers, could feel it clinging to the sweat on his back. Bonnie barked once as the bathroom door opened, and she got up from where she lay on the floor behind his chair.

"No," he said. "Bonnie, sit." Bonnie sat. She had better for the amount he spent on her trainer.

Berry Rich came out of the bathroom with his white bathrobe tied loosely around her waist so he could see her chest from the belly button on up. He hurt inside just to see it; the way the robe barely covered half her breasts, letting him see their inside curves bulge against her sternum but not her nipples. It melted something inside him.

He wanted to take a drag of his cigarette, but instead he found himself just thinking about it. No action. She actually made him nervous, he realized—a feeling he couldn't remember having in a long while. She stepped across the rug to him barefoot, her dark red toenails something he'd pay for down the road. If he was really going to take her on, install her in her own spot in this tower, then he'd have to pay for every detail on down to her beautiful feet.

He could live with that, he decided.

After Shirleyann, he was ready to step it up again, get with a woman who could hurt him inside just from how she looked. Fuck if it didn't do things to him that his boys would say to stay away from: Black Jesus, the rest of them, they'd speak out if he gave them the chance, but that wasn't their function. They brought in the money, worked the streets, corners and hallways with their boys, carried out his orders, but did not speak on how he should handle his heart.

She took the Kool right out of his fingers, ashed it into the tray next to his coffee, and sucked it hard enough for the cherry to burn white. She winked at him, exhaling through her nose. "How you feeling, my man?"

"Rich," he said. "I'm feeling Berry Rich."

She smiled her smile, the one that was going to make him give her an apartment on eighteen, fill it with furniture, a TV—whatever she wanted—buy her clothes. Without taking another drag, she lay the Kool down in its ashtray, then pushed out her lips.

With her hair wet, Rock could smell something like fruit, not an apple, something better, like a fresh fruit you would only get in the tropics. She smelled good. Then she leaned across the table, reached in front of his face for the pack of smokes. As she did, her smell overwhelmed him; this scent that he couldn't describe, a soap he'd never known before, washed over his face and down into the hot place near his lungs. When he opened his eyes again, he saw the robe fall open to reveal the lower curve of her breast and its nipple. He wanted badly to put that nipple into his mouth—her whole breast!—and he pushed into her, his nose and mouth against her hot skin still wet from the shower. She let him touch her like that for a moment before she pulled away.

"Funny," she said. "That's what I was hoping you'd do." She pulled a Kool from the pack and brought it to her lips. "Light me?" she asked, dropping the pack onto the table.

He did and then cleared his throat. He was ready to lay down his proposition.

"I—" Something caught in his mouth, stopped right there at the front of his idea. "I was thinking," he said.

Someone knocked at the door, and Rock wasn't sure if this was him getting saved or rudely interrupted. "Hang on," he told her, then got up and went to cross the living room. He passed by the couch with the leopard skin blanket draped over its back, reached the door just as more knocks came.

"This better be fucking important," he said.

Black Jesus's voice came through the door: "Yeah, it is."

Rock unlocked and opened the door part way, then stopped its progress with his foot. In the hallway stood Guardy Little, the one everyone else called Black Jesus because of the Jheri curl he used to wear. Now he kept his hair buzzed short, tight on the sides and on top, practically bald, but he couldn't get away from the name. The motherfuckers in this community could be ruthless like that, completely unforgiving like they were when Rock moved to Cambridge with his mother back in the early 70s from Haiti. For the few Haitian kids in his class at Tobin, life had been a daily hell, and especially for him, being just off the boat and still speaking with a heavy Creole accent. Yeah, they had made things hard, but sometimes he wanted to thank them, show his appreciation for hardening him early. And sometimes he did show thanks in the form of small discounts or an extra hit in the weed bags he sold.

When he joined the Marines at seventeen, he knew he'd learned a few things about toughness from those kids at school *and* from the towers. Enough so he wasn't bothered by anything the U.S. Government ever asked him to do—even the odd missions in Haiti and Central America, the ones no one ever mentioned out loud.

Now he was giving back an even bigger gift: the wonders of crack cocaine, with its bigger hits, faster highs and stronger addiction. This community was lucky to have him around.

Black Jesus tried to push the door open, but Rock's foot held it in place. "What up?" he asked.

"Some shit on the roof. Shots fired."

Behind Guardy, Rock could see Hammer showing a funny look on his face: he was one of the ones who did the shooting, that much was clear. And with some luck, he'd done a good job, not wasted shots.

"Who started this?"

Black Jesus turned toward Hammer. "Someone up on Marlene's roof. Bucked out and we followed up."

"They was packing," Hammer said. "Think I clipped one of Marlene crew."

Rock nodded. It was bad news, but if it was the worst he heard all day he could live with that. "Good job," he said. "Now?"

Black Jesus frowned. "Now there cops in the towers. *The other* towers. They know to stay outside 412."

"Good. You shut down sales below the second floor?"

He nodded. "No lobby and no outside. Both shut off."

"Then people know to hit the landings. Keep up eight and sixteen. Nothing else. Who downstairs on watch?"

"Roughneck."

"Good." Rock started to shut the door, but Black Jesus stood in the way. "What else?"

"I—" He shook his head and stepped back. "We got things under control."

Rock started to shut the door, then asked, "You seen Clarence?"

"Nah. C Dub ain't been around all day. Where he at?"

"Motherfucker supposed to be looking for Young Junius."

"Oh," Black Jesus nodded and stepped into the hall. "The niggah who shot Lamar? Word to that."

When he closed the door, Rock turned back toward his Berry. She slipped her hand down the front of her white robe, loosening the belt until it fell open to show she had absolutely nothing on underneath. He saw her trim dark patch of hair and just about forgot everything else in the world.

"Come here," she said, sliding up onto his glass table and opening her legs to show him the fine moist coochie. She took a last hard drag off her Kool and ground it out.

"Fuck," he said, taking off his own robe as fast as he could. "Here I come."

4 0

The hall was dim, and no one was around. As Junius stepped out onto the cheap carpet, he closed the apartment door softly. When it clicked, he was out. He wished he had a watch, thinking he could try to come back at a specific time, before Elf got crazy and knew he'd been left. He'd get back before two, he decided. If he saw a clock.

He headed to the stairs, knowing it wasn't safe or smart to take the elevator with police in the building. At first he wasn't sure which direction made more sense, up or down, but as he got closer to the stairway, he decided that up only limited his options, cut him off from choices. He'd been to the roof already and that hadn't gotten him anything but shot at. Maybe if he had a bigger gun he could do something at long range from up there, but this Tec-9 wasn't making it.

Going down he'd have choices, options.

As he made his way toward the lobby, Junius saw police knocking on doors and talking to residents about what they'd seen. He passed a few officers on the stairs who barely noticed him.

That they were knocking on doors, trying to find people home on a weekday to talk about shots fired on the roof, that was just crazy. They had a better chance of finding out what happened if they stood in front of the building with a megaphone, asking the shooters to come out.

Here he was, fourteen, over six feet tall and carrying a loaded semi-auto in his pants, and no one stopped him or said boo.

In the lobby, he looked outside and saw two cops standing together talking. One of them was waving at an Oldsmobile as it drove off, a 98 that looked too much like the car he'd seen Clarence in earlier, the one that almost ran them down on Mass Ave. Then the older cop, a white guy with crazy hair, started yelling and pointing in the other cop's face. The first cop was getting chewed a fresh one, a big one, and Junius shook his head. He hated to see a brother, even a cop, getting treated like that.

He looked out toward the street and saw a total of four police cars. With the boys upstairs knocking doors and some still no doubt looking over the scene on the roof, Junius guessed they'd be around a couple hours. He took a good look over at 412 and didn't see any officers. He wondered if they even realized 412 was where the shots that killed Jason had come from.

Junius watched the lobby and saw Milk, one of Roughneck's boys. He wondered again about the sign Rough had made up on the roof.

Milk looked like just another soldier, and Junius doubted whether the message from Rough would extend to his boy. He couldn't just walk right in to 412, could he?

The cops on the front walk yelled at each other for a bit longer, or really the white one yelled at the black one, and then the white cop pointed toward 410 and the other cop headed off in that direction.

Junius looked away just as the white cop turned around. He faced Junius and examined him with cop's eyes. Junius shoved his hands into his pockets, acted like he was waiting for a ride, someone coming to pick him up from the direction of Route 2.

The cop stepped forward, and Junius could feel the cold air rush in when he opened the door.

"You." The cop pointed at Junius. Even though he knew no one else was around, Junius glanced back toward the stairs.

"Right here." The cop jabbed his badge. "You see anything suspicious here today, young man? Anything I should know about?"

Junius had to think hard about his answer. Anything strange? What *wasn't* strange?

Finally he just shook his head. "Nah, Officer. I ain't seen nothing."

"You live here in these towers?"

Junius said he was just visiting.

"Visiting who?"

Now Junius wanted to say Marlene, that he was here consulting the Oracle to find out who killed his brother—and how were the cops doing at solving that case? But this was a Cambridge cop and Temple got killed in Somerville. They probably didn't even share the case.

"Just visiting a friend on sixteen."

The cop asked for his friend's name, and Junius gave the name "Todd Bridges," who played Willis on *Diff'rnt Strokes*. He didn't know the name of the kid sitting watching TV with Elf, but neither would the cop. "Apartment 1611," Junius said.

The cop nodded, acted like he was writing it all down.

"You got anybody looking at that building?" Junius asked, pointing to 412.

The sergeant shook his head. "No. Should we?"

Junius lifted his shoulders. "I'm just saying. There's three buildings—"

"We'll get to it. Three buildings and you come here to 411, want us to go check out 412. Let me guess: someone you visiting is down with Marlene's crew, right? You don't like Rock?"

"Who?"

The cop laughed. "Stick to the day job, kid. Your acting career ain't going to work out." He patted Junius on the shoulder and started toward the elevator.

Patrolman Gary Johnson stared off in the direction the 98 had gone: the dirtbag had driven past 410 and made a turn toward the back side of the towers. He hadn't even taken off, just driven around the lot.

And now O'Scullion the scallion wanted him to check out 410 for anything that seemed out of whack. Well, he could do that for old Onion Head. He walked into 410 through the front entrance and the lobby was empty. *That* was definitely suspicious. These towers crews never left a lobby unguarded, without someone watching or selling. Something was going down connected to the shooting on the roof.

Johnson looked at the elevator and decided to play his other hunch: to go after the 98 instead of knocking on doors. His knuckles hurt just thinking about twenty-two floors of it.

He went into the right-hand stairwell, then back around to the rear hallway. Yet another problem with these damn towers and trying to police them was these back doors: sure, they stayed locked from the outside, for the most part, but from the inside you could always slip out, making the buildings impossible to lock down.

There was always another way out.

Johnson took the back door and came out among the garbage dumpsters along the rear of the building. He almost tripped over a broken-open trash bag, stepped past it and saw another one, this one hanging off the side of the dumpster and spilling half its contents onto the ground. A flap of white plastic blew in the breeze. He looked for the 98 but didn't see it.

"Shit," he said. Around the dumpsters lay a scattered mess of trash bags, both black and white. Looking up, it was pretty obvious what was going on: instead of bringing their trash down through the lobby and out the back door, some of the residents on the back side were just dropping their bags out the windows, hoping they landed in the dumpster where they belonged.

Looking at the debris, Johnson could guess what floor the bags had been dropped from—just based on how badly split apart they were.

He stepped farther into the back lot. Fewer cars were parked here, and as he went along, he saw the back half of the Olds, its taillights go on and then off as it parked.

"Motherfucker," Johnson said. He thought about whether O'Scullion the Onion would be checking up on him in 410 and realized he didn't care. This guy in the 98 was more suspicious than anything he'd see in an hour of knocking on doors.

He started around the back of 411. As he did, he heard the slam of a car door—one of the doors of the 98.

Clarence slammed his door closed and headed around the side of 412. He might check in with Rock and see about the cops, or he might go up to his apartment to kick back, hit some Ready. He wasn't sure which, but did know he had to lose Pooh before either. No way he was sharing his pipe.

"Yo," he said, stopping along the side of the building. "Drop around back and make sure no cops saw us."

"Yeah?" Pooh stopped, looking hurt that Clarence didn't want him along. The welt on his forehead was starting to calm already, even without ice. Clarence remembered when he could get in a fight and tagged up like that, then let it go away on its own. Back when he was young things healed so easily. Now, catch a punch and he had a yellow bruise on his face a week later.

Fuck good getting old did you.

Clarence shook his head. "Yeah. Drop around back and meet me down the lobby in ten minutes."

"Cool. Ok." Pooh took off, heading toward the old train tracks.

Clarence knew those tracks and the space under the rusty metal bridge about a hundred yards down where he used to hide and smoke weed when he was even younger than Pooh, hiding from the rain or snow or school—the world even, whatever else was out there.

Alone in the lobby of 411, Junius found himself in a world of choices. He felt the Tec-9 pressing into his waist, a gun he was supposed to use to kill Black Jesus and Rock. Both of these men seemed far off. He didn't know much about them or where he was now.

But he did know enough about 411 to understand how the stairways worked, where the roof access was, and where you could hide yourself if you had to. He guessed 412 had the same layout, which could help.

The 412 building loomed above, reaching up beyond where Junius could see. Coming to the towers was a risk, a big one, but going into 412 was like entering a fortress of enemy power, something like the hall of mirrors that Bruce Lee went into at the end of *Enter the Dragon*.

Junius knew the problem and the situation, also that his path lay right outside, just in front of him. His path took him to 412. He could see the simple gray concrete sidewalk on the other side of the glass, out in the cold.

He looked at the building again and saw Milk disappear from the lobby. A moment later, Roughneck appeared in his place, standing by the front entrance. This, Junius recognized, was a sign.

42

Johnson walked along the back of the buildings toward the car. He saw the guy and his boy both get out of the Olds, then they disappeared around the side of the building. When that happened, Johnson started to run. If they were heading up into one of the towers, especially 412, the one Onion O'Scullion was keeping the patrols out of, he'd have to catch them before they hit the elevator and left the lobby.

He crossed the back of 411 and the gap to 412, thought for a second about using it to come up toward the front again, but then realized if he did, Onion Head would see him. So he continued around the back of 412, got a little more than halfway, and that was when he saw the boy come back around to the Olds.

His eyes lit up when he saw Johnson running at him, so Johnson slowed. "Hey," he said, from about twenty-five feet away. "Stop."

The boy stopped.

Johnson came up on him slowly, watching to see if the other guy would pop out from somewhere. "Put your hands up."

"Why?"

Johnson touched the handle of his gun. "Are you fucking joking? *Why?*"

"I don't see no point to why you doing this, Officer. What I do wrong?" He raised his hands.

Johnson was about ten feet from him now. He looked at the side of the building and didn't see the man. "What's your name, son?"

"Pooh."

"*What?*"

"Jacob Stevens. I'm just going home now, man. You know, up to 412."

"That's good." Johnson started patting him down, looking for what, he didn't know, but doing it just the same. From the look on his face, Jacob Stevens could use a weapon to protect himself. Johnson found a student T pass that read "Steven Jacob" on the back.

"You sure your name 'Jacob Stevens,' now?"

He smiled. "You know. Jacob Stevens, Steven Jacob. They call me what they call me. To me? I don't care. Pooh be fine."

Johnson turned to look back in the direction he'd come. He wasn't looking for worried about his back, just couldn't believe this line of shit and needed to get away from it for a second. But when he looked away, he saw they were alone in the back of the towers here, just him and this bullshit-spewing kid who would not give him a straight answer.

He studied the gray, rough asphalt of the back lot.

"You know there was a shooting here today, Steven Jacob?" He could feel it coming already, the stupid answer, but more than that too: he felt his whole right arm go tense from the strain of how hard he was making a fist. His neck hurt with it.

"Nah, yo. I didn't know that. I didn't—"

That was when Johnson spun, brought his fist from down around his knee and twisted his hips to bring the punch around hard, lining it right up with the boy's jaw and—*bang!*—knocked him clear over and onto the hood of the Olds.

Damn if he didn't hear the crack of a bat, and just like that something came loose in all the tension he had from the bullshit details, O'Scullion's crap, too many stupid answers, all of it.

The hood of the car made a pop when Pooh slid off it onto the ground.

Johnson watched him lying by the bumper. "How about that shit, young man? You got a stupid answer for *that*?"

He'd never knocked anyone out before, and maybe the chance to throw a wide open cold cock like this was just too much.

Or maybe he was pissed off to see the lack of cooperation from this population he was trying his best to help. Maybe he just couldn't hold himself back from doing what he wanted to when faced with the blank fucking reality of how hard it was to make anything right. Or maybe this was the kind of police work he really needed to do.

Regardless, the punch had worked. Maybe too well.

The boy was down in an awkward position, his head rolled back under the car and his eyes closed. If it was a cartoon, he'd have little canaries flying in circles around him.

Johnson shook out his hand. It didn't even hurt. "Yeah," he said. "Now tell me your fucking name. *Pooh!* Fucking Winnie the bear?"

His leg kicked, and Johnson drew his gun before he could even think. Then an arm twitched and Johnson realized it was just a spasm. For a second he worried he'd actually hurt the little fucker, but he'd seen people laid out way worse than this and get up. He came around the side of the car to look at the boy, and his leg was shaking a little, Johnson had to admit.

He heard a sound behind him and spun with the gun.

Roughneck watched Junius walk out of 411 and turn right toward 412, then come up the path. Even with the cops around, there was no way he should be making a move to 412. He should have made that clear up on the roof, made sure Junius knew not to come on Rock's ground. He tried to wave him off, but just as he lifted his arm to do it, he caught sight of Clarence coming up from the other side of the building.

"Shit."

He liked Junius, didn't want to see Clarence get ahead with Rock, but if C Dub was going to drop a body right out in front of 412 like this, he couldn't stop it now.

This kid made his own rules. He'd have to live or die by them.

Then Clarence stopped and turned back around to where he'd come from. He still wouldn't be able to see Junius for another few feet, so Rough waved toward 411, trying to stop him, but Junius kept coming. From where he was, he wouldn't be able to see Clarence until it was too late.

Then a sound came from around the side of the building, and Clarence took a step away from the doors. That was when Junius would have come into Clarence's line of sight. But he wasn't looking. He took another step toward the back of the building and then disappeared in a run.

Just after that, Junius hit the doors and walked right into the lobby. Rough knew they were alone, but for how long?

"Fuck you doing here?" he asked, even knowing he didn't care about the answer. He didn't care and didn't have time to hear it, because if Clarence came back and saw him, he'd drop Junius fast.

"You know," Junius said, and Rough came up on him.

He knew Junius had a gun, had seen it in his hand on the roof, but Junius couldn't be *that* fast. He stepped to him in three quick moves and scooped Junius up at his shoulder and between the legs. Before he could fight back, Rough had him two steps closer to the stairway, and threw him through the door feet first.

Clarence heard the noise of something hitting his car and started running back around toward the Olds. He saw the cop standing over Pooh, and Pooh laid out flat. The cop drew his gun, and that was enough to stop Clarence cold.

Suddenly the cop spun on his heels and pointed the gun at him. Clarence threw up his hands. "What the fuck?"

"You seeing this?"

"Seeing what? I don't see shit." Clarence shook his head. The gun was small, just a little revolver the cop-pussies carried, but its black eye looked right at him. He kept his hands raised.

The cop started toward him.

"Yo. The fuck—" The cop pointed the gun at Clarence's face, and he stopped talking.

He also knew a small revolver like that would have a hard time hitting his head from twenty feet away, at least. Twenty feet of jump, Clarence figured, and with this his only chance, he took it.

"Yo, look out!" he called, pointing to the tracks, a trick that didn't get the cop to turn but at least stopped him for a moment. And in that time, Clarence spun and began a sprint for the front of 412. He knew if the cop actually took a shot, he'd have to explain firing in a public area to the rest of the police force. And if he actually hit him, would have to explain why he shot a man in the back. So Clarence was banking on him not to shoot.

True to form, the cop didn't fire. Clarence made the turn to the front of the building and rushed into the lobby.

He paused for a second just inside the doors. Roughneck stood before him, just next to one of the stairwells, and Clarence wasn't sure if he'd try some shit. He raised his fists in case it came to that, but Rough held up open palms.

"Yo," he said. "Why you running?"

"Cop."

Roughneck pointed toward the left stairs, telling him to go and that he'd cover the lobby. Clarence paused a hard second, weighing whether Rough would send the cop after him—it didn't matter now—and hit the left-side stairs at a sprint, busting through the door and ready to kick it up the eleven flights to his apartment.

Roughneck still had his hands up when the cop came around the side of the building with his gun drawn. He knew Clarence would trust him to follow the code—the law to never say shit about any other member of Rock's crew or another resident of the towers to a cop.

"I don't know shit," he said, as soon as the officer came through the doors.

The cop paused just inside, spread his legs and leveled the gun at Rough. This wasn't the first time he'd looked down the barrel of a cop's gun, and he knew it wouldn't be his last. Since it had first happened six years ago, it scared him less every time.

"Yes, Officer," Rough said, his hands high above his shoulders. He could hear Junius moving on the other side of the door just behind him. If he came through it holding a gun, there was no stopping this brother blue patrolman from firing.

"Where that motherfucker go? The one just ran through here?"

"Him?" Rough pointed to the other stairwell. "He just ran up the stairs to his apartment. He live on—"

"Give me his name."

"Yo, that dude is Lee Dal Monte. He live on six."

The cop lowered his gun and started jogging to the stairs, then stopped short. "Is that where he's going?"

Rough held his hands higher. "Fuck if I know. But check his apartment: 611, sir."

Something squawked out of the cop's walkie-talkie: an angry voice asking for Officer Johnson. He pulled it off his belt with his left hand as he ran for the stairs. "Just doing a routine check—"

The slam of the door behind him cut off the rest of the sentence. Roughneck could hear boots pounding up the stairs. Keeping his hands raised, he turned to face the other stairway door.

"You all right to come out now, young buck. Heard who was just here?"

Junius opened the door, the gun out of sight, and Rough lowered his hands. "Clarence?" he asked.

"C Dub *and* a cop going after him. You don't want to be near that."

Junius nodded. He stayed inside the stairway with the door open. "He really live on six?"

"No. Fuck no." Roughneck started to the front of the lobby, and told Junius to hang on. He went outside to the buzzers and rang up to Milk's apartment.

Milk answered after two buzzes. "What's up?"

"Need you down here. I got to be out."

"Five minutes."

Rough pushed the buzzer again, then hit talk. "Nah, niggah. You got two."

He was already through the doors when he heard Milk say he was on his way down. He still knew how to respect the man in charge.

The one thing Roughneck *didn't* want was to be here in the lobby when the cop came back looking for Clarence. Anyone, especially a pissed-off cop, would be hell to deal with after finding 611 was the home of the meanest bitch in the towers: old Josephina and her five crazy girls. When he didn't find Clarence, the cop was going to want Roughneck too.

"Come on." He waved Junius toward the elevator then pushed the button hard like you had to. He was glad to hear the whir of the motors running in the shaft.

"Where we going?" Junius asked.

"Just the fuck out of here."

Junius rode up in the elevator with Roughneck to fifteen. He wasn't sure what was going on and didn't fully trust Rough after the way he'd slammed him through the stairway door, but what else was he going to do?

"You know Clarence was coming when you put me through that door?"

Rough nodded. He wasn't saying anything now, something else that made Junius unsure.

"Where we going?"

"Chill. You be all right."

Junius bit his lip. He wanted to be cool, just grip the handle of his gun and know he could deal for himself if anything went wrong, no matter where the elevator took them. Instead, he wanted to know more.

"Why you doing this?"

Roughneck turned. "Can't shut up for a minute, can you?"

Junius shook his head. He was inside 412 alone with no one to back him up. He licked his lips. "Calm my nerves. Clue me in."

Rough shook his head. "Call this my vendetta against C Dub. Just say me and him don't get along."

"And what about Rock? Lamar?"

"Yeah." Rough nodded. "Best just leave that alone. I haven't figured them out yet myself."

The elevator whined and creaked as they moved upward. Roughneck looked at the floor beneath their feet, the dirty tan tiles, and said, "But you know the truth? I think you could use a friend."

Junius tilted his head to the side, and turned to the front of the car. He did need a friend; he wasn't going to argue that.

On fifteen, the elevator doors opened and Roughneck stepped out into the hall. It was empty and smelled like fried goodness. Junius could hear the sound of a TV. He followed Rough to an apartment like the others, not close to the elevator or to the end, just another one in the middle. When Rough opened the door, Junius stepped into a world that looked like it hadn't come past 1975. There was a big wooden couch on the right: ugly plaid pillows and white crocheted doilies over its arms. A macrame throw rug with a landscape design—mountains, maybe?—hung behind it on the wall. In front of the couch, a dark wood coffee table with white doilies under the magazines to match the ones on the couch.

Beside the couch was a wooden rocking chair, the kind that slid back and forth on gliders. An old woman sat in it with a multi-colored blanket over her lap. She smiled when she saw Rough, even turned the smile on Junius when he walked in.

"Hello, my boy," she said.

Roughneck nodded—almost a bow. "Hi, Miss Emma."

"This your friend?"

Roughneck nodded. "This Junius."

"Welcome." She held her hands up to greet him, and Junius realized she was still working on the blanket at one end, crocheting it even as it warmed her legs. "Do I know you?"

Junius looked at Rough, then shook his head.

"Who your people?"

Roughneck closed the door behind them as Junius stepped onto the thick rug. "I'm not from these towers, ma'am."

"No. 'Course not. If you were I wouldn't be asking. I'd already know you."

"I'm from near Teale Square. My people are Gail Ponds and Aldo Posey."

"Ahhh." She nodded. "Your brother is Temple? You must be the younger handsome one."

Junius looked down at the rug; at the mention of his brother's name, a chill ran through him. He wanted to know what the hell he was doing now in this old woman's apartment when he could be out in the halls finding Black Jesus and then working his way toward Rock. But Roughneck stood still in front of a bookcase filled with book. Without Rough telling him where he could find Black Jesus, Junius had little choice but to walk the halls and see who he came across.

Either he could do that or he could start at the top of the building and work his way down.

"You all right?" Miss Emma asked. "How about some Kool Aid? Randall, get your friend some Kool Aid out the 'frigerator."

Roughneck looked at Junius for a moment, then started toward the kitchen. He opened the refrigerator and took out a pitcher of red Kool Aid.

"I'm a be out, man," Junius said.

Rough came back and handed him a glass. "Where you going?"

"Tell me where I can find Black Jesus."

4 5

Clarence shut the door of his apartment hard behind him. The place was a mess and he didn't care. The blankets and sheets on his bed were in knots from how fast he got up to get the phone. Dirty clothes and a towel hung off the back of his old couch.

He leaned against the door, breathing fast and listening for footfalls in the hall. If Roughneck told the cop where to find him, he'd kill the cop *and* go kill Roughneck. That much was simple. But the loudest sound he heard was his own breathing. Time to quit the smokes, maybe. If he couldn't run up the stairs to his apartment without close to dying, wheezing, then he'd have to quit or lay off soon. Even as he thought this, his hand found the pack and started it out of his pocket. Fuck if the body didn't know what it wanted sometimes before the mind.

He lit up and started to feel better after the first drag. Even the burning in his lungs started to subside. His heartbeat slowed. He took another long drag and thought about how good he'd feel when he got some of that Ready. He had a piece on the nightstand, the last of his stash. It would be enough for a few hits, enough to get him through the now, but he should have gotten more while he was out. Another way this hunt for Junius was fucking him up.

He couldn't just come real and buy from Hammer or Milk, either. That broke the first rule, and he couldn't let it get back to Rock that he was smoking crack.

As his heartbeat slowed, he could hear it was quiet out in the hall. Rough must have done something right, sent that cop somewhere else. Maybe he was still good for something. But the cop? He had dropped Pooh like a bad case of crabs, just put him down. That was no way to treat a citizen *or* a minor. Just let Clarence put that truth in Rock's ear. Rock would know who to pass it up to. O'Scullion or somebody even higher, and then Officer Dickhead would really find out what kind of crime scene he liked to handle.

Clarence took off his heavy jacket and threw it on the couch. He hacked something up and wanted to spit, but this was his apartment after all, so he went to the kitchen and used the trash can. That settled, he rested a few moments, hands on the counter, and finished his cigarette, ashing into the sink. The cocaine he tooted was just a little, nothing to match what he was about to get into. That Ready Rock was exactly what he'd wanted all day.

Even just a few weeks from the first time he tried it, he couldn't stop thinking about its high. The shit was like his whole body bloomed on it, like it reworked his mind.

And now here he was with it waiting for him, and he was just standing there.

He went to the bed and sat down, picked up the bag with half a rock in it and shook it out. The little white nugget sat right in front of his eyes.

"Fuck yeah," he said.

Smoking the rock was still new enough to Clarence that it fascinated him: how he had to break off a piece and put it on the burned scrap of Brillo, then cook it up at the end of the Love Rose tube until it melted into the fibers. He liked watching it disappear under the flame, but that was a tiny pleasure compared with sucking the white smoke out of the glass. When he did that, he felt like there wasn't anything else in the world.

Willie told him not to inhale it way down like with weed smoke, but Clarence didn't care. Shit, he'd smoked menthols for ten years, so what could this do to his lungs? Plus, holding it down gave him a better, bigger high.

"Damn," he said, burning it into the Brillo. He was starting to feel crazy already. This was way beyond anything he'd ever had from cocaine. He listened again for a sound from the hall.

Rock always said never to use what they sold, but Clarence knew a few of them baked the weed out and even had a snort once in a while. What he *didn't* know was if Rock understood that the new shit, was this good, if he even knew what it could do to you when you got that shit in your lungs. Fuck, he had a blunt, his Kools, and a few toots today and that still wasn't anything, not beside the Ready.

He brought the glass up and hit the end with his lighter, watching the white smoke fill the pipe. The hair on his arms started to tingle as soon as he hit it and the apartment stood out like he wasn't even paying attention before, like the fucking lines of the room started to wiggle.

"Fuck," he said, sitting back a little. He put his finger over the hole to hold in the smoke. "Fuck me, niggah."

Then he hit it again. He hit it for the next few minutes until the rock was all gone, and then he lay back on the bed. He rolled in the covers a bit and shook his head until he got a pop in his neck that felt like he just realigned his whole spine.

He jumped up off the bed and hit himself in the chest a couple times. He wanted that cop to walk through the door now, have him come in at this second so he could deal with his ass exactly how it needed. Clarence knew if the cop was here now, he'd be too fast for him, would see the cop's movements before they happened, maybe even be able to read his mind.

And Junius?

Clarence turned, faced the window and looked out over the highway at the hills to the west. He could hear footsteps in the apartment above, a door sliding open, maybe the fan in a bathroom. Junius was in this building—he knew it. He closed his eyes and somewhere in 412 he knew he could feel the boy he needed to kill.

If he could ice Junius, *then* maybe Rock would make him his strict gun man and he'd be off dealing with Dee and Ness. No more worries about sales, corners, stairs—none of that shit! He'd be the man with the burner, the one who bucked shots. Maybe then he could tell Rock about the Ready, let him know how good it was and buy from Hammer.

Clarence smiled. He knew he had this coming. All he had to do was keep this high and feel out everything he needed. So what if Rock found out he was smoking crack. He'd be alright when he knew what Clarence could do on it.

He'd go down to the lobby and get more first, hit that, and then go out to deal with Junius and the cop, clean up the whole fucking towers, maybe Marlene too.

All that after he got another rock.

He took his Walther out of the dresser and tucked it into the back of his pants, then hung his shirt over it and crossed the room to the door, leaving his jacket on the couch. Everything he had to go after now was inside this tower, right here in the 412.

He knew it, could feel the building telling him it had everything he would need.

"I'd hate for you to run off already," Miss Emma said. "At least sit and finish your Kool Aid."

Rough turned to the old woman. "He's trying to find Guardy Little."

"Oh." She turned back to the blanket in her lap and her crocheting. "Best I should stay out of that, then."

Junius drank the red Kool Aid. It tasted sweet, with just the right amount of sugar. It didn't taste like cherry; it tasted like red Kool Aid was supposed to—like red itself was a flavor.

Junius looked at Rough, but Rough didn't say anything. Behind him, the clock on the wall read one fifteen: only forty-five minutes left until he told himself he'd be back to get Elf. Junius downed the rest of the Kool Aid in one long swallow, trying to be polite. "You going to tell me where he be?"

Rough shook his head, shrugged. "I can tell you his apartment, but he won't be up in there right now."

"Why are you so angry?" Miss Emma asked. "You're such a young man."

Junius set the glass down on the coffee table, in the middle of a doily, and backed toward the door. "I apologize to you, ma'am, if I seem rude today," he said. "Thank you for your hospitality."

"He mad because his brother dead," Rough told Miss Emma.

"What?" She looked at Rough and then back to Junius. "Is that true? Temple dead? He's so young!"

Junius looked away from her. Why he had to be the one to confirm his own bad news, he didn't know, didn't like.

"Randall?" She waited for an answer.

Rough nodded. He'd just said it plain and straight, and now he confirmed it with a nod. "Yes, ma'am."

"And your mother?"

Junius could hear the glider creak in the quiet. Dust spun and circled in a ray of light on the other side of the room.

"She ok," he told her. "Upset, but—" He stopped because he didn't know what else to say.

"That is no good," Miss Emma said. She sucked her teeth. "No *damn good.*"

And Junius knew it wasn't.

He knew that more than anything. He also knew it hadn't helped that he dropped Lamar, or that Jason was now dead on the roof. None of it did any damn good, and still he wanted to take it further, take more bodies with him. If he had his reasons, and he did, then anything he did made more sense than the way the rest of it.

"Who did this?" Miss Emma asked. She looked to Rough for her answer, but he stayed silent until she asked again.

When he answered her, Junius watched his eyes, watching for the lie when he said someone other than Rock or Black Jesus. Instead he said, "I don't know."

Junius didn't blink, kept his eyes on Rough's for any sign that he did know, that it came from someone he knew, but he didn't see anything. Two weeks on the street was enough to know when someone was lying: you worked a corner and you had to know who told the truth, who had the money, and who was a cop. Junius had worked Teale Square for two years.

Rough wasn't lying.

"Don't know? No damn good you are!" Miss Emma started to get out of her chair. "Get me that phone and I'll see who up in here knows what! Think we don't know what's going on? I can tell you how this terribleness happened in two calls. You watch me!"

Rough smiled. He helped her up out of her chair after Miss Emma had set her blanket and her crochet hook on the table. She shuffled toward the empty kitchen, mumbling to herself that she knew who she would call and that she still had friends who could tell her what was happening. "Think we women don't know what's the what," she said.

Rough laughed, then he saw Junius's face and he stopped. "Sorry," he said. "But you know she gone come back saying it came from nothing. No good reason and she's right."

Rough tilted his head toward her. "Or, she could find out clear as day what went down. Who did what. She could come up with most anything. No telling."

"Yeah, well I ain't about to wait."

Rough shrugged. "Guess you know where you headed."

"Thanks for your help."

"It's cool. But watch out for Clarence in here. That niggah *wild*."

"Yeah. I heard that." He clapped his palm against Rough's and nodded at the bigger man.

Rough nodded back, and Junius slipped out into the hall.

He didn't break stride when he was out of the apartment, walked right to the stairs and opened the heavy steel door. Inside the stairwell, he listened, wanting to hear voices so he'd know who else was around.

Clarence stepped into the hall. He wanted to punch holes in walls, shoot people who needed shooting.

"Fuck," he said, drawling out the word, listening to how long he could stretch out the "u" sound. He rubbed his fingers and it felt good to feel the slide of his thumb across the others' pads. This was not a moment for the stairs, though he felt like he could sprint down them; it was time for a nice, slow ride in the elevator. He'd ride like the king he was. His apartment seemed to let him out directly in front of it, as if he'd only blinked and was already pushing the button. He heard the pulleys spinning and the cables stretching from the other side of the doors, wheels rolling up supports to bring the elevator car his way.

This was how it was supposed to be.

"Fuck." He punctuated it with a fist to the right elevator door. Satisfied that he had made a dent, Clarence checked his knuckles: they looked like normal, and he didn't feel a thing. He punched the same spot on the door again, deepening the dent, and nodded. He was ready for anything that came his way.

"Yeah," he said, and at that moment the elevator doors opened. The car was empty.

He got in and rode to the lobby by himself, punching his fist into his empty left hand as he listened to an imaginary beat in his head that felt like it was tailor made for the situation. He tapped his feet. No one got onto the elevator as it made its descent; no one stopped it between the eleventh floor and the lobby. Clarence wasn't even sure if he cared who was there when the doors opened: if it was Roughneck, he was getting fucked up; if it was someone else, the same; if it was that cop who had dropped Pooh, he was getting *beat down*.

The elevator dinged, which struck Clarence as odd; he couldn't remember the last time he heard it make a sound. Then the doors opened, and he was looking at the place where a fancier elevator might have a series of numbers to mark the floors, so he didn't see the lobby immediately.

"Mo-ther-fucker!"

He heard it before he saw who was speaking, but as soon as he did, he knew exactly who he'd find.

"Yes, sir," Clarence said, stepping out of the car to stand in front of the cop. The lobby was empty but for Rough's boy Milk standing by the doors, and the cop, Officer Johnson, Clarence now read off the tag above his badge. The cop had his nightstick in one hand and was smacking it into the palm of the other. He looked almost as happy to see Clarence as Clarence was to see him.

"You fucking run?" Johnson said. His eyebrows came together above his nose; his mouth pursed into a thin smile. "We love it when you motherfuckers run."

"I'm here now." Clarence held his hands out by his sides. His arms felt just a little heavier and the beat in his head was getting softer. But he knew how to get it back.

He stepped to the cop. "Come on."

Johnson swung with his nightstick, and Clarence raised his arm to block it. The stick hit his forearm, and Clarence heard a crack, felt his first pain since hitting the rock upstairs, but the pain was just a tiny feeling compared to the roar it started inside him. The new strength of the bass track made him quiver. He ripped the stick from Johnson's hand and threw it across the lobby.

"We won't have that," Clarence said, and grabbed the front of the stiff blue uniform with both hands. He pulled the cop toward him, brought him close enough that he could smell the cop smell. "You want me? Clarence right here for you."

The cop swung and hit Clarence in the kidney with a tight hook. He might as well have tried pinching him for how much it hurt.

"Yeah," the cop said. He headbutted Clarence in the middle of his face, connecting with the top of his forehead against the bridge of his nose, and Clarence saw black. He felt his eyes tear up and his face squeeze together on its own.

He heard, "This is exactly where you should be, you fucking crackhead."

He was still seeing black, but Clarence knew exactly where the elevator was behind him and he'd already heard the doors close. He spun with the cop's uniform in his hands, and twisted Johnson's body as he did. In the last second before they made impact, his sight came back and he saw the silver doors of the elevator just a second before he smashed the cop's face into them. The cop's body went limp a little, and Clarence tasted his own blood on his lips. He spit against the doors and saw red.

"Yeah." With one hand he pushed the cop against the metal doors at the shoulder and with the other he grabbed the back of the cop's head and pulled it toward him so the cop could see his face. "You see me?" he asked.

Then he slammed the cop's face into the elevator doors again.

"The fuck are you doing, C?" Milk tried to grab his shoulders. "This dude's a fucking cop, and we got more cops all over this piece!"

Clarence brushed him back. "So be the fuck out, you don't want part of this."

Milk took his hands away, and Clarence heard his feet on the lobby tiles as he went for the stairs.

"Just you and me now, Officer."

"Good." The cop hit Clarence in the stomach with an elbow that made Clarence want to double over. He rested his forehead against Johnson's shoulder and breathed hard. He could feel Johnson getting stronger, pushing back against the elevator doors, and he tried to slam the cop's face into the doors again, but this time the cop held himself still, didn't let Clarence control him.

He spun and hit Clarence in the gut for real this time, up under the ribcage. Clarence wanted to vomit or sit down and take a shit, he didn't know which. He felt his buzz from the crack slipping away and wished he was upstairs again, sucking on another hit—or three—and ground his teeth together. When he looked up, he saw the cop's chest in front of him and jumped at his face. The crown of his head connected with the bottom of the cop's chin and the cop went slack for a moment. He heard the back of the cop's head hit the elevator doors.

"You!" he shouted, hitting Johnson in the hip with a low, hard right. "Do not!" He followed with a left to the cop's stomach, doubling him as he stood to go higher with his next punch. "Come into this tower!"

The last punch, an uppercut, landed under Johnson's chin and spun him into the doors. The cop went slack, but Clarence held him up. He reached around to his back and brought out the Walther in his right hand, holding it around the barrel to use like a mallet.

"To fuck with us!"

He punctuated this last exclamation by jabbing the barrel of the gun into the cop's lower back, the soft place above his belt and hip bone, exactly where he thought he'd hit kidney. The cop squirmed and reared back. His knees buckled, and Clarence let him fall.

Behind him, Clarence heard the jingling of keys and the front door of the building. He turned and saw a woman in her sixties holding a brown paper bag of groceries. "Oh my God," she said.

Clarence raised the gun at her and ground his teeth. "Get the fuck out!"

She hurried back out of the lobby with her groceries.

"Fuck with Pooh!" Clarence said.

He kicked the cop in the side, then pulled his foot back to kick again, thought about kicking the cop in his face, and then stomped down on his fingers instead. That got the desired reaction from Johnson, who cried out and rolled into a ball against the elevator doors, his back to Clarence. Clarence kicked him in the back this time, and, coming to his senses a little, he pulled Officer Johnson up by the back of his uniform. He had to pull on it hard to get enough loose fabric to grip each shoulder, but when he did, he started to drag the cop toward the back stairway doors.

The cop started kicking and spun in Clarence's hands to try to get free. That was when Clarence cracked him twice in the side of the head with the butt of his gun. After that the cop was out.

Clarence pulled him out of the lobby, through the stairway doors, and around to the back of the building where they were supposed to put the trash out.

He dropped Johnson to open the back door and realized he still had his Walther in his hand. As he stood to tuck it into his pants, he noticed the cop had left a trail of blood along the floor. Maybe some of it was his own, too. He wiped his hand across his lips and saw red when he brought it away. He wiped this blood off on the cop's uniform. That was when he saw the cop's gun.

He pulled it out of the holster and looked it over. On the side it said, S & W—Smith & Wesson. It was silver with a nice-looking black grip. Cold steel! This was a cop-gun, the kind that would only be traced back to a cop. He wasn't sure if he'd get away with capping Junius with it and have that go back to a cop, but it was worth trying. He tucked it down the front of his pants, then carefully took the gold badge off the front of the cop's shirt and pushed it down into one of his back pockets.

"Motherfuck you," he said to the cop. "This is why you do not come up into this tower, you fucking piece of shit cop." He kicked Johnson again in the side.

Now he'd need to call Rock and get someone down here to do a clean-up. He needed more of that Ready, too; his high was gone and not only did he feel tired and spent and empty, but his forearm, his back, and his nose all cried out for some kind of self-medication.

He kicked the cop again and then left him, headed for the stairs and the second-floor landing where somebody's boys would be selling. There he could tell a young one to go clean up the blood and get another rock to take back to his apartment.

Marlene took a deep breath and raised the glass of white wine to her lips. She sat on Malik's couch, his TV set off and no sound in the apartment but the sound of someone else's TV coming from across the hall.

The wine tasted crisp, like an apple or a pear, and it was cold. Since Malik had gone away and left an empty refrigerator, she'd been using it to store her whites: the wines she was trying to get used to so she could talk about them with Anthony. She kept the reds under her counter, away from the light, but she liked those even less. Truth was, none of the wines tasted to her like something people would go crazy over.

Usually she had to send someone over here to get her a bottle or two every now and then. Now she scanned the layer of dust on the coffee table and on top of the TV. She needed one of the girls to come over and clean this place more often. Who knew what amount of dust she was sitting in on this couch.

But she didn't want to think about that, not when there was so much else going on.

Seven Heaven sat on the love seat across from her. He'd have ideas about all this, but she knew he would wait to hear hers first.

"What you think?" she asked. "How long until those young bucks get us all killed?"

Seven laughed, shook his head. "They with the TV-boy, Shari's kid on twenty. They hold up fine there."

She nodded. "How about us?"

Seven shrugged.

Marlene took another sip. "Just tell me I did the right thing."

"You did the right thing."

"Shit." She laughed. Seven always told it to her straight, so if he was willing to lie to her now, it meant she'd really fucked this up. "You think it's that bad?"

He folded his arms. "It'll be all right. Just so long as they don't tell Rock who said it was him killed Temple."

"We could pull them off."

Seven frowned, shook his head. "We go get them out of TV-land and tell them to go home, we gone have a problem with them too. They young, but now they had a taste."

"No." Marlene stood up. "Get them out before more shit comes down. We made a mistake." She drained the rest of her wine.

Now Seven Heaven stood up. If he wasn't her brother's closest friend, she'd let herself act on their attraction again, make their relationship more than just the work level. She thought back to the one time they made love on a Sunday afternoon, fallen into what they both really wanted. She could still smell his scent, the cigar smoke on his sweatshirt.

"No," he said. "We don't—you don't—make mistakes. That's not how we run this. You tell them what you told them, then it be right. Rock our problem and now we sent them his way. They get killed, it's on him, not us."

She bit her bottom lip, pushed up her sleeves. Malik's apartment was warm—all that free project heating pent up in one place. Soon it would be safe to go back to her apartment; she'd be more comfortable there.

"Maybe I did do the right thing. They wanted guns, we gave them guns, sent them in the right direction. But—" She let it hang, thinking the next part through to be absolutely sure.

Seven waited. When she was ready, she said, "But find out what really happened to Temple. This comes back, I want to have the truth in my hands. Use whatever leverage that can give me."

Seven nodded. "I get that." He raised his shoulders. "But you know how these things be. Niggahs popping off, getting shot at for nothing. Just some bullshit."

"I know." She looked down at the long strands of her brother's shag rug. She'd have to ask one of the girls to just throw the damn thing away. "You're right. But let's be sure."

He nodded.

"And put an end to this shit between you and Pickup. You hear me?"

Now he looked toward the door.

"Just know you're my number one, ok? Nothing going to change that. So dead this. I want you and Pickup to get along."

Seven turned to head for the door. "Hey," she said. "Let them go at Rock, but go see them first. Make sure they still ready, then pop them free from TV-land."

Seven nodded. "They gone want to know where to start again."

"What'd you tell them last time?"

"Told them Black Jesus. Sent them to watch from the stairs."

"No," she said. "Fuck it. Send them into 412. Send them after Rock. This comes to a head right now."

She crossed her arms, watched him turn to leave. Seven was nodding the whole way to the door.

At Mike's diner, Dee and Ness had each had a steak and cheese sub with extra peppers and two Cokes, and still nothing was going on. Across the restaurant, Willie Stash sat in a booth with two of his boys, talking shit and playing cards. They were all supposed to be friendly with one another now because Clarence said they were up here waiting for Junius and Little Elf, but Dee didn't like it one bit: hanging out in wack-ass Somerville, up in bullshit Davis Square.

He was as tired as he could remember being. Cokes or no Cokes, he'd been up all day yesterday, slept on and off during the night in the car, waiting outside Junius's mother's place, and now he was supposed to hang out in a diner, watching the main intersection at Davis Square for two kids who weren't going to show. Just the fact that they were headed toward Porter when they first came out in the morning meant they had somewhere else in mind. No way they were coming to see Willie, and Clarence should have known that, *would have* if he wasn't stoned out *and* high on coke.

"Yo, this is bullshit," Dee said, tapping a quarter against the red tabletop of the booth. "C Dub losing his grip."

"These benches ain't shit." Ness tried to slide sideways to rest his back against the window and put his feet up, but that didn't look comfortable—and it kept him from seeing where they were supposed to watch. "I'm fucking ass out, son."

"Heard that." Ever since they'd smoked up in the 98, things had been ok for a little while and then gotten worse. "You got any trees?"

Ness shook his head. "Shit, niggah. We smoked all my shit up last night."

Here they were supposed to be selling, and neither of them had any shit to smoke.

"Yo!" Dee sat up straight. The car! It was only a few blocks from where they were, close to Porter, but walkable from Mike's Diner, and he had a stash of papers and a nice bag inside.

"Fuck this. I got *my* shit in the car, still. Those niggahs come back by Davis, let Big Willie handle it. He fucks up, he can tell Rock himself."

"What about Clarence?"

"Shit." Dee had already pulled his jacket up onto his arms. He sucked down what was left of his second Coke. "I got trees in the car, niggah. Tell me you don't want to hit that shit and head home."

Ness got up fast, hustled to get out of the booth. "I'm a hit that bed like I hit yo moms!"

Dee punched him. "I tried to fuck your moms, but Clarence was already there."

"Oh!" Ness's face soured like he swallowed a whole lemon turned inside-out. "That's nasty! *Please* don't be talking about my moms and Clarence, yo. Ok?"

Dee pushed Ness toward Big Willie's table, and his crew looked up.

"Yo. We done. You see your boy J, you know who to call."

Willie nodded. "Yeah, we hit you. Don't you worry your pretty little dome-piece."

"Good." Dee took a few seconds to decide if he should come back at Willie with something, then made his move for the door. The car and the weed were both calling.

He waved to Willie and gave him the finger. "Fuck all you, niggahs, alright?"

One of Willie's boys shuffled up to start, but Willie pulled him back.

"We catch you," Willie said, giving one upward nod.

Dee put his hands in his pockets as Ness opened the door, getting ready for the cold. "Not if we catch you first," he said at last, then spit a short stream onto the floor of the diner before stepping out to the sidewalk.

Elf looked at the clock on the wall. *I Love Lucy* was over and it was coming up on one thirty. He'd been sitting on this couch for close to an hour.

"What you say about them chicken nuggets then?"

"Yeah, that's a really good idea." The kid hopped up off the couch and padded into the kitchen. He wore a horizontal-striped turtleneck with brown corduroys and thick slipper-socks. "What do you want to watch next?"

"Damn. Where you get them clothes from? You know your momma dresses you funny?"

He stopped at the refrigerator with the freezer door open and looked back to Elf. "You think I haven't heard *that one* before? And may I remind you that you're the one who's a guest in *my* house? And that I'm considering feeding you?"

Elf rolled his eyes and looked toward the dingy window of the apartment. It was made from the same thick plastic material that the windows at school were made from, the kind you weren't supposed to be able to break.

"My bad."

He heard the freezer close. "And do you realize that you've been here an hour and haven't even bothered to ask me my name?"

The kid stood waiting, now holding a box of frozen chicken nuggets in his hands. Shit, if he had real food, Elf was not about to take any chances. But the first thing he said was, "How long those take to cook?"

"Did you even hear what I said?"

"Yeah." Elf nodded. "My bad. What your name is?"

"Malik." He smiled. "And these take about twenty-five minutes to cook, once we get the oven pre-heated."

"Shit," Elf said. "Don't you got a toaster oven?"

Malik set the box of nuggets down on the counter and disappeared behind the kitchen partition. "Don't worry about it. It'll all seem quick in the end."

Elf heard him light a match and then open the door to the stove. A few seconds later, he heard a *whoosh* as the gas caught.

"Put some in for Junius," Elf said. Then he turned back to the TV. "What be on next?"

"Six for fifty. Six for fifty."

Junius looked up when he heard the voice above him in the stairwell.

"Six for twenty on that Ready Rock, niggah. Weed bags six for fifty, hundred get you twelve."

A younger voice said, "Ten dollars?"

"Ten get you one, my niggah. Ten get you one."

"What about on that Ready?"

"Twenty get you six," came from another, deeper voice. "Back the fuck up and wait your turn."

The talk came from no more than two flights up. Junius rubbed his hand across his eyebrows. He was grinding his teeth again. This was what it would come down to sooner or later. Time was ticking—on Elf, on Rock's crew knowing he was in 412, on Clarence. Then the rest of them would come in waves, unless he was the first to the punch.

And this was fine with him, Junius decided. Punching was what he came here to do—punching toward the top, where he knew he'd find Rock.

Junius took the Tec out of his pants and looked it over. A part of him sparked inside—a part that wanted blood and revenge for what happened to Temple, a part that was mad Roughneck thought Temple was killed over nothing.

Just the drug trade: the answer for everything bad. Drugs and more drugs. Everybody wasted and losing their lives in the game.

But not Temple.

He closed his eyes and thought back to when he shot Lamar. Even that last shot, the one at point blank that ended it all, had not felt wrong. It felt like he was taking something back.

He'd heard about people worrying their whole lives over someone they killed, even seeing dead faces in their sleep, and he knew already that that wasn't going to be him. Lamar's face wouldn't keep him awake at night. He was glad he'd killed that bitch.

Rock's boys played for real, too. They didn't give a shit about killing someone.

Jason's blood had spread across the pebbles on the roof, the red mixing into the dirt, staining the stones. Jason knew his brother. Now they were both gone.

He didn't care if Marlene was the Oracle, a prophet, or just a woman who wanted to run these towers; Willie wouldn't protect him now, so it was prove himself to Marlene or leave everything he'd known his whole life.

That wouldn't be him.

Like the heroes in the kung fu movies, you had to get up and stand against the tower, or whatever was in your way, find your path to the man who needed to be killed. He wasn't going back to spend years training. He was going on up.

He was already more than halfway to the top. No more waiting.

He held the Tec-9 in both hands, low alongside his waist, and started up the stairs.

5 0

Randy watched Clarence head down the hall to the elevator. Nathaniel had just passed him three rocks, and Clarence told them to get the money from Rock. Rock wouldn't like that, and neither would Roughneck. As Clarence waited for the elevator, he turned back to them.

"What I told you?" he asked.

"We heard you," Nathaniel said. "And we on it." He pointed his chin at Randy. "You heard him?"

"I heard," Randy said.

Nathaniel offered him his fist, and Randy bumped it. That was Nathaniel's way of telling him to get going. Down the hall, the elevator doors opened, and Clarence stepped inside. He turned back once before disappearing, and pointed directly at Randy. "Get on that," he said. And then he was gone.

Randy turned to Nathaniel. "You for real about this shit?"

Nathaniel looked up at the ceiling. "Let me see: C Dub said there be a mess in the lobby. You be new as shit and trying to get on. You need to get your dumb ass *down* there and clean that shit up." His eyes opened wide as he said this last part, and his forehead wrinkled, as if he couldn't believe he had to explain it. "Now get on that shit!"

Randy shook his head, turning, and felt the smack of Nathaniel's hand across the back of his head.

"Don't you shake your head at me, now."

He felt a push from behind that almost sent him face-first down the stairs, but he caught himself against the wall and started to run.

"That's right. Get on that shit. You find a mop and some sponges in the closet by the back trash door."

Randy waved at Nathaniel without looking. At the next landing, he risked a peek back up and Nathaniel was still watching. "You finish and you buzz Rock at 2208. Tell him what C Dub did."

"Ok."

He trotted down the steps toward the lobby.

His cousin had hooked him up with Rock's crew for the vacation week as a trial run, and he'd come through the first two days fine. All he had to do was stand with Nathaniel, watch the count, and back him up if needed. So far, the only one to get bullshit on them was Andre's moms, the bitch who always yelled at people up on eighteen. She looked skinny as nobody's business these days, real bad, and she smelled like she needed a shower. When she came to them with in her nightgown with no money, trying to pick up some rocks, Nathaniel wasn't having it. But Randy had to push her down the hall and into the elevator, and he hated every second of that. Even if Andre never found out—his moms didn't seem like she even recognized him—it felt wrong to be treating her that way. The worst part was when she went for his fly, tried to open his pants by the elevator doors. She offered to suck his dick for the crack, and when he looked in her eyes, he could tell she meant it.

That was the worst part of the two days, but today was looking like things could really start popping off when they got the word about shots fired on the roof and cops patrolling the towers. That fucked with Randy's head because he didn't want to get caught doing *any*thing wrong. He knew if someone had to go to jail, it'd just as likely be him, the man on the bottom rung.

Then Nathaniel got word to move up on eight to keep selling. So they did. All in all, the day had more action than the previous two combined, but Andre's moms still ranked as the worst of it.

That was until he hit the first floor and came into the back hallway, where he found a cop lying against the back doors in a pool of blood. Then things all of a sudden got *much* worse than dealing with Andre's moms. This was way worse than any of that shit.

He knelt down next to the cop and looked at his face: there was a welt above the cop's temple that looked like you could fit a mouse inside it. His nose looked bad, and one of his eyes was swollen shut. Blood was coming from his nose and his mouth, mostly, but it also looked like there had to be another place it was coming from, just from the amount of it.

This cop was busted up, and if C Dub was the one who did it, then he was in for some serious shit. The cop was black too, and that almost made Randy feel worse. Then again, he was a cop. What could you expect? Better this than him in jail.

He followed the trail of blood, careful not to step in any of it, one word—evidence— burning into his head the whole way. The blood led him back up the hall, into the lobby, and straight to the elevator. The doors there had more blood on them and a mess of it where they met the floor. Right in front of the elevator there were streaks in it, places where feet had slipped and someone had fallen. From there, the blood was like someone had been dragged through it for a few feet and then after that it was just a trail.

The fight had been right here.

The front doors rattled behind him, and Randy spun fast, half expecting to see a whole crew of cops watching him with their guns drawn.

Instead, an old woman carrying a grocery bag opened the door, intentionally looking away from the elevator and Randy. She started right for the east stairs, the ones Rock didn't use, where she wouldn't have to walk past Nathaniel or anyone selling drugs. She didn't stop on her way through the lobby, not to check her mail or to ask what was going on. She made that line for the stairs and then she was gone. If she'd been around the towers for any amount of time, she knew it was better that way.

But just like she knew that, Randy knew a cop getting fucked up in Rock's tower was not something that would just go away—especially not on a day where shots had already been fired and more cops were on the scene. Either C Dub had completely lost his mind *and* his shit or—*shit!*—Randy looked around and didn't see any other explanation.

Self-defense? Fuck that. A cop put a beat down on you, you took it and asked questions later.

But there was another problem: that cop wasn't even dead. *That* would be some trouble when he woke up, some *serious* shit, and Randy didn't want to be there for it.

He went right to the buzzers in the outer lobby, holding the door open as he went to the panel so he wouldn't get locked out. He didn't have to think about who to call, either. Nathaniel said to buzz Rock at 2208 when he was done; well, he wasn't done, but this job was definitely going to need more than just him.

Black Jesus had just sat down on his couch when the phone rang right next to him on the table. It had been one hell of a morning already, what with Berry Rich making her trip to the towers, the shootings on the roof, and now the police going door to door in 411.

Now Black Jesus had just gotten to sit down for a minute and the phone was already on ring. Rock was steady fucking; Hammer was back up on the roof trying to watch what the cops would do about the body; Roughneck was in charge of sales in the stairs; and Mike Only, Rock's driver and Jesus's sometimes love interest, wouldn't be calling him in the middle of the day, not on a day that was already this crazy. So he didn't know who'd be on the other end when he picked it up and said, "Yeah."

"Yo, we got a issue down the lobby." It was Rock's voice. Rock was not happy.

"We not *in* the lobby."

"Oh, we ain't selling. We got bigger shit. Just got buzzed up from downstairs. Clarence busted the fuck out a cop."

This took more than a second to register. "A cop? What you mean busted?"

"I mean he fucked the niggah *up*! Beat down. Blood all over the place."

"C Dub gone crazy?"

"Fuck." Rock's voice trailed off, and Black Jesus pictured him naked, his chest heaving from what he'd been up to with Berry Rich. Jesus boxed with Rock three times a week at the gym, and Rock would go topless, so Jesus knew Rock was cut. He looked good.

When Rock came back, he said, "Clarence sent this kid down to clean shit up, and he sees it's a blood storm, more shit than he can handle. Boy's got some sense in him. We should recognize that." Rock paused a few beats and Black Jesus thought he could hear the man drinking. Then he said, "I want you to get your ass down there and see to this. Take who you need. Just get shit fixed."

Rock hung up before Black Jesus could say anything more. He had no idea how you took care of a cop that was beaten up. A dead cop was one thing, but the prospect of one who was fucked up *and* still alive?

Black Jesus did not want to be the one to kill a cop.

He started dialing Mike Only. Mike might know what to do about this mess, and even if he didn't, it would be good to hear his voice.

5 1

Seven Heaven didn't bother taking the tunnel on his way back to 411. If the cops wanted to fuck with him, search him, or ask him questions, he was down. All of his answers would come back to Rock and Rock's boys. It was Hammer shooting on the roof, Hammer and his boys trying to start shit and make a play for Marlene, Hammer who had shot and killed Jason.

Time had come to fuck all the treaties and cop silence rules; the war with Rock and his crew was about to heat up whether or not Marlene knew it, wanted it, or was ready.

Marlene might be wrong to dig in and deny the towers their upgrade in fuck-you-up from crack, but if that was her decision—and Seven understood the logic behind it every time he saw what the crack users looked like after just a few weeks—then he would help her make her stand. Malik didn't get it, that much was sure. He was out of the game, couldn't see the street. So they were on their own with this strategy; it was their fight.

If they fucked things up, they would have to answer to Malik. Seven was ok with that.

The elevator doors opened onto the lobby of 410, and Seven saw a few boys and girls playing outside and an elderly couple waiting to ride up. He stepped out of their way coming out and then held the doors open, trying to make things easy, but they still wouldn't look at him or stop to say thanks. He'd go down in a war trying to stop the further destruction of these towers, and these people would still hate him for the way he made his money.

"Have a good day now," he said as he let the door close. They turned to face the front of the car, and the man stared him down, refusing to speak, hate in his eyes until the doors closed and he was gone.

Meldrak and Big Pickup stood sentry by the front doors, waiting to sell or act ambassador if the cops decided to head into the building. They both gave him the upward nod, and he returned their stares.

If Big Pickup was going to make a move, it would come soon. But Seven knew it wouldn't work: the way Marlene looked at him was different than how she looked at Pickup. Only one of them fit what she wanted in her bed, and even if Pickup carried her from here to Harvard Square, his fat gut and big legs just weren't going to be that. Plus, she and Seven had history.

"You two doing the right thing," Seven said, winking at Pickup. "Definitely holding it down. The cops come through, buzz up to Marlene and be sure she know."

Drak just nodded; only Pickup continued to stare. Drak had less at stake, less ambition, even if he was smart. So Seven gave him a pound as he stepped to the doors. Big Pickup he put a big soul clap on, brought the man to him in a one-arm hug.

He slapped Pickup on the back. "Yo, let's dead this, my man."

If it was what Marlene wanted, he'd do his best to try—at least on the outside.

"Oh, word?"

Seven felt Pickup pulling back, drawing away from him.

"Dead what? What is up here to dead now?"

Now Seven let him go. He looked Pickup in the eyes, waiting for the other to acknowledge what they both knew, but Pickup didn't blink. He wouldn't come clean about it and that meant it was even worse than Seven thought. But shit, he'd done his best to try. What else was there for him to do?

"Oh, that's cool," he said. "Guess there nothing to be dead then."

Pickup nodded. He patted himself on the chest, almost as if he wanted to wipe Seven's touch off his hand.

"Ok, my man," Seven said.

Seven brushed past Pickup and headed out the doors. He needed to watch now: Pickup would come at him from behind.

Sun Tzu, the master of war, would be his guide in this time of strategy. And Sun Tzu, bad motherfucker that he was, would guide his ass through into the clear. Go into a war, you had to know who your loyal soldiers were. That's what he'd read.

Seven knew both sides of the equation. Now he just needed to wait for an opportunity to make his move.

The kids outside didn't hate him, instead they smiled and said, "What up?" as Seven walked through the doors. He caught their ball on a high bounce as it came off the wall and for a second acted like he would tuck it under his sweatshirt to keep.

"Hey!" one of the bigger boys said, and then pulled himself back, realizing who he was talking to. Seven smiled and tossed the ball back. Maybe this one would make a good soldier some day. Seven winked.

The cold greeted him more harshly than the police. There didn't seem to be anybody on patrol outside 410 yet. Maybe the cops were with Rock now so much that they'd just target 411. Maybe he'd paid them *all* off.

Seven stepped to 411 and saw the old white cop standing out front. Let this captain cop search him down. He'd left one Tec-9 back in Malik's apartment and he had another waiting in the freezer on sixteen.

"Hello, young man," the cop said.

"Hello." Seven saluted him halfheartedly, walking up to the front of his building. "Everything ok here now?"

"Oh, some bad shit went down up in here," the cop said. The tag over his badge read "Sgt. O'Scullion." This was the guy Rock had bought out completely, according to Marlene.

"How about up in there?" Seven pointed to 412 and watched the sergeant shrug as he expected. "Nothing up there?"

"Not that I know of at present. Shots fired on the roof of this tower, is what I heard." O'Scullion pointed up at the top of 411 and his eyes narrowed. "You know anything about that?"

"Just a citizen with concerns," Seven said, showing the palms of his hands.

This cop knew Seven; they'd seen each other enough times on his drive-throughs of the towers, shared enough eye-fuckings that they were both aware of the games. The Sergeant couldn't declare all out war on Marlene's crew yet—it would generate too much attention—but he usually acted like he wanted to.

"Why aren't you working today?"

Seven had reached the spot in front of 411 where he either made his move to the lobby, turning his back on the cop, or turned to have a real conversation. Instead of either, he stopped where he was, half-facing the doors and half not.

"Just my day off," Seven said. "Today my day."

O'Scullion squinted like he was trying to decide what to ask next. "Really, how much you know about what happened here today?" he asked. His face went slack when he asked it, almost like he was taking off a mask. The real face underneath was concerned, just wanted a clue, some idea of why there was another dead body on the roof. "We could use a little insight."

"Just the shit," Seven said. He took another step closer to the cop. "You know the shit, Sergeant, and how it be."

O'Scullion nodded.

"Bullshit, is what it is. Same thing left Lamar out here." He gestured behind them. "Same thing that's bound to happen a few more times this week before everything cools off."

O'Scullion chewed on his lips, sucking the bottom of his mustache into his mouth. A cold wind whipped across them both, and Seven realized the cop had been standing outside for a long time. His cheeks were a deep red, his nose, already red from drink, was like a shining beacon lined with veins.

"The shit?"

"My guess? It's gone get worse before it gets better."

Seven dug his hands into his pockets, waiting for what was next. He'd presented the truth, and the cop could choose to see it or turn a blind eye.

What worried Seven most was the cop almost seemed ready to care and get involved. There was no telling where that would lead.

But just as O'Scullion opened his mouth to speak, the radio unit on his shoulder squawked to life. "Sergeant, we got a body out back in the alley. Second body. Looks like this time we *will* need an ambulance. Back side of 412 closest to the freeway." The radio squawked and then came back again. "Sergeant, we got a body."

O'Scullion leaned his head toward that shoulder and pushed the talk button. "10-4, Officer. I am en route." He let the radio go quiet and stood in front of Seven for a moment.

He'd been about to say something real and now that was gone. The disdain was back on his face, and he was a cold cop again.

"I see you got a hand in any of this shit," he said, raising a finger to point at Seven's face. "I am one hundred percent intent on taking you down."

Seven didn't say anything, just waited for the cop to turn around and run where his radio had called him. O'Scullion started to trot sideways, still looking back at Seven and eyeing him for a few strides before he turned full around to run for the alley.

When the cop was gone, Seven spit a stream onto the ground. "Fuck you," he said, hands still in his pockets.

He turned to go inside.

"Twenty get you six. Step up here."

"Ten get me three? Can I get three?"

"Whoo! You want that crack rock? Yo, little niggah need that crack rock!"

"Then give him the crack rock," the deep voice said.

"Word. Ten get you three, little man."

Junius reached the next flight of stairs, halfway between fifteen and sixteen. The voices were closer now, just back above where he came out the door on fifteen. He peered around the edge of the stairs and saw two legs in jeans standing partway up the next flight. This would be the one with the deep voice: not the salesman, but his support, his backup. This would be the guy closest to his gun.

But not as ready as Junius was with his.

The steel felt familiar in his hands now, comfortable enough that he was ready to fire shots. He was ready to start punching.

He heard the slap of the palms as the baggie changed hands, heard feet shuffle, perhaps another person waiting in line, and then he moved.

He jogged up the next few stairs and turned, threw his body toward the next landing and raised the gun at the same time. Like he expected, the closest one was the soldier—black as night and arms crossed over his chest, a gun handle sticking up from the waist of his pants.

Junius aimed and pulled the trigger once, twice, then again. The gun bucked, and he kept moving until he felt the wall behind him. First he fired low, hitting the soldier in the left leg about thigh-high.

The soldier's eyes went wide and he started for his gun, but not before Junius fired four more times—four quick trigger pulls, four quick whistles from the barrel—each shot hitting higher on the soldier's chest.

"Fuck me." The soldier looked at his hands and saw his own blood.

He fell forward them, down the stairs, and landed in a bad way on his head, then flipped once and wound up splayed out on the landing, just above Junius.

Junius looked up and saw a kid about ten or eleven years old staring back at him in disbelief.

The salesman ducked around the corner out of sight, a Latino not much older than Junius. Junius shot at him once, missed, and started up the stairs.

"Who the fuck is you?" the salesman yelled, throwing a handful of singles down the stairs.

The soldier reached around and grabbed Junius by the legs with what strength he had left. It brought Junius down, but he was able to kick free. He saw the gun raised in the soldier's other hand and kicked at it, heard it bounce and fall down the next set of stairs.

The soldier tried to punch, but Junius moved, scrambled up the rest of the stairs just as the salesman reached around to his back for his gun.

Junius raised the Tec and shook his head, but the salesman pulled out a small black revolver.

Junius fired again—twice more. Both shots hit home and the salesman buckled. When Junius fired a third time, he hit a shoulder and punched it back into the wall. The salesman let out a quick scream as he slid down the wall onto his butt, leaving a line of blood above him.

Junius had a moment of fear as he finally saw the next flight, then sighed with relief when all he saw was a woman in her pajamas holding a twenty-dollar bill. The boy was down against the wall now, sitting on his haunches and holding up both hands: one with the crack bag and one empty.

"Please," he said, his eyes closed. "Please don't kill me."

"Shut up." Junius slapped the crack out of his hand. When he was out on the corner for Willie, he *never* sold to anyone this young. "Who you buying for?" he asked.

"This for my momma. She sent me down to get it."

"She can't come down to buy her own shit?"

The kid's nose started to run, and he began to whimper, crying with as little noise as he could manage.

"Go on. Go back upstairs."

He opened his eyes and grabbed two of the crack baggies, then took off.

"Don't—" The rest of the thought had something to do with him not telling anyone what he'd seen and not giving the crack to his mother, but Junius realized the impossibility of each before he could finish.

A bubble of blood popped over the salesman's mouth; he was still breathing. He cradled his stomach with bloody hands, dark red spilling out between his fingers.

"Please," he said through another blood bubble. In addition to the shot in his stomach, Junius could tell he'd hit something hard— bone—in the saleman's shoulder. He looked wrecked, his life dripping out of him and soaking into his clothes. Junius didn't want to pull the trigger again, see more of his body explode at close range. He didn't hate this kid like he hated Lamar.

This kid was basically him. Doing the same job for a different person, in a different place. But Junius didn't sell crack, and these towers—this woman in her pajamas and the boy buying for his mother—was a whole different world then the one Junius knew.

"You best kill me, son," the soldier said from below. Junius looked down and saw him crawling up the stairs empty-handed.

He raised the Tec again. "You sure?"

For a moment, the soldier's conviction held, then the fight dropped out of his eyes. His anger subsided, and he shook his head. He turned to sit on the steps.

Junius turned away. Killing wasn't what he wanted to see.

He turned to the woman on the stairs: she wore a light blue nightgown that hung long to her shins, probably flannel, and her stomach puffed out perfectly round below her breasts. Her hair spread out from her head at all angles, like she hadn't given it any thought for today at least, if not longer.

"You here to steal them rocks?" she asked. Her crusty eyes fixed on the Latino's jeans, his pockets bulging on both sides. "You let me have them," she said, "I suck your dick."

Junius didn't know what to say. The wrecked body of the salesman, his eyes pleading at Junius as he tried for breaths, and this woman: neither were things he knew how to deal with.

He brushed past the woman, leaving it for the two of them to work out as he climbed the next flight of stairs.

Roughneck stood in the lobby looking at a bloody mess in front of the elevator. If Miss Emma came down and saw this in her building, she'd be so far gone she'd have to move. He couldn't have that. And what if Rock or someone else started asking why he wasn't in the lobby when all this went down?

He could say he was pulled off the first floor after the shooting, that he was up watching his boys on eight and sixteen. That'd work well enough as an explanation—shit, it was pretty much exactly what Rock had told him to do—but now, looking at the mess, he felt like things were getting ready to explode.

Milk stood behind him at the foot of the stairs, watching Randy wrestle with the mop. So far he'd filled the bucket of the roller with water, and now he worked to squeeze the mop dry using the wringer. This kid had clearly never mopped a floor in his life.

Roughneck nodded at the blood. "How the fuck C Dub gone do some shit like this and we're supposed to handle it?"

Milk spit a thin stream out the side of his mouth onto the tiles. Now that the lobby was a mess, Rough guessed it didn't matter. "Seems like he out of control today. Coming up on you like he did before and now this shit?"

Rough didn't say anything; Clarence was a subject he planned to avoid.

Milk went on, "Should have let me cap a bitch right then. At least scare him with the gat."

"Yeah. And Rock come back with love. You go up the ladder on him, pull a gat on a bigger man?"

Milk unfolded his arms and held his hands out. "Oh! Self-defense, my man. Self-defense! C Dub wilding. What could I do?"

Rough laughed. It might even have worked. "Maybe." He tilted his head to the side. "But what we do now?"

"We take the fucking trash out. Throw that cop in the dumpster around back, hope he wake up and only think about C Dub."

Rough turned back to the lobby. The elevator doors opened just as he was considering the thought; as long as the cop didn't wake up while you were throwing his ass in the dumpster, this might not be such a bad plan. Then the doors opened, and Black Jesus and Mike Only stepped out of the car.

"Yo," Rough said. "Glad to see you stopped wearing that hat."

Mike Only ran his hand over his temple. "Fucking true that shit. Least I only have to wear it in the car."

"Yo, *hell*, no. You got to tell Rock to straight up fuck that shit. You ain't no chauffeur."

The two men stepped out of the elevator to its side, careful to avoid stepping in the blood that the kid still hadn't started to mop up. Milk yelled at him to start.

He took the too-wet mop and slopped it onto the floor, spreading the blood around, watering it down and making a bigger mess. Rough didn't bother to say anything. At least it was something.

Mike Only said, "Check out how he paying me, and you think twice about wearing that hat if it was you."

Roughneck looked at Mike Only and thought about it. Could Rock really be paying him that much? If he wasn't in charge of pushing product, just washing the car, driving it, making sure it stayed clean? Even if Mike Only had done his time with a crew selling in back of the projects and trying to run shit out from under Malik, he still wasn't doing shit now but driving. Anyone could do that job.

"Yo, help this fool," Black Jesus said to Milk as the kid pushed blood and water around in circles. Then he came right out and said, "Show us the cop."

Rough gestured toward the door that led to the alley. It wasn't hard to follow the trail of blood, either. He considered letting the kid use paper towels, if the mop was too much of a skill-job for him to handle.

"Yo, this shit best get cleaned up," Black Jesus said. He bent down and picked up the police baton that lay next to the door.

"Milk!"

Milk slapped the kid in the head and took the mop himself, dropped it into the water and put it in the wringer right, then cranked the lever to really get it dry.

At the back of the building, the blood trail had thinned. It ended in a pool around the cop, most of it up by his head. He looked like he might just be asleep if it weren't for the lumps on his temple, his busted lips, and his swollen eye.

"Yeah," Rough said, as the other two stood looking. "C Dub did this shit and took three crack rocks off the boy on eight, then went up to smoke base. We got to shut his ass *down*."

Black Jesus sucked his teeth. He pointed the baton at the cop and shook his head. "C Dub is just not fucking right today. Not right at all."

"Let me take his ass down. Give me ten minutes alone with that bitch and his problem be solved for the week. *The month*."

Mike Only turned back away from the cop's body to look at Rough. He frowned, but not like he wasn't thinking about it. He looked like he might come around. Then Black Jesus shook his head. "What we do with this cop? That's first."

Rough waited until it was clear that neither of them had a good suggestion, and then he offered Milk's idea about throwing him into the dumpster.

Mike Only laughed, but Black Jesus still stood facing the body.

"Let's do it," he said.

Roughneck felt as surprised as Mike Only looked, but he hurried to go for the feet so he wouldn't get blood on him. Also, if the fucker woke up, he did not want to be the one the guy saw.

The three lifted the cop's body awkwardly: Rough at the feet and the other two each took a shoulder. They pushed through the back doors, and the good part was the cop didn't wake up while they took him outside.

He didn't wake up until the first time they tried swinging him up into the dumpster. The first time it didn't take: Black Jesus stopped at the last second, when he saw they didn't have enough height to clear the front lip of the dumpster, and the cop crashed into the its side with his shoulders and head, the part Mike was still trying to shove over the top.

"Fuck," was the first thing the cop said. Then he started to squirm. But Black Jesus and Mike Only just exchanged one look, a fast glance of recognition, and then they both swung his upper body into the side of the dumpster, knocking his head against it hard. It made a sound like a gong. The cop stopped squirming.

"Let's just lift," Black Jesus said, hoisting his end of the cop over his shoulders. Mike Only did the same, and Rough got the legs high enough to follow when the other two brought the body right to the edge of the dumpster and then hand-passed him in onto the trash.

From the sound of it, he had a soft landing on the bags. They all three listened for a minute to make sure he wasn't squirming or kicking around, then Black Jesus tossed the baton in after him and they went back inside to get that blood cleaned up off the floor.

5 4

Seven had the 411's elevator all to himself as he rode up to twenty, but at each floor he worried it would stop and a cop might get on.

On twenty, the doors opened and nothing happened. Seven looked out into the empty hallway.

It wouldn't have surprised him if the building turned out to be haunted, what with Jason and the other dead brothers all out there somewhere, ready to come back and fuck with him from the beyond. He laughed to himself, hoped that would never come true.

Maybe he would get by without any more shit from the police today. That wasn't such a big thing to ask, was it? No. He didn't think it was.

Seven got out and walked the few steps to the TV-land apartment and knocked. He could hear the sound of a woman's voice talking.

The door opened and Seven saw the TV set before anything else: the old show where a hot chick with black hair and long legs tried not to get into too much trouble. Just a few years back, he'd rubbed out more than a few watching her run around in her short-ass 70s dresses from back in the day. Too much leg on the show and not enough pussy in his life left him to fantasize at home in the afternoons when he skipped school. What else was a growing young man supposed to do?

"Hey, Seven, what's up?"

He looked down and there was Malik. "Yo." Then he looked right and only saw one of the boys from before: Elf sat by himself on the couch.

"Yo." Seven nodded at the TV and walked into the apartment. Instead of giving dap to Malik, he ran his hand over the top of his head, then palmed it and shook him around. "What's up?"

Elf pointed at the TV. "This bitch kind of hot, tell you the truth. Boy knows his television."

"Damn right this boy know his TV. This here TV-land."

After shutting the door, Malik stepped up next to Seven. "So we've confirmed that Marlo Thomas is unquestionable more attractive than Lucille Ball."

"Oh, most *definitely*," Elf said. "No doubt."

"It's true." Seven then came right to what worried him. "Yo, where your boy?"

Elf looked to the couch next to him, as if Junius might just appear. "He coming back. Said he was going out to look for you."

"We're making some chicken nuggets for lunch. You're welcome to stay."

Seven reached down to pull Elf off the couch. "But Pickup left you both up in here, right? He told you to stay."

Elf nodded, mumbling something.

"How long ago he leave?"

"Oh, he left before Lucy even started. So that's been almost an hour."

"Damn." An image of Junius cuffed and being led out of the building to a squad car flashed through Seven's mind. "Where he at now?"

Elf looked serious for the first time since Seven walked in. "Yo, I'm sorry about that shit up on the roof, man. I fucked up."

Seven glanced away, avoiding Elf's eyes. He didn't want to think about whether giving them the guns was right. He shook his head.

Looking down, he saw Shari had a crazy ass rug on her living room floor. It had so many colors, you could throw up on it and no one would know.

"Drak has my Tec now, anyway," Elf said. He pulled up his shirt and drew two Berettas from his waist, aimed them down at the ugly rug.

"Yo! Put those guns away in here right now. This is a no guns, no swearing household." Malik looked up at Seven like he wanted to know if Seven could believe this.

"Put them away. I see what you got. Now you know how to set those safeties?"

When Elf said he didn't, Seven stepped over and took the guns, set their safeties one at a time, showing Elf how it was done. Malik complained, but Seven waived him off. He handed one gun back to Elf and pushed the other down the back of his pants.

"I'm a keep this for now," he said. "So your boy, where he be? Because we need to find him. This place *covered* with Five-O."

Elf's eyes stayed on the TV, but his chin nodded at Seven.

"You guys don't want to stay for chicken nuggets? They'll be ready in eight minutes."

Now Elf turned his full attention to Seven, who nodded toward the door. "We out. Eat that shit cold if you want it."

"I wouldn't—" Malik started, but Elf was already up and heading for the kitchen. It was the fastest Seven had seen him move.

Elf opened the oven door and pulled out a nugget. He bit into it and started nodding as he chewed. "Just a little cold in the middle," he said around the food. "I can eat these."

"Make sure you leave me some."

Seven turned and opened the door to the hallway as Elf leaned into the oven to grab more of the nuggets. Malik made a face, but didn't say anything.

"Come on," Seven told Elf. "We out."

The part Junius couldn't believe was the silence, the still quiet. Here he'd shot two in the stairwell, perhaps killed one and left another bleeding and there was no sound. No screaming, nobody crying for the police, no vengeful crew-members yelling after him.

It was just the normal sounds of the building as he made his way up the floors: mothers yelling at their children, boys and girls playing in the halls, girls just a few years younger than him talking on the phone. And the TVs. Seemed like most of the noises he could hear when he stopped to listen were from TVs: the regular weekday game shows, soap operas, and random old sitcoms on UHF.

It was all quiet in his head, too: no voices second-guessing, no wishes that he hadn't done something, no background buzz about anything at all. Somehow, he felt like all of his thoughts had been cleaned, put on mute.

Maybe it was the desperation of the woman, the way she offered to blow him with that nasty mouth. She was worse than anything he'd seen up in Teale Square or Davis, anything Big Willie put in his way. These towers were a whole different world. Even the air here felt dead.

In Teale Square, everything was open—you could see the sky. Here, it was drab hallways with their dirty, off-white paint, flickering fluorescents, stairways that held the same noises and smells all the way up, as high as you could go.

No air, no light; a world like one underground.

These towers.

It was enough to make you do anything to get out.

He continued up the stairs slowly, listening, his gun still drawn and his knees bent so he'd be ready to move fast.

He tried to walk like the heroes in the kung fu movies on Saturday afternoons, the ones with the wide black pants and the shirts tied across their chests. He moved like a cat, or as close to how a cat would move as he could manage.

Another floor up and the sound of the TVs began to die down. The other noises peeled away. Junius was getting closer to Rock.

Gary Johnson smelled bananas. It wasn't the smell of fresh-sliced banana bread or a nice cut-up banana on his morning cereal, it was the smell of old, black bananas and peels, a strong smell that hit him as he opened his eyes for the first time. Make that one eye. Even before he knew where he was, he realized that his left eye was swollen shut. Johnson touched that side of his face and felt a bruise the size of a golf ball sticking out where his eye should be.

"Fuck me." He heard the words come out, felt pain, and then moved, shifted how he lay. He heard the rustling of plastic bags. It felt soft, where he was lying, but there was that smell and something hard and pointy sticking into his lower back. As he came to his senses, the smell grew to include vomit, soiled diapers, and rotting food. By the time he could see his surroundings, it didn't surprise him to find the rusty metal walls of a dumpster.

Toward the sky he could see one of the brick buildings of the towers. Now he started to hurt. He squirmed to get up, but moving only made him sink deeper into the trash.

He tried to sit and something sharp poked his ass. When he pulled it out, he found a broken-off TV antenna with one end burned black. He threw this against the dumpster's side.

Last he remembered, he was in the lobby or back hall, fighting or being dragged around by that freak drug addict. Now that his consciousness opened, his pain started to center itself in certain key points: his lower back on the right side, his hands, his head.

His head felt like it had been hit about the temples with a golf club, as if someone tried to hit the ball over his eye with a driver and missed. The front of his face hurt too, but he couldn't tell whether that pain came more from his eye or his nose.

The nose.

The nose hurt worse than the eye by a long shot. In fact, the eye barely hurt at all. It was just there, a pressure pushing on his face, obscuring his vision. He'd seen worse in all-city boxing, once had *both* eyes puff out on him, but never had one swollen like this.

His nose was broken; it felt like he was breathing through a chewed-on straw.

Then he remembered his gun. He went for it immediately, but it wasn't there.

He hissed through bloody lips that split as he stretched them. Next he patted his front down with cold, brittle hands, and when he couldn't find his badge, it didn't surprise him.

He rolled to the closer side of the dumpster and clawed at the metal. By working his body against the trash and pushing his feet down into somewhat-stable bags, he managed to stand up and look out over the side.

The first thing he saw was the last thing he wanted to: more officers.

To his right along the fence, a handful of bodies were huddled around the back of the Olds 98. They were all looking down at something—or some*one*.

That was when Johnson knew they were looking after the boy he laid out.

Kelley was bent down by his head, checking for vitals. That would be just what Johnson needed: to have reports filed about him for a lost gun *and* assaulting a minor in the same day. That would go over great with his superiors. He'd probably be lucky to keep his job.

He swore softly against the rusty metal. The other officers still hadn't seen him.

But if the boy was just knocked out—*Pooh!*—then why were they spending so much time examining him?

Then Johnson got the whole set of details: something about the tilt of the boots on the ground clued him in and made him realize the boy wasn't going to get up. He wanted to swear again, curse the fucking project gods that put him in a situation as fucked up all around as this one—where he probably needed some medical attention himself and couldn't face the rest of his detail for not one but *two* reasons.

"Fuck." He said it even though it made his lips hurt. He lowered himself back down into the stink and the trash, touched his nose and felt blood caked onto his upper lip and around its sides.

"Motherfuck," he said, and he thought of the crack-head fuck who did this to him. Johnson had to take that fuck out himself—right here and today—so he could get his gun and his badge back. Of that much, he was sure.

He checked the radio on his shoulder to find out why he hadn't heard the talk and realized it was broken, smashed in his fight.

He pulled the unit off his uniform and dropped it into the trash. He'd be better off without it now. What he had to do today he'd be better off doing all by himself.

Aldo Posey woke to the sound of a phone ringing in the adjacent room. His eyes hurt; overnight the pain had returned—the dryness that only loosened with the day's first drink.

A clock on the dresser read one thirty and, from the light coming in the windows, it was definitely afternoon. That was when it hit him where he was: the clock had been in its place on her dresser for more than ten years. He was home, in his ex-wife's bed again.

He wanted to forget everything he'd done wrong, the ways he'd fucked up, being pushed by his wife and oldest son out of his own house, all that had happened the night before.

It was his drinking, of course, that had led him to this. Aldo wouldn't argue that. He'd let a great part of himself go. When Temple was twelve, he'd helped his mother kick the old man out of his own house. Temple, the little man, her man. Truth was, Aldo had been proud of how Temple took care of Junius and taught him how to play ball. Even proud of how he stood up for his mother.

But still.

Still, for just this moment of hearing the phone and looking at the old clock on her dresser, waking up in his old bed, he felt like he was home.

The phone rang again.

That was when last night's events started coming back to him in full. He looked down, saw his clothes and the sheet wrapped around his legs and was grateful to his wife for letting him sleep, not pushing him back out into the world.

He sat up. It was one thirty in the afternoon, plus Gail's extra five minutes to make sure she was always early meant it wasn't quite that late. Still, this was what Gail would call "sloth." The answering machine picked up the phone, and his ex-wife's voice slowly explained that no one was home, not her or her sons. She'd taken his name off the recording. Of course.

The machine beeped and a woman's frail voice started in. "Mrs. Posey? This Miss Emma Lawrence calling to say I'm sorry about your boys."

Aldo's heart skipped a beat. Had she really said "boys"? He remembered the business from last night: the guns in the living room and those hoods of Rock's he helped force their way in. He prayed it hadn't led to Junius getting harmed.

Then and there, Aldo swore that if Junius was dead because of him, he'd never take another drink again in his life.

"I extend my condolences to you about Temple, that beautiful boy. May he rest in peace. And I wanted to call and let you know that I just seen your youngest son, Junius, here in the Rindge Towers looking to get himself into no good."

Aldo slid his feet off the bed and onto the floor. Junius was alive. He wanted his happiness to come from that fact alone, but he knew it came too from the fact that he'd have another drink today.

"I just saw him when my nephew Randall brought him in for a visit. It isn't good that he's over here. And looking for the boy they call Black Moses? Guardy Little, is what his name used to be. That boy ain't never up to no good. Your son here looking to find him, then you got a worry."

"Shit." Aldo shoved his hands onto his knees and forced himself to stand. When he'd come last night, he'd brought Clarence. Clarence did not mean anything good for anybody. He was close to Rock and crazy, liable to do any damn thing he pleased.

And he was looking for Junius.

Aldo walked across the floor into the living room, his back hurting and his sciatica, shooting flashes of bright pain all the way down his right leg into his toes. The floorboards creaked under him to match his knees. He really had put some miles on his old body, that was for sure, and he'd be lucky to get many more if he kept up like this.

Two steps more toward the phone and the sciatica was so painful he just wanted to lie down and have a drink.

"You know Guardy be dealing with that man thinks he own my building, Mrs. Posey. You know the one calls his self Rock? Boy think he the Prudential or some craziness! Never can stand that fool. But—"

Aldo picked up the phone and heard the answering machine screech feedback from its speaker like a broken guitar. Sounded like Little Joe Cook from up the Cantab Lounge, singing about "The Peanut Man" whenever Aldo was trying to enjoy a drink.

"Hello?"

"Hello?"

"Mr. Posey?"

"Yes. This Aldo Posey. I thank you for calling."

"Mr. Posey, I'm happy to hear you there today. You better head on up here to do something about your boy. I was just leaving a message to tell your wife."

"Uh, ex- Miss Lawrence. We not—" He stopped. "She Miss Ponds now. Took back her old name."

"Well. You mean you ain't married to Mrs. Posey any longer? I am sorry to hear that, but times do change us. What you doing answering her phone?"

Aldo stumbled back a step. He looked around and saw his old living room surrounding him. Maybe this woman was too quick to be talking to this close to waking up. "I—"

"Perhaps that's just none of my business. But I did want to say I'm making a few phone calls to find out what happened to your older boy. I will get to the bottom of this."

"You don't—"

"I'm also sending my Randall after Junius to make sure everything ok. Wouldn't want him bumping into some of the wrong folks round here, you understand?"

"Yes, I—"

"Because you know things may happen. I heard police sirens out on the street today and yesterday they took that boy Lamar off on a covered stretcher."

Aldo closed his eyes, trying to think of a way to get himself off the phone. In the kitchen he could see the tall, thin cabinet along the wall where he used to keep his good gin.

"They *young ones* now," she said. "Getting they selves into all sorts of trouble. It's no damn good, I tell you. No *damn* good."

"Yes ma'am," Aldo said. "I— Let me get going so I can make my way over there to see about my boy."

"Yes, I—"

"I do appreciate your call."

"I understand. But let me ask you: when I find out what happened to your Temple, where you want me to call?"

Aldo shook his head. He didn't need her to tell him what'd happened to Temple. Didn't need anyone to tell him what he already knew.

"You just call back here," he said, hoping she wouldn't. "You could call back here, and I'll check on you when I come to the towers."

She was in the 412, she told him, the one closest to the highway. The one Rock owned. Where Clarence lived. Junius had been inside.

He shuddered against what could be happening and hung up the phone without saying goodbye.

One of his sons—his *only* son now—needed him. That was enough to make him move.

In his apartment on eleven, Clarence sat down on the bed after sweeping his sheets and blankets onto the floor.

In his hand he held three little bags with white rocks in them. He nodded, replaying his fight with the cop in his mind's eye. He showed that pig who ruled these towers, taken what the cop had to sling and stood strong to beat him down.

He tossed the badge and the gun onto the bed beside him—the gun silver, shiny, well cared for. Its cylinder held five bullets, and maybe he had more .38 shells around in a drawer.

The Smith & Wesson 60, genuine cop issue. It would bring no less than five hundred on the street, or he could use it himself to get that interfering pig into any amount of trouble. He looked at the clothes in his closet, trying to decide if he had a suit nice enough to pass for a cop if he showed the badge. Maybe down in Central Square or Boston where they didn't know him. He might score some serious shit that way. Even, and if he could pull this off Rock would *really* be impressed, a couple of fake drug busts: confiscations and all that shit. That could lead to more guns and drugs that he might as well sell for himself rather than turn over to Rock.

Yeah, there was plenty he could do with this badge.

He thought back to the morning, how he'd run out of the apartment, chasing Dee and Ness, the dumb fucks, and that damn kid who didn't even matter. Junius Posey and his boy Little Elf. They could both suck his dick now. Fuck Lamar too. Let Junius put a cap in him. Just one less asshole that he, C Dub, had to deal with in his house.

"This my house," he said out loud. He thought of Eddie Murphy's routine in his live stand-up movie. "*My house,*" Eddie said, imitating his own father.

"My house," Clarence said, and beat his chest. He looked around his apartment and thought about Rock up in the penthouse with a whole wall of windows. This was no way for Clarence Williams to live. He'd take it all, everything he deserved, which was, as Tony Montana put it, "The world, chico … and everything in it."

Clarence pushed two of the rocks into his pocket and squeezed the third out of its baggie. He broke off a piece and put the rest on the night table. The glass pipe was right where he'd left it, ready with the Brillo.

He pushed the shard onto the metal pad and lit the glass. That was when he heard a knock.

He tapped the glass with the lighter and lit the flame, holding it under the Brillo again. There was nobody on the other side of that door right now more important than his hit. He brought the flame toward the pipe again and put his lips to the other end.

The knocking turned into banging. He hesitated, took a deep breath and said as loud and as menacingly as he could, "Who is it?"

Gary Johnson had to wait for the ambulance to come, the paramedics to load Pooh into it on a stretcher, and finally for the CSI dicks to start working on the scene before he felt like he could crawl out of the dumpster. Until then, there were just too many cops around, too great a chance he'd be seen.

They'd want to know how he got fucked up, where his gun and badge were, and if Sergeant Onion-Butt O'Scullion found out about that—well, Gary Johnson just couldn't let that happen.

He tried to avoid looking at the stretcher when they wheeled it into the ambulance, wanting to avoid more bad news. He still saw it, though, and he was relieved when it went in uncovered, even if that meant the boy would tell what he'd done.

If Pooh was alive, Gary Johnson knew he still had a chance to make everything right.

When the ambulance was gone and the CSI crew started, he noticed his nightstick in among the trash bags—a small blessing. He squeezed the plastic grip in his hand for the feel of something hard and real. Finding assurance in that, he slipped over the lip of the dumpster.

The ground came up to hit his feet like a punch in his spine, and he blacked out for a second, then discovered himself slumped against the rusty metal. He stepped slowly toward the back door of 412 and dropped the business end of his nightstick into his left hand. The impact didn't hurt; no, it felt good. Feeling something solid felt better than the loosely fastened connections of his body.

He brought the stick down onto his palm again.

He was going to feel even better when he used it on the crackhead who did this.

5 8

It took Milk doing half the lobby himself, but now Randy finally had the hang of using the mop. Black Jesus and Mike Only had left long ago, gone back up to Jesus's apartment to chill out.

Milk stood with hands on his hips and his lips pushed out like he couldn't believe any of this shit, just watching. "You know this bullshit," he said.

Rough nodded. "What we gone do?"

Milk spit through his front teeth in the direction of the mop, managed to land a stream right in front of it.

"You know what I think."

"That I'm a go up and handle Clarence myself? Just roll up on him?"

Milk nodded. "That's what I been saying. Not like he didn't try his shit on you this morning."

"True." Rough thought it over, knew Clarence had gone rogue, way past what was alright. Maybe Rock would even thank him for handling the situation if he did something.

"Niggah need a beating. He gone too far."

Rough held his hand up to quiet Milk and listened. Other than the sound of Randy sloshing the mop against the floor, he couldn't hear anyone. But for a second, he thought he heard something, someone listening.

"Hold up." Randy stopped the mopping and the three of them stood still in the lobby. From somewhere above them, Rough heard the elevator moving, listened as it started up and then creaked to a stop a few floors later. He heard its doors open and close. Then the building was quiet. A siren squawked and rolled from the back alley, most likely the ambulance that had passed through the parking lot ten minutes earlier.

Rough turned to see it cross in front of the building and then wind through the parking lot, headed toward Route 2, its lights flashing and spinning, the horns blaring.

"Shit. Now we got ambulances carting off niggahs I don't even know about. Who was that?"

Milk shook his head. "Fucked up, yo."

"This day just hopping the fuck off!"

"It won't get fixed until you start righting it."

Rough rolled his eyes. "One note you blowing, all damn day."

"Because it be right."

"Yeah. Ok." Rough stepped toward the elevator and pushed the button. "That's what we do, then. We roll on up to eleven and gat down this motherfucker to make shit right."

Milk clapped Rough's shoulder. "*That's it*, my brother. *That* is what I'm talking about."

Rough shook his head. "No other way to shut you up, apparently."

Above them the elevator started to whir its way down. Even if it was Milk's idea and Milk pushing him, maybe it he wanted this all the way.

Maybe that was why he hadn't turned in Junius and Elf when he saw them on the roof or tell Clarence when he and Junius both came through the lobby. The truth was—and he'd known it a long time now—Clarence was a fuck-up, someone who would bring down their organization. Rock, Rough, Black Jesus—whoever was in charge—would have a problem until Clarence got dealt with. Maybe Milk was right about Rough being afraid, but you could only train karate katas on the roof for so long. Came a time you had to stand up and act.

The elevator opened and Rough and Milk got in. Milk looked at Rough before pressing the button for eleven. Rough nodded. "Time to take this shit on up."

When the elevator doors closed, Randy stood up straight and rested his arm on the mop. He'd be fucked if this shit was what he signed on for, if this was any of the work he wanted to be doing during his week off from school.

Sure, he was in this shit now, and he'd carry it out—he owed it to his cousin to at least do that much—but after this week he was going back to school. This life didn't have *shit* on school. Maybe you could make a buck here and there, but he didn't see a future in it. He'd be just as happy to keep his ass in class. Even if Tobin sucked, maybe he could roll his grades up a bit and talk Mrs. Johnson into getting him to the Intensive Studies Program over at Longfellow. Last year they took Tasha up there, and she came back saying she loved it.

Shit, reading a book definitely beat mopping blood off the floor.

The back hallway door opened and Randy froze. The blue uniform stopped his body, but it was the face that came in attached to it, the one he last saw laid out in a pool of blood, that stopped his breath cold.

The cop walked in as if loose pieces of him were shifting around inside his middle. His legs plodded onward with fluid determination, but the person above them, especially the face, looked like it was from another place or even another body. In his hands, he carried the nightstick Black Jesus had picked up. He squeezed it tight enough to brighten his knuckles.

The cop wheezed and his voice came out like a sucked-in breath. Whatever he said, Randy didn't hear. Then he barked, "Where they go?" Randy could see the determination on his face and the white around the cop's irises that said he was going to *really* do something.

Randy pointed to the elevator.

"What floor?" The cop's lips were tight, his teeth clenched around the words. He still had dried blood in his mustache.

"Eleven." Randy pointed again at the doors. "They up on C Dub floor."

"Motherfucker who looks like he been in a fight? Crackhead son of a bitch?"

"C Dub? Yeah, I guess you could describe him like that."

The cop nodded. He removed one hand from the nightstick and steadied himself against the wall. "That's who I want." He scraped himself together enough to close the distance to the elevator doors and then jabbed at the call button with the end of his stick.

Randy held the mop, guessing how hard it would be to get into the ISP program. Sure, he'd mop up the floor today, but that was the extent of what he planned to do for Rock.

59

"It's Sheila," the voice said: Sheila D, and Clarence knew it was her. No other woman had the sixth sense to know exactly when a man had drugs to shake her ass out for. Sheila *always* knew.

Clarence looked down at his lap, considered if it was worth a blow job to let her in. That didn't take long to decide; Sheila didn't just give a *good* blow job, that woman knew every bit how to give a god-damn masterpiece performance. She'd leave a lipstick ring around the base so dark you'd remember her the next time you took a shower, get to thinking about her again so you wanted more.

Clarence looked at his pipe.

"C Dub," she said. "You hear me out here! What you doing?"

Clarence checked the lighter. He knew she had the x-ray hearing to know if he lit it, but he didn't care. For all she knew, he could be lighting up a Kool. He laughed. The woman just knew, like she had crack-rock radar. Even when he had a good stash of coke she knew to come around. It was like she could smell it from three floors away.

But even Sheila couldn't keep him from his hit. He flicked the lighter.

"C Dub!" she shouted.

He brought the flame under the pad and sucked hard.

"Mmmm!" he hummed to her as he watched the tube fill with white smoke, hoping if she heard him she'd shut the fuck up and just wait. Then he tasted the blast and sucked it down hard into his lungs. He pushed a breath in behind it to go deeper, and then he hit the pipe again to get more on top of that.

Lung capacity: that's what it came down to. Ever since he started smoking weed at thirteen he'd been increasing how much he could suck in. Now he held it, watching the world go cloudy and gray for a second before it all came clear and turned to a new set of colors. That was the boom; the boom-bang. He checked his forearm: even the welt left by Johnson's nightstick didn't hurt. He stood up. Nothing hurt anymore.

"Clarence!"

He let a little smoke seep out through his teeth as Sheila resumed kicking the door. He crossed the room and checked the peep hole. Sheila stood holding up her middle finger like she knew exactly where he was and when he'd look. He unlocked the door and held it open just an inch, put his lips to the gap and blew smoke out into the hallway; he emptied his lungs in a steady stream at her face.

"Ooh," she said, "I know you got that *good* stuff now!" She leaned into the door trying to open it.

"Mmmm hmm," he said.

"Now let me in, baby. You know I make it worth your while."

Clarence moved his foot and let the door swing open for Sheila to come inside. She took the pipe out of his hand and walked toward the bed like the place was hers.

"Yeah, baby. Come on and bring yourself in." Clarence glanced out into the hallway and shut the door.

"You know you want it," she said. She sat down.

Sheila was dressed like always: with a shirt that revealed cleavage pushed up by a too-small bra that offered it to the world on a tray. She'd already lost some of her game: the shirt she wore over her tank was worn, a flannel plaid worn more for warmth than look; her jeans were last year's tight acid-wash instead of the black leggings girls were wearing now.

But Clarence didn't care.

Shit, half his clothes were still from the 70s and he liked their style better than the overpriced Girbauds and Z. Cavariccis that brothers wore now. Pants showed you were a man, he'd always thought, and so, true to form, he had on a dark pair of brown work pants like his father wore when he worked for the city. When he wanted to get wild for a club or something, he had a pair of black nylon parachute pants with a lot of zippers in the back of his closet.

Shit, even if the wash on Sheila's pants was wrong for the year's fashion, the tight-ass seams didn't hide a thing. She'd gained a few extra pounds, but what woman in her thirties hadn't. Her hair could use a new cut, but she had shed that Jheri curl like the bad habit it was, and now sported a 'do that Clarence could actually put his fingers in. He shrugged, knowing Sheila wasn't much. Still, he'd had good times with her. It touched something inside him to have her around.

She sucked on the pipe and reached for the lighter to heat the Brillo again.

"Nah," she said, "this here's done." She held out the pipe for Clarence to add more rock.

Clarence set her up again with a bigger piece. He cooked it and brought the pipe up to his mouth. Sheila started to protest, but he put his fingers over her lips.

When he dragged in the smoke now, he didn't take it into his lungs; instead he kept it in his mouth and leaned forward, brought his lips to hers and kissed her, pushing the smoke in. She moaned her approval and leaned back onto the bed, pulling at his shirt. He resisted, stood up and hit the pipe again for himself now, dragging deeply. He was hoping that if he stood in front of her long enough she would go for his belt.

By the time he had his hit, though, she was reaching for the pipe again, greedy for more. Clarence didn't care: his blood pumped hard in his veins and everything was all right with his world. What he loved so much was to hit the rock *and* have Sheila hit his cock at the same time. He stood and waited, then flopped down onto the bed next to her when the feeling moved him. She smoked what she wanted and then leaned toward him, started running her hand across his chest.

"So where you been at?" Sheila reached for his belt. Thin, warm rays of light shone through the blinds and onto the side of her face. He took the pipe as she went for his buckle and pulled on the belt's end to open some slack. Clarence licked his lips and brought the glass up, thinking about what would come next—a beautiful idea that got interrupted by a knock at the door.

He sat up, put his finger to his lips. Sheila hummed her agreement as she opened his belt and pulled at the button, already unzipping his fly with her other hand.

"C Dub," someone called from the hall: a deep voice that sounded like it might be Black Jesus or Rough. Rough he didn't care about, never had to deal with if he didn't want to. Black Jesus was a different story. Clarence sat up and listened. That was when Sheila started licking her lips, and he saw them shine as she put her hand down his boxers and pulled him out. He was sprung from the crack. Nothing like it. Then she kissed him, and when he felt her lips on his cock, he fell back onto the bed.

"C Dub! Clarence!" He heard calling from outside, but in his world all that existed was his dick and Sheila's mouth on it. He knew only lips, tongue, warmth. Then her hand was a part of it too. That was what he liked.

"Fucking Clarence!" He heard and knew it was Milk's voice. Who could miss recognizing that little fucker? It had to be Milk and Rough outside then, two brothers he definitely did not give a shit about.

"*Fuck* off!" he yelled. Sheila stopped in surprise, but he grabbed the top of her head. A moment later, she started again.

The next thing Clarence heard was a bang—a sound like someone hitting his door with more than fists or feet. "The fuck?" he said. He opened his eyes to see the ceiling tiles above him like a chess board.

Then the sound came again and this time it was more ragged, like wood breaking, and he looked up to see the door pop off the frame, lock and all, opening inward from the hall.

"Motherfucker!" He sat up.

Sheila stopped, and he felt cold air on his wet cock as soon as her mouth was gone. Roughneck came in behind the now-broken door and Milk was right behind him.

Sheila screamed at them to get out.

"Yo!" Rough looked like he'd been about to say something else, but when he saw what he interrupted, he froze.

"Oh, shit!" Milk said.

"What's wrong? You niggahs have never seen a man's dick before in your little lives?" Clarence pushed Sheila's hand off his shaft and waved himself at them. "See this shit, niggahs! I'm a beat you with my dick!"

Roughneck turned to Milk like he had no idea what they were getting into, and he was right. They had no fucking clue.

Clarence stood up, Sheila right behind him. She said, "Ya'll niggahs get the *fuck* out or I will fuck you up my *damn* self!"

Clarence was hard and he liked the look of it, liked it even better when he squeezed the base with his hand. "Yeah!" he said. "You like that?"

Rough stared with eyes wide, his eyebrows halfway up his fore-head. "Put that shit away," he said, holding his hand in front of him so he could meet Clarence's eyes without seeing his lower half.

Clarence walked toward them. "No. Hold up!"

He went back to the foot of the bed and picked up the cop gun, turned to them with his dick in one hand and the gun in the other. "Now what? Tell C Dub which one of these you want between your lips!"

"Hold up!" Milk raised his own gun, a small revolver.

Sheila smiled at Clarence; she did not seem to be upset at all by the gun. She put both hands on her hips and started to say some-thing, but then she put one finger across her upper lip. She was try-ing to keep from laughing.

"What?" Clarence said.

"Forty-four Charter Arms Bulldog, motherfucker," Milk said. "Paid for!"

Sheila smiled wider, and Clarence looked down.

"Best put that away now," she said.

"Bitch!"

"Yo, listen to the lady," Rough told him.

"I'm a shoot that thing off." Milk lowered his gun, still pointing it at Clarence.

"You afraid to fuck with a man got his dick out?" Clarence asked.

Rough held up his hands and took a step back. "No way I want to get some AIDS up in this shit."

Milk stepped back as well, but kept his gun pointed. Clarence felt his pants start to drop and then fall to his ankles. A cold breeze rushed across his bare legs.

6 0

Marlene put down the phone after her call with Anthony. She'd only called to say hello and to tell him what was going on here, that she was handling it. All she wanted was to talk, hear herself say the events out loud and have him listen.

But Anthony wasn't like that.

She got to the part about the shootings on the roof and the police all over her tower, and he went into his ultra-lawyer mode, talking about citizens' rights, illegal searches and motherfuckers needing warrants to get into people's apartments—even if only to talk to them. She sighed and barely listened.

Of course he would think these things, have all the crap from right out of his books ready at the tip of his tongue. Next he'd want to come down and say it all to the police.

Of course he would.

She knew it would do less good than sending Seven to talk to the cops, that the Harvard Law School bullshit would do less to impress these North Cambridge cops than waving twenties at them.

But he got his fictional, optimistic, idealistic fire up and now he was on his way over to defend her rights and those of everyone in her buildings.

Maybe it was time to just cut him off.

She'd wanted to sound him out on Junius and Elf, the only part of her day that actually seemed a strategic decision, and he'd barely responded.

He was far more concerned with her stash of Tec-9s hidden in an apartment refrigerator than her giving them to kids. Of course, he totally missed the nuance of her lying about who killed Temple Posey. So now he was coming over and she'd be damned if she'd be available at the front of the building when he started talking his shit at the cops.

She was damned if she'd stay up in her brother's apartment, either. The heat still blew her away, she was bored and the white wine wasn't worth any of it. She was starting to think about heading home when she heard a knock at the door.

"Marlene," Pickup said. "Yo, it's Big P."

She crossed the room to the door and opened it. Big Pickup stepped in onto the thick shag rug.

"I seen Seven break out and wanted to make sure you had everything all right."

"No, that's good. I was just thinking that I should get back to my own apartment. You want to walk me over?"

"That's word," Pickup said and nodded. "I can take you back there." He gestured toward the hallway, knocked on the apartment door. "I'll make sure they ready for us and send Drak back on over."

Marlene put her cigarettes and lighter back into her purse and left the wine bottle and empty glass. "You want that?" she asked Pickup.

"What it taste like?"

She shrugged, offered him the bottle. He picked it up around the neck with one hand and poured some into his mouth, not letting the glass touch his lips. Then he made a sour face and shook his head. "Nah. That ain't my speed. Give me a four-oh over that anytime."

"Plus it's the middle of the day," she said.

"Plus that." Pickup winked at her like they'd just shared a private joke. "You want to take the tunnel or go around front?"

"We still got cops outside?"

"A couple."

"What you think I should do?"

"I'd take the tunnel. Might as well stay warm much as you can. It be *crazy* cold outside."

Marlene exhaled. "Sounds good. Let's go down and through."

Raphael stuck his head in the door. "We ready." Behind him, Marlene knew Sean Dog waited in the hall.

"Let's go."

They rode the elevator down to the basement of 410—Marlene, Big Pickup, Raphael, and Sean Dog—and crossed back through the tunnel into 411. Once home, they called for the elevator to take them up, and Marlene used her maintenance key to disable the other calls in the building. They rode all the way to twenty-two with no stops, no interruptions, no police.

Just the express.

Meldrak stood outside her apartment when they got there. He was glad to see them, glad to have Marlene suggest he get some rest and let Raphael and Sean take over the hall. After all, he had seen a friend gunned down in front of him.

As Marlene unlocked her door, the phone rang.

Seven had stopped on the sixteenth floor to get himself one of the cold Tecs. He pushed the Beretta down the back of his jeans and the nine down the front, pulled out his sweatshirt over them and his Triple Fat Goose over that.

Now he and Elf stood in the lobby of 411, and Elf asked where they would go.

"To find your boy."

"Where he at?"

"Exactly." Seven stepped to the front windows of the building and looked across at 412.

"You think he up there?"

"We gone find the fuck out." Seven looked at Rock's lobby. Elf didn't see anyone out front or inside either. He saw two police cars parked between the buildings, but they were empty as well.

Seven rapped on the glass twice with his knuckles and headed out the door. Elf watched him, then followed.

He didn't think Junius would go after Rock and Black Jesus on his own, not without him, but didn't know what telling Seven Heaven would do. The truth was, Seven scared the speak out of him, and he'd just as soon keep quiet.

Outside, he followed the big man toward Rock's building. The wind whipped at his face and stung his eyes. Back toward the train tracks, he didn't see anything or anyone. Other than the two empty cop cars, there weren't any police around at all.

What had he been doing upstairs watching TV then? Someone was supposed to come get him. He was ready to act and stand up with his own weapon; the time for him to do his thing had come.

"I—" he started to speak, but it was clear Seven wouldn't hear him, not with this wind. He wasn't even sure what he wanted to say.

Then he saw the whole lobby of 412, and a boy his own age using a mop to clean up.

That was all the security he saw.

Nothing else.

Maybe this wouldn't be so hard.

Marlene answered the phone and it was Anthony. Sure enough.

Anthony calling back from his Harvard Law School apartment—
Anthony the son of a New York lawyer mother *and* father just like he
was out of the Huxtables on a Thursday night. Anthony who looked
good enough to eat cake off of with his clothes off but who was now
calling to tell her that he wouldn't be coming over.

"I just don't think it'd be prudent for me to get involved with
what you have going on over there right now," he said. "I mean, what
good would it do to have me pointing out civil injustice to the police
at this point?"

"You right," she said. "I don't think you should come either."

"You don't?"

Marlene held the phone tight, looked around her own apartment.
She was glad to be back.

"Nah. You best just stay away until it's time for us to have play-
time. Best just to come up here for our fun." He tried to interrupt, but
Marlene kept talking. "See, you don't be involved here. Maybe later,
when you making paper to come in the courts and defend a person,
that's when you put your shit in. But now—"

"Marlene, I really don't think—"

"I'm sure. Right now you best to keep away."

"It's just that I spoke to my father and—" But she was already
hanging up the phone.

"Fuck you," she said. Whether he talked to his father, his mother,
his Harvard advisors, or just checked his gut in the time it took her
to get from Malik's place to hers, she didn't care. It was time he saw
how big the wall was between their two worlds.

She needed to see it too.

Then Pickup was behind her. "You say something?"

"Nah." She turned around, saw Pickup waiting for her to tell him
what to do. "Seven down with Shari's kid grabbing up Elf and Young
J. Who you got on the lobby?"

Pickup told her which of his soldiers he'd set up in the lobby of each building and where he had others camped out on the stairs. If the cops left, there were sales to be made, exchanges to be handled. Business needed to buzz again, get back up and running.

"Follow Seven and catch him up, see if he still down there. If not, hit the lobby and find if the cops gone. They is, get shit rolling. Then get over to 412. That where Seven gone go. Watch his back."

"But—" Pickup's face turned to one of doubt.

"He doing something for me now. And he need your help."

Pickup's eyes narrowed. Seven had said something about making amends on his way out of 410 before, and now he knew that it came from her directly. What she didn't know was how he'd respond.

Seven did what she said.

Now it was time to find out if Big Pickup would too.

Junius sat down on the stairs. He'd lost track of what floor he was on and knew he had to be careful around the higher floors, even more careful than he was already just to be in 412.

One step after another, lifting his leg high and bending his knee, he took each stair in the last few flights to the top. He wasn't worried about Black Jesus because he had no clue how to find him. He wanted to go straight to the root: Rock.

Fuck whatever Seven advised, or where he thought Junius should start. Going after somebody you didn't know how to find in a tower of your enemies did not make sense. In Bruce Lee terms, you got into the temple and went straight for the boss. You tried your best to take him down and his boys found you along the way. You had to go through the right hand man eventually, but that didn't mean you hunted his ass down. If he was worth anything, he'd be there when you found the boss, protecting his right hand.

And so Junius marched.

He passed the twentieth floor, the twenty-first, and started up to the twenty-second floor. Then halfway up, he stopped.

He could hear talking in the hallway above and, craning his neck to look through the bars, didn't see any legs or sign of a person waiting guard. There was very little to see where he was: just the next landing above him and a few stairs leading up to the twenty-second floor. He got down low and started to crawl up a few steps to the landing. With his feet out behind him and the Tec-9 in one hand, his finger off the trigger, he crawled up onto the next landing, imagining soldiers in Vietnam doing the same. Here he was in the middle of his war zone, a soldier without a side, looking to find his way.

He could hear the talking more distinctly now from the hall: two men, at least, standing guard outside of Rock's apartment, just talking shit. Neither of them were Black Jesus. Nothing ever came that easy.

"Motherfucker," Clarence said. He grabbed his boxers and pulled them up to cover his bad self. He went for his pants, still trying to match Milk gun-for-gun. Sheila turned away laughing and sat down on the bed.

"This just beats it all, don't it?" she asked, reaching for the pipe and lighter on the bed stand.

Roughneck stood with his fists in some kind of karate pose, ready to throw. It was a moment of embarrassment for Clarence, but one he mentally wrote of as just another dope fiend move. He wasn't afraid or ashamed of being a dope fiend anymore.

"You niggahs need to get up out of here." His high was somewhere in front of him, just above him and out of reach. He looked to Sheila sitting on the bed, getting set to light the pipe again. "You ruining a moment. Get the fuck out!"

Milk stood still, his gun on Clarence. "Fuck with him, Rough."

And then Roughneck moved—fast. He was in front of Clarence in a blink and then below him, doing some kind of sweeping kick. Clarence fell backward. He fired, and then saw Roughneck's fist crack down on him. Clarence saw black, heard Sheila scream, and felt another stiff punch. He'd fired into the ceiling or the wall facing the street. One of those two.

Then he was off the bed on the floor, and Roughneck kicked him in the ribs and stomped on his gun hand.

Clarence let the gun go. He bit down hard, keeping his mouth shut and refusing to scream.

"You fucking up, C," Rough said. "Fucking up for the whole of 412."

Milk said, "You can't beat on a cop, yo!"

Clarence opened his eyes, looking to see if it was over, but Rough came in quick with a left from the hips that caught the side of his face.

"Yeah," Clarence said, when he stopped spitting blood on the rug. "That's cool. You got me. Now what you gone do? Just be on out."

"Man, fuck," Milk said. "Tell me why I don't just shoot his ass."

"*Because murder is a capital offense.*" This was a new voice that came from behind Rough: a tired one that sounded like gravel on concrete. Something hard banged against the doorframe, and when Rough moved aside, Clarence saw the bald, black, raisin-headed cop he'd beat down in the lobby.

"What you want?" Clarence said. "Come for more?"

The cop knocked his nightstick against the doorframe, beating out a rhythm. Then he smashed it down against the broken door as hard and loud as he could.

"I come for my gun. My gun and my badge and your ass."

Rough chuckled and stepped back. "Shit. Be my guest to it."

Officer Johnson stepped inside. Clarence could see now that he had one eye swollen shut and his nose was a mess. "You welcome to my ass, Officer. Matter of fact—"

Clarence got partway up and dropped his boxers. He turned to show the cop his cheeks. Rough moved in, kicked him in the hip and bounced him off the end of the bed, onto the blankets.

Clarence rolled to his back and started pulling up his boxers, laughing the whole time.

"Get out," the cop said. He was talking to the others, Milk and Sheila and Rough.

"You want no witnesses so you can give me that proper cop-style brutality?"

Johnson hit his nightstick into the palm of his hand. He ground his teeth as he spoke. "I want everyone else out, so I can have you all to myself."

Sergeant O'Scullion stood with his men in front of the three brick towers. Though these were technically part of his detail, they were completely unlike anything else in it, except for Jefferson Park, just a few hundred yards back up Rindge Ave. Down here at this end of things, just off the highway, was a no man's land he preferred not to consider.

Jerry's Pit, Dougay's Supermarket, and these two sets of projects. If it weren't for poor Joyce Chen, the best Chinese food in town, he'd write off the area entirely. Sure, he heard from civic leaders that he needed to police the towers, if only so the mess didn't spill over to the other side of Rindge, where the working whites—Italians and Irish mostly—had their two-families, but most of the time he thought the projects would be better off eating themselves alive in the war that was always brimming to the surface of this cesspool.

The radio squawked from his shoulder and dispatch came across with a three-car accident on Mass Ave. and Walden—a busy intersection that would create a mess in both directions if it didn't get cleared. Getting close to rush hour on a weekday afternoon, he'd hear about it if that wasn't avoided. He had three cars now at the towers and another up on Mass Ave. at Pemberton Market, looking into the scene of a shooting from the night before.

The boy from the roof of 411 had been bagged, tagged, and taken to the morgue. If homicide came up with anything on his shooting, it wouldn't be until the end of the week or later. Just like O'Scullion, they were sick of coming here and ready to write the kid off as another unsolved.

Covering the whole city, they had even more bullshit to take care of than O'Scullion. Another death on these roofs? Hardly worth writing up: no witnesses, as always, and no clear motive other than the usual—drug war.

The ambulance had taken the other kid from the back lot. No one had any leads on who laid him out, and Johnson doubted that would change.

"Fuck this," he said to his men. "Accident up on Mass Ave. needs our attention. This shit?" He raised his hands. "A waste of our time."

One of his men—Officer Roberts—spit on the ground. His face was ruddy and cold from the wind. At least he had the good sense to keep a dip in. The other officer, Kelley, pointed back up to the front of the first building. "Johnson's car is still up there, sir."

O'Scullion looked in that direction, saw the car nosed in behind a civilian's parked Datsun. "Shitbird was supposed to canvas the building," he said.

He called Johnson on the radio and got no response. He tapped at the radio with his fingertip, hoping the damn thing hadn't frozen up again. But then it squawked: dispatch reminding him about the accident, upgrading it to an all-units call.

"I am en-route," O'Scullion said.

He looked at Officer Kelley's thin blond mustache and polished badge. Kelley, a five-year cop raised North Cambridge all the way. Catholic School, confirmed at St. John's. Father was a fireman. A good boy.

"We roll, Officer. Johnson can't see to keep himself in radio contact or respond to an all-unit, then that is his problem, not ours."

What he didn't say was that he didn't care what Johnson did or if he got himself fired. Johnson was a Roxbury boy fresh from the academy and City Hall made the detail hire him as a part of affirmative action.

He spit onto the ground, reached into his jacket for a smoke. "We get up there fast enough, you can stop at Pemberton to get us all coffee."

"That's what I need," Roberts said. "Let Johnson stay here with his kind. Maybe he can clean up their shit." Roberts started back toward the front of the buildings and his car. "I know we can't."

Kelley looked to O'Scullion, who nodded at Roberts. "Better stay with your partner, son."

O'Scullion stuffed a Marlboro between his lips and stared at Kelley until he turned to do as he was told. O'Scullion wouldn't have put things as plain as Roberts—as a commanding officer, he knew better than to say these things out loud—but he agreed all the way.

As Junius crawled up the first steps from the landing—he was less than a dozen stairs from Rock's floor, probably no more than thirty feet from the door to the man's apartment—he could hear the talk from the hallway more clearly. This top hallway and the one beneath it didn't have doors. They were wide open onto the stairs, unlike all the hallways below.

"Celtics just too white," someone said, "now Rick Mahorn, that's my niggah. You just watch how he fuck with people. That is a niggah playing some ball."

"Vinnie Johnson."

"That bitch come out, he don't give a *fuck*. What I'm saying. Motherfucker don't care about nothing but shooting!"

"Microwave get hot."

"But that's how I play. Shit, talking about Bill Lame-beer. Motherfuck *is* lame. You know I wouldn't pass him the ball. Look at Isiah: fucking Indiana. You have to be a punk to let Bob Knight fuck with your shit!"

Junius crept up one stair at a time on his belly, straining to see who was on the hall and where they were.

"Dumars ain't no punk."

"No. No. Motherfucker some straight gumbo-ass Southern type murderer shit. Mean as dirt. Don't say *shit*."

"What about Parish, then? He black."

"Shit."

"From Louisiana—"

"Motherfucking *Chief*? The Chief? How you gone be a tough motherfucker and people call you Chief? Plus he hang around too much with Larry Bird and Kevin McHale. Don't get no whiter than them two!"

"True. It's true."

"And don't start on no Dennis Johnson, neither. You tell me one niggah you know with freckles and a red-ass afro. Tell me!"

"But he *black*."

"He *something*—Cedric Maxwell, Tiny Archibald, shit, even M.L. fucking Carr black. Bill Russell! Way back! *They* brothers. But D.J.? Please. He like them punks. Danny Ainge: Mormon. Jerry Sichting? Please. Scott motherfucking Wedman?"

"Greg Kite."

"Oh! *Please* don't even *say* that name. Oh my god. They can't be serious!"

"Bill Walton."

"You need to stop."

Junius had come up three stairs and could see partway down the hall, but where the talkers were. He could see the first four doors, and Rock's apartment had to be either all the way in the middle or at the other end.

"But Parish—"

"Wait. Parish? Cetentary? The fuck is Cetentary? You ever heard of that shit? What *is* that? He studying for his priest test or something?"

Now Junius could see one of their backs. The quiet one faced the opposite direction, and Junius saw the back of his head. He'd come up just another two stairs, staying as low as he could. He could see the guy's short black hair, a buzzed-up fade with a bit of a Gumby. He was shaking his head.

"Exactly. You don't even know what that shit is."

"Charles Oakley, that's my man."

"Yeah, yeah. He raw. He raw. But I'm saying the Pistons, they my team right. I like those motherfuckers. Even Dennis Rodman. Shorts high as shit and that motherfucker cannot shoot a shot to save himself, but he do something right. Something."

"A.D. my man too. Mark Aguirre."

"That's what I'm *telling* you. Look at that team all up and down: niggahs! Exactly! That's what I been saying to you."

"Dantley a pump-faking motherfucker!"

They both started to laugh.

"Yeah! He be like—" And with that, the other one, the one Junius couldn't see, suddenly popped into view. Maybe Junius had come too far up, but he wasn't expecting a move like that. As soon as he moved, Junius recognized him as the one who did the shooting up on the roof—Hammer.

Junius ducked against the stairs, pulled his head down. He'd seen Hammer for just a moment, saw him stand and start throwing imaginary pump-fakes.

Now it was quiet from above. Neither of the two spoke. Junius listened closely. Then he heard one of them hiss.

Elf followed Seven toward 412. Seven banged on the glass, and the kid with the mop looked up.

Elf recognized him now as Randy: one of his brother's friends he used to see in the summers playing basketball at the courts up behind Pemberton Street. Randy was a set shooter, barely got both feet off the ground, but he could hit it. Elf had to give him that.

When Randy saw him, Elf nodded. Seven kept banging on the doors. "Open the fuck up." Randy pushed the mop into its bucket, splashing water onto the floor, where Elf noticed the white tiles had red streaks across them. The black tiles still looked the same.

"Come here," Seven told Randy, and Randy came to the doors. "Now open the fuck up."

Randy had to look up to meet Seven's eyes, and when he did, he pushed the door open immediately. He tried to keep his body in the way, ask what they were doing, but Seven pushed past him immediately. "Who here?" he asked.

Randy looked puzzled.

"What up?" Elf gave him the nod and they bumped fists.

Randy said, "Ain't seen you playing ball."

"Nah." Elf shrugged. "Business."

"Who the fuck is here?" Seven asked, louder this time.

"Just me." Randy pointed to the mop. "Niggahs got me cleaning up a mess of blood because Clarence up a cop. Now Rough and Milk gone up to see about Clarence, and the cop went up too."

Seven's eyebrows climbed his forehead. "Cop?"

Randy shook his head. "Clarence *fucked* his ass up. Niggah beat him *down*."

"Clarence." Seven didn't say anything else.

"You seen Junius?" Elf asked.

Randy shook his head.

Seven crossed the lobby and pushed the elevator button. "Come on," he said.

"To where?"

The elevator doors opened. "Up, niggah."

Seven looked down at Elf as they rode up.

Elf tapped his fingers against the side of his leg. His head bobbed a little, like he had some song in him. He stared straight ahead at the elevator doors. Neither him *or* Junius had come up in these projects and, from what Seven knew about Willie's boys, they probably didn't come up in projects at all. Where Willie's crews rolled it was mostly two- and three-families, houses on streets with sidewalks, even a few trees. There was one project over there, six or seven buildings that looked bad but held nothing like the pain of the towers—none of them were more than three or four stories tall.

"Yo, you know those projects up on Powder House by Broadway?"

Elf nodded. "North Street Projects," he said, and Seven could tell he wasn't from them by the way his mouth didn't curl around the words.

"Your man J come up there?"

"Nah. Neither us."

Just a kid was all he was. Even if he was older than Junius, Elf didn't act it. Maybe Junius knew that and left Elf behind on purpose. He might've had something there.

The doors opened and Seven stepped out onto fifteen. "Come on."

He walked halfway down the hall to an apartment that he hadn't visited in years. Just before he knocked on the door, he looked down at Elf. "Stand up straight."

He knocked and heard her inside, saying she'd come in a minute, that she was on her way. Seven smiled at the sound of her voice and looked away from Elf so the boy wouldn't see. Then he shook his head when she said, "One minute!" She was the same as always.

She opened the door without asking who it was, still trusting the insane world around her, and then brought her hands up to her mouth when she saw him. She smiled through her hands, laughed even.

"Steven," she said. "Where you been, boy? You know it's too long since I seen you!"

"I'm here, Miss Emma. Here now to pay you a visit."

"Well, isn't that—" She stopped and invited them in, stepping back and waving them to the same old couch that had been there before. The same plastic was still on it and she probably had the same pitcher of red Kool-Aid in the refrigerator.

"Who is this now?"

Seven glanced back at Elf, but didn't know his real name. Miss Emma wasn't one for nicknames. "This—"

"Elvin. Elvin Jenkins, ma'am. Pleased to meet you."

Seven patted his back. At least the kid knew when to show some manners.

"Sit, sit." She commanded them to the couch. "So what brings you to my door today, Steven?"

"We looking for a friend of ours, and I might have to go upstairs. Thought I could leave *Elvin* with you for a minute."

Elf turned to Seven fast, confused.

"What you mean, *Steven*? I thought we were here to find Junius."

"Oh, Junius just here," she said.

Seven felt his jaw drop and he closed it fast. "He was?"

She nodded. Steadying herself with a hand on the armrest, she slowly let herself down into her glider. "Randall brought him, but they didn't stay long. He seemed real upset about his brother."

"Randall?" Seven asked.

"Temple?" Elf said.

She laughed. "Yes to both. He said he was here looking for Guardy Little. Seemed real eager to find him, too."

Seven bit his lip. The boy had gotten further than he expected. He didn't know if that was bad or good. Under his breath, he said, "Black Jesus," to let Elf know who she meant. The fact that he was with Roughneck didn't make sense.

"Black—" Elf said, and stopped himself.

"How long ago?"

"Mmmm, not more than a half hour, I'd say. Enough time for me to call around to his people and let them know where he be at."

"His people?"

"Course Randall left right after he did. Hardly stayed long enough to say a proper hello."

Seven stood up fast. "I—" he said.

"I just spoke to his father on the phone ten minutes ago. Told the man to come up here and see about his boy. Young man all upset like that, no telling *what* he might do! Nothing good, though, I'm betting."

Seven took off his jacket and set it on the couch. He pulled his sweatshirt around his waist, making sure not to betray any of the bulk of his guns to Miss Emma. That would be the *last* thing she could handle.

She stared at the jacket, and he picked it up fast before she had to tell him where it went—on the old coat rack next to the door.

"I think you right about him getting into trouble," he said. "Especially looking for Guardy. He don't even know where to look."

She shook her head. "The things that happen here these days. And what happened to his brother?" She started to cross herself and then stopped. "Makes me so I don't *know* what to do."

Elf stood up, but Seven held him where he was with a hand. "Miss Emma, it all right if my friend stays here with you while I try to find Junius?"

"That's ok," Elf said. "Really."

"Of course it is. I'm happy to have him. Always nice to have company."

Elf stood up. "Nah. Nah. I'm a come."

Seven opened the door behind him and pulled Elf into the hall. "Just one second, Miss Emma."

"I'm not—"

Seven grabbed Elf with both hands and lifted him onto his toes, then shoved him against the wall. He brought his face close, so Elf could hear him whisper, "You stay the fuck here. I bring you out in this hall, I knock your ass out myself and leave you in a janitor closet. Ok?"

Elf started to speak, and Seven shoved him into the wall again, harder, hoping Miss Emma wouldn't hear. "I don't give a fuck what you think you gone do. Your boy up in here and I'm a get him out. Neither one of you up to killing Rock *or* Black Jesus. Just two young bucks and that's how you need to stay."

Seven reached down the back of Elf's pants and pulled out the Beretta, stuffed it into his pocket. He worried a little that if something happened to him and Junius, he might need a gun to get himself home, but the chances of that leading him to help instead of harm were small; he'd be better off walking out with his hands raised.

Otherwise he'd probably drop the gun on Miss Emma's rug and scare the shit out of her or worse.

He let go of Elf's jacket, smoothed where it'd been bunched.

"Now I'm going back in there with you and you make nice. Talk to her until I get back with your boy."

Seven didn't wait for Elf to answer, just pushed him back through the door.

"Niggahs be leaving me behind all day!"

Seven shoved the back of his head. "I apologize for not being able to talk more right now, Miss Emma, but I think you're right about someone finding Temple's brother before anything goes wrong. Do you mind?"

She shook her head, started to get up, and Seven waved her down. "Sit," he said, "Sit. I'll see you later."

Seven glared at Elf once more, hard. "Bye, *Elvin.*"

Then he was gone.

Rough watched the way the cop stood there, uneven on his own feet, like something had bent in his middle and made his top half kink to the left. This was the same cop he threw in the dumpster. He couldn't be more surprised to see the man back on his feet.

"Go on. The rest of you just get on out."

"That's cool with me," Rough said, holding up his hands. Milk shot him a look.

"I just be getting on then," Sheila said, taking the pipe and Clarence's lighter off the bedside table. She pulled her flannel shirt around herself, trying to cover her chest. She made a production out of the way she walked, practically sashaying across the room like she had just won something. It was hard not to notice. She tipped her head to the cop as she passed him, said "Officer" just as sweet as you please.

"I'm a get to work now," the cop said. He was black and not someone Rough had ever seen before. Definitely not from around here. Boston maybe? He weaved farther into the apartment. "That my gun?" he asked, pointing at Rough's feet with his nightstick.

Rough looked down and saw the Smith & Wesson. He bent and picked it up, holding it by the cylinder with the barrel pointed down.

The cop reached out for it, but stood where he was until Rough stepped forward to place the gun in his hand.

"Thanks."

Clarence was pulling his belt tight around his waist, smiling like he wanted to see what would happen. He showed his hands and then started to get up.

Rough gestured to Milk to put his gun away. "This a cop here. Police."

"He don't see nothing. Do you, cop?"

"I don't see anything now, but something happens, I'm a to see that."

"Milk my titties," Clarence said, squeezing one of his pecs. He pushed his lips out. "Go on. Get ghost, son. Me and my officer got something to settle."

Then Clarence held the badge out for them to see it: it was round at the bottom and with a crest on top. He held it up to his chest, smiling like a true crackhead, as if nothing mattered in the world.

"Who's the cop now, pig? Why don't you come show me?"

At that, the officer pointed his gun at Clarence, aiming low toward his legs, and shot. Clarence howled, collapsed sideways onto the bed, and went for his knee with both hands. He cradled his shin, both eyes squeezed tight. Rough started to imagine what getting shot in the shin might feel like, how it'd be to have that bone shattered, and he didn't think about it long. Didn't want to. The blood wasn't gushing from the wound, but Rough saw some of it seep through Clarence's hands.

"C Dub," the cop said. "Show me a smile."

"That's cool," Milk said. "We out, right?"

Roughneck and Milk both stepped toward the door, the cheap piece of hollow metal that would no longer go back on frame.

Clarence made a sound that was part pain and part something else. Then he smiled at the cop, showing all his teeth and wildness in the eyes.

The cop hobbled forward toward the bed and tucked his gun into its holster. He gripped the nightstick with both hands. "Go on," he said, over his shoulder. "Don't make me tell you again."

Rough grabbed Milk by the sleeve of his sweatshirt and pulled him out into the hall. He did his best to close the door, leaning it against its frame from the inside. When he turned, Milk was already halfway to the stairs and past the elevator. He didn't look back, and Rough didn't either, not even when he heard the nightstick hitting something hard.

Seven Heaven pushed the elevator call button.

It came and he got on, but as soon as it started up he realized how bad it would be if he got to the top and the doors opened on Rock's boys. Even with his Tec ready, he'd be looking at guns in his face and no time to talk. He pushed the button for seventeen and the car stopped. Better to go softly up the stairs, where he could listen and creep, than to drop onto an upper floor in Rock's building.

In the hall, he didn't see anyone—just the dim fluorescents and the dirty walls. Then he heard a sound, something like scratching from the stairway, and he turned in that direction. When he did, the door opened and a thin, frail woman wearing a worn bathrobe and light blue fuzzy bedroom slippers walked out. She was holding the robe closed against her body, but even with her arms around her, Seven could tell she needed to put on weight. Her collar bones stuck up around her neck on each side, and he could see the tendons leading to her jaw as she came closer.

Her stomach poked out, distended below her arms like the Ethiopian kids you saw on TV with the flies buzzing on their faces. Like that or like she was pregnant. She looked hungry and cold but smiled wide, revealing teeth connected to gums that wanted to leave her mouth altogether. She cradled a big handful of crack rocks against her side with one arm.

Behind her, Seven thought he saw a white and black Air Jordan in the stairway through the gap in the door. Then it was gone.

"Handsome," she said.

"What happened?"

The woman didn't answer, but instead caught his arm and held it. "You Seven Heaven?"

Seven shook his arm free and pushed past her toward the stairs. Behind him, he heard the elevator doors close.

When he didn't answer, she yelled, "Fuck you then! Stank dick motherfucker!"

Seven didn't look back. He got to the door and peered through its square window. It was dark on the other side, but he could see something black against the brown paint of the wall. He turned the handle and tried the door. He could only open it a foot before it hit something. Then what it hit moved and made a sound. He saw a Jordan kick once on the floor.

He pushed through the door into the stairway.

There on the floor, he saw a Latino kid lying in his own blood. He shifted when he saw Seven, smiled through the blood in his mouth. He was holding his stomach with both hands like he was trying to hold his life inside with his fingers. There was money around him on the floor: fives and tens in the blood, some bills crumpled between his fingers like he'd tried to use them to plug the holes. His breaths came slow and far apart, but his eyes moved, following Seven.

Past this, Seven saw more blood on the wall down the stairs, a trail of it leading away from the next landing.

Seven turned back to the Latino with the Jordans. "Who did this?" he asked.

The pusher smiled, blood between his teeth. "Ambulance."

Seven saw a few weed bags on the floor and up around his head. The rest of what he held had probably been picked clean by the woman in the robe—the reason for her smile.

"Ambulance," he said again.

Then Seven saw a shell casing on the floor by the far wall and he wished he hadn't. He could tell the gun it had come from, but pretended he wasn't sure until he picked it up and held it himself in his own two fingers. He still didn't want to know.

Seven looked back at the slinger, who knew what he was getting into when he decided to play the game. He wasn't going to live long enough to see the inside of an ambulance.

The white uppers of his Jordans were stained with blood. Such a shame to fuck up a nice pair of $120 sneakers like that. Not that that mattered; not that there weren't much bigger things to deal with.

Seven started up the stairs, hoping to get to Junius before Rock did.

66

Junius crawled back down the stairs for the first landing down from twenty-two. If he took a shot, he wanted to be standing and ready to run. He crawled down to the landing and then made the turn around the corner for the next flight, holding his gun over the rail, ready to take a shot at legs or feet if someone started toward him.

He glanced at the doorway to the next floor, the twenty-first, and this doorway was empty also, exactly the same as above: someone had taken the doors off their hinges to leave empty doorways here on the top two floors.

Dropping down into a crouch to see the other end of twenty-one, Junius made out feet on the stairs—a pair of legs and even, suddenly, a face with a gun.

He fired.

Junius didn't dream of making the shot at that distance—all the way down the hall—but he hoped letting off a shot would stop the guy from coming, give him the time he needed.

He vaulted over the rail and onto the first flight down from twenty-one, then jumped down to the next landing. He turned and nestled himself into a corner, his back to the walls, where he could see the stairs above and below him, the stairs and the landings and the hall.

A shot echoed from above, from somewhere at the other end of the hall, and this one was *loud*—a real gunshot, not like the whistle of his silencer. Something landed in his hair, and Junius brushed it off, looked up to see a small cloud of plaster dust a few feet above him. A shot had hit the wall there, maybe three or four feet from his head.

Junius ducked lower, gripping the Tec in both hands. He slipped a fresh magazine from the back pocket of his jeans and switched it for the one he'd partly used.

He watched the stairs and the hall.

Elf sat on the couch trying to make nice with Miss Emma. She was a nice old lady and after she offered him the Kool-Aid a second time, he agreed to have a glass.

It was good, too. Elf felt his stomach grumble and he knew he was hungry, that the chicken nuggets weren't enough. But he couldn't ask this woman for food straight out either, and Seven told him not to leave until he and Junius got back.

Bullshit, is what it all was. The second time today he'd been left behind. He knew he could handle himself in these towers. He smiled at the old woman, did his best to act interested in what she had to say, but what was she talking about? Something about all the phone calls she made around North Cambridge to folks.

"That's how I came up on the truth about it, *finally*," she said.

"Truth about what?"

She shook her head. "Boy, ain't you been listening to anything I just said?"

Elf smiled. "I apologize, ma'am. I guess my mind started to wander. I tend to do that when I'm hungry." She crossed her arms, went back to gliding in her chair. She didn't make any motion to pick up on his comment about being hungry, but there it was.

"What was you saying?" he asked.

"Something important. I'm talking about your friend's older brother, Temple. Ain't you the least bit interested in how I found out what happened to your friend's brother?" She looked down to her lap. "Such a shame, really."

"What?" Elf said, forgetting his stomach for the moment. "What you mean, 'What happened to Temple?'"

She sucked her teeth. "Can't even think beyond your own stomach is the problem with you, is it? That all you got on your mind: food?"

"Tell me what you was going to say about Temple?"

She stared back at Elf, pursed her lips in front of her face until they stuck out almost as far as her nose. "Boy, now you want to know about how Temple died? Feel like listening?"

"Yes, ma'am," Elf said. "Yes, ma'am."

Gary Johnson crossed the small, dirty room in two limping strides and swung the nightstick down hard on Clarence, who tried to block it with his right arm. It hit the forearm, which made a sound like it broke, and a memory in the back of Johnson's mind sprang to life, telling him he'd done damage to that same arm earlier.

Clarence bit down hard, gnashing his teeth, his lips pulled back. He was on the floor at the end of the bed. His face shook but he didn't make a sound, didn't scream. Instead, on his next breath, he moaned like something good had happened, said, "Yeah, motherfucker!"

Johnson tried the other direction now, swinging from his ankles in an uppercut and going for Clarence's face, but he lost some of his balance, and Clarence caught the end of the nightstick with his left hand. Now he made another sound, this one more like pain, and pulled on the stick. But Johnson shoved it at him, pushing the end into Clarence's neck. That stopped him, and Johnson swung again, brought the stick down hard at Clarence's chest now, hitting him between the shoulder and neck. He heard the collar bone snap.

"Yeah, motherfucker," Johnson said. "How you like that?" He slapped his badge across the floor with his stick, knocking it away from Clarence.

Clarence fell back against the blankets, nodding and sticking his tongue all the way out to lick at his chin. "Mmmm," he said, nodding.

Johnson sat down on the bed, breathing heavy, his lungs pumping. He could hear a rattle in his chest and hacked, trying to catch whatever was loose, and spit something red and thick onto the floor.

"Nice," he said. "Aren't we a fucking pair." He coughed and spit again. "How about I kick the shit out of you and then we both us go to a hospital?"

Clarence spoke through clenched teeth. "Fuck off, pig. Just get your badge and get out." He pulled in a big breath of air and shouted, "Leave!"

Johnson looked to his badge on the floor, not ten feet from where he sat. The crackhead was right: he should just get out, get the fuck gone and leave this mess in his wake. Get back to his unit, if it wasn't on blocks by now, and drive his own self to a hospital. But getting up off the bed, picking up the badge, and walking were not actions that would come easy.

He reached for the radio on his shoulder, then remembered that it wasn't there. Lost or broken, he couldn't remember which, and at this point it didn't matter.

"Fuck," he said, looking down at his legs. "Look at us both now."

Big Pickup didn't like finding TV Malik alone in his apartment. That Junius had left a long while back and that Seven and Elf went on to find him didn't sit well either. Pickup knew this wouldn't go over well with Marlene. She wanted to know what was going on at all times; she wanted control. Now, with Seven Heaven and the boys gone ahead, after who knew what—maybe even Rock—the other part that Pickup didn't like was it meant he had to follow.

That was what Marlene had asked him to do.

He had to go after them, and since he they weren't in Marlene's towers—he'd been in and out of those plenty to know—all three must have gone on to 412. Pickup thought back to the stare-down that morning between him and Roughneck—Roughneck *and* Black Jesus. They were not his friends.

He was not meant to go over there. Doing it was like trespassing, and trespassing made it open season—open season on his ass.

"This ain't good."

"Nah. They've been gone for a while now. My guess is they've got the jump on where you're going."

Pickup shook his head. "What you say?"

"I said—"

"Nevermind." Pickup cut him off with a wave of his hand and left the TV-land apartment behind.

He rode the elevator down to the bottom of 411 by himself. No cops were out front, so he told the boys and the slingers in the lobby and out front to get back up on sales. Shit had come apart a little today with the cops on the scene, but now it was time to make sales. Even though Pickup liked giving the order, it made him pissed at Seven. Seven wasn't doing his job.

Seven was the top man, the one supposed to be in charge.

No matter what was going down, it was Seven's job to be on top of it all, to make sure areas were covered for sales: lobbies, stairs, wherever.

Pickup would have to make Marlene aware of this. She had trusted him to do it, too. That was a note of confidence.

But first he had to find what was what in 412. He had to find Seven Heaven and Little Elf and Junius Posey. Those motherfuckers still stood in his way.

He came out into the cold air and looked around. The sun sat low over the old Polynesian restaurant on the other side of the highway, stretching its rays along the bottom of a few thin clouds. The wind had increased and the temperature was dropping.

"So what you gone do now?" one of the soldiers asked, a boy barely seventeen.

"Shit." Pickup didn't want to say it, didn't want to think it, and *definitely* didn't want to do it. He shook his head, pulled the Tec-9 from the back of his pants and tucked it inside his jacket. He pulled back the bolt and slid it forward, setting a round into the chamber.

He spoke into the wind, didn't care if the others heard him or not. "Lock and load, son. I'm going up into the 412."

6 8

Seven had just come up a few flights when he heard the shot. He heard the familiar whistle first, the sound of a silencer he'd customized himself. The shot was fired from above him on the stairway, *his stairway*, and Seven knew Junius couldn't be far.

Then he heard a second shot, and this one was *loud*. It sounded like it had come from the far side of the building, maybe the other end of a hall.

That shot was from a handgun. Possibly a Beretta or maybe a Walther. No silencer.

He felt the side of his jeans for where he'd slipped two of his fifty-round clips into the pocket that some jeans company had meant for a hammer. His hammer was like this: nine millimeter and ready to go bang.

The Tec-9 in his hand was one of the few he'd modified to go full auto. If shit came down to seriously fucking something up, he was not about to be letting off a few shots. He'd be letting off many. He fingered the trigger guard and felt his pulse quicken.

Yeah, something was getting ready to go down.

At the next hallway up, nineteen, Seven hit the door and raced down the hall. If someone was shooting from the far stairway, that was the one he would take. If he was coming up on somebody from behind, he didn't want it to be Junius, he wanted it to be one of Rock's boys so he could open up and ask questions later.

He was quiet at the doorway on the other end of the hall, looked through the small window onto the stairs. No one was there. Then he opened the door slowly, turning the knob all the way before pulling the door.

He slipped out into the stairs and closed the door himself, letting the knob and the bolt settle softly. Then he made his way around the outisde wall, keeping his back against it, the Tec in front of him He climbed the stairs sideways, watching the next landing and the flight above, staying slow and careful, making sure he didn't see anyone above him up on twenty.

He was on the landing between twenty and twenty-one when he heard the blast of a shotgun from the other end of the building. He could see the hallway on twenty-one didn't have a door on it, and that explained the clarity of the sound.

Seven made his way along the wall, watching above him. He was close to where the first loud shot came from. That he *knew*.

Clarence reached across his body with his left hand, straining to get into his right-hand pants pocket. He could feel two rocks in there but getting at them would be hard. The cop still sat on his bed, breathing hard, something inside him rattling and wheezing. Slowly, Clarence managed to slide one of the rocks upward by trapping its bottom half and pushing it against his skin, squeezing it toward the opening at the top of the pocket. He finally felt the tip of the baggie against his fingers and pulled at it, brought it out so he could see the white hardness inside the Ziplock.

This would cure him. This would push away the pain, at least for the time being so he could get up off the floor or just get away from the hurt.

His shoulder was broken. He'd been shot in the leg. His right arm wouldn't move, or it would, but each time it did he wanted to cry out. All this, but looking at the rock in his hand gave him at least a little hope.

"Cop," he said. "Cop!"

Johnson grunted. Clarence couldn't see him from the floor, but he knew where the cop was from the sound of his breathing.

"Cop!"

"What?"

"You see that pipe beside you on the bed table?"

He waited, listening to the cop breathe, feeling his own blood slow in his veins.

"Ain't no pipe there, motherfucker. Your bitch took that shit when she left. She fucked you, niggah."

Clarence groaned. He had other shit in the apartment he could use to smoke a rock, but he'd have to look for it. There was at least an old one-hitter and bat inside the night table itself. "You see—"

"Man, fuck you!" The cop stood up, the bed creaking beneath him.

"Is there a lighter on the table?"

Now the cop turned to face Clarence. He looked gray, like he was half-dead, but he smiled. "Bitch took that too, niggah."

He swung the stick at Clarence's left hand, knocking the baggie out of it. It flew across the floor, and into the corner.

"Shit, niggah. Why you *do* that?"

"Don't do drugs." The cop laughed and then started coughing, his whole frame rocking with the force of the hacks. When he was done, he said, "Just say no. Motherfucker, didn't you know Nancy Reagan told your ass."

The cop laughed again, holding his sides with his arms like he was cradling a bag of broken bones. Despite it all, Clarence had to smile, if even just a little. "Niggah," he said, grabbing his crotch. "This be your brain on my dick. Any questions?"

"Yeah," the cop said. "Yeah." He coughed again, laughing as much as he could, then stepped to where his badge was on the floor and, bracing himself against the couch, he bent slowly and picked it up. "That's Officer Johnson to you."

When he had straightened, Johnson hobbled toward the door.

"Fuck you, cop!" Clarence said, trying to get up. But feeling a shot of pain across his chest when he started to move kept him planted. "Fuck you in the ass with your nightstick!"

The cop didn't say anything else, just pushed the door away from its frame. Before he was gone, Clarence said, "Wait! Wait. Cop? Just help me find something I can use to smoke this rock out? Please?"

He waited. It sounded like the cop was waiting at the door, like the origin of the hacking-breathing had paused.

"Please, man. Just help me smoke this shit and I be ok."

"Fuck you." That was all the cop said, and then he was gone; Clarence looked up and saw just the empty door frame.

He let his head fall back against the blankets, counting his breaths. He would rest for a little while, let himself count to fifty or maybe even one hundred, and then he'd get himself to the night table to find the rest of the Brillo, his one-hitter, and maybe even some matches. He had to have matches.

Or maybe Sheila would come back. Maybe she'd been waiting outside in the hall the whole time, just waiting for the cop to go away.

He felt his right pants pocket again with his left hand; he could still feel one rock left.

Elf stood up from the couch. He'd done just like Miss Emma said: sat and thought and figured out what to do next. He had to do what was best for his boy.

As far as they'd come together, wherever Junius was and whatever trouble he was in—if Elf could get to him before he got to Rock or tried to go after Black Jesus, tell him Marlene had put them on the wrong path—he needed to find his man and get them both out of 412.

"So you made up your mind now, have you?"

He nodded.

"What's it going to be then?"

He patted his thighs, trying to figure out what to say. "I think—"

"You *think*? Son, you better know what you planning if you going to make a move up in these here towers. These are not a place for a boy to tread light."

Elf stood up straighter. "Yes, ma'am. I have to go find my friend and tell him what you just told me. He on his way to get into a world of trouble."

"That's good," she said. "Friendship worth something. Not as much as your own hide, but you can't just watch that all day. Got to be some give and take." Miss Emma nodded. "You know where you're going, then?"

Elf guessed: "Up?"

"That's right. If your friend went after Rock, he went up top and wouldn't stop. But—" Now Miss Emma started to stand. She put her crocheting on the coffee table and steadied her body with both hands on the glider's arms. Elf took hold of one elbow and helped to steady her. She thanked him as she crossed to the kitchen.

"Come here," she said, when she was in front of the stove.

Elf followed, and when she pointed to a cabinet above the stove, he took a small footstool and set it in front of the oven, then climbed on it to get to the cabinet. He still had to stretch to reach the knob.

"You reach in there," she said.

Elf stood on his toes and felt inside the cabinet, expecting to touch dust and things that were dusty, but instead he felt the metal end of something with a scored surface. He worked it toward him and when he had it in his hand, he knew it was a gun.

What he brought out was a small revolver with a black handle. "What?"

"That belong to my nephew Randall. Boy don't know I knew it up there. Damn if I know why it is, but that be where he put it." She raised her shoulders and then dropped them. "Might be of use to you, not that I want that. But things come to pass, you might have a need for it.

"Looks like you were in a fight already not too long ago." She touched her lips, where Elf knew he had a scab.

She turned and walked back into the living room as Elf shut the cabinet and got down from the stool. He looked down at the gun in his hands: it had a short barrel and a cylinder that held six shots. Along its side, he read *Smith & Wesson*.

It was smaller than the Beretta, and definitely less gun than the

Tec, but that suited him fine. He tucked it down the front of his pants easily; it fit better than the other guns.

"Thank you, ma'am. I'm a be careful."

Miss Emma waved her hand. She'd already reached the rocker and begun her process of sitting down. "Times changing round here and it's no place suited for me. Not no more." She shook her head. "Uhn *unh*." She waved at Elf again. "Best you go now, boy, before I change my mind."

Elf watched her settle into the chair. Her eyes were closed. "Go," she said, but he was already at the door, letting himself out into the hall.

He shut the door quietly behind him.

Out in the hallway, it smelled of burned food or cooking oil. Something was wrong in the air.

Dee and Ness got into the 412 elevator so stoned and tired that it took them a full minute to realize neither one had pushed a button for their floor. Dee noticed it first, and laughed. "Damn, niggah. You know we just been standing here, right?"

Ness opened his eyes and turned to Dee. He looked like he might ask a question, but then he just waved his hand and closed his eyes again.

"Damn, yo. You dead on your feet up in this bitch. I mean we ain't slept but—"

"Yeah," Ness said, his voice quiet and barely there.

"Ok. You asleep then, fine. Tell that to Rock."

"Who we going to? Rock or C?"

"Fuck C."

"Heard that."

"Leave us up in front that house all night, then up in that budget-ass diner. Unh unh. Fuck him. We talk to Rock today. Black Jesus at least!"

Dee stepped up to the buttons and hit twenty-two. The doors creaked shut. A Dee watched them, he thought he saw red marks on the lobby floor.

"That blood?" he asked.

Ness didn't answer.

Inside the elevator, he heard the motors whir and the machine creaking as it took them up.

After leaving Clarence alone with the good Officer Johnson, Roughneck followed Milk to the stairs at the end of the hall. They started to make their way down at first; Rough didn't know their next move, but the least they could do was see how Randy had managed with the mop.

They came down a flight and a half before they heard the first shot. Rough froze, his hand on the railing. It'd been a handgun, one shot from inside the same stairwell they were in; with the echo, it couldn't have been fired anywhere else.

"Fuck was that?"

Rough turned to start back up the stairs. "Means some shit going down."

He broke into a run, knowing it was more than ten stories to Rock's floor and that running them would be faster than the elevator. If shit was going down, especially if it involved Junius—Rough still didn't know why he even cared—he wanted to be there. If he could do anything to help Rock or protect Junius he wanted the chance.

He shouldn't have let Junius leave Miss Emma's without more of a fight, didn't know why he hadn't just talked him down and sent him out of the building.

Milk yelled back something about the elevator, and Rough called him a pussy, told him to come on.

Rough never thought Junius would reach Rock, but he was so far outside the towers' norm he was unpredictable. Maybe that norm didn't work anymore and Junius was here to shake it up. Maybe rough might want to help make that happen.

He hit the landing between thirteen and fourteen exactly as he heard the second shot, this one from a shotgun at the other end of the building. "Shit," Rough muttered. "Hammer."

Below him, Milk trailed Rough by more than a flight. He swore again and called down for Milk to hurry it up.

At the next landing, on fourteen, he hit the door and opened it hard. No one stood in the hallway, just a clear path down to the other end and the opposite stairwell. If Hammer was at that end of the building, Rough wanted to be on those stairs when he got close to the action.

He waited for Milk to come into view and then started for the other end of the hallway at a run.

Seven made his way up the last few steps to twenty-one with his back against the wall. He had his gun trained on the next staircase the whole way, but by the time he reached the top step, he knew the next flight was empty. Whoever had fired had moved on.

Seven pushed back against the wall and up sideways until he felt his shoulder rub the edge of the doorframe.

He'd never done this before but had seen the cops on TV, T.J. Hooker especially, do the duck in to check a room enough times to know how it was done. He raised the Tec to his chest and set it to full auto. Whoever was down that hallway better be ready.

Seven stood silent, loaded for bear.

He heard someone yell at the far end, and then another blast from the shotgun. Hammer wouldn't care who he went after or what kind of property damage he did. Hammer was Lamar's boy. They were both crazy.

Seven had heard Junius's and two more guns; he knew there could be more.

He did the quick, slight turn around the corner so he could tell if anyone was close to him. No one was.

The next move, he figured, meant holding the gun between his bent knees and spinning into the doorway while he swung his arms up to point the gun down the hall. In his head, he could picture Hooker's boy, Adrian Zmed, doing this. Adrian Zmed, that pussy from *Dance Fever* who always took his shirt off. No, that was not the guy he'd copy.

Instead he ducked his head around the corner again, getting a better look down the hall: he made out the back of someone's black track suit.

Seven swore into the quiet. He'd never pulled and fired on someone, but this time there was no chance to ask questions. He'd come all the way inside Rock's tower, just below the man's floor, and now he only had room to act.

He nodded to himself, agreeing with it. Even if Junius wasn't the one to slide up on Rock and make things different, even if Marlene had been wrong to send a boy to do a man's job, it was still the right job to do. They saw what crack was doing to their people, and it was time to take a stand.

Seven closed his eyes and tried to clear his mind; he saw Adrian Zmed with no shirt on. That was enough to pop his eyes back open. He wanted to swear again, louder this time, but he didn't dare. Instead he ducked to his left as he raised the Tec-9 in both hands—arms out straight—and dropped down onto one knee in the doorway.

Halfway down the hall one of Hammer's boys, Deacon Speakin, crept toward Junius.

Seven opened a quick burst from the Tec that punched a series of holes in the back of Speakin's black sweatshirt. He turned around, and Seven lit him up again.

Speakin fell against the wall and then down onto his knees. He looked at Seven with empty eyes and then fell forward onto his face. His legs scrambled for a few moments, and then he was still.

That was all it took: a turn, a few fast, quiet bursts from the Tec, and the boy was down. Seven had fired about twelve shots in that quick moment, all of them hitting home.

From somewhere above him, Seven heard the persistent sound of a dog barking: Rock's Bonnie.

He stood and stepped into the hall.

Black Jesus and Mike Only sat in Mike's apartment smoking cigarettes and listening to *Bitches Brew* by Miles Davis, the latest jazz album they were trying to figure out. They'd made their way through Coltrane and Charlie Parker, started at *Kind of Blue* for Miles and got hooked. They understood *Sketches of Spain* well enough and decided it wasn't their thing.

They fell in love with Herbie Hancock's *Headhunters* and *Watermelon Man* even before *Beverly Hills Cop* and "Axle F." But Miles kept changing things up, was an enigma they felt deserved more attention and listening before they could fully understand all he'd done. The first few times they heard *Bitches Brew*, they had no idea what Miles was thinking, though they could imagine what he'd smoked.

Mike sat on his Eames lounge chair, the one luxury indulgence in his apartment, and Black Jesus sat on the old couch. He bent forward toward the coffee table, holding his Kool over the ashtray.

"That," Mike said, after a familiar refrain that could have been stolen from "So What."

Black Jesus nodded. He took the ashtray off the coffee table and leaned back into the couch. If Mike had an ashtray balanced on the arm of his chair, there was no reason why he shouldn't have his own also.

The phone rang.

"Shit," Mike said. "That be him, then."

Black Jesus ground his smoke into the ashtray and picked up the phone. "Yo."

Rock's voice came through the line. "You heard that?"

"Huh uh. What?"

"Shit popping off now. You best get on up."

"Berry wilding?"

"Worse. Hammer letting off blasts. I'm a leave Berry in the place, pack my Uzi and go out."

In the background, Bonnie barked like she was really after something.

"We coming." Black Jesus hung up the phone and stood. Mike was already up. He cut the record player just in time for them to hear a blast from a few floors above.

"Shotgun," Mike said. "That's Hammer."

Black Jesus had already pulled his S & W .44 from his shoulder harness and flipped open the cylinder. Just like always, the first slot sat empty. He pulled another round from his jacket pocket and slipped it in.

Elf stood in the hallway on fifteen in front of the elevator. He could hear the creaky old car moving inside its shaft. That was when he heard a strange sound: something echoed loud in the stairwell on his right.

He stopped and listened. He knew it had been a gunshot from the floors above—where Junius would probably be. If Junius still had Seven's Tec-9, the one with the silencer, it was *not* a shot from his gun.

He turned back to the elevator and definitely heard the car moving close to him. He jabbed at the call button and it lit up just as he could hear the car pass above. He'd missed it by less than a few feet, and now he could hear it keep on going.

"Fuck!" He pounded his hand on the door of the elevator just before he heard another blast from above, this one even louder than the first.

Dee turned to Ness in the elevator. "You hear something?" he asked.

He'd heard a couple of different sounds, all of them muffled, but one sounded close, as if someone was banging on the outside doors of the elevator. "The fuck was that?"

Ness didn't say anything, still had his eyes closed, so Dee shoved him against the wall. He fell easily, slumped down and then started to collect himself.

"The fuck?"

"You hear that, niggah?"

Then Dee heard something much louder, a shotgun blast from above. "Goddamn," he said, reaching for his gun.

Big Pickup didn't see Roughneck, Black Jesus, or Hammer out front of 412. He saw the sun dipped low behind the Polynesian place, almost gone from sight, and the cold of dusk sweeping trash along between parked cars. The night's first star and a thin crescent moon hung over the horizon.

The police cars had all gone, and the front of the towers was like a dead zone. Perfect time for sales to pick up.

Pickup patted his chest over his heart as he made his way toward Rock's building. An older man crossed the parking lot from the direction of the T, heading his direction. The man looked like he'd been through some hard shit, maybe even a fight in the last few days. He walked with his coat open, like even the cold didn't bother him now.

Pickup knew this man wasn't from the towers. At first, he didn't recognize him, but then about ten feet from the doors, he knew him as the old drunk who was father to Temple and Junius.

Lord only knew what he meant to do in Rock's building. If he tried to go in playing drunken savior, especially without a gun, it would not turn out well.

Pickup gave him a nod when they were closer, held the lobby door open for the older man. "What up?"

"Ain't shit up," the father said. He didn't exchange Pickup's nod or meet his eyes, just walked inside the tower and crossed the lobby straight to the elevator. There he pressed the call button and waited.

Pickup followed him in. He saw signs of a mess on the floor tiles, what was left of a bloody struggle, but he didn't think much of it. There'd be more spilled blood in this tower soon, he would bet.

Junius had lowered himself onto his haunches and slid along the wall into the lowest corner when the first blast from the shotgun came. It hit the wall above him and to his left. A shower of plaster rained down.

"I'm coming for you, motherfucker!" Hammer's voice was unmistakeable.

Junius slid to his right, toward the next down staircase, still holding the gun up at the end of the twenty-first floor hallway, hoping he wouldn't see the guy who'd fired the first shot come out of it, but also watching to see if Hammer would come around the corner.

He ground his bottom molars against the tops.

A stream of thoughts flew through his head, but he tried to concentrate on his sight and just breathe. So far it was only two people coming. He knew there'd be more soon: Rock, Black Jesus, and he had no idea who else. He definitely didn't want to see Clarence.

He would hold his ground here, not continue down. Maybe he could get the jump on Hammer or his boy.

"Yeah," he said softly, steeling himself for what was to come. "Yeah, motherfucker. This your time."

He inched back toward the stairs, keeping his head well below where the first shot hit, his gun trained on the next hallway. He held his arms straight, ready for the recoil of the Tec or to swing the gun up if Hammer started down.

"I'm coming for you," Hammer said again. It sounded like he was on the landing just above. Hammer was waiting.

In the hall on twenty-one, Junius heard the quick whistle of another Tec firing through a silencer. It fired much faster than his. He heard Hammer swearing and then he fired the shotgun again, this time into the hallway; Junius saw the blast eat up the second door on the hall.

Another quick burst came from the hall above, more whistles from a Tec. Junius didn't know who could be firing. A series of bullets sparked against the black metal railing above him.

Junius stayed put, holding his gun ready, both hands on the grip.

Seven stepped into the hall and went down on one knee again as he fired. God help Junius if he was down the other end of the hall, but Seven wanted to scare Hammer back. If Hammer fired again, let off down the hall while Seven was walking it, he'd get carved up, plain and simple.

So he fired off a few rounds. As long as Rock and his boys stayed on twenty-two, Seven could handle things, but a partner to watch the other stairs could help. Maybe Junius, even as young as he was.

"Yo, Junius," Seven called down the hall.

No answer came back for a few breaths. "Just us killers down here," Hammer called back. He fired his shotgun again, ate up another chunk of the wall.

Seven wondered how many cartridges the shotgun held. He heard its slide pulled back and knocked forward.

"Yo, J?" Seven tried again, hoping to let Junius know he was here.

"Who that?"

"Seven Heaven, Junius! I just took one boy down and now I'm a come for Hammer. Stay where you is to back me up."

Seven saw movement at Junius's end of the hall, then Hammer was at the open end, and he fired the shotgun down the hall. Seven fell back against the closest doorway, but he still felt the sting of buck-shot penetrating his shoulder.

Hammer turned fast to shoot down the stairs, but Junius was good, got a few shots off that made him duck back out of sight. He might even have taken a hit.

"You feel that?" Seven called.

"Yeah, niggah. How about you?"

Seven bit his lip, wouldn't answer to give Hammer the pleasure. "I'm coming," he said.

Officer Johnson heard the sound of the first blast as soon as he left Clarence's apartment. He expected to go straight to the hospital, turn in his badge and gun and get the treatment he required. He didn't care how long it took or how long he'd be out on disability, either. The crime on the streets could take care of itself.

But then he heard what sounded like a shotgun, and he felt the call of a whole new situation.

"Fuck," he said, limping toward the elevator. He checked the cylinder of his gun, saw it had just been fired twice. Steadying him-self against the side of the hallway, he pulled two shells off his belt, took out the empties, and slid in the new. Then he flipped the cylin-der closed.

He tapped his belt with his left hand, feeling the hard nightstick hanging where it should. He started moving again, his right forearm bracing him against the wall with each step, the S & W 60 in his hand the whole time.

He would take the elevator to the floors above and find out exactly what was going on. Banged up and hurting or if he was even shot—*thank God he wasn't*—Johnson still owed it to the city and its people to investigate a shot fired in a residential tower. Even with a population as fucked up as Clarence and the rest of his crew, Johnson couldn't give them all up. There were good people who lived in this tower.

He pushed the call button when he got to the elevator shaft, and it didn't light. That was when he heard a second shot.

Junius thought he'd hit Hammer.

And Seven Heaven was above him in the next hallway. How Seven got this far into Rock's building, Junius didn't know, but at least now he wasn't alone.

He'd hit Hammer. It wasn't a body shot and wouldn't kill or stop him, but Junius had fired before Hammer could shoot the shotgun and that had saved his ass, at least for now.

He sat on his heels, looking up and waiting for Hammer's next move. That was when he heard a sound on the stairs below him and dove sideways, flat along the ground against the wall. If someone was coming up from below, they had to come up a lot farther to see him if he was flat to the floor. He pulled his legs in, trying to keep them from where Hammer would be able to see if he turned down the stairwell again.

Another quick burst of shots—the familiar whistle of Seven's Tec—echoed against the railing above. Junius heard more sounds from the stairs below him and crawled forward to get a look. He pulled himself along by his forearms, keeping his head low.

Someone told someone else to hold up.

Junius peeked over the top of the stairs: he saw Roughneck and Milk below him on the next landing, Milk holding a big, silver gun pointed right at Junius.

He pulled his head back fast and heard Roughneck swear, then hit something. Milk fired, but it sounded like the shot went high, way over the landing.

"Fuck you doing?" Milk said.

7 3

Rock told Berry Rich to stay in the bedroom. She started panicking as soon as she heard the first shots in the hall, and Bonnie started barking too. Problem was, if Bonnie got too worked up and there was a stranger around, you didn't know how she might act.

Better for Berry Rich to keep her beautiful body up in the bedroom, save those pretty legs and arms.

He took his top gun, the Uzi, out of the cabinet by the door. Even knowing her as well as he did, paying for all that damned training, Rock couldn't look at Bonnie now without having just a little worry. She'd never been worked up like this before, gone this wild.

She snapped her long canines at the door, slobber starting to foam and drip around her mouth. Rock considered just letting her go out there and tear at whoever was causing the fuss, but he knew Hammer was the closest and either he or his boy Deacon Speakin would get torn up. He also knew he couldn't take it if Bonnie got shot.

"Shut it," he yelled. "Down, girl!"

Rock stuffed three clips for the Uzi into the pockets of his black track-suit and pulled on the jacket with no shirt underneath. Damned if he had time to find one now.

At the door, he shoved Bonnie out of the way, got it open just enough to squeeze through, and slid out into the hall. He shut the door fast to keep her inside.

Bonnie's barking sounded even louder now in the hall, but not loud enough that Rock didn't hear the elevator chime its arrival on his floor and turn with his gun ready. He didn't know where Hammer or Speakin were, but they weren't in the hall and he was the only one here to protect it. He raised his Uzi at the elevator doors and watched for who'd come out.

As the doors slid open, he heard someone inside fall. Then he heard laughing.

"Who the fuck there?" he asked, just before he heard a quick burst of shots from a silenced gun coming from a lower floor—too close. He'd be damned if he was ready for a war in his tower today. Not when he'd just spent all morning fucking and shooting his precious juice.

"Bring your ass out," he said to the open elevator, and Dee stumbled into the hallway. Dee, one of the young ones coming up under Clarence, a corner boy who worked the Alewife bus stops. The boy looked stoned as hell, his eyes like slits, his shoulders slumped. He didn't even have his gun drawn.

"Who with you? And where the fuck your gun is?"

Dee reared his head back like it took that effort to open his eyes wide. Then Ness fell out of the elevator as if someone had tipped up the car and shook him out. He fell against Dee.

"Damn," Dee said.

Hammer's shotgun went off again in the stairwell and Rock turned to look. The sound got the boys' attention. They both stood up straight, and Ness even shook his head like he was trying to jar something free.

"You hear me now," Rock asked. "Where your guns?"

Dee lifted his shirt and took a Walther by the handle; Ness pulled a Tec-9 from inside his coat.

"We up," Dee said, his eyes still narrow.

"Right." The elevator doors closed. "Hit that!" Rock pointed to the call button, hoping to keep the car on his floor and avoid any further surprises, but by the time Ness reacted, the car had started its way back down.

"Fuck me! We got shit popping off up here! This real. Now wake the fuck up and get ready to defend yourselves!"

"Clarence kept us up all night watching that boy Junius's momma's house. Then we—"

Rock shook his head. "I don't give a good *fuck* about that shit." He pointed up the hallway. "Get your ass down those stairs and find out what the fuck going on."

They started down the hall.

As soon as it occurred to Rock, he asked, "Where C Dub at?"

Dee turned back and shrugged, said he didn't know.

Rock wanted to hit somebody.

He squeezed the grip of his Uzi and ground his teeth. "Get gone." He waved them toward the other end of the hall.

As he started toward Hammer's stairwell, he heard another quick whistle of shots.

Milk pulled his arms away from Rough's hands. "That's that niggah we supposed to want dead."

"Shit ain't right. He just young."

"*Right?* Who say right? That niggah kill Lamar. Rock put out his
all-points APB!"

"He just a kid. Let him be." Rough couldn't see Junius on the landing; he'd ducked at the sight of the gun and had to still be lying low.

"Yo, Junius," Rough said. "I'm coming up. It's cool." Milk still
held the big Charter Arms in front of his chest, and Rough tried to
take it.

Milk wouldn't let go. "Nah, niggah. You crazy? There be shots up
in here and I'm keeping my fucking gun."

"Then don't fuck with Junius."

Milk met Rough's eyes. They'd been friends for a long time,
longer than either had worked for Rock. Milk had two hands on the
gun to Rough's one, but Rough outweighed Milk by more than fifty
pounds; he could take the gun if he really wanted.

"Ok," Milk said, finally. "I leave him be, but no way I give up the
gat."

Rough let go. He turned up the stairs, showing Milk his back. If Milk was going to choose Rock over him and take a shot, Rough wanted to know sooner instead of later.

When he got halfway up the next set of steps, he saw Junius go from a prone position to a crouch, a Tec-9 in his hands trained on the next set of stairs up.

"Who shooting?"

Junius shook his head. "Hammer and his boy. Plus Seven up on the next floor. I'm not sure if he hit, but I think I touched Hammer one time."

Junius looked scared: he was dug in like an animal in its hole, and his right eye twitched as he watched the stairs. The muscles flexed along his jaw.

"It's cool," Rough said. "All gone be all right."

"How you know?"

Then Hammer yelled down the stairway. "Roughneck! Shoot that niggah. What be wrong with you? Motherfucker up here to kill Rock!"

Rough heard Milk from behind him. "I'm saying."

"We settle this without the guns. What this shit about? This about who killed Temple? Lamar?"

Junius nodded.

"No! Not no more it ain't!" Hammer called down. "Fuck that shit! This niggah shot me. Now this be about blood, war, and his ass!"

Milk said, "War, motherfucker. Now who the fuck's side you on?"

Rough stopped. He wanted to hear Milk say "we"— "whose side we on"—but he knew he hadn't. Milk was saying "you" now, like this was going to turn into every man for himself, or like Rough wasn't calling the shots for them both.

"Yeah, motherfucker," Hammer called again. "You not gone help me defend our tower?"

Junius narrowed his eyes.

"Get that somebitch," Hammer commanded.

Roughneck heard a series of shots from the next floor up, a quick burst from a silenced automatic—Seven's gun.

On the fifteenth floor, Elf heard the elevator approaching him in its shaft again. He pushed the "Up" call button.

He'd heard a few more shots coming from above, shots that sounded like they came from the stairwells, and that was enough to keep him from walking up. Whatever he was getting himself into, it was going down and he didn't need to rush. He wanted to get his man Junius the fuck out, but still.

He gripped the Smith & Wesson tighter, felt the sweaty handle against his hot palm. He would not drop this gun, but he might be a little nervous. He transferred it into his other hand and wiped his right palm on the thigh of his jeans.

The elevator sounded close. He fell back along the wall, holding the gun up by his head. He'd be ready if the car opened and someone stood inside. Just like the shit with Lamar yesterday, Elf had come through and was ready now to step up and be a man.

He knew how to shoot a gun, had played Duck Hunt for hours with his brother.

The elevator came to his floor, creaking down the shaft, and kept going. The call button light stayed on.

"The fuck?" he asked.

He looked at the other call button: the still-dark button to go down. No, he hadn't pushed that one; he'd made the decision not to go home.

Seven found himself breathing hard in the middle of the hallway. He's seen Junius hit Hammer, he thought, and he'd fired again in that direction, but it was just to keep Hammer back. He hadn't hit anything but the railing of the stairs.

Now was as good a time as any to change clips. He could hear Hammer yelling at the end of the hall, calling down to Junius and someone else about what to do.

Deacon Speakin lay not ten feet from him on the floor, still as a coffin, gun in his hand.

Seven's left shoulder stung from the buckshot, but he knew it wasn't going to fuck with him. He wouldn't lose a lot of blood; the shit was just going to hurt. Hammer was a son of a bitch was what Hammer was; Seven had never liked him—Hammer and Lamar always on the other team in baseball, cheating and causing some shit. He bit his lip.

That was when he saw a fast movement on the stairs to his right, back the way he'd just come.

It was feet moving, not even someone being careful or coming down slow; they just walked down like it was a normal day. Seven reached across his body and aimed the Tec down the hall at the stairs. When he saw the legs come around the landing and hit the next flight, he ripped off a quick stream of shots that dashed along them just below the kneecaps.

The man on the stairs crumpled, screaming. He fell forward down the steps and rolled head over ass once before he stopped.

Seven saw it was Ness, just another of Rock's street soldiers. He had a Tec-9 in one hand, but he let it go and got his hands up fast, which was good because Seven wasn't planning on waiting to let him think it over.

Down in the lobby, Pickup waited for the elevator with the older man, trying not to attract too much attention and watching the stairways on either side to make sure no one was able to creep up. The old man ignored him, acted like he didn't want to acknowledge that he was in the towers now, on Pickup's turf.

"You Temple's father, right?" Pickup asked.

Aldo Posey shook his head, stared straight ahead at the elevator doors. He pushed the call button again.

"That was your boy."

Aldo bit his upper lip, didn't respond.

"Yeah. I know Temple. Good pitcher in his time. Threw the heat." Still no response. "Junius your boy too, then?" This got a quick glance in Pickup's direction, then back to the doors.

"Yeah. I seen him here today earlier. You come down to find him?" The older man gave a slight nod.

"I figured. But you don't have to worry, he didn't get hurt in that shooting we had up on the roof. I seen to that myself."

"Shooting?"

Pickup shrugged. "Just some shit. But I got him out. He all right last I seen him."

Pickup saw more of the other man's face now, and that he hadn't been drinking today, though it looked like that was having an effect for the worse—his skin looked gray, his eyes bloodshot and small.

"But now he up in the wrong house."

Pickup wished he had something he could offer the old man for a pull. He patted his jacket where the Tec was, hitting it extra hard with his ring finger so his gold clinked against the steel of the gun. "It be all right, though. I'm here to help him, so he be ok."

"I wish you wouldn't do that for him. He in enough trouble already." The father knew what he was saying, had seen enough to know exactly what his son was involved in. "This my family," he said. "And I take care of it."

"Can't do that now," Pickup said. "This be my business. He in my towers."

Aldo Posey turned away; he faced the elevator doors again and took another step forward, moving away from Pickup.

He shook his head and said, "Leave my boy alone," without meeting Pickup's eyes. Then he pushed the call button.

Rock heard one of the boys he'd just sent down cry out in pain from the stairwell. By the sound of it, someone had shot him up bad. Rock could only hear the screams.

When he glanced down that end of the hall, he saw Dee, the other one, staring back, unsure of what to do. Rock pointed one finger and then made a pronounced movement down so Dee knew with no uncertainty where he was supposed to go. If someone was shooting at you, you crept up on them and took them out. You did not turn around and ask for more orders.

If he'd had this crew with him when he went through boot camp for the Marines, they'd have all gotten buried. He looked at Dee again, saw him start down like he was supposed to. Then again, even back in boot camp he'd been older than these boys by a few years.

He made his way toward Hammer's end of the hall, Bonnie still barking in his apartment.

"Yo, Hammer," Rock called. "Please hurt those motherfuckers!"

From the stairwell the shotgun blasted out, followed by the sound of Hammer chambering a new cartridge and shooting again.

"Yeah," Rock yelled. He let off a spray from his Uzi down the stairs, cutting into the plaster.

"Hear that, motherfuckers? This Rock, baby! Coming to get ya!"

He stepped up the hall.

Seven saw Ness still holding his hands up, crawling back up the stairs without his gun. Tears glistened on his cheeks.

Rock was yelling on the floor above them—yelling and shooting off his Uzi for no cause. Seven would be damned if he let one of his buildings come to shit in a fight like this. Shooting up your own walls and doors? It just didn't make sense.

But Rock probably figured he'd bring in workmen tomorrow, get them to spackle and paint over the whole mess for just a few hundred dollars. He was probably right, but the people who lived here— they'd find bullet holes in their walls, their space torn up like a war went down. And how could they not care, not know everything was wrong? Even if they weren't home now, cowering in their bathrooms as they heard the shots, they would know and realize it was time to move. If they could.

They had no choice. That was why they'd stay; there was simply nowhere else for them.

Maybe Rock figured a few hundred dollars' worth of spackle was a small price to pay for defending his home, but Seven wanted something better for the people who lived here: better than watching those around them turned to zombies by a new drug, better than living in a war zone.

Seven wanted to explain himself to the people in the hallway. He wanted to tell them why he was doing this: for *them*.

Rock yelled down for Hammer to start shooting, and Hammer bucked off another shotgun blast on the stairs.

He loaded again, and Seven was watching for him, but he didn't bring the Tec across his body fast enough.

Hammer spun into view and leveled the shotgun at his waist. Seven saw the barrel flash and he squeezed himself up against the doorway to hide. Buckshot chipped the wall in front of him, but the bulk of the spray carried on down the hall. He felt the front of his sweatshirt, looked down to see if he was hit. He wasn't, but standing in the middle of this hallway where people could take shots at him from both ends was no kind of place to be.

"Fuck this," he said, resigning himself to damaging Rock's building. He shot a few rounds into the lock and handle of the door across the hall, and kicked it open with all he had.

The door banged against the inside wall, slapped back against its frame, and fell open. As it did, Seven saw a sudden movement from the end of the hall where Ness was, heard the loud report of a handgun and a bullet ricochet off a wall.

He hoped there wouldn't be a family freaking out inside, yelled out a warning and jumped through the doorway and into the living room of the apartment across the hall.

The elevator doors creaked open in the lobby, and Pickup stood aside to let Aldo Posey go first. The older man crossed to the back of the elevator and stared at the buttons, waiting to tell Pickup his floor.

"Which one you want?" Pickup asked.

"Fifteen."

Pickup pushed the button, ready to let the old man get off and do whatever he needed to. If Junius was really going after Rock, he'd be on a higher floor. Pickup pushed the top button, then thought better of it and pushed the button for twenty as well, not sure he wanted to end up right in front of Rock.

"All the way up, huh?"

"I need to see the man."

"That's right, then. You see him. But if he has my boy with him, tell him I'm taking Junius on home."

"I can do that. Unless you want to just come and tell him yourself."

The older man shook his head. "No. I need to see an old friend first, find out what all this is about."

The doors crept shut and the elevator shuttered, then started crawling up the shaft. Pickup turned to face front, his hand inside his jacket on the grip of his Tec, his finger outside the trigger guard. Now was not the time to get jumpy.

The old man started to whistle as the elevator climbed, and the whistling made Pickup nervous. But he'd be damned if he would ask the old man to stop.

Pickup felt the elevator slow. He squeezed the Tec, brought his finger onto the trigger.

The elevator came to a complete stop and the bell chimed. Pickup raised the barrel of his gun, still inside his jacket.

Aldo Posey stopped whistling.

The doors opened slowly to reveal a cop: the last thing Big Pickup wanted to see. He pushed his finger hard against the front of the trigger guard, making sure with every bit of him that he didn't panic and let off shots. This wasn't what he was here for, and he hoped this cop wasn't here for him.

Pickup pointed the gun back down, took his hand out of his

jacket, and folded one hand in the other; he cupped the two in front of his groin like a boy in a choir.

The cop's face looked gray, like he'd lost a lot of blood. His cop life-force had been drained out and he was running on fumes. The side of his face was one big bruised cut from the forehead to his chin, but his eyes were cold.

He looked to Aldo and then to Pickup as he stepped into the car. "Gentlemen."

He stepped in slowly, like his leg might have a broken bone, and then he turned around to face the front of the car just like Aldo and Pickup.

The elevator doors began to close.

As the car started its way up again, Aldo Posey resumed his whistling.

Junius heard a scream above him, from down at the other end of the hall. Whoever it was, that person was *in pain*. The scream sounded like they had just been stabbed in the eye, what you'd yell like if that happened.

Rock called down the stairs that he was coming, and Hammer fired off a couple more rounds. Rock tore shit up with whatever gun he had—something big and automatic. Junius did not want to get involved with that.

Roughneck was still partway up the steps to Junius's landing, looking like he wasn't sure what to do. He held his hands out empty in front of him.

"What now?" Junius asked.

"Yeah!" Milk came up next to Rough. He waited for an answer.

Roughneck shook his head. "I *know* Seven, man. Me and him came up together. This ain't just business."

Milk was older than Junius but too young to have grown up with Rough and Seven. He looked to be about as old as Temple.

"You known me a long-ass time, too," Milk said, his face sour. "You and 412 the only family I know. What it gone be?"

Rough looked down and chewed his lip. "You do what you need, then. But you not shooting this niggah here." He nodded at Junius.

Milk sucked his teeth. "This shit ain't right. Brothers choosing new sides, splitting shit up? Huh uh." He waved a hand at Rough, dismissing him, and started back down the stairs toward twenty. "You don't know what you want? I'm ass out. Come get me when you know who we play for."

Rough watched him go. He called to wait, and Milk turned on the landing, looking up before taking the next flight. He raised his eyebrows. "What?"

"I respect that."

"Get with me when you know your shit right."

With that, Milk kept going down the stairs. Rough turned back to Junius. "What can I say? Ain't no one way in this game. Not no right and true always. Sometimes? Ain't even no *up*."

Rough stepped up the stairs. "You hear that? Don't trust no one: Marlene, Rock, Big Willie? No one. They all fuck you over."

"But not you?"

A new voice spoke behind Roughneck, a very deep voice. "You done talking shit?"

Rough turned. From the next landing down, Black Jesus held a cannon on him.

In his hand, Black Jesus had the biggest gun Junius had ever seen. It looked like the gun from the Dirty Harry movies, the one where he said, "Go ahead … make my day."

But no one was copping any dumb lines, and the gun looked even bigger in real life than it did on the screen.

"Shit," Junius said under his breath. "There you is."

Elf waited on fifteen for the elevator. He could hear it rumbling in the shaft, getting closer, and he tightened his grip on the pistol. He heard his own breaths. The building had gone completely silent except for the shots from above, as if everyone turned off their TVs and radios and stopped talking to listen—like the whole building waited, wondering and thinking about what would happen next.

Elf listened to the movement of the elevator and waited like the rest.

When the elevator bell let out a "ding" above him, Elf started. He stayed still as the doors crept open, and then he turned fast to look inside the car and smacked right into Mr. Posey.

Elf knocked him back into the car and stumbled. A blue uniform cop who looked half-dead caught Mr. Posey.

"I'm sorry," Elf said.

"You my boy's friend?"

The cop helped Mr. Posey get firm on his feet.

"What up, boy?" Big Pickup stood in the back of the car, next to the cop and behind Junius's father. The scene was getting weirder to Elf by the moment. Then he heard another shot from above, the loud blast of Hammer's shotgun.

"Let's go," the cop said. "Move along now."

Mr. Posey stepped out of the car, and Elf stepped in. "You know where my son is?" he asked, turning to look back into the car.

Elf shook his head. "Maybe up top," he said. "That's where I think he be."

Mr. Posey just looked at him, squinting as if big thoughts were running through his head. The elevator doors started to close. He lifted his hand as if to stop them, but then pulled it back. He looked confused, like a man unsettled, pushed out of his place.

"What up, son?" Big Pickup asked when the doors had closed.

"Nothing. What up?"

The car started its climb.

The buttons for twenty and twenty-two were lit. Elf decided he'd get off on twenty. Anything he could do to keep from going right to Rock sounded good. He tried not to look at the cop. He didn't want to seem odd, but he couldn't help himself. He wanted to see how much the cop was alive.

"You come with me," Pickup told Elf. It was not the first time Elf wanted to question the day's decisions.

As they neared the top, the cop pulled his gun. Elf took a step back, bumped into Pickup, and then found himself shoved against the doors of the car. He turned and the cop was staring him in the face.

"What?"

"Huh?"

"Where you think you're going? Don't you know there's trouble up here?"

Elf swallowed hard. "I'm looking for my friend. He's—"

"Go back on down," the cop said.

"Enough of this shit!" Pickup pulled his arm out of his jacket fast and, before anyone could move, he had the barrel of his Tec up against the back of the cop's head.

"You in the wrong place, blue boy. Now you the one don't know what the fuck you doing."

The cop didn't say anything, just turned to look at Pickup, the gun barrel sliding across his bald head as he did, tripping past his ear to rest at the corner of his forehead. His eyes were cold, thin. "What you gone do, boy? You want to shoot me right here in the head?"

Pickup didn't move. The car kept rising.

"Do it then. Show me what you got!"

Pickup moved fast: he hit the cop in the back of his head— just where the skull meets the neck—with his elbow. It was what Elf heard the boys at football practice call a "forearm shiver," but the cop didn't shake. Instead he fell hard into the corner of the elevator, slumping to the floor like the sack of skin and bones he looked like he was. Pickup didn't wait to see what'd happen next; he turned the Tec in his hand and brought the side of the barrel down hard against the top of the cop's head. Then he reared back and backhand-slapped him again across the side of the face with it.

The cop fell onto his side and didn't get up.

Elf blinked. "You serious?"

Pickup just laughed, wiped the barrel of the Tec off on his pants. "Where we going, we don't be needing no police. Now get your ass ready."

Elf nodded once and reached around to his back for the Smith & Wesson.

The elevator stopped. They were on twenty.

"What up, son?" Rough turned all the way around to face Black Jesus. Mike Only stood to his side, holding a semi-auto .45 on Junius. Rough stepped in front of it.

"Son, the fuck you doing?" Black Jesus said. "Stand back."

Rough shook his head. "Can't do."

He didn't know what he *could* do, only that he had to be here to stop them from killing Junius.

"The fuck you say?" Mike Only stepped around Black Jesus to get a clearer look. "You sure you know what you doing?"

"No."

"Say what?"

"I said, 'No.' But this where I be. And you not coming through me."

"What he say?" Mike Only turned to Black Jesus in disbelief.

"This where it ends," Rough said. "No more. We got niggahs wild up above, Seven and Hammer trying to kill each other, and killing *this* kid for Lamar ain't gone make none of it right."

Black Jesus put one foot on the bottom stair of the flight. "We here for Rock. People fucking with this building, we protect it."

"This boy ain't about fucking with Rock." Rough nodded at where Junius was. "He just young, don't know what he doing. Let me get him out."

From above them, Rock screamed: an angry yell like he was going into some kind of impersonation of the last scene in *Scarface*, trying to shoot up everything in the building. He followed it with another long blast from the Uzi, though Rough couldn't guess who it was directed at.

"Rock just crazy. Has been. You know that."

Black Jesus paused to look at Mike Only, and it was Mike who spoke. "Nah. You the one acting crazy. We represent. This a family. Family where Rock be the head."

"My man," Rough said. "But we leave this kid."

"Yo, Hammer!" Mike Only called as he started to climb the stairs. Rough looked up and got caught completely off guard by a series of shots from right behind him, a quick whistling burst from Junius's Tec.

He spun and saw Junius flat on his chest. He'd crawled forward to the edge of the landing to look down at Black Jesus and Mike Only. Now he'd fired on Black Jesus and all this was going to get crazy real fast.

"For my brother," Junius said.

Rough spun back around in time to see Black Jesus fall. He bent in the middle like he'd been punched, his chest caving in toward the stairs, and as he fell, his gun went off. Mike Only turned fast to see his man, firing blind in Junius's direction.

All Rough could do was duck against the railing.

"Mother fuck!" Mike Only caught Black Jesus and held him up.

Rough saw a blood bubble form over Black J's lips. He turned to Junius. "The *fuck?*" he asked.

Junius was up against the wall now with his gun in front of him, pointed at Mike Only.

Mike pulled Black Jesus to him, smearing blood across the front of his jacket. His chin went all wrinkles and his eyes were squeezed tight. "Fuck," he said, drawing out the word in a groan.

"Goddamn," Rough said. He thought about stepping to Junius and taking away his gun, but instead he went forward, to Mike Only, and that was a mistake.

"Killed my brother," Junius said so softly that no one seemed to hear. "Killed—" But he couldn't say it again. He saw the pain in how Black Jesus went down and now he saw the hurt on Mike Only's face: more than just the hurt of losing a friend, he looked like he lost his brother.

And that was when Junius understood there was no revenge or payback or evening out the pain.

There would always be new mourning in the long fucked-up war that was these towers, all of their projects, everything he knew.

It didn't matter.

In the bigger sense it was all a circle, just a snake eating itself; all the people he knew killing one another: his brother gone, Lamar's brothers losing him, and now anyone who was close to Black Jesus had lost one of theirs. Same for Jason, killed on the roof because Elf fucked up. Should someone come after Elf and take him down because he caused that?

Probably not.

There wasn't any taking things back.

Maybe if he waited—*and lived*—long enough he'd have a chance to take out Rock. And maybe that'd be worth something.

Or maybe it wouldn't.

Rough stepped toward Mike Only.

"The *fuck*!" Mike yelled, with tears in his voice. Junius heard a shot, and Rough spun half-around, fell against the railing holding his shoulder.

"Fuck *you*!" Mike was saying, standing now and shooting up the stairs.

Junius broke to his left, unconsciously shooting in Mike's direction. Then the Tec clicked on nothing and the bolt shot forward. The trigger wouldn't pull.

Mike started up the stairs at him, shooting, but Rough tripped him up. He grabbed Mike Only, and they both went down backward toward the landing below them, Mike still firing as he fell.

Junius heard himself say, "Shit," and then he saw Hammer.

First Hammer ducked into the hall and fired, then he started to turn Junius's way. He yanked at the clip in his Tec and it was stuck. He pulled it again, then found the release. Now the clip came free. With it in his hand, Junius didn't waste any time: he threw the magazine at Hammer with all he had, his best pitcher's motion, but it spun wild and barely glanced off his shoulder.

Hammer shrugged and pumped another cartridge into the shotgun's breech. He shook his head in what looked like disgust.

Junius patted at his pants with his left hand until he came across another clip. He jammed it into the Tec and the bolt shot forward.

Hammer shook his head and leveled the shotgun at Junius's chest.

Clarence lay on the floor at the foot of his bed. He'd managed to crawl as far as that, just drag his body, really; with the pain in his chest, what felt like a broken collarbone, and a bullet in one of his shins, he couldn't do much more than pull with one arm and push with the one good leg. He was moving, though, and what more could anyone ask of him.

That he still had one rock in his pocket was getting him through.

It hadn't been an entirely bad day. He'd beaten the shit out of his first cop, ever, payback for a lifetime of anger at any shit a pig had ever put on him—beat-downs, eye-fuckings, interrogations, arrests, and general bullshit. All of it. This was for that.

He'd taken that much out on the pig and that motherfucker would not be walking right for a long time. He'd seen the pain in his eyes. Shit, he'd even dragged that bitch out of the lobby unconscious, leaving a trail of cop's blood on the tiles.

The truth was, this shit they called the Ready—the Ready Rock—this shit was a ride like no other. And he still had one piece left.

All he had to do was get to the nightstand, find his Brillo and something to cook it in, and he'd be chalked up on another ride—

something he knew would get him over the pain enough so he could get to the phone, call himself an ambulance, and get some help.

But then he froze. What if he did go to the hospital? When they saw this shit, they'd know something bad went down and then maybe he'd have to hit the lockup. None of the sweet Ready in that piece.

"Fuck," he said. Then he had the best idea of the whole day: police brutality. That was all it had been, that asshole cop just beating on him for no reason. He did his best to protect himself, in self-defense of course, and look where it had left him. Just look at him: he was fucked up.

Just trying to protect himself from the cop who'd laid out Pooh.

It was as good a start as any, and all that was *after* he smoked the rock he had. Maybe just doing that would open up a whole new world of options.

He dug his right forearm into the floor, the thin red carpet worn smooth from years of getting in and out of bed. At the same time, he kicked with his leg, trying to dig his toes in to push toward the night stand. In his right hand, he held the little baggie with its precious content.

"This your ass on my dick," he said, and laughed. He'd said that to the cop before that motherfucker left. No, it was more like that egg-in-the-frying-pan TV commercial. *This is your brain. This your brain on drugs. Any questions?* That was it.

"This your brain on my dick."

Pausing to laugh made him feel just a little bit better.

Laughter, if it couldn't get you through, what could?

"Niggah, who your ass talking to?"

He looked up and saw Sheila, precious Sheila, returned from the far and gone.

"My baby," Clarence said. "You are a sight for sore motherfucking eyes! Where you been at?"

She held a hand up and sucked her teeth. "I ain't staying up in here with no cop around. That motherfucker gone?"

Clarence nodded. "He gone. Now give my ass that pipe and help me smoke this."

"Smoke what?"

"Bitch, what you talking about?"

Now Sheila put her hands on her hips and slid her head side to side. "Bitch, that what you calling me now? Because I don't see nobody else here you talking to."

Clarence closed his eyes. He breathed in, an act that actually hurt. Something got caught in his chest and he couldn't catch a full breath. But he had to calm down.

"Forget it, baby. Forget that, ok? You got my pipe? Baby? I thought I saw you walk out with it back when."

"You mean this?" Sheila produced the glass pipe out of her jeans-jacket. "This what you want?"

Clarence rolled back onto his side against the bed, relieved. He reached out to her with his good hand. "Pass it here."

"What you gone do with it?"

"Smoke this rock." He showed her the little baggie in his hand, gripping it tight between his thumb and his palm. She'd have to kill him to take it. Before she could start to bargain, he said, "Bit—baby, you let me hold that pipe and get mines. I definitely give you a hit of this sweetness, but you have to help old Clarence out. Clarence a bit fucked up here, you see?"

"Yeah, I see it," she said. "And momma gone be good to you now." She came over and sat on the floor next to him, her back against the bed. She held the pipe out in front of him, even showed him his lighter in her other hand. "I'm ready for you, baby. Let's smoke this."

"You gone be good to me?" Clarence asked her. He looked in her eyes and knew he couldn't trust whatever she'd say.

She winked at him. "I'm with you, baby," she said, and that was it: as good a comfort as he would get.

"Just help me smoke this. I only need a taste, girl. Old Clarence be hurting."

She smoothed her thumb across his temple and brushed it over his ear. His back and neck were starting to hurt. He opened his hand to her, held out the baggie. "Just—" But that was all he said.

She took it from him and squeezed the rock out its open end, broke off a piece and slid it down on the Brillo. He watched her heat it with the lighter.

Whatever was there on the other side of this ride, Clarence wasn't sure he wanted to know. But the ride, *that* was all he needed.

"I'm here now," Sheila said. She kissed the top of his head. "Momma be here for you now. Everything gone be ok."

When she melted the rock and it started to run, she held the pipe up to his mouth. She brushed a thumb across his cheek and brought the lighter up under the pipe. She flicked it once, then again and it caught, danced a little flame along the bottom of the glass.

Clarence could see the smoke.

Then he tasted the subtle change, the first touches of vapor along the back of his tongue. He sucked harder, taking in the smoke with everything he had.

Seven heard the shotgun blast at the end of the hall. He'd heard a lot of shots from that stairwell: everything from a semi-auto to a re-volver and, finally, somewhere in the middle of it all, the whistle of Junius's Tec. He heard yelling and more than one cry of pain. But what he hadn't heard again until now was the sound he'd been wait-ing for: Hammer shooting his shotgun down the hall.

Hammer wouldn't forget him, couldn't possibly now that he'd come this far. When he heard the shot tear down his hall, he knew it was worth a look out, that Hammer just might have fired to scare him back. If that was true, then this was his time to act.

He pushed up against the frame of the apartment door and looked out: first down toward Hammer's end and then back down the other. Nothing either way.

Then he leaned out even farther, watching for Hammer to be waiting. Instead he saw Hammer's back, the shotgun barrel coming up over his shoulder as he cocked it, and Seven took his chance.

Being right-handed, he had to come all the way out of the door to shoot down that end of the hall. He leaned out, stepping out of cover, and brought the Tec up fast to shoulder height with his arm extended.

All he knew at the other end was Hammer and possibly Rock, and if Junius was lucky, he'd be down the stairs and out of the line of fire.

Seven pulled the trigger.

Time slowed as he watched the individual bullets punch into Hammer's back and cut through the black cotton of his sweatshirt, letting up a patch of fabric and a burst of blood with each entry. Two shots went across Hammer's left shoulder and then another shot, then two and three crossed across his back.

Hammer stumbled forward, and that was when Seven heard the loudest shot he'd ever heard: the report from a handgun that sounded like it came from just a few feet behind him, echoing into his ear. As soon as he heard it, he wondered if it had just come, or if it had come a few seconds ago, when his world started to slow. All of a sudden, he didn't know how time worked anymore.

He fell hard against the doorframe, his Tec cutting a line of shots across the opposite wall, then fell into the apartment, rolled onto his back, and looked up to see Dee step into the doorframe. Dee, the one who rolled with Ness, who he'd shot on the stairs. The first thing he thought was he should have known better: where there was one, there was always the other.

But that wasn't as important as the second thing in his head: that he'd been shot—shot bad.

Junius was still raising his gun when the shots tore through Hammer. From the *quip, quip, quip* of the silencer, he knew it had to be Seven shooting, Seven taking Hammer down. Then he heard a louder shot from above, and the silenced Tec stopped firing.

But it had already done its damage. Junius could see the dead, torn up look on Hammer's face: like he had touched a state of shock, begun to experience the kind of pain his body wouldn't allow him to feel. Some of the shots came straight through his shoulders, one of his arms, even his neck. He shuddered in pain, stumbled toward the stairs.

The barrel of his shotgun fell as if the strength to hold it had passed right out of Hammer's arms. He started to smile, then he coughed and blood brimmed up over his lips. With his free hand, he tried to catch some of it. As the blood slipped through his fingers, he turned his eyes to Junius and winked.

Then Hammer started to fall. It happened so slowly, like Junius could watch the different events going on around him, all of them, without missing anything. Another set of shots echoed from an automatic above.

Halfway up the steps below, Mike Only struggled to free himself from Roughneck's grasp. "Let me go, motherfucker," he yelled, clubbing at Rough with the butt of his gun.

Roughneck pushed him back into the wall, his forearm at Mike's neck. They slid down as Mike groped his way farther up the stairs toward Junius.

"Motherfucker, chill," Rough said.

The shotgun dropped out of Hammer's hand and clattered down the stairs, falling end over end. Its butt hit a step and it changed trajectory, angling so its barrel faced diagonally up. It flipped again, then slid down the rest of the stairs and came to a stop.

Junius compared his Tec-9 to the much bigger shotgun and immediately wanted to trade up.

Above him, Hammer pitched forward, his head angling toward the steps and the rest of his body following. His hands were at his waist, his face already dark. For the first part of his fall, his body stayed straight, then he bent at the hips and knees. He fell forward and hit the steps with the top of his head. His body crumpled on contact, neck bending chin toward his chest. He somersaulted, hit the steps with his back, then on the next rotation his face hit a stair hard, and Junius thought he heard teeth break.

"He dead," Mike called out. "Jesus dead, motherfucker!"

He flailed at Rough's arms, hitting him about the shoulders until Roughneck caught his wrists and leaned his weight onto Mike's body. They were stretched out, almost at the top of the stairs. Junius could see a red hole in the back of Roughneck's jacket where the feathers were stained with blood. The big man was favoring his right side, but still outweighed Mike Only by enough to hold him.

He had saved Junius once already and was trying to do it again. Junius pointed his Tec at Mike and tried out the phrase, "Freeze, motherfucker." It didn't sound right, didn't fit in his mouth.

"You bitch!" Mike Only tried to point his gun at Junius. "I'm a *kill* you!"

Rough rolled over onto Mike, pinning one arm down and wrestling for his gun. Mike shot a bullet at the stairs and Junius cringed away.

"What you doing?" Rough said, his eyes meeting Junius's. "Waiting on what?"

Junius picked up the shotgun and, holding it by the pump, stepped to Mike and swung it up over his head. He chopped the stock down hard into Mike's forehead.

"Fuck!" Junius saw blood spray out onto the wall. The look in Mike's eyes as he brought it down—one of pure anger, panic, and disbelief—seemed carved onto the back of Junius's head. "Fuck," he said again, louder, as he hit Mike with a straight jab from the shotgun's stock.

"Goddamn." Rough let Mike Only go limp in his hands. "You shoot his boy and then beat his head in with a shotgun?"

"You said move. What I'm supposed to do?" Junius turned the shotgun around in his hands.

Rough took the gun by its barrel and settled the stock against his side, under his good arm. When Junius met his eyes, he shook his head. "Lucky you didn't kill yourself. This thing cut you in half."

Junius picked up his Tec.

Hammer's crushed face almost made him feel sorry. He was upside-down, blood running up from his broken mouth into his nose.

"Fucking mess," Roughneck said, shaking his left hand. Junius could see the hole in the front of his jacket now, marked with red feathers like the one in the back.

A single shot, then a series of silenced ones came down from the floor above, somewhere just past the doorless entrance to the hall.

"Come on," Junius said. "We going up."

8 0

Aldo Posey knocked on the door of the apartment Emma Lawrence had given him over the phone. He'd seen Junius's friend going up in the elevator and he knew the worst was the case: that he'd have to go up there himself if he was really going to do what he came for. But it made sense to check with Miss Lawrence first, didn't it? Of course it did.

He knocked again.

"Come in."

Aldo rubbed his face with his hand, wished he'd taken the time to shave. He suddenly felt bad he hadn't. But he couldn't do anything about it now, so he turned the knob and opened the door. Just as he did, he heard gunshots from somewhere higher up in the building. He cringed. Even with all he'd been through, things could always somehow get worse.

Inside the apartment, Miss Lawrence sat erect in a glider with her hands in her lap, like an animal who was focused only on hearing.

"You heard that?" she said. Aldo nodded. "Not the first, either. Been going on like this." She shook her head, her body slumping down into a normal sitting position. "Like it's a war going on."

"Is my son in that?"

She sighed, nodding, and he closed the door behind him. Suddenly he had the strong urge to sit down.

"Thought you come to get him?"

"I have." On the couch now, he put his head in his hands. Another string of shots echoed from above, softer now that he was inside. "Why don't you put some music on, or something?"

She buttoned her lip and shook her white-curled head. "This my life," she said. "I won't tune it out. Those boys up there? The ones doing the shooting? I seen them come up, gave them Kool-Aid on that couch you on now."

Aldo waited but that was all she said. He needed a drink. "Could I—"

"Bottom cupboard," she said. "To the left of the stove. That's where I keep it and don't go telling me any stupidity about how the oven could make it warm up and ruin the taste. Been keeping it there for long enough and I ain't never had a bottle go bad."

He nodded at the kitchen, pulled down on his cheeks. "I told myself I wouldn't drink today."

"Then *don't*. But if you do, don't look at me for no explanation or sympathy. You hear?"

"Yes, ma'am." He stood up and then sat right back down. "I can weather this."

"Damn right you can! Drinking? Nothing but a crutch. You want to live your whole life that way, limping on the help of a bottle? You do, you no better than them." She pointed up.

"Drugs, all the same," she said.

He returned his head to his hands. "Guess I just need to go up there and get my son."

"Just sent two his friends to go up and do it. Was trying to tell you that on the phone." She shrugged. "They probably better suited to the task, being young and a part of it all."

"Used to be he'd get in a fight or something, I could just go down and fix things, pull him out and set him straight."

"When was that?"

He tried to think it through, count the years, but he'd lost track. "Seems like it wasn't that long ago."

When she didn't answer, he said, "I lost my older boy this week."

She slid back and forth in her glider, the blanket she was making on her lap. "I'm so sorry about that. He was a good boy, much as I can remember. Now your youngest here trying to fix it, but the problem didn't start here."

Aldo sat up and looked at her. "That's what I came to hear. How this happen?"

"Shame." She shook her head and turned to him. Their eyes met for the first time, and Aldo looked away. Her lower lip was pushed out in disgust at it all.

"Didn't even involve these towers, though that's not what Willie told your Junius. Then the boy come up here, looking for trouble, doing what he thinks needed doing. You know how that goes. Been there yourself, I imagine."

Aldo nodded slowly. He was back to looking at the kitchen again. It didn't matter whether he stopped drinking today or tomorrow. Or at all.

"Now he taking on these towers, trying to prove hisself a man."

Aldo got up and stepped around the coffee table, across the rug, and onto the linoleum.

"Might as well," she said.

In the cabinet by the stove, he found a bottle of malt liquor unopened, cooking sherry, and a fifth of good scotch.

"Malt liquor ain't mine," she told him. "So don't go telling me I should keep it cold. That swill can rot for all I care."

He turned the bottle around to see the label: Olde English 800, the Eight-Ball, one of his favorites.

"Shit," he said. Even now it felt a shame to see the bottle left forgotten. He wanted to put it in the refrigerator. Instead he took out the whiskey. "Just one pull."

He straightened up and screwed off the cap. It stuck, sugar crystalized inside it, but he got it off and brought the bottle up to his mouth before he realized it was bad form.

The old woman watched him. "Don't stop on my account."

Careful not to let the glass touch his lips, he poured just a little under his tongue. It brought a sense of warm he hadn't felt all day.

"Talk to your wife today?" Miss Lawrence asked. "I'm thinking she be home by now."

"Not my wife."

Aldo wiped his mouth with the back of his wrist. He opened a cabinet and saw white mugs lined up on a shelf, took one, and set it down onto the counter. Slowly, carefully, he poured two fingers of the whiskey into it, then set the bottle on the counter and raised the mug, knocked that off in one pull. Now he was warm; he could feel the strong heat of the drink spreading through him, burning down his neck and settling at the pit of his gut.

"What is wrong with these boys?" he asked, raising his voice a touch so she would know he was serious. He poured out three fingers this time and turned, ready to meet her eyes and accept any criticism, any doubt.

But she wasn't even looking. She'd gone back to poking with her hook.

"I can fix this." He took a small sip and set the mug on the counter. "They won't take both my boys in one week."

"One bad enough," she said. "Sure is."

Then another gunshot came from above, louder than the others.

"Shotgun," she said. "That belong to Harold. Poor child, he *never* was any good." She shook her head. "What you gone do? Tell me how you fix this mess?"

She looked at him without anger, disappointment, or even concern for his drinking. She sat there taking it all in, every bit: the building, his drinking, the shooting.

She went back to her blanket.

"I'm gone go up there and take that boy home."

He watched her hook dip in and out of the yarn, raised the mug and took another sip.

Elf stood aside to let Big Pickup choose where they went and what they'd do. The hall they were on looked exactly like the one on fifteen, just like all the others he'd seen in these towers. They all smelled the same too—like old funk mixed with piss.

Pickup turned toward one end of the hall and told Elf to come on.

"Yo, you fucked up that cop," Elf said. "That pig got bitch-slapped." He tried to laugh, but the truth was he hadn't liked it.

Pickup didn't respond. Elf heard another series of shots from above and behind and jumped. He spun with his gun out, but it hit against the wall and fell to the floor. He stooped to grab it quickly, hoping Pickup hadn't seen.

Pickup reached the door at the end of the hall and stooped to look through the small, rectangular window into the stairway. Its glass was crisscrossed with thin red wires.

"See what I'm saying?" Pickup asked. "That's why you weak."

He turned the knob and opened the door partway. As soon as it opened, Elf heard the whistle of air rushing up and down the twenty-two floors. Then he heard another shot go off, and this time it was much louder, echoing up and down the hard walls.

"Fuck."

Pickup blocked his path into the stairwell with his body. Before he moved through the door, he turned to look back at Elf. His eyes were small, his brows pushed together. "You scare like a bitch on me, I shoot you myself."

"I—" Elf said.

"And you drop your gun again, you'll deserve it."

Pickup stepped into the stairwell as a huge gunshot boomed from the floor above. Elf cringed, trying not to jump.

"Yo, shit is loud is all."

"Gone be louder when you pull the trigger. You handle that?"

Elf caught the door and stepped through it. As soon as he did, he saw blood on the railing. When he looked up, he saw it dripping from the flight above. He saw another drop fall and turned, watched Pickup start up the steps along the wall, his Tec out in front of him.

Elf thought he could hear crying, like someone was bawling but trying to keep it quiet. Then he heard a big sniffle. Someone was worse off than he was. He had that to keep him steady.

As Pickup walked around the outside of the stairwell, aiming up, Elf did his best to cover their backs. He held his gun with two hands and aimed it down the stairs, stole looks above them at the blood but tried not to think about it, his lips sucked into his mouth to keep from swearing.

The crying was louder as they came higher, and now Elf could see the blood trail down the side of the stairs. Pickup had reached the next landing. He put the first finger of his left hand to his lips and the crying stopped at a final sniffle.

Elf came up behind him, stepped in front to see who was there: it was Ness crying with snot running down his mouth, his face all mashed up like it got when you were just a little dude, bawling your ass off because someone knocked you down.

Pickup kept his finger over his lips as he walked sideways. He swayed his head toward the hallway like he wanted a better look.

Ness raised his hands above his shoulders. "I promise I won't do nothing," he whispered.

"What happened?" Elf asked, coming up the rest of the stairs. Pickup shot his left arm out in front of him, but Elf could see all of Ness now through the rails and what he saw looked bad: Ness bled heavily from his legs just below the knees. All Elf could see was blood—a mess of it covering his pants, sticking them to his shins; blood covering the steps, dripping down to the landing below.

Elf swore, and Ness started crying again, but Pickup gave a look and Ness covered his face with his hands. For a moment, this quieted the sounds, but then Ness screamed, full on howled into his palms and let out a cry so full of pain and frustration that Elf stumbled back against the wall.

The scream echoed around the stairwell.

Big Pickup swore, and Elf heard silenced shots firing from his Tec-9. He turned to see the muzzle flash from the gun as the shots kept firing up the hall, then he tripped down a stair or two and landed on his hands and knees. He was about to swear, but Pickup looked down at him, and the disgust on his face was enough to shut Elf up.

Pickup stepped into the next hallway with his gun by his side, following the direction he'd just shot. Elf collected himself, slowly got back to his feet and went up to the next landing to see what he'd done.

Ness had stopped crying. He looked at Elf like he couldn't believe what was happening.

"Who he shot?"

Elf looked up the hall. He saw Pickup's back, mostly, his body taking space, but then he noticed a mound on the floor: body parts and clothes.

"Is that Dee?" Elf asked.

"Fuck," Ness said. "Bitch capped my boy."

Elf could barely believe what he was seeing. "Yo, he fucked him up."

"Shoot his ass for me, then. Fucking blow him away."

Elf looked down at the gun in his hand, the one from Miss Emma, and then back at Ness.

"Shoot me, then," Ness said. "Just kill me now."

"What happened to your legs, niggah? Who did that?"

"You hear what I said? I said kill my ass."

Elf looked back up the hall. Pickup had stopped by Dee with his gun pointed down. Another series of loud shots echoed down the far stairway, and Pickup got low.

"Everybody shooting," Ness said. That was when Elf noticed the Tec on Ness's other side, just laid out on a step, peaceful as a puppy.

"Who shot you?"

"I just fucking smoke weed son, get high like Apollo 7." Ness looked at Elf. "You holding? I know you can see I be hurting."

It took Elf a second to register what he was hearing and another to take mental inventory of his pockets. "I got trees," he said. "But how you gone smoke with all this shit?"

"Watch me."

"Ok." Elf took the rolled ziplock bag out of his jacket and offered it to Ness. "Smoke, brother."

"Got papers? A pipe?"

Up the hall, Elf watched Pickup stand to full height. He'd seen something beyond Dee and started talking. It looked like he was speaking to someone in an apartment on the right side of the hall.

Then Pickup raised his Tec and held it at an angle, as if he was pointing it at someone on the floor.

Rock had come halfway to the end of the hall when he heard the elevator doors open behind him. He cursed, then flattened himself against the wall and aimed the Uzi back at the elevator. Just to keep anyone from thinking they weren't in the middle of some serious shit, he shot a few rounds down the hall.

"You do *not* want to come up in here now, motherfucker!"

Watching both stairways and the elevator doors as best he could, he inched forward; if he could get to the elevator and flip the manual hold button, the damn thing might come in handy as a way out. He thought he still had the special key that would keep it from stopping on any other floors on its way down too. If shit went wrong, that was an out he might have to take.

Bonnie barked louder from inside his apartment. If she was fucking up things inside it, gone to town on his leather sofa or torn up his Persian rug, she'd be out on the corner come morning. Fuck that shit. For the amount he'd spent on her, she could tear up the couch and still stick around. But if she did anything to Berry—

He stopped himself; that was a possibility he didn't want to consider.

"Shut up!" he yelled at his apartment. "Bonnie! Sit!"

For the moment, the dog stopped barking.

He got to the elevator and spun quickly into the car, holding the Uzi at his waist, ready to fire.

But he didn't need to. All he saw was the slumped body of a black policeman, probably the same fucked-up cop that his soldiers had been trying to get rid of all day. And now someone was fucking with him: sending this cop on up to his floor to show him he still had *this* problem on his hands.

Rock swore again at the air.

He heard more shooting from down on the next floor and stepped into the car.

He kicked the cop hard in the thigh, then again in the top half of his arm. The dumb pig just crumpled against the floor, limp against the wall.

"Yeah," Rock said. "Motherfuckers sent you to fuck with me, huh, dead cop? Fucking dumb ass pig?" Rock kicked him again. "Stupid, stupid motherfucker! You should *know* to stay out my towers!"

The cop's head looked like it'd just been barrel-slapped by someone's gun: his bald scalp was split open over his ear and fresh blood trailed down his neck.

"Stupid ass," Rock said. He turned away from the cop and pulled the manual stop button on the elevator before stepping back into the hall.

He looked up and down the corridor, heard more shooting from the floor below and knew it was time to act. It was time to man up and show people some shit.

"Yo, Hammer!" he called. "Hammer!"

When no one answered, he popped a new clip into his Uzi and started up the hall.

Marlene couldn't wait.

She'd smoked a half-dozen Newports and her throat hurt. Today's pack was down to its last three and that told her it was time to go. They called her the Oracle for many reasons, but one of them was supposed to be her knowledge of when to act and what to do in a given situation. Whether the title applied or not, she believed in actions defining themselves, that you pushed ahead and the world formed to meet your moves—a self-fulfilling prophesy.

Now it was time to listen to the voice telling her to go, that things were taking too long; something, everything was fucked up.

Seven Heaven, Big Pickup, *and* the two kids had all been gone for too long. First Seven had left and not come back, then Pickup disappeared. They both liked to keep her away from any action, high up in her tower, but she was no one's princess. No, she was a woman capable of handling whatever came her way.

If either of those two got hurt, or worse—the young bucks she sent over to do a man's job, a job she should have done *herself*—that shit would be on her conscience in a big way.

Out the window, the sky had grown dark, but below the streetlights Route 2 and the Alewife T station lit the night. Even Rindge

Ave. and the area in front of the towers was well-lit. Just another ben-
efit of life in the towers: it was never fully night, never time to pack
up shop and go to sleep. A 24/7 candy store—that was her home.

She saw a Honda Accord turn off Rindge Ave. into the parking lot;
she didn't recognize the car, which meant it was probably a customer.
She laughed, just one short breath, thinking that with all the commo-
tion and the warring, she wasn't even sure if someone was downstairs to
sell. Then she laughed again at her concern. There was always someone
downstairs, always ready to sell drugs and make some money.

Marlene crossed the floor from the windows, toward her door, then
stopped at the coat rack and pulled on her shearling and a warm hat.

It was Seven she worried about most. Just Seven. And maybe it
was time she acted on those feelings, did something about the man
who considered himself her brother's best friend. In the year since
Malik went to prison, Seven had become *her* best friend— the person
closest to her and most on her mind.

She slid open the hall closet and took a fresh pack of Newports
out of the carton on the shelf. This went into one of her outside pockets. Behind the carton and underneath some old clothes was her gun
box. She pulled it down and set it on the floor. When she'd dialed the
combination on its locks, she lifted the lid and looked down on her
little black beauties: two Taurus Model 85 small-frame revolvers, .38
specials with Rosewood grips and gold finish. She loved her .38s, their
gold triggers and safeties accentuating the color of the Rosewood. She
took each one out of the black foam that lined the case, kissing their
barrels gently before sliding the guns into the two inside pockets of
her coat that she'd had fitted specifically for this purpose.

After putting four speed-loaders into her outside jacket pockets,
she shut the lid of the case and slid it back into the closet along the
floor. As she stood up again, she reached into the way-back corner of
the closet, feeling around for the cold steel behind all the coats and
umbrellas. She brought out the Benelli M2 tactical shotgun. Semi-auto

and loaded for bear, this would be her first line of defense, the stopping power she'd need if she came up against anyone from Rock's crew who was armed. Marlene jiggled the weight of the gun, getting her sense for it. She knew it was loaded—cleaning these three guns and making sure they were loaded was as much a part of her morning routine as drinking her coffee.

She knocked at the door before opening it onto the hall. Even if Raphael wasn't every bit the soldier she expected, she didn't want to know. When she thought he'd had enough time to get presentable, she opened the door.

Meldrak *and* Raphael both stood there, hands behind their backs like this was some kind of gentlemen's army.

They both tried not to look surprised when they saw her holding the Benelli across her chest.

"You boys ready for a little errand?" she asked.

They both nodded in agreement.

Seven Heaven lay on the floor of the apartment looking up at Dee. He couldn't believe that this stupid kid had gotten the drop on him and put a bullet in his back. He couldn't believe it or that Dee was right here standing in front of him, waiting and not shooting him dead.

Seven had the Tec in his hand, looked down his arm and could *see* it, but it wouldn't move; his fucking arm would not lift the gun up to shoot.

"You better shoot my ass," Seven said. "Because if I get this gun up and squeeze the trigger, your ass dead."

Dee's eyebrows rose up his head. "Really?" He shook his head. "Tell me how you feel first. How it feel to have a bullet in your back."

It actually didn't feel that bad, didn't feel bad but for the fact that he couldn't *feel anything*. Seven looked down his body like it was foreign soil: nothing seemed attached to him anymore, not attached or a part of him. He couldn't move his arms, couldn't move *anything*. He tried shaking his feet: nothing.

"Fuck me." Seven let his head fall back onto the apartment rug. At least he had control of that. "Just kill my ass, you piece of shit."

Dee shrugged. "That's all you got, son? Nothing but that little piece of fight left in you?" His gun hung down along his thigh, but now he started to raise it. "I'll shoot you," he said, pointing the revolver at Seven's chest. He raised it higher, pointing at Seven's face, the black eye of the muzzle staring him down like a cyclops.

Then Seven heard a loud scream of pain from the far end of the hall, and Dee turned. A series of silenced shots rang out in the hall, whistling down and ripping through him. Seven got his head up enough to see Dee cut to pieces: first across the chest and then down again across his torso as he fell. Finally he crumpled into a heap.

Seven tried again to move his hand and now something felt a little different; his finger started to move. He could feel the rough pattern of the Tec's grip against it. "Who there?" he called out.

He watched the hallway, listening, waiting to see who'd shot Dee. The bullets had come from the wrong direction for it to be Junius, but with the sound of a silenced Tec, it had to be him.

"Junius. I'm fucked up."

When Big Pickup stepped to Dee's body, Seven wanted to laugh. Not because it was funny though. Instead, he let go: dropped his head back down onto the floor of the apartment. The old rug had little cushion left. It was a shag rug, the kind that had fat strands of yarn sticking up. They stretched all the way from him to the kitchen and beyond.

Seven closed his eyes, waiting for Pickup to make a decision.

Then he heard a series of loud shots out in the hall, down the other end—what were probably shots from Rock's Uzi. He looked up and saw Pickup crouched low by Dee's body. Then Pickup saw Dee's gun and he took it, stood up, and turned to face Seven.

"What's up, my brother?" Pickup asked.

Seven felt himself go weak. To get through Rock's building, avoid getting killed by Dee, and then to get to *this* motherfucker; Seven just could not believe it.

"Yo, what up, son?" Pickup looked down on Seven, the Tec in his left hand and Dee's revolver in his right. "So tell me how it went down, my brother. Dee crept up and shot you in the back? It like that?"

Seven tried to move his arms, tried to sit up. Nothing.

He could feel his finger slide along the grip of his Tec, so he focused on that, concentrated on getting his finger to tighten around the trigger. He felt like his head existed in space with nothing below his neck, as if he'd been cut off from his body. Out of that emptiness, he could feel his right hand's forefinger and thumb

"Can you stand up?"

"Yeah. Just give me a minute." Seven looked up at Pickup's face, trying to gauge what was going on in his head. He realized it didn't matter; he had no choice but to put all his trust in this brother.

"You might have to carry me out, man. Think you up to that?"

Pickup's eyes narrowed. "So tell me how it be. Dee roll up on you?" He raised the revolver to point it at Seven's chest. "He got you in the back and then one time in the heart before I could rush him?"

Seven looked Pickup in the eyes, but Pickup wouldn't meet his gaze. He kept staring at Seven's chest, aiming the gun and his eyes at the same spot.

"You would do that shit," Seven said. It wasn't a question; they'd passed that stage in a hurry. "All that to try and get up closer to Marlene?"

"Shit, I just come up on you. How was I supposed to stop something that happened before I got here." Pickup kicked Dee. "Don't worry though, I capped his ass for that shit. Evened it out."

"You ain't talking to a dead man."

Pickup's eyebrows went up. "I ain't?" Now he met Seven's gaze. "Tell me I ain't."

"I—" Seven didn't have anything else. He could feel his palm against the grip of the Tec and his finger on the trigger, his thumb on its other side. But what good would that do if he couldn't lift his arm? Shooting at Dee's corpse wasn't going to get him anywhere. Even if he could shoot Pickup in the foot, that would only get him dead sooner.

"What you want? Want me to tell Marlene you her man? I get out of here I be in a chair for the rest of my life anyway, won't be no good to nobody. You still run shit."

Pickup's eyes narrowed and then he shook his head. "You done? It be you and then it be Rock. That's how it go down."

Seven strained his hand. He could feel his wrist move barely, and he angled the gun closer toward Pickup, hoping the other man wouldn't notice. If he could just raise it high enough to shoot his shin, maybe Pickup would fall and Seven could shoot him again, get a shot at his body or his head. Maybe. He strained to move as much as he could, trying not to show the effort on his face.

More shooting from the other end of the hall, where Junius was. "You hear that?" Pickup raised his chin at Seven. "*That* is this game. First and last, niggah. Straight up."

Seven couldn't wait. Whether he had the gun turned far enough to hit Pickup where he stood—foot or shin, or just a part of his sneaker—the opportunity to use whatever he had left would soon be gone. Pickup was getting ready to move. Rock, Hammer, who knew who else was down there and what they'd bring—the concern was taking over Pickup's eyes. This part of his game would be over soon.

"Yo, what you doing, man?" It was Elf's voice, plain as could be. He was coming up the hall and then Seven saw his face dip into the doorway. "You ain't thinking about shooting Seven, is you? He your man. What up with that?"

Pickup glanced at Elf like he was dead either way. "Niggah, you either blind to this or you next."

Seven knew it was time to do what he could. He felt the metal trigger move slightly and then really take hold as he gave it everything he had and brought it all the way back and ...

It clicked on an empty chamber.

"Niggah, you crazy." Pickup kicked the Tec out of Seven's hand, sent it across the rug. "You fucking crazy in this piece."

Pickup's mouth curled down and his eyes went wild, as if Seven had been the one to do something unforgivable.

"Shit."

"I—" It was all Elf got out before Pickup spun and smashed him across the face with Dee's gun. Then Elf was down in the hall, and Seven knew it was over.

"Niggahs *all* wilding up in here," Pickup said. He pounded his chest with the gun. "Know whose day this be, motherfucker?" He pointed the gun down at Seven again, aiming at his face.

"Yours?" Seven answered.

"Mine," Pickup said. And he pulled the trigger.

Junius followed Roughneck up the last flight of stairs to the twenty-first floor. It wasn't the first time he'd climbed them today, but it was the first time he had to climb over a dead body. Hammer lay upside-down on the stairs, and below the landing, Mike Only lay with blood trickling down his face. Black Jesus bled on the landing below.

Rough did his best to aim the shotgun up. He couldn't use his left arm, so he bent his knees and leaned against the wall, angling his body to raise the shotgun across the stairs toward the next hallway up. He swung it back and forth as he pushed himself up the steps, ready for someone to come at them from either the hall or the stairs.

"Yo," Junius said, coming up behind him. "Let me help you." He stepped in front of Rough, taking care not to put his head up above the landing where someone would see it all at once.

"You hear that?" Rough asked.

Junius listened: he could hear a dog barking somewhere above them and someone talking softly in the hallway. At the far end of the building, it sounded like someone was crying.

"Where?"

Roughneck whispered, "Above us. Come back."

Junius didn't hear anything from above them, just wanted to see who was in the next hall. It had to be Seven still; he thought he'd heard Seven call to him a minute ago. Now it was just that soft talking. No shots.

Junius couldn't resist. He set both hands on the steps in front of him and eased his body forward, keeping his head low.

"*Come on.*"

He turned his head sideways, almost touching the cold concrete with his cheek, and raised his head to look down the hall. There he saw Big Pickup standing about halfway down. He looked down—at something or some*one*. Junius looked up now, unafraid to show his face, and saw Big Pickup was standing over Dee, holding a Tec on what looked like his dead body.

Junius was about to call out when he heard something above and behind him on the next flight.

Shots rang out all around him. Some hit the metal railing and its supports, singing off the metal like the sound of thick ice under your feet.

Then Roughneck fired the shotgun, and Junius felt something hit his face. His ears rang. He scrambled back down the stairs on his chest, almost falling over Hammer. He saw white ash and plaster in the air, felt it on his cheek and neck. Looking up, he could see the chunk Rough had blown out of the stairs.

Rough had to jam the butt of the shotgun against his thigh and grab the pump to reload it.

"Here." Junius scrambled to give him the Tec.

Rough took the semi-auto and let Junius grab the shotgun.

"Who down there?" Rock's voice called from above.

Rough started back down the stairs, stepped over Hammer to the landing. He was still Rock's man.

"What we do?" Junius whispered.

Rough held the Tec's silencer up to his lips like it was one too-long finger telling Junius to stay quiet.

Junius felt his teeth grind and his pulse quicken. He had reached the top of Rock's tower, had the man himself just above. The thought of Temple flashed through his head. He squeezed the shotgun, liking its feel and its weight.

This was what things came down to.

"It's Junius. Who you looking for, and I got your soldiers laying all at my feet."

Roughneck shook his head, slicing the silencer in front of his neck.

"That Hammer's shotgun you holding, boy?"

"And Hammer laying dead right here."

Now Rough threw his hand up. He moved back down the staircase and crouched into the corner to aim the Tec-9 up through the bars at the next flight.

"Hear that dog bark? How about I go on up and let my Doberman loose on these stairs. Think you like that? Think she give a fuck who you be?"

Junius could hear the barking. Like anyone who grew up in the city, he feared Doberman Pincshers. He bit down, took a step up the stairs.

"Bring whatever," he said. "I'm here." Marlene's words echoed in his head. This was all for Temple now, his family, his life.

"Ho!" Rock howled. "You are *fucking* crazy, son? Do you even know who the hell you dealing with?" Rock's Uzi stuck through the bars above and he shot a spray of bullets along the wall. Junius pointed the shotgun up at the flight Rock had to be on, but it was eight inches of concrete, at least, between him and the man.

Rock said, "I like that, tell you the truth. You got something."

Roughneck shook his head. "Get down here." He waved the Tec.

Junius hoped Big Pickup was listening. If he came quietly up the hall, maybe he would get the drop on Rock. That's what Junius was counting on: if he could get Rock down those stairs and onto the next landing, maybe Pickup would have a clear shot.

Rough grabbed the back of Junius's sweatshirt and pulled him back. "That niggah will wreck your shit. I guarantee." He pushed Junius down onto the landing.

"So what we do?"

"We wait, motherfucker."

"For what?"

Rough didn't answer. Mike Only was right next to Junius, looking like he could wake up at any moment.

"What if this niggah wakes up?"

Roughneck stood. "Yo, Rock. I'm down here too, so chill for a minute and hear what I have to say."

"The fuck? Roughneck? Niggah, I *knew* Clarence was right about you. Fuck you doing down there that don't involve killing?"

"I—"

"Shit, I'm coming down now to do it myself! I had known—"

"No." Rough said it loud and defiant. "I said chill. I'm shot and this niggah here just young. Dumb as shit and don't know what the fuck he doing, but this a war."

"Tell me shit I don't know."

"Yo, Black Jesus down here. He shot. And Mike Only shot me and—"

"Mike O down there too? Yo, Mike! Mike!"

Rough waited for the call to echo away on its own, for the stairs to go quiet again. He moved up with the Tec by his side.

"Man, I been shot. He lost his brother. Now we fucking up our whole building. Motherfuckers dead. Even we kill everyone here, we lose the people who live in this piece. They bound to be still scared as shit." Rough waited. "You hear?"

He gestured with his gun toward the stairs, but not even like it was a weapon he held, more like it was a piece of bread, just like he was talking to someone at dinner.

"And what, motherfucker? They still gone buy my product, get high off my shit, and keep coming back for more. I want these motherfucking towers. I *want* this war."

Rough shook his head. Junius hadn't moved except to get farther from Mike Only; he had a feeling Mike was going to wake up and didn't want to be within arm's reach when he did.

Then Rough stepped onto the next stairs. "I'm saying it's time we move up and see things different, conquer in a different way of enlightenment."

Just as he said it, another loud shot rang out from the hallway above. Junius sprang up, hoping to see Pickup in the door. Instead, he didn't see anyone, just more fluorescent lights in the hall.

That was when Junius heard a loud cough and laugh from above them. "Niggah, please," Rock said. And Junius saw the muzzle flash of the Uzi through the railing. Rock stood at the top of the stairs, letting shots rain down on Rough. The slugs from the Uzi knocked Rough back against the wall. He started to sink down.

"Enlightenment? Now I *know* you been smoking too much product, niggah! *Shit!* Enlightenment? Where the fuck you get that?" Rock started down the stairs, and Junius raised the shotgun to his chest. He knew it would have a kick.

"Tell me you got that shit from Villari's," Rock said. He jabbed the gun at Rough like he was throwing a punch and let off more rounds.

Rough collapsed against the wall, made a noise like he was trying to speak. Blood pumped out of a hole in his neck.

"Let a niggah get a *little bit* of knowledge from a guinea kung-fu bitch and he come off like he the fucking Confucius. *Shit!*" Rock shot more rounds. He was still coming down the stairs.

Junius eased to his left, keeping his back against the wall.

Elf lay on the thin carpet in the hallway, his head still ringing from where Pickup had pistol-whipped him. He'd heard firing from the far end of the hall, an automatic weapon on the stairwell.

He saw his hands in front of him. He could feel the rug's thin, scratchy fibers and the hard concrete below it. Just beyond his reach, he saw Miss Emma's gun.

Big Pickup crept up the left side of the hall, the Tec-9 in his hand.

Elf shook his head, trying to make the ringing stop. He pushed himself up off his chest and onto his hands and knees. In the door of the adjacent apartment, Seven Heaven lay on the rug—Seven or what was left of him after Pickup had finished shooting.

This game had no mercy; you cut down your brother just like you cut down an enemy. Sometimes your own brother turned into your enemy.

Elf thought about his own brother playing Nintendo. Terrence stayed home weekends and nights, tap-tapped that little controller hour after hour. Even got good grades. He'd probably make a good friend to Malik with his *I Love Lucy* and *That Girl*. Both of them were nerds.

Shit, with Dee dead on the floor in front of him and Ness fucked up so he'd never walk again, Terrence was starting to look like he had it right.

Elf scratched the rug, came up with the handle of the .38, and slid it toward him. The grip was still warm. More shots from the far stairway—more automatic fire.

Elf struggled up to his knees, both hands on the gun.

He whispered, "Seven thought I have this trouble. But I can shoot."

That was when Rock jumped into the doorway with his back to Elf, the Uzi at his waist firing off a string of loud blasts.

Elf dove face-first into Dee's body, trying to get down.

Pickup had been sliding along the wall to get his jump on where the real killing was happening: the stairs. He looked back at Elf and then Rock appeared in the stairway, gun drawn on the landing and firing down.

Pickup dodged back against the wall. Now the big man was right in front of his Tec-9, less than ten feet away.

He had heard that Uzi fired plenty and knew it wouldn't be long until Rock turned around to spray the hall. Barely looking, he sheared off a few rounds from the Tec. They caught Rock's right shoulder and pushed him away from the hall. The Uzi went high and wild, firing at the ceiling, and Pickup pulled the Tec, still firing, to shoot across Rock's back.

When the Tec clicked on an empty chamber, Pickup looked down at it, then back up, and just that quickly Rock was gone. He hadn't screamed or made any sound of pain.

"Caught me," he said from the stairwell, out of sight. "I seen you now."

Pickup flattened himself into the door of an apartment and fumbled at his back for another clip. He released the empty magazine from the Tec and rammed a fresh one into its well.

That was when he heard a shotgun echo on the stairs. He ducked fast, hoping it wasn't Hammer. Of anyone in the towers, Hammer and Rock were the only two living, un-jailed residents he feared.

He heard a grunt from Rock, this time with a note of pain in it.

Junius eased toward the next flight up keeping along the railing in the middle of the stairs. He had seen Pickup with the revolver in the hall; he *knew* Pickup could get the drop on Rock.

Junius stepped up a stair and kept the gun trained above. He thought about trying a blind shot at the next flight.

Then Rock jumped onto the landing and fired more shots down the stairs at Roughneck, just missing Junius wide. He didn't know how he hadn't been hit.

Then more shots came from a second automatic, a silenced Tec— Seven Heaven?—punching into Rock from close range. Junius could see them tear through his back. Rock fell back against the wall. He closed his eyes and said something. When he opened them, he faced Junius.

Their eyes locked for a brief moment, but in it Junius saw all the anger and hate he would ever need to see in the world.

He had the shotgun raised to fire, and he squeezed the trigger as fast as he could. The gun kicked more than he expected, and his shoulder flew back away from the rail. He lost his footing and slipped in Hammer's blood, hit his head on the rail, and went down on his knees. The barrel of the shotgun bounced up and hit him in the face.

But he'd shot Rock, had lined him up, taken a good shot and hit him in his side or his chest. Maybe his hip. He hit him; that much was certain. He'd seen the blood.

Junius got the gun back in his hands. It had blood on it now where he touched it: Hammer's blood from the stairs and maybe Rough's, too.

He looked up: Rock was gone.

Junius saw where his shot hit the wall. Part of the blast marked off the space where Rock had stood. On the wall there was also blood, scattered like it had flown off someone.

His forehead hurt.

The sound of laughing came down from the stairs above. Rock was on the move.

Sometimes the war had to be more tactical than brute force. Rock knew this.

Sometimes you played the hand you held and sometimes you had to think, even go back to the deck and draw your aces in the hole.

He'd been shot a few times in the shoulder and the damned punk that had caused all of this, Junius, had shot him in the side with Hammer's shotgun—a lucky shot.

They had both been lucky, Pickup and Junius. The shotgun had given him an emergency appendectomy is all. Just a fucking organ he could do without. He could still run, too, even if he had to hold the rail up the stairs.

He'd caught worse shots in Nicaragua, gotten through those and brought his ass home. This too would pass. In those days, he mainlined coke to get by and survived far worse. Those jungles weren't something you could just step out of; they did not have a back exit, only a body bag as an alternative to fighting.

He tripped up the stairs, watching behind him for Pickup and his Tec, the Uzi raised and ready.

He laughed at Junius, the way he'd fallen. Kid got lucky and shot straight but was badly unprepared for the shotgun's kick. It knocked him back like a mule, and just like any other dumb kid, he wasn't aware of the blood at his feet. Stupid.

Rock laughed, but that turned into a cough. He spit blood—a big, thick gob of it that trailed down the wall.

"Fuck me."

Maybe he'd been state-side too long. Could he be losing his edge? Too much pussy would soften a man—that and delegating shit out to his soldiers instead of keeping a hand on the streets. It was enough to tender you up, make you fall.

He hoisted himself onto the next stair and with a quick look back fired off a string of shots. Fuck it, if he could get lucky and hit Pickup that was fine. If not, he'd keep that fuck back at least.

Rock dropped the clip from his Uzi and pulled another from his back, jammed it in. He almost reached for a grenade on instinct, this shit taking him back to the jungles again. There was no grenade at his shoulder, just his track suit, fabric wet with blood.

He slapped himself across the face, first once and then again harder. The second slap brought him back to the moment: he was in *his* tower, had a few cuts from some shooting. He would get through this.

As he stepped into his hall, Bonnie barked from the apartment. "Ho, Bonnie," he called. "I'm coming for you, girl."

In a flash it occurred to him that if Marlene's soldiers were up in his tower trying to get *his* ass, then maybe she'd be without protection. If he could slide up in there and kill her now, he'd take control.

This thought made him smile.

Rock looked back for a sign of Junius or Pickup and didn't see either, which meant they might be trying to creep up from the opposite stairs. He fired a few rounds down the hall.

Shit, he'd cut down anybody on *either* of these staircases if they got in his way.

Rock spit blood again and pushed himself forward off the wall. He noticed the marks of blood left behind: a handprint and a splotch from his shoulder.

He pressed forward, steadying himself against the wall. As he reached his doorway, the door shook from Bonnie leaping against it and scratching to get out. She was a good dog, wanted to come out here and fight to save her man from the heat.

"Good girl," he said. "Good girl, Bonnie. Sit!"

She calmed for a moment, and Rock tried to listen for Berry.

"Berry," he called. "Yo, Berry!"

She didn't answer. Rock felt for the keys in his pocket. He thought about opening the door and going in for her, but knew Bonnie would run out. She'd be on Junius and Pickup too fast for them to do anything, but then she might be in trouble. He'd be damned if he would let Bonnie get shot.

"Good girl," Rock said, touching the door, leaving fingerprints in blood.

"Berry! Berry, baby. Stay in the bedroom."

He thought he heard her answer, but Bonnie was barking too much for him to be sure. "Be a good girl, Bonnie. Don't hurt my Berry if she to come out, you hear?"

Bonnie threw herself against the door again, and the impact pushed Rock upright.

He touched the door a last time, smearing his blood on the white paint, and shoved himself toward the elevator, glad he'd left it as an escape.

He was not abandoning, just retreating for tactical reasons, seizing an opportunity to get the drop on Marlene.

Junius collected himself and called up the stairs, "Yo!"

No one answered.

"Who there? Pickup?"

"Yeah."

He heard a grunt and then he stood up, slowly, watching above him for movement. Rock was not someone to count out.

The blood was all over his hands, the gun, and his sweatshirt.

It could be worse; at least the blood wasn't his. He wiped it off on his jeans, made sure his hands were dry, and then used his sweatshirt to wipe blood off the shotgun. He thought about trading it out for the Tec that now rested in Roughneck's hand, but there was something about pulling a gun away from a dead man he didn't like. He'd stay with the shotgun.

He started up the stairs, saw Big Pickup step out of the hallway to stand above him.

"Yo," Pickup said.

Junius nodded, stepped around Hammer and made his way up to twenty-one.

"Shit," Pickup said when Junius reached him. "Fucking blood bath in this piece."

Junius didn't need to look back to know the body count. And Pickup probably couldn't see Black Jesus or Mike Only from where he was either. Junius nodded.

Up the hall, he saw Dee's body shot up on the ground, and then, just beyond that some clothes shook and turned into a person who sat up: motherfucking Elf.

"Yo, Elf!" Junius called out. "The fuck happened to you, niggah? How you get up here?"

Elf smiled. "Yo, you all right?"

Junius started up the hall. "My man!"

"Ness fucked up," Elf said, his face going soft. Junius could tell he'd been crying. "And Dee dead! Seven, too."

"Seven?"

"We gone put Rock on that list in a minute," Pickup said. He still watched the stairs.

Elf said something else that Junius didn't hear but for one word: *Pickup*. He cut his finger across his neck. "Pickup killed Seven," Elf said.

"What?"

Pickup came back from the stairs, his Tec-9 still trained up the hall.

"He upset I had to dead Seven. What he don't know is Seven cross over, came up in here helping Rock."

Junius stepped back, pressed himself against the wall. "Seven Heaven? With Rock?"

Elf shook his head. Pickup said, "True enough, niggah. For real."

Junius couldn't believe it. Seven had been the first to reach this floor. He'd heard Seven's voice; they were on the same side.

"He killed Hammer." Junius pointed down the stairs at Hammer's body. "Why would he do that?"

Pickup looked at Junius hard, tilted his head like he wanted to see things from a new angle. "You saying I lie?"

Junius inched along the hallway toward Elf. "No, I—"

Pickup stood still, waiting. "Come on. You want kill Rock, or what?"

"Yeah," Junius said. "I'm with that."

Instead of moving toward the stairs, Pickup stepped into the hall, coming closer. Elf was slow getting up.

"You alright, yo?" Junius asked.

Elf nodded. "*You* all right?"

"Come to save my ass?"

Elf smiled, but it was thin, fragile. "Dee dead." The boy's body lay at Elf's feet. "Seven, too."

"Lots of people dead now."

Elf shook his head. "Ness shot up bad. He could die too."

Junius looked back at Pickup. "What now?" he asked.

"Yo, fuck that niggah." Pickup started toward the stairs. "We move on Rock, *now*—with the quick."

Elf looked nervous, like he wasn't sure what he should do. He had a gun in his hand, but dropped it. He shook his head, but Junius didn't know what that meant.

Elf said, "That's Miss Emma's gun."

"Miss Emma gave you a gun?" It sounded weird to say, but holding the bloody shotgun of a dead man, Junius could see that anything had become possible.

"Is this our fault?" Elf asked.

Aldo Posey put both hands on the counter and looked across at Emma Lawrence. The woman rocked back and forth in her glider, doing her crocheting and paying him no mind.

He was drunk. He pushed his lips out in some imitation of a duck's bill, found his eyes swimming from one side to the other. He finally felt good: the anxiety, worry and feeling bad about everything he did had all left. Now it was just him, back in his old skin.

"Yep," he said. "This me here."

"About done with that bottle?" Miss Emma asked without looking up.

Aldo checked the bottle of whiskey beside his mug: sure enough, it was empty. "Yes, ma'am." He tipped it up over the mug, waited for the last few drops to trickle out. "Guess so."

He studied her now, this older lady who had let him into her apartment, trying to decide if anything about her looked good. Sure, she had extended her hospitality out of concern for his boy, but maybe her hospitality was meant to go further. Sure, she was old, but he was getting up there himself. Weren't people like the two of them meant to keep each other company?

He held the counter with both hands as a chill ran through him. The last bit of it made his head shake. No, he wasn't supposed to be keeping time with some Bible-loving rug-maker. That wasn't him. Another bottle somewhere, that'd keep him company.

"You got the courage up to go see about your boy?" She paused her hook to look up.

"Hmmm? What you say?"

"Your Junius. Who you came here for. You ready to go up and see if he ok?"

Aldo remembered the sound of gunfire in the hallways, the man in the elevator who looked ready to eat a child, and the beat-up police officer. Those two were riding to where the shots were. His son's friend, too.

"No. Huh unh. I won't get myself shot at."

Emma nodded, her lips pursed. The crocheting hook started moving again. "Just checking," she said.

"Yeah. I mean I go up there if I had a gun. Do you have a gun?" He watched as she shook her head.

"No. See I don't think I should go up there. A son get himself into just so much a father can help him out of. Come a time where we have to raise our hands." As if to illustrate this point, Aldo raised his hands. It took him a second to get used to standing on just his two feet, but then he was alright, even felt more clear-headed than before.

"Right." He knocked off what little was left in his mug and told her it had gotten to the time he had to leave. He thought of the supermarket and liquor store next to the towers, tried to recall how much money he held. For the briefest moment, he thought of asking this woman for a loan, but then decided against it.

A man had to draw the line for his dignity, especially in a situation like this. He'd make do with what he had, even satisfy himself with his old standby—a bottle of Scope mouthwash—if it came down to it.

"I thank you for your hospitality." He came around the counter and stood by the door. "Sorry I couldn't be more help to you, Miss Lawrence."

"Help me?" She looked puzzled. "Do you remember what I told you about your son Temple?"

Aldo nodded, not quite sure what she meant, but ready to do his best to make her happy. "I do. And I appreciate your condolences."

"That's good." She turned back to her crocheting. "I *am* very sorry for your losses."

Aldo turned toward the door. Reaching for the handle, he stopped. "Loss," he said.

"Yes," she said. "My mistake. Your *loss*."

"Thank you." He turned to the door, opened it, and went out into the hallway. His eyes took a few moments to adjust to the flickering lights.

He wobbled up the hall to the elevator and pushed the button.

When it hadn't come in what felt like ten minutes, he decided to take the stairs.

Gary Johnson felt like a fly that had hit the windshield of a car doing seventy-five: as if everything inside him had been broken and smashed, his bones and especially his skull. The only difference that he could tell was in his case the momentum hadn't carried his asshole through his face. He had that to feel good about.

When he started to open his eyes, his head hurt so bad he had to rest it on the floor. Wherever he was, the floor was his pillow and resting his head there made his body hurt less. Keeping his eyes closed from the bright light around him—Was he in heaven? Could heaven actually feel like this?—he ran his fingers across the floor and felt a thin, ridged rug, like it had lines built across it. His face pressed against a cold metal wall with a bumpy texture. Maybe someone had taken pity on him and just planted him in a box.

But a box wasn't heaven, so he knew he had to be alive. Of course he was; a dead man couldn't hurt this bad.

He forced his eyes open, rubbed his temple to ease the pain. When his eyes adjusted, he could see he was in an elevator.

Then the rest of it came roaring back: he was in the terrible tower, the last one in the Rindge apartments. He remembered his encounters and fights with a drug dealer named Clarence, punching out a boy called Pooh, and an elevator ride with a big guy who hit him in the head with a gun.

His head rang.

He tried stabilizing himself by putting both hands on the rug. Something ran through him, made him retch. He heaved and spit out a yellow gob of bile, coughed, rested his head against the cold wall. Cold felt good against his cheek.

Someone tripped into the elevator, rocking the floor. He stumbled, stepped, and fell against the back wall. The whole car shuddered. The other person said, "Fuck," and pounded on the wall.

Johnson kept his head down, trying to appear dead or out cold. Either of these were his best choice for how to play this. He felt his gun on the floor under his ribs. It couldn't be anything else but his Smith & Wesson. He heard a rattling of keys and then the elevator shook, actually started to hum. The doors creaked closed, and then the car began to move.

They were headed down.

"Rock!" Pickup yelled. "We coming."

Junius pointed at Elf. "Stay there."

"I'm cool," Elf said. He held his hand up.

A dog barked in the distance. Pickup took off and hit the stairs before Junius moved. As he rounded the turn on the landing and headed up the last flight to twenty-two, Junius started up the hall. He'd expected Pickup to creep up on Rock stealth-like, but instead he charged up. Junius was halfway to the landing when Pickup called back, "He in the elevator. Call that shit on twenty-one, niggah. Hit the button!"

Junius called to Elf, "Hit the button!"

Elf stared at him.

"Go!" Junius said. He pointed at the elevator, and Elf stepped to the doors and jabbed the button.

Behind him, Junius heard Pickup. "He coming down. Stop the elevator."

Junius didn't know what Elf would be able to do against Rock, but then Pickup knocked Junius out of the entrance to the hall and he charged at Elf with his gun ready. Junius caught himself against the wall.

Elf turned toward them with his hands up. "It's not stopping!"

"Motherfuck." Pickup ran down the hall and pushed Elf aside. He stabbed at the button, then gave up and slammed his fist against the elevator. "Fuck me. Twenty floors, motherfucker?"

At that, Pickup came back up the hall at a run, lumbering toward Junius with his frame filling the hallway. Of the three big men— Pickup, Seven Heaven, and Roughneck—Junius could see now that Pickup was the biggest. Not that it mattered anymore, if he was the only one still alive.

Junius stepped back out of Pickup's way. That was when he noticed Mike Only pulling himself steadily up the stairs, one hand on the railing and the other holding his gun, a trickle of blood still sticking to his forehead.

Pickup burst out of the hallway and onto the stairs. He jumped halfway down the first flight and booted Mike Only in the face, knocking him back. Mike fell, hardly looking up to see who'd kicked him.

Pickup opened up with the Tec into the bodies, spraying bullets. He landed heavily on the landing, slipped and swore, then punched the wall to right himself and ran on down the stairs.

"Motherfucker!" he called out as he turned the corner.

Now Junius stepped to the edge of the stairs. Looking down, he saw blood, bodies, arms, legs.

Maybe it wasn't safe to be going around unarmed in Rock's tower, but he was ready to find out. He tossed the shotgun down onto the remains.

"Rest in peace, niggahs," he said.

When Junius turned back to the hallway, Elf was waiting. "I pushed the button," he said. "I really tried."

Junius patted him on the shoulder. He could feel Elf shaking through his clothes.

Sergeant Jerry O'Scullion heard the call again. It was the third time dispatch had tried to raise him, but he didn't care what they had to say—*whatever* it was.

"Fuck, Sarge, will you answer that shit?" Roberts spit tobacco juice onto the sidewalk beside their cars.

He was right, of course, but O'Scullion deserved a break. It had been a day's worth of shit already—six hours of chasing idiots in the towers, then a pileup on Mass Ave., a robbery at the pizza parlor where Cameron met Harvey Street, and then the one that sucked all the life out of him: back on Rindge Ave., a six-year-old girl molested in a bathroom at Notre Dame Church.

After taking down her story, shit he had not wanted to hear, he'd come out to find Roberts and Kelley waiting at his car. They'd stayed on scene up at Tony's pizza to get the last of the witnesses' testimony, and he'd come up here to handle the girl himself.

He was the unlucky one.

Now he just wanted to sit against the back of his patrol car in the cold and smoke a stogie. Let it all wash over him. He shook his head, looked Roberts in the eye. "You know what that girl just told me in there?"

"Sarge, I—"

"No. Listen. That girl, six years old, comes out of the bathroom to her mom after a guy busts out the women's room she was in. Think her mother wants to see that? Wants to clean her daughter's face after the guy just finished?" O'Scullion could only shake his head. "Mother of Christ." He sat down heavily against his patrol car, thinking of his own daughter.

Kelley was the one who spoke next. "We got to roll, Sergeant.

Just stopped here to collect you. There been more reports of shooting up at Rindge Towers. Sounds bad. Multiple apartments calling in automatic weapons fire."

O'Scullion took his hat off and looked into it. At the crown of his head was his transcription of the Miranda rights, but sticking up from the headband, above the spot where his forehead had worn the leather shiny with sweat, was the yellowed piece of paper he'd kept inside every hat he'd worn since his first day on the job.

The writing on it, his writing, was still clear: *There but for the grace of God, go I.*

"Motherfuck me," he said. O'Scullion straightened and stood off the car. "Ok, Officer. Roll out and I'll be right behind you."

His legs were tired, and the six-year-old girl's eyes still looked back at him from the inside of his skull.

Marlene led Raphael, Sean Dog and Meldrak around to the back of 412.

No one stood on watch at the back side of Rock's building. Sure, the easiest path would be to just walk up to the front of 412 and see what was kicking, but that wasn't how she was doing this. Tonight things were under *her* control, and she knew to check the back side first.

She told Sean Dog to stay on the rear. Above the other two, he was best suited to stand guard by himself. Like her, he carried a Benelli M2 semi-automatic and had the stopping power to cut down anyone who came his way.

She led the other two around to the front side of the building and had them post on each side of the front glass. Then she walked across casually, trying not to look obvious. She stopped short when she saw the lobby was empty—no one on guard, nothing happening.

Meldrak came up behind her. "Big Pickup and Seven came through, they would not leave no one behind."

She shook her head. "Huh uh. But something else wrong. Rock wouldn't leave his front without someone on sales."

Meldrak shrugged. He pulled the front door open and held it for her. A rush of warm air blew out.

"Ok," she said. "We go in."

She walked into the lobby with the Benelli ready. The elevator doors were directly ahead. To either side of them were twin doors to the stairwells. She knew the layout well: it was exactly the same in 410 and 411.

The towers.

The right door would also lead around to a hallway for the back and the dumpsters, the trash area, where they'd find Sean Dog.

She nodded Meldrak toward the right door. "Go around and get Dog, will you? We might need his gun."

"I'm on it."

Raphael came into the lobby. "Too quiet in here."

She nodded.

That was when she heard sounds from the elevator; it was coming down.

"Something bound to happen soon," she said, nodding at the elevator.

She stepped to the right side of the lobby and waved Raphael to the left, then raised the shotgun to her shoulder and aimed it at the dull, metal doors.

Officer Johnson rolled his head to the side as he thought a dead man might, trying to make it look like the movement of the elevator was jiggling him from one position to the next.

When he'd gotten himself to a precipice, the point where he could rock sideways from his shoulder, he let himself fall. The gun was still under him, and he did his best to slide it forward. Then he waited, breathing breaths so shallow that no one would notice, playing dead as best he could.

Nothing happened, and he allowed himself to open his eyes a little—just a quick look through his lashes. He saw DeShaun Thompson slumped against the other side of the car.

Smooth Rock Thompson was what they called him at the station, but this time Rock looked anything but smooth.

He looked bad was the truth of it, like if the elevator got stuck between floors, he might just bleed out and die. On the other hand, given the way he felt and the fact that Rock didn't seem to have any problem presuming him dead, Johnson doubted he looked any better.

He allowed himself one full, deep breath when he saw Rock wasn't watching. The man was focused on breathing himself, had his head tilted all the way back to face the fluorescents above. Johnson shifted his weight to free the gun from under him, sliding it closer within reach.

The elevator bumped and he slid his good hand over the gun. He wrapped his fingers around the grip and lifted it.

Rock's hands were still tight on his Uzi—the big, black automatic. Rock wheezed and launched into a coughing fit that finished when he straightened up and looked Johnson dead in the eyes.

"What up, cop?"

Johnson held his weapon, but it pointed toward the doors. He was too far from moving it and getting his finger on the trigger to get the drop. Rock's Uzi wasn't likely to offer any second chances.

"Just wondering the same thing."

"You having a good day, Officer?"

Johnson didn't take his eyes off the other man's face. He wanted to laugh, but knew from recent experience that it hurt too much.

"No. Matter of fact, this one of my worst."

Rock nodded. "Lot of that going around."

"So what happens when we hit the lobby?"

Now Rock looked hard at Johnson. He hadn't so much as glanced at the Smith & Wesson or changed the angle of his Uzi. "I heard my boys tried to throw you in the trash. That you?" He smiled.

Johnson didn't answer, but he sat up farther against the wall. He felt at a disadvantage being on the floor with Rock standing above him, but that wasn't going to change.

"*And* I heard old Clarence got a piece of your ass still in his teeth."

Even if Rock asked him to stand, Johnson wasn't sure he could. He slid the gun closer to his leg, turning it toward Rock.

Rock sucked his teeth. "You know you best leave that gat right where it be. That's not how we play this."

Johnson didn't move.

"You have a license for that firearm, citizen?"

Rock laughed outright. His head flew back and his shoulders shook. He wiped tears from his eyes. "You are a funny motherfucker, cop. Know what else?" Rock lifted his eyebrows, as if he really had an interest in Johnson's answer.

"What?"

"I want to tell you it pleases me to see a black man wearing the uniform. You hold on to this job now, brother. You know?" Rock made a fist with one hand and clenched it in front of his chest.

The elevator stopped, and Rock stood up off the wall. He pointed the Uzi at the ground, holding it along his leg as he stepped forward to the panel of buttons. At the top was a set of keys dangling from a lock. He held the door-closed button and removed the keys. They went into his pocket.

Now Rock stood off to the side of the doors and faced Johnson. He raised the Uzi.

The Smith & Wesson hadn't moved, but now Rock stood almost in front of it; all Johnson had to do was raise it and pull the trigger.

"You ready, cop?" Rock asked.

"Ready for what?"

Junius walked up the hallway behind Elf. He had to step around Dee's body. Then, inside one of the apartment doors, Seven Heaven lay sprawled on the floor, a Tec-9 still in his hand. His chest now featured a pool of blood and part of his face was gone, mashed into the rug by a bullet. Whoever lived here would have one hell of a mess to deal with.

"Pickup did this," Elf said.

"Seven wouldn't cross over."

"No. Pickup just evil." Elf moved on up the hall, and Junius followed. At the next stairs, he saw more blood than he thought possible. Even after what he'd seen, the mess around Ness confused him.

"A lot of blood," he said.

"Shit, you think I should be just about bled out now." Ness held out the roach of what looked like a big-ass Jamaica-joint.

"Nah." Junius held up a hand, but Elf took the joint and puckered the side of his lips. He curled them around the roach and sucked.

Junius looked at the mess that was Ness's legs.

"That help any?" he asked.

Ness nodded. "Shit, man. I think I got full-on cut off from feeling anything about ten minutes ago, but now I feel even better than that." He wrinkled his brow in thought, then nodded. "Yeah, it do help. It do."

Elf passed what was left of the roach back to Ness, who tossed it into his mouth, chewed it, and swallowed.

"You can walk?" Junius asked, even though he knew the answer. Ness's legs looked like they'd been cut open at the shins with an ice pick—again and again.

"We carry you out," Elf said. "Come on. We got to get him to a hospital."

Elf got under Ness's arm and started to lift, so Junius got under the other. They lifted. Ness wasn't light, and twenty floors was a long way to go, but Junius didn't want to tell Elf that he wouldn't live anyway.

Ness gasped, and Junius knew he was in a world of pain as soon as they moved him. His feet would bump down every stair they took. Twenty flights of pain.

"Set me down. I wait for the elevator. Paramedics. Whatever. This shit ain't working."

Junius looked at Elf. "Rock just took the elevator. You want to wait for it?" Then, before Elf could answer, "I can't wait, man. Shit."

"You gone be alright," Elf told Ness. "We send someone back up for you."

"Yeah." Ness held out his hand and Elf gave him a pound. Junius did the same.

"I'm a just wait here." Ness leaned against the railing. He pointed at a Tec-9 on the stairs. "You best take that heat."

Elf looked at Junius. "We might need it."

Junius waited, knowing Elf wouldn't pick up the gun. After a few moments, he hit Elf's arm. "Come on."

Junius started down the stairs. When Elf followed, he dropped into a jog.

He heard Ness say, "Don't forget me."

They ran down the stairs, Junius leading, pushing to get out. He didn't want to catch Rock in the lobby or see him confront Big Pickup. He needed to get out of the towers altogether. The stale air had become oppressive; it smelled of blood.

Around the thirteenth floor, Junius heard singing—bad singing with slurred, broken words. He stopped. He knew the voice and the song.

If Junius hadn't built a lead, Elf might have hit him from behind. Instead, he stopped a few steps above Junius.

"What?"

"You hear that?"

"I saw him in the elevator. Said he came to get you out of this."

"Yeah, right." Junius tried to laugh, but it wasn't funny. He'd heard this song too many times.

He started down, and then, before he saw his father, he heard the old man say his name.

"Junius, *my son*!" The man leaned up against the wall, drunk. He raised a hand to reach out, but Junius kept his distance. "You ok?"

Junius stood on the landing above his father, who was partway down the next flight.

"I be alright."

"That's good, son. I was concerned about you."

Junius started down, but it didn't look like there was enough room for him to slip past. He considered going back up and taking the other stairs.

"Today I made some resolutions."

"Ok. Good."

Junius tried to move along the railing, but the old man slid into his way. He smelled of whiskey. Junius wanted to say something about his father bringing Clarence and Dee into his mother's house, letting them hold her up, but that seemed like so many words. Just a waste of breath.

So much had happened since then: too many deeds, too much changed; it felt like a different life.

Junius put his hand on his father's shoulder and tried to ease him out of the way.

"What you doing?"

"Just let me by. I need to go. I got to get outside."

"Yeah? That what you need?"

Junius tried to pass again, but his father put his arms out to block the stairs.

"That's it? You just gone run out?"

Junius looked his father in the face. His father glared back, his eyebrows sliding together in concentration. He blinked hard, steadied himself against the rail.

"That's it, old man. That be all."

"So that's how you gone see it?" He shook his head and spit down the stairs. "Fuck it then," he said, and stepped out of the way. "Go on, but you come to see. One day, you gone see what it's like."

Junius had a dry, sour taste in his mouth. He wanted to spit, but didn't have the saliva. Elf waited. Their only move was to keep going, to head down the stairs and out of the building away from it all. To get away into the night.

"I—" Junius watched his father's eyelids lower and then glide back up. "Alright, then." He turned to start down.

When he had gone just a few steps, his father said something that made Junius stop.

"What you say?"

"Big Willie," his father said, for the second time. "He the one kill Temple. I came and heard it from someone who know. They got in a fight over some shit, and Willie took him out. That's it.

"So what you did here, whatever shit you did today? It all because someone told you some shit." His father spit onto the landing. "Just some bullshit lies!"

Junius turned to look back at his father. The steel railing was cold in his hand, even in the warm air of the stairway. His father's eyes were half-lidded, yellow and bloodshot. They met his gaze full on.

Elf shook his head. "I heard the same thing." He stood right next to Junius, but the words sounded miles away. "I was going to tell you."

"For some *bullshit!*" his father spit. "For someone else's bullshit you did whatever you did today. Fucked up your whole life for a fight that wasn't yours."

"You don't know nothing about what I did today." Junius wanted to tell his father he didn't know what he was talking about, that Rock and Black Jesus had been the ones who killed Temple, that everything he did was for a reason. But he didn't know anymore. Whatever conviction and anger and reason he'd had were gone.

"You don't know shit," he said.

Aldo waved at his son with the back of his hand. "Go on. Keep telling yourself it was all for your brother." He nodded. "Keep walking. Keep thinking that be true."

Elf reached out to touch Junius's shoulder. "Come on."

His father raged now in the stairwell, yelling, his voice echoing off the walls. "Keep thinking that and let me know how long you can hold to it! You come tell me in ten years how you see it."

Junius watched his father turn away and head back up the stairs, farther into the building.

He waved again as he left. "You just a stupid kid is all. Don't know shit."

Junius stepped up one stair. "Fuck you!"

His father kept going. Toward what? Junius had no idea.

"Fuck you!"

His father didn't stop, just waved again as he climbed. "The fuck
you been around long enough to see? Nothing, niggah. Too young to
have seen shit."

Then Junius said it again, quietly. "Fuck you."

He waited for someone else to speak—his father or Elf, either
one—but neither did. His father kept on up the stairs with his back
turned. At the next landing, he opened the door to the hall and disappeared inside, never looking back.

Slowly, Junius turned away. He started down the stairs again,
telling Elf to come on.

Rock released the door-closed button and the elevator shuddered. The doors started to part, and as soon as they did Gary Johnson saw a woman aiming a shotgun at them.

Johnson didn't have time to raise his gun, didn't even think of it until it was too late.

He thought about the moment a lot later, for weeks and even months after the events he considered it, and in all the time spent, he came to the same conclusion his mind flipped to in that fraction of an instant: he was just trying to save his goddamn ass.

Whether he'd been through more than enough already in the one long, horrible, violent day or whether his natural instinct to seeing the hole at the end of a shotgun was to duck, it didn't matter. He put his head down on the floor of the elevator car, forehead to the rug, and curled his arms around his face. He went full turtle on the mother-fucker, just flinched and ducked.

But that wasn't what Rock did, or the woman either.

Rock stepped calmly out of the elevator pointing his Uzi at the first thing he saw, a nineteen-year-old resident of the 410 tower named Raphael Michael Rodriguez who, despite holding a pair of loaded nine-millimeter Browning HPs in good condition, cleaned recently and well cared for, with both hammers cocked, did nothing.

Rock cut him down in less than five seconds as he emptied half the Uzi's clip across Rodriguez's chest and face before the woman, Marlene Brown, of the 411 tower, shot Rock twice in the center of his chest from ten feet away with a Benelli M2 semi-automatic shotgun, killing him instantly.

This was exactly how Officer Johnson would write it all up in his report later, as he reconstructed the events in the lobby of 412 Rindge Avenue on the night of February twenty-second.

But at that moment all he knew was the sound of shots fired and the feel of something wet splattering across his hands and neck as Rock fell back hard onto the floor of the elevator.

After a series of breaths, Johnson looked up. He saw the woman, Marlene Brown, staring him straight in the face like she had no idea what to do.

She looked angry, but also about as confused as he was.

The elevator doors started to close, but they hit Rock's legs at the thigh and rushed back open. They slid forward a moment or two later and tried to close again, only for the same thing to happen.

Johnson heard a door off the lobby open and two men walked in: one holding a black shotgun similar to the woman's and the other holding a Tec-9. The shotgun man, one Sean Robertson, stood in front of the elevator. He glanced down at Johnson, and the other went right to Marlene Brown. "We got to get on out," he told her.

"This a fucking cop here," Robertson said.

Johnson held his hands out to show they were empty, pushed the Smith & Wesson away from him with his wrist. "I didn't see shit. I did not *see shit*."

"But I just—" the woman started to speak and pointed at Rock's body. The doors started to close again and this time, mercifully,

Robertson stepped forward to hold them with a foot. He lowered the muzzle of his gun.

"Self-defense," Johnson said. "Everything I just saw. Self-defense. I'll testify to it."

Johnson knew Rock had been shooting, and for him that constituted enough for a self-defense plea, regardless of how the woman came to be holding a Benelli M2 there in the lobby of a residential building.

Given all he'd seen that day, carrying a loaded shotgun didn't seem like such a bad idea.

"We trust this cop?" Robertson asked.

"Trust him or kill him," the other man—one Meldrak Mohammed—said, matter of fact. "And that's not much of a choice."

All three of them lowered their guns. Mohammed tucked his into his jacket. "Maybe you need us to issue statements," he said, "but perhaps we can do that back in our own building?"

Johnson looked up in time to see the man wink.

"Other than that, we can assure you of our full cooperation."

Johnson heard sirens in the distance, police cars coming. He wasn't sure if he'd even be able to stand. He coughed and waved his hand in front of his face. "You better wait. My backup take you over. They hear your statements."

Both of the men started to protest, but the woman cut them off. She stepped into the elevator and flipped the red Hold switch.

The elevator buzzed once and then stopped shaking.

"You be alright?" she asked. "Maybe we should call you an ambulance."

"There be one here, soon enough."

The sirens roared louder; the cars were closer. Johnson could see red and blue lights reflected in the glass of the lobby.

The others put their guns down and started toward the doors.

Johnson heard another door off the lobby open and saw them flinch.

They turned and looked calmer. "Big Pickup," Mohammed said.

A bigger man than the other two came into the lobby and gave one-armed hugs to the others. He gave the woman a big kiss on the cheek. "You all ok?"

"What else happened up there?" she asked.

Johnson pushed himself up onto his elbows. He recognized the big man who had last whipped him in the head with a gun barrel. It would not go unmentioned.

"Nothing good," the big man said. He turned and Johnson saw him start to smile when he noticed Rock dead on the floor. He stopped himself fast when he saw Johnson.

"Nothing good at all," he said.

By the time Junius and Elf got to the lobby level, they could hear police cars on Rindge Ave., sirens calling from the front-side of the building, and loud voices in the lobby.

"Fuck that," Junius said. He nodded toward the back door. "We best be out."

"What about Ness? We said we bring him a ambulance."

"Yo." Junius tilted his head away from the lobby, already taking a step in that direction. Even worse than fucking with whoever might be in the building, the idea of talking to the police and waiting for the paramedics was not one Junius liked.

"We could tell them—" Elf stopped, both his feet planted.

"He gone die." Junius put it out there. Whether Elf was fragile or not, they didn't have time for decisions.

"I'm out," he said, taking a step closer to the door. "You should come."

Elf teetered toward the lobby and rocked in Junius's direction. He almost fell forward. Junius laughed. He hit the back door and knocked it open, didn't even look around as he started to run.

By the time the door slammed closed, they were both past the dumpster and running along the cold, rusted fence behind the towers.

The door slam echoed into the night. Someone would hear it and come looking, but by the time they did, Junius and Elf would be gone.

They came to a hole in the fence and crawled through it, ran down the rocky slope to the tracks, their breaths puffing out in front of them in the night.

Careful not to trip on the wooden cross ties, they ran on until they couldn't run anymore, then they walked, knowing the tracks would lead them through Cambridge and back to Porter Square or even farther—into Boston—if they kept going.

Junius knew the tracks were just a start. He didn't have a choice anymore—no way he could go back home after all that had happened.

His mother told him to leave on a bus for New York City. She had been right. Much later, he would realize it didn't make a difference either way.

Now he walked on into the cold night with Elf. He said he was going to take the Red Line to Boston and then straight to South Station to get on a bus bound for New York City. He'd find his aunt and fade in and disappear, never to be found again by Rock or Marlene or Willie Stash.

"What about me?" Elf asked.

"You be ok. Don't worry. You be ok here." Then, as an afterthought he added, "Didn't kill no one, so you be alright."

"Did you?" Elf stopped.

Junius didn't answer him, just kept walking along the cold tracks, his hands in his pockets.

"Think they won't find you? Come up to New York and track your ass down?"

"I change my name," Junius said. "Never liked Posey anyway. It belong to him: that sack of shit back there on the stairs."

Elf caught up, and they walked on. Eventually he asked, "Who you gone be?"

"Ponds," Junius said. He looked right at his boy and clapped Elf on the back, then started to run again.

Up ahead he could see the lights of the new Porter Square T Station and he knew there would be a train along soon to take him into Boston to South Station, to the bus depot where he could buy a ticket for New York.

"Junius Ponds," he said as he ran.

"Junius Ponds."